Richard Dacre and The Murder Room

>>> This title is part of The Murder Room, our series dedicated to making available out-of-print or hard-to-find titles by classic crime writers.

Crime fiction has always held up a mirror to society. The Victorians were fascinated by sensational murder and the emerging science of detection; now we are obsessed with the forensic detail of violent death. And no other genre has so captivated and enthralled readers.

Vast troves of classic crime writing have for a long time been unavailable to all but the most dedicated frequenters of second-hand bookshops. The advent of digital publishing means that we are now able to bring you the backlists of a huge range of titles by classic and contemporary crime writers, some of which have been out of print for decades.

From the genteel amateur private eyes of the Golden Age and the femmes fatales of pulp fiction, to the morally ambiguous hard-boiled detectives of mid twentieth-century America and their descendants who walk our twenty-first century streets, The Murder Room has it all. >>>

The Murder Room
Where Criminal Minds Meet

themurderroom.com

Richard Dacre (pen name of Donald Thomas) (1926–)
Donald Thomas was born in Somerset and educated at Queen's College, Taunton, and Balliol College, Oxford. He holds a personal chair in Cardiff University. His numerous crime novels include two collections of Sherlock Holmes stories and the hugely popular historical detective series featuring Sergeant Verity of Scotland Yard, written under the pen name Francis Selwyn, as well as gritty police procedurals written under the name of Richard Dacre. He is also the author of seven biographies and a number of other non-fiction works, and won the Gregory Prize for his poems, *Points of Contact*. He lives in Bath with his wife.

By Donald Thomas

Mad Hatter Summer: A Lewis Carroll Nightmare
The Ripper's Apprentice
Jekyll, Alias Hyde
The Arrest of Scotland Yard
Dancing in the Dark
Red Flowers for Lady Blue
The Blindfold Game
The Day the Sun Rose Twice

As Francis Selwyn
Sergeant Verity and the Cracksman
Sergeant Verity and the Hangman's Child
Sergeant Verity Presents His Compliments
Sergeant Verity and the Blood Royal
Sergeant Verity and the Imperial Diamond
Sergeant Verity and the Swell Mob

As Richard Dacre
The Blood Runs Hot
Scream Blue Murder
Money with Menaces

Scream Blue Murder

Richard Dacre

An Orion book

Copyright © Richard Dacre 1988

The right of Richard Dacre to be identified as the author of this work has been asserted in accordance with the Copyright, Designs and Patents Act 1988.

This edition published by
The Orion Publishing Group Ltd
Orion House
5 Upper St Martin's Lane
London WC2H 9EA

An Hachette UK company
A CIP catalogue record for this book is available from the British Library

ISBN 978 1 4719 0448 6

www.orionbooks.co.uk

For Carol

Note

The events of the following novel occupy almost a year in the career of DCI Sam Hoskins. Canton and Ocean Beach are a creation of the novelist's imagination. Their police forces, politicians and citizens exist only as a fantasy. In one sense, Canton is any city. In the near future, it may be every city.

1
SUMMER

1

'Playtime'. The green electric script faded like old silk in the bright haze of the summer morning. Beyond the white freshly painted pier pavilions the tide's sluggish ripples caught the misty sunlight in a glitter of glass fragments. The light wind dropped as the tide slackened. Women in the striped canvas chairs were shrugging off their cardigans, drawing up skirts above the knee, exposing pale winter flesh to the promise of Sunday warmth.

Elaine stood to one side of the green electric sign. Overhead two rows of white bulbs flashed on and off in sequence, creating a dance of light round the eaves of the amusement pavilion. Beneath her, the iron girders of the pier echoed a rush and rattle of waves on sand-coloured shingle.

In her short skirt with grey pleats, her white blouse and school tie, the regulation knee-socks, she looked more like a lumpish ill-mannered child than a young woman. But even at fifteen years old, childhood was something for which she felt only good riddance.

At that moment she was looking for a man, somewhere in the slow-moving crowds of Sunday trippers. She had no idea of his name, age, or appearance. Such things were not important to her. He was there, all right. Somewhere. In a few minutes more she would probably find him. And then he was going to be very sorry that he had ever set foot in Ocean Beach. Very, very sorry indeed.

The girl glanced across the sands towards the duck-egg-blue rails of the Cakewalk promenade. All the deck-chairs were full by eleven o'clock with the crowds that had come by car from the valley towns or by the metro-rail from the shabby streets of Canton itself. The pages of the *News of the World* or the *Sunday People* were spread out against the growing heat. Their headlines ran in ceaseless repetition along the rows of pier deck-chairs, like messages tapped out from a doomed

3

liner. SABOTAGE IN CAPE AIR RACE ... DEAD BABY SENT THROUGH POST ... A pre-war photograph of the Duchess of Windsor in a black dress filled a centre page.

Del and Sonny were waiting as patiently as the girl. They leant on the promenade rails, near the kiosks of the pier-approach and the painted scrolls. 'Jokes, Tricks, and Magic' ... 'Films and Cigarettes' ... In the warm sheltered air the smell of fresh marine paint was stronger. A perfume of tobacco smoke lingered between the stalls. Like a dozen other young men nearby, Del and Sonny each rested a sharp toecap on the lower rail and waited for the fun to begin.

Fainter still in the strengthening sunlight, the white electric pearls danced unnoticed round the pavilion roof. Someone inside turned a switch. The green script flickered 'Playtime' once more and then went dead.

It was Del who caught the movement of Elaine's head first as she leant on the pier rail and looked at them. He threw away his half-smoked cigarette with an impatient gesture learnt from the movie screen.

'C'mon, Son!' he said. 'She's got one.'

They pushed forward, nudging and jostling among the crowd, to reach the turnstile. Passing through it, they came up level with the girl. There was nothing remarkable in their appearance. Any one of a hundred shabby terraces or high-rises in Barrier or Orient, or the dockland of Canton's Peninsula district might have been home to them.

Elaine was the youngest. The lank hair lay loose on her shoulders from its central parting, framing the broad oval of her pale face with its narrowed eyes and thin mouth. The pleated grey skirt of the uniform scarcely covered the pallor of her sturdy adolescent thighs. Tossing her fair hair into place, she looked up the deck towards her prey, directing the attention of the other two.

Del, at twenty, was two years older than Sonny Hassan. He appeared an easy-going fair-skinned giant, somewhat overweight. A blond kiss-curl and a humorous twist to the mouth suggested good nature and gentleness. A closer look showed that the heavy upper lip was curved in a slight but rigid deformity, resembling a sneer rather than a smile. He moved down the pier deck with a lounging walk, something between a sailor's roll and the flat-footedness of a cartoon animal.

The rings on his right hand were not worn from sentiment or for display. Their edges were sharpened brass. With his fist clenched, Del could break a man's nose on the brass edges or lay open a cheek with no more effort than knocking on a door. He stared down the pier deck. Hot nougat smells from the sweet-stalls hung in the warm air. He could spot the target fifty feet away. The upper lip moved in scornful self-confidence.

''s a piece of piss,' he said.

Sonny Hassan looked at him quickly and grinned. Sonny's long dark nose and quizzical eyes, like his name, were the legacy of a lascar seaman who had visited his mother rarely and briefly in a dockland house off Martello Square. But though wiry and fast as a bantam, Sonny was apt to defer to Del's authority in business of this kind.

With a quicker eye for commercial value, it was Sonny who already had two girls working the street for him. They might be shopgirls during the day. But when evening came they were ponies in Sonny Hassan's stable. He walked with a short energetic swagger, proud of his investments. Del disapproved but tolerated the arrangement. He cared nothing for the girls. Even so, there was something unmanly in living on a woman's money, however it was earned.

The target was in full view now. He was a beauty, Del thought, in his middle forties with dark hair and red neck. He looked short and stocky in grey flannels, his sports shirt hanging over fat hips and beer belly. Two brilliantined flaps of hair lined the bald division along his skull. The man's face wore the expectant, purposeless expression of the casual tripper. His woman was plump and pale, a timidity in her brown eyes and soft freckled face.

The couple wandered into the amusement pavilion half-way down the length of the pier. Del and Sonny closed the distance a little. The fluorescent-lit pavilion with its bare decking and iron rafters echoed like the din of a machine-shop. Del stood by the leather punch-ball on its stand of varnished wood. He grinned at the 'Test Your Strength' dial. Steadying the ball with his left hand, he danced on his toes and delivered a short downward jab with his right fist. The ball rattled violently against the wood. Del hoped the mug and his woman were watching. No need to waste a coin and see the needle measure his strength on its dial. Better than anyone else, he knew how strong he was.

The man and woman wandered past the electric pintables with their mushroom scoring-coils and comic-strip images of glass display panels. 'Playboy' . . . 'Top Card' . . . 'Diamond City' . . . 'Spaceman' . . . The punter and his woman walked slightly apart, not speaking or touching one another. They had now assumed a vacant, uncomprehending look of boredom or sudden bereavement. Electric colour flashed and machinery rattled. Sonny knew that Del's instinct was right.

Elaine had gone ahead and chosen her place. It was beyond the amusement pavilion, just short of the Pleasure Palace at the end with its bars and arcades. She was standing at the pier rail, where a row of older machines had been set out as an antique curiosity. 'Artist's Model' and 'The First Night', peep-shows of old cards in cast-iron cases. There was a horse-racing game, two metal animals wound along green linoleum by a pair of handles. In another glass case the gates of a little prison opened to show a toy figure, bound and hooded, being hanged by a pair of companions.

Elaine leant on the rail, as the crowd moved slowly on towards the pier bars and the glasses of beer at sunny tables. She looked down at the bottle-green swell of the tide where it made little whirlpools round the girders. Her pose was assumed as carefully as any model on the peep-show cards. The hem of the little pleated skirt was drawn higher, baring her rather heavy young thighs suggestively above the white knee-socks. Slovenly but provocative, she offered a calculated glimpse of white elasticated web, the cotton briefs outlining her hips and buttocks. The tight material was awkwardly twisted and gathered, so that one fattened swell of pale flesh was half uncovered. Del smiled and knew that every pair of male or female eyes passing by would register the image.

From time to time, she tossed clear her fair hair and glanced back over her shoulder. The dark narrowed eyes with their fleck of green, the tight sullen mouth, conveyed her adolescent impudence to the adult world.

Del nudged Sonny. The mug and his woman were close now, not more than twenty feet from the girl.

'Watch it, Son!' he said quickly.

The man and woman drew level with Elaine, the woman nearer the central glass wind-break, the man closer to the pier rail. Beyond the Arabian helter-skelter, an amplified steam-organ blasted out 'The Good Old Summer Time'.

Elaine jerked suddenly and straightened up. She swung her arm back at the level of her hips, as if lashing out at an insect that had bitten her thighs. The eyes were narrower still in fury as she spun round and bellowed after the man.

'You dirty filthy thing! I'll get the police to you!'

Del and Sonny were beside her now. The sunbathers in the deck-chairs looked first at the girl and then for the man at whom she was shouting. To Del's delight, the punter handed them a bonus. Hearing the shout just behind him, he turned round to see what the fuss was. His movement had the appearance of guilt as he stared at the girl.

'Yes, you!' she bellowed with childish indignation. 'That's the second time! Filthy thing! You do that again, I'll have the police to you!'

Del and Sonny came up to the man. Sonny was on the outside, Del stepped between the punter and his woman. As the man tried to turn away, they jostled him back with their shoulders and folded arms.

'You mucky old sod,' said Del pleasantly, almost as if they were sharing a joke at the girl's outburst. 'You want to keep them hands to yourself a bit more. Don't you? Eh?'

'I done *nothing* to her!' The punter's voice was strained in an effort to convey the exasperation of an innocent man. 'Never *touched* her! Never even been *near* her!'

'Don't come it,' said Sonny Hassan quietly. 'You was bloody seen! And you tried it back there by the amusements. Only you didn't get worse than a look from her then.'

Del turned to Elaine, as if they were strangers.

'You want a witness, my love?'

Again the punter tried to turn away, showing the first sign of panic. Sonny and Del hemmed him in easily. They shouldered and blocked him in a small ring of spectators, who gathered at the sound of Elaine's shouts. The woman stood apart, her face drawn in a look of repulsion, either at the two young men or perhaps because she believed them. Pathetic and silent, she left him to his own defence. But the man himself had recovered his wits and began to argue.

'What's this game, then?' he said grimly. 'I was never near her. And if you was watching, you know that. So what's this game?'

Del nudged against him, chewing casually, letting the spearmint breath into the man's face.

'Two saw you. Crafty old bugger. Touching up little girls on the side? Old lady not enough for you, is she?'

'Let him alone!' It was the voice of the punter's woman at last. 'He done nothing! He was with me! Leave us alone!'

The 'us' worried Del a little. Whatever the woman thought, she was going to stand by her man. He caught Sonny's glance briefly.

'Right.' Del stepped away from the man. 'You're alone, then. And you stay alone. I don't never want to see you trying that on again with a girl. All right? Understand?'

The punter stared dumbly. He was no match for the two young men and he knew better than to prolong the argument. Del was satisfied that the sullen silence would be taken for guilt by the onlookers.

'Other thing,' he said quietly to the man. 'I don't want to see you on this pier again. Not while I'm on it. Never!'

To impress the point, he folded his right hand into a fist. The sunlight caught the square faces of the brass rings with a fogged gleam. The deformed lip lifted in a slight involuntary sneer. For a moment it seemed that the punter was prepared to argue again. But Del and Sonny moved away, strolling towards the arcading and the bars at the pier's end. Del knew it would be all right. He could hear the woman pleading with her man, on the verge of tears, coaxing him into submission for his own sake. Whatever defiance he felt, his woman only wanted to get away, to hide from the knot of puzzled spectators.

Where the pier opened out round the bars and arcades, the whoop of the Ghost Train and the electric splutter of dodgem poles was overlaid by the climactic chords of the steam-organ.

> *I'll be your tootsie-wootsie*
> *In the Good Old Summer Time . . .*

The Atlantic Bar was already doing business, wooden seats in the bright morning occupied by shirt-sleeved men with pint glasses of dark ale. Sonny and Del walked round the side of the wooden arcading, out of sight of the crowds. The wind was cooler at the end rail of the pier, the ocean glitter fading in infinite haze. The two young men faced one another and went through a pantomime of silent agonised hilarity.

Del glanced back to make sure they were not being watched. Behind them, cars shone in the sun along the promenade like the carapaces of insects, blue, yellow, and black. From his pocket he took the punter's wallet. The black leather bill-fold was worn to a dingy brown but fat with its contents. Sonny wrinkled his nose and did comic fast-breathing in anticipation.

'She picked one!' he said jubilantly. 'She's got a nose for it!'

Del snapped the wallet open. He unfolded the banknotes and counted them.

'Fifty-two quid,' he said admiringly. 'Not bad for a start.'

Sonny slid a long finger into the leather pouch and hooked out a slip of paper, endorsed with a name. He read it and grinned.

'Mr Jonas had a day at the races,' he said mockingly.

'Lucky day for Mr Jonas!'

They looked at one another for a moment, heaving with silent laughter. Del counted out twenty pounds for Sonny and twenty for himself. He folded away the remainder for Elaine. Then he looked at the rest of the wallet's contents. Two metro-rail tickets from Canton Orient to Ocean Beach. Two scraps of paper with addresses, telephone numbers, simple arithmetical calculations. An old handwritten letter, its single sheet of paper discoloured toffee-brown along the folds. Two small photographs, one of a child in a garden, the other of an elderly couple sitting in a front doorway. The edges of the snapshots were bent and their glaze flawed by tiny creases.

He crumpled the paper scraps and dropped them in the sea, the tickets also. The letter and snapshots he tore into fragments and scattered them on the green water below. Last of all, he pitched the wallet out as far as it would go and saw it sink slowly.

'Rubbish like that could hang us, Son,' he said humorously.

Then he brushed his blond kiss-curl into place and turned back towards the shore.

2

As Del and Sonny moved out of sight, Elaine turned her back to the pier rail and leant against it. No one paid her much attention now. The punter and his woman had turned away towards the toll-booth. They walked with high dignity past the pier gates, shouting a final backward threat of reporting the incident. The girl knew there was no risk of that. Even when the mug found his hip pocket empty, he would think twice before repeating Del's accusations to the beach patrol. Elaine had cultivated an unerring gift of recognition. It was as if she sensed in her victims the tendencies of which she accused them. That made it all the easier. It scared them into silence.

Raising the two curtains of her lank fair hair on her thumbs, she drew them back behind her ears. The dark eyes with their fleck of green had narrowed again in the strong light. Now that the excitement of the sudden quarrel was over, the newspapers were spread out down the row of canvas chairs by the wind-break. Apart from a few surreptitious glances, the men and women who sat there had lost interest in her.

Except for one. She had not seen him at first. He stood watching her through the glass of the wind-break from the far side of the pier deck. Elaine knew him as the man who had watched her scores of times in the previous six months. Just watching. Looking at her as if he was fixing her image in his mind. Never approaching, never speaking. Watching and, perhaps, waiting. He was a secret in her life, a secret kept even from Del and Sonny. She thought of him simply as The Man.

It had begun early in the year. Walking home from school in the afternoons, Elaine was aware that The Man shared the route with her at the same time. About a quarter of a mile of it, from Shackleton Road and the school gates, past the Redlands estate, up the hill to the cement-coloured houses where she lived with her mother and stepfather, her unmarried elder sister and that sister's daughter, who was referred to by family custom as being the parents' third child.

The Man did not follow her every day, only once or twice a week. And sometimes there was a week or a fortnight in which he was not to be seen. But then he would reappear like a ghost or a shadow. After his absence, Elaine would abruptly sense him there, without glancing round. It was like the shock of an invisible electric pulse between them. Or like knowing in the dark that someone was hiding on the path, silent and without moving. And when at length she looked round he was there. Always the same. Always walking about twenty feet behind her, watching.

Elaine reacted with scorn rather than fear. She did not quite know whether The Man was dangerous or pathetic. Certainly less dangerous than most boys of her own age. She had learnt about men early, from Billy and Steve in unfrequented corners of the school grounds. It was common knowledge that there were men who had a preference for girls of her age. They were middle-aged men, she imagined, and she thought it possible that all middle-aged men shared these desires. There were magazines catering for such tastes, sold in the little newsagents' shops beyond the station. They were full of photographs showing girls in school uniforms and men or women in mortarboards and gowns, carrying canes. They were punters' rubbish, from what the girl could see. No one at Shackleton Comprehensive ever wore a gown, and canes had been illegal for several years.

It was not in tribute to the magazines that Elaine wore her grey skirt as high up her legs as possible. There was rebellion and contempt for the adult world in her display. She found it indefinably exhilarating. And there was a feeling of triumph in knowing that she could make such a fool of The Man, more than twice her own age. Each afternoon when she walked home up the steep pavement ahead of him, high above the view across the Peninsula and the waveless dock-water, she taunted him with a display that she hoped would give him sleepless nights for a long time to come.

On those afternoons, as she turned from the pavement and went up the steps that joined the estate path, The Man stood at the bottom of the bank and stared up at her. Elaine had once or twice shaken her hair back and looked round at him. But he stood there without expression, seeing more and more as she climbed. Whatever his motive he made no secret of his interest.

She was not the least scared, as girls were supposed to be of such men. Perhaps that was because The Man's appearance was ridiculous. His gabardine slacks and brown jacket were ordinary enough. The oddity was in his brown shoes with white piping, like an American actor she had once seen in an old film. And despite the crisp black hair, he seemed ancient to her. Forty, at least, and perhaps much more.

The Man had only once followed her home in the evening, after she had been to a Blue Moon concert with Claire and Viv. Still Elaine was not frightened. It amused her to have an admirer who was far too timid to approach. On that evening, she had been tempted to give him a fright, to swing round and confront him. Or she might look down from the top of the bank and ask him if he had now seen everything he wanted. But that would be like breaking the rules of a private game. Then, perhaps, The Man might become dangerous.

So it had gone on, from January until June, the strange consenting game. It was like a courtship ritual on the steep streets of Lantern Hill, the headland suburb across the water from Peninsula and the Canton Railway Dock. Elaine had said nothing to her mother or stepfather. There would have been questions about her own part in The Man's conduct. Questions, too, about boys of her own age like Steve and Billy. Sooner or later, her answers would be unsatisfactory, they always were. And then her stepfather's strap would be taken from its drawer. The strap and not the police represented the rule of law in the cement-coloured houses. No one had the least use for the police. It was thanks to them that Elaine was living with her mother's second husband and not her own father.

Leaning against the pier rail in the morning sunlight, it was easy for Elaine to pretend that she had not seen The Man beyond the glass partition of the wind-break. The tables were turned against him, the spy being spied upon. She turned and once more stared down at the whirlpools of the tide, her stomach pressing on the varnished rail. In an awkward lethargic posture she balanced like this on the polished wood. Once more the curve of her body drew the short skirt and the hem of the pants higher, the length of her thighs and the pale weight of her buttocks partially bare. She was sardonically aware of giving The Man the biggest treat of all.

From time to time, she shook her fair hair back and glanced round, as if looking for Del and Sonny. In the corner of her vision she could make out that The Man was still staring at her through the glass partition. He was like a ghost in a darker world, the kingdom of the dead. She could just see that he had something dark in his hands, perhaps a camera. Elaine supposed that he was taking pictures of her to be enjoyed at leisure. A private collection of surreptitiously aimed snapshots.

The thought of this engendered an acid contempt for him. He was pathetic, even sick, after all. Elaine straightened up, denying him the view with which she had taunted him so far. She saw that Del and Sonny were walking back from the end of the pier. When they reached her, she need only complain to them of The Man, the annoyance caused by the stranger taking suggestive photographs of her. Suddenly she decided that she would like to see The Man's scared face, even to watch him fisted once or twice by Del's armoured knuckles.

But that would be risky, so soon after the lifting of the wallet. In any case, by the time that Del and Sonny reached her, The Man had vanished, as he always did. Whenever he watched her, she was on her own. Whenever she was accompanied, he was nowhere to be seen. Never a witness. There was something about The Man that suggested he was not merely another punter, after all. The thought of it nagged her like a faint and premature warning.

She walked with Del and Sonny in their jackets and slim-legged trousers. The three of them passed through the pier turnstile on to the promenade. Along the Cakewalk, the crowds from the car parks and the metro-rail were packed still deeper, moving slowly as the tide. The 'Old Timer' corporation buses with their royal blue livery and ancient advertisements had been brought out as a novelty for the season on Bay Drive. Their sides were painted with long bright slogans in summer colours. Jupp's Ales . . . Zambuc Ointment . . . Gilbey's Odds–On Cocktail.

The little grey skirt fluttered against the top of Elaine's pale thighs in a light quirk of wind. She tossed her fair hair into place contemptuously and put The Man from her thoughts.

The public address system on the pier had begun to blast the warm air with its promotion for that night's rock concert at the Blue Moon Club. Elaine narrowed her eyes against the glitter of the warm sea.

'C'mon!' she said impatiently. 'Let's have some fun!'

3

The afternoon streets between the clock tower and the pier were deserted in the Sunday heat. Behind tinted display-glass, the sales concourses of the big stores lay dark and still as ancient temples. Lunch was over. The trippers had left the fish restaurants and milk-bars of Rundle Street, returning to the deck-chairs along the Cakewalk and the sands of Ocean Beach. Elaine walked between Del and Sonny, the three of them eating warm food from plastic cups.

'You gotta think of it sooner or later,' Sonny Hassan said sharply. 'Unless you want to spend all your life knocking over punters' wallets. Not too big, the first time. I don't say you could take over Canton city and Mel Cooney just like that. But what's Ocean Beach? It's not Canton and Cooney. Cooney don't want it. Just old Pruen. Old betting-shop dodger with a wedge of hot money. When the rest hear he's had a proper kicking, they'll be good as gold. Girls. Clubs. The squires and the queers that run them. All they want to know is who's in charge. Old men, mostly. I could take the lot. One-handed.'

'Piece of piss,' Del said. 'Any case, with what you could take off Pruen, we could set ourselves up. Buy some rations and flog them round the Blue Moon concerts. Buy a piece of the Blue Moon or the Petshop.'

With a quick turn of his wrist he screwed up the plastic cup, spun it in the air and batted it into the gutter with his fingers. Despite his lumbering walk, the movements had the self-confident dexterity of a stage juggler.

Sonny, walking with a tight-hipped swagger, thought about it. He talked of squires and their clubs as his contemporaries did about football. There were stars and contenders, scores and feuds. The game was mostly timing and nerve.

'We could be big,' he said. 'All you need is to want it. Most don't. Word is, Cooney gave up the Beach when he got to city councillor. More important things. And Neville the Mouse got topped in the Town River, doing a runner from the law. Stupid little half-chance bastard he was. There's no one else standing in the way. Fuck-all. Even the law only wants a quiet town.'

Del slipped a wafer of spearmint from its wrapper and began to chew.

'Wanker like Pruen!' he said contemptuously. He crumpled the silver wrapper and shied it after a man walking several yards in front of them.

Elaine's hair spilt aslant her face again and she tossed it back into place.

'Pruen's old woman? You going to fist her too?'

Del chewed and thought about it, but not for long. He grinned.

'Would if we had to. If it was her or me. Only we won't have to. Not the way it's going to be. She'll do what Pruen says. And Pruen won't give bother. When a prat like him sees his old lady about to get a smacking, he won't make trouble. Never. Cuts the balls right off his kind.'

'If there's any hitting,' she said doubtfully, 'you two can do it.'

Sonny Hassan had walked ahead a little in the broad empty shopping parade. He gave a short helpless laugh of exasperation at such stubbornness and turned upon the girl.

'There *won't* be! What's in Pruen's place is mainly dog-track money. That and a bit of casino and whorehouse. It's what's taken in cash at the tables and never seen in the books. He's not going to want the law and the income tax inquiring after that. See? He can't go round screaming about money he's not supposed to have in the first place. Right? He's made for being hit. Any case, he's got up everyone's nose round here. There's no one going to weep for old Pruen.'

'He could fight,' Elaine said resentfully. 'Him or his mob.'

Del came to Sonny's support with a scornful grin.

'Old Pruen? He might have fought twenty years ago. Not now. Not with two on him. No chance. He's well gone fifty. And he's got no mob. Not any more. Just an old dosser with his savings put away.'

'There's bound to be others,' she said.

'In the house?' Sonny's eyes slanted with a gleam of mockery. 'There's Pruen, his old lady, and a horsey that works as maid or something. Gives old Pruen a blow through on his birthday and Christmas. That's all. Three gag-rags, some handy cord, and you could do what you liked with 'em. Five minutes with a razor or a lighted match. Pruen would be begging you to take his last penny. And if I should have to fist an old bag like Muriel Pruen, I'll do it. All right? Good and strong!'

Rundle Street was like a canyon, the walls of the high buildings dark as cave-rock, and the sky above a pale soaring blue. The three of them crossed from the fish restaurant to the Luxor Palace, its cinema modernism all black glass and white tiles. The square white tower of its ventilation shaft, the name embroidered in red neon, rose against the hot depth of holiday sky. In the chromium-edged display cases, Joseph Cotton and Joan Fontaine regarded one another with the intensity of monochrome romance. Elaine looked sidelong at her escort.

'Who's the skivvy?'

Sonny shrugged, casual in his contempt.

'Some scrubber. Noreen something-or-other. Eighteen or nineteen. Ma Pruen's companion, so called. Pruen gives her a gallop when they can get enough spinach into him.'

'She might give trouble,' the girl said.

Del touched his upper lip with his tongue, humorously. 'I'd love her to try. I'd enjoy that.'

Sunday afternoons were the Luxor's 'Golden Dreams' at half-price. No one cared about the films. It was a place to take a girl in the dark or just get out of the sun and the crowds. Somewhere to wait until tea-time. Del watched Elaine while Sonny paid for their three tickets. Despite her caution, he could see that she was beginning to enjoy the prospect of turning over Pruen's place, smashing and looting. It was a good feeling. Del had already promised her that. Knowing that everything in people's lives was yours. Strong and good was how it felt, even smashing and tearing the things that couldn't be carried away. Especially then. Stealing was anonymous. Smashing a place was personal, like a message. Del had learnt that for himself when he was nine or ten.

A man in dinner-jacket and black tie stood incongruously in the full afternoon sunlight, a relic of 1950s style that was now in vogue again. He tore their tickets and watched them go up the shallow steps from the poppy-scented vestibule, the carpet soft as snow under their feet. Sonny led the way up the Circle stairs, the chromium rails cool to the hand, the pillars of opaque peach-coloured glass illuminated from within by electric light. Beyond mirror-doors the Circle lounge was a deserted landing whose narrow silver-rimmed casements gave a soundless glimpse of sparkling tide and a pale glare of sand.

Sonny turned to the other two and inclined his head towards the private staircase from which the distant clatter of a projector was just audible.

'That's offices up there. You want to take a good look some time. They don't bank after Thursday until Monday. What's up there Sunday night is the best of the week's takings.'

He led them past the old-fashioned colour portraits of Hollywood stars to the heavy doors that closed off the auditorium, recessed like the portico of a pharaoh's tomb. On Sunday afternoon the soft, twilit interior had the vastness of an empty cathedral, couples sitting here and there among countless rows of seats. The curtains purred open in a lime-green flush of cyclorama and the advertisers' slides filled the screen. Yardley's Bond Street Salon ... Horowitz on HMV ... The sleek lines of the new Humber Pullman. Del sat between Sonny and Elaine. A censor's certificate, the writing old-fashioned as a mediaeval manuscript, proclaimed *September Song*.

Each of the three was there for a different reason. Sonny Hassan had business to discuss with Del. Del was to exercise certain rights over Elaine. Elaine might watch the film if she chose. Sonny stared with incomprehension and contempt at the opening scenes of middle-aged romance, the swelling piano chords of the Rachmaninov concerto booming and soaring.

'You ask anyone,' he said firmly for Del's benefit. 'Cooney's given up this town. Got to, hasn't he? Being on the city council. Any case, he's old and soft. He can't hold the streets any more, not even if he wanted to. They've heard that down Peninsula and Barrier, the people that matter have. If some old queer like Pruen gets a real spanking now, they'll know Ocean Beach is wide open.'

'Cooney mightn't like it.'

'All Cooney wants is managers. I know a bit about him. If we can manage a few interests out here better than a prick like Pruen, he'd as soon have us.'

'Suppose he would,' Del said. Half his interest was in the film now. The lovers were in Naples, the piano on the sound-track bonging out its insistent theme, the orchestra sweeping onwards. He cuddled the girl towards him, his free hand brushing down until it touched the cool smoothness of her bare thigh just below the hem of her short pleated skirt. There was no protest. She did not even take her eyes off the screen.

'The Blue Moon Club,' Sonny said. 'The Petshop. Even Ocean Park. They need managing. Mel Cooney has to keep his distance now. He'd be glad of a few names to do the work for him.'

Del's hand moved up, stroking the top of her leg. Elaine turned her mouth up for an awkward kiss, then returned her gaze to the screen with the look of having paid a debt. Del moved her slightly and slid his hand inside the elastic waistband, stretching it round the warmer smoothness of Elaine's bottom. They stared at the screen.

Just as Sonny Hassan was about to say something else, a man and a woman came in and sat down in front of them. Sonny stared at them for a moment.

'There's enough in the Blue Moon Club to cut half a dozen ways. And you could run a string of ponies out of the Petshop. That's what it's there for.'

'Cooney's scared of that.'

'Not if he's got a name doing the work and taking a cut.'

The man in front turned round and stared at them, the flicker of light from the screen illuminating his frown.

'And not if there's rations being put out through the Blue Moon concerts.'

Sonny spoke louder, his face close to the neck of the man in front. The man turned again.

'Would you please mind keeping quiet?'

Sonny leant forward.

'And would you mind going and fucking yourself, sunshine? We was here first.'

Del sniggered.

'He wants to go and do it up a rope while he's still got something to do it with.'

'Him?' Sonny rocked the man and woman to and fro with his feet in the back of their seats. 'I shouldn't think a girlie like him ever had much. We could shave him clean and sell him to Iran.'

Del snorted with laughter and Elaine giggled. The woman said something to the man and they got up, their seats squeaking and clattering back. Sonny watched them as they sidled down the row to the far side of the cinema.

'Wankers like that!' Del said contemptuously.

Sonny waited impatiently for the film to end, indulging Del and the girl.

'Pruen lost his grip years ago,' he said. 'It's doing Cooney a favour. That's all.'

He stared at the screen without seeing the film. In his mind he played out a fantasy of being Cooney's lieutenant in Ocean Beach with Del to mind his back – and then being King of the Beach in his own right. He was aware of Del beside him, one hand moving under Elaine's skirt, feeling and fumbling. Sonny Hassan had no taste for such courtship. He preferred to call one of his two working-girls, Mandy or Sharon, and make his demands as if ordering from a restaurant menu. Apart from that, sex was an inconvenience and a complication.

They left by agreement before the film was over. While the other two walked to the Circle exit, Sonny moved like a slim and wiry shadow along the empty row, behind the man and woman. In the dimness it was impossible to see his hand move. Only when Sonny had passed behind them and reached the far aisle did the man put his hand to the back of his neck, as if stung there by an insect. Then he looked quickly round, this way and that, the hand still covering the back of his neck. Sonny had caught up with the others at the door. He slid the fragment of razor-blade from under his long thumbnail and closed it in a match-box.

'There's one that wants to watch his manners,' he said casually.

Del grinned and combed his hair into place as they went down the deeply carpeted stairs, past the manager in his evening-jacket and black tie. On the pavement of Rundle Street they stood blinking in the strong light of early evening, its brilliance mirrored by the windless and tranquil tide at the end of the shopping parade.

'Main thing is,' Del said, 'when we decide to do old Pruen.'

Sonny Hassan hunched his bony shoulders and scuffed his neatly polished shoe on the pavement.

'What's wrong with now?' he asked simply.

4

At the western end of Ocean Beach the seafront curve of Bay Drive climbed sharply through a series of tight bends. It rose between overarching boughs of chestnut and spruce on the wooded hillside until it came out at last on the overcliff drive of Highlands Avenue. For a mile or two the toy castles of Victorian ship-owners and the green-tiled Spanish villas of the 1930s rose massive and secure behind fortress walls of rhododendron.

The trim lawns and tall windows of the new executive class looked out across the same calm and rippling bay that the coal-owners and shippers of Canton had known. Their view stretched from the eastern headland which concealed the Railway Dock to the flat and sunlit finger of Sandbar with its shingled houses and yachts riding at their moorings in a light swell. But the houses had changed. Where ornamental wooden gates once marked the driveways in the dark rampart of rhododendron, there were now barred panels of dove-grey steel that purred open electronically in response to the correct signal.

By six o'clock on the warm Sunday evening the horizon line of the Channel had gathered a first band of fogged gold in the sun's descent. The sky was patterned golden-grey and the sea-blue began to fade. Del and Sonny, the girl walking between them, turned off the overcliff drive towards the roads behind, the residential area known as The Links. Its leafy avenues were set with municipal acacia trees at regular intervals along the uneven brick of the pavements. Apart from a street of small and expensive shops, The Links consisted of Edwardian villas with cream gables and verandahs, their cherry-coloured brick matching the pavement.

The houses were set well apart behind each garden screen of lime trees and chestnut, the high front walls dashed with pebble and flint.

'You don't want a car for a job like this,' Sonny Hassan said quietly. 'Too soon noticed in an empty road. And Elaine won't need a stocking. They don't know her from nothing.'

The Edwardian villa at the corner of Douglas Road and the Priory might have belonged to a surgeon or a retired colonel. Its tall black-leaded gate was spiked and locked; only the gap between the hinges gave a view of the garden. Walking past, Sonny Hassan glimpsed a long section of trimly shaven lawn and a quiver of light on the duck-egg-blue water of a swimming pool.

'Old Pruen's done well for himself,' he said, sardonically admiring. 'Hasn't he done well?'

They turned the corner into Douglas Road, where the side gate of the house stood barred and locked. But Sonny took another view through the crack.

'That's nice,' he said to Del. 'Garage door shut. No cars on the hard standing. No visitors, in other words. Just three of them. Not even a servant until tomorrow morning. We got all the time we need.'

At that hour on a Sunday evening the long seaward avenues were deserted. In a yellow flush of sun, the sky faded from azure to the first violet haze of twilight. The purr of lawn-mowers had given way to a murmur of ice in tall glasses, the woollen tone of a Palm Court Orchestra on an old recording. A warm breeze, moving with the tide, carried a peal of bells from one of the town churches.

Sonny Hassan glanced up and down the road.

'Watch my back for me,' he said.

Del leant against the wall and pulled Elaine towards him. He was Pruen's kitchen-boy now, slipping out for a kiss and a fumble with his girl. Sonny took a running step and sprang for the top of the wall. His boots thudded on the flints as he levered himself up and looked over. Almost at once he landed deftly on the pavement again.

'They got nothing. Not even a dog,' he said breathlessly. 'Nothing. There's the horsey out tidying the garden, Pruen and his old woman indoors. I researched this lot down to the last detail. I told you it was going to be easy.'

'They got an alarm?'

'Oh yes,' said Sonny derisively. 'They would have, wouldn't they? They're going to wish they hadn't!'

From the direction of the preparatory school, a double file of small boys in grey flannel suits crossed far down the avenue that ended half a mile away in a shaft of opalescent sea. The peal of bells dwindled to a measured tolling, as if for a burial.

'Alarm,' Del said.

Sonny nodded at the phone box across the road.

'Probably not switched on, with them being in and out to the garden. If it is, it might be a niner, through to the police on the phone line. All you got to do is keep the line engaged and it blocks the outgoing alarm call. See?'

Leaving the others, he crossed to the phone box, lifted the receiver and dialled Pruen's number. A woman's voice, quavering a little, answered him.

'I'm a neighbour of Noreen's mum. Can I speak to Noreen, please?'

Someone lodged the phone on a table. Sonny grinned at himself in the little mirror on the kiosk wall, seeing the flat almond eyes and the long levantine nose. In his mind he pictured the girl straightening up from the flower border, crossing the wide lawn and going indoors. He heard her voice.

'Hello,' he said quickly. 'Noreen? I'm across from your mum. There's been a bit of an upset. Nothing serious but she wants to speak to you. Hang on. I'll go and get her.'

He signalled to Del, laid the phone down, and walked casually back across the road. Del was up, astride the wall, helping the girl over. Sonny followed, dropping down the other side on soft earth.

'Stocking,' he said, holding out to Del a woman's nylon. In a moment their features were flattened to imbecile anonymity by the dark film drawn over their heads, the spare length knotted at their crowns. Each of the two then drew on a pair of cheap woollen gloves. Del and Sonny moved cautiously along the wall, intending Elaine to approach the front door. But even that was unnecessary. Noreen had gone in through the French windows, one of which was still open. The built-in safe and the reinforced door might be connected separately to the alarm. Not that it mattered, Sonny thought. The alarm was never going to ring.

On this side of the house there were two ground-floor openings. The dark panelled dining-room with French windows was the way by which Noreen had gone in. Across a passageway was the bay-windowed drawing-room with the yellow glow of a standard lamp beyond the gathered curtains. A thickening rose-light of evening sun threw Del's bulky shadow across the step of the open French windows.

5

'The rules are simple,' Sonny said quietly. 'Really simple. They're not hard to understand at all.'

He looked at Pruen and the woman. Each sat on a dining chair staring up at him. They seemed like a pair of travellers who had just missed a train and were waiting to be told where to go. They wanted to hear the rules now. Sonny knew it. They wanted to know in order to obey. In order not to be punished. It was going to be even easier than he had thought. Behind him he could hear Pruen's girl gasping, still resisting a little. She was quite strongly built, but Del had got her arms behind her back, twisted them up and knotted the cord round her wrists. Probably it was the ache of being twisted rather than defiance that made her gasp now. Sonny looked down at the two Pruens, their gaping anticipation.

'First of all,' he said quietly, 'anyone that yells gets smacked. Smacked hard. You speak when I tell you to. I say things once. Just once. When I ask questions, you answer. See?'

Muriel Pruen's grey hair straggled about her face. She quivered a little, thin and nervous, with a look of brittle bones.

'What do you want with us?'

Sonny smirked.

'You'd like to know!' he said. 'Wouldn't you like to know!'

'This is bloody absurd,' Pruen said. He was a plump man with a grey fringe and horn-rimmed glasses. He might have sold insurance. 'If there's something— '

'Shut it!' Sonny said. 'Shut it and listen. Your time's up, Pruen. Now on, you do as you're told. Else you and the old woman, and the young horsey, are going to star in a horror-show of your very own. Understand?'

The Pruens sat in their tall drawing-room with its gathered velvet curtains and overstuffed cushions, the expensive glass pendants and the mahogany veneer, not daring to speak. In the next room, Elaine had kept the phone off its rest and dialled the speaking clock to block the alarm-line. Smooth as cream stout, the distant voice intoned its litany. 'At the third stroke, the time sponsored by Accurist will be eight-fifteen and twenty seconds . . . '

Elaine left the phone and came into the drawing-room.

'Them!' Sonny indicated the Pruens to her with a nod. 'Hands behind their backs and wrists tied tight as you can to the frame of the chair.' He watched her obey his instruction and spoke to Del without turning round.

'You having trouble with the horsey?'

'Good as gold now.'

Sonny waited until Elaine had tied the Pruens into their chairs. Then he turned to Noreen, whom Del was still holding. She was quite tall and strongly built, dark hair and fringe contrasting with the anger in her firm, fair-skinned features. Sonny took a step forward. With no preliminary sign of movement, he patted her quickly across the face with the backs of his ringed fingers. She gasped in alarm and dropped her head. Sonny undid the belt at her waist and used it to pinion her ankles. Del pressed her down till she lay curled on her side. Noreen's head rested against the skirting. The swell of her hips in the faded jeans protruded tightly and suggestively from under the occasional-table. Sonny turned back to the Pruens.

'She's a lucky girl,' he said gently, 'considering what a booting I could give her now. Still, it'll be worse than booting if I don't hear answers.'

Mrs Pruen emitted a whimper of self-pity.

'Shut it!' Del said impatiently. 'You was told before!'

From the next room the distant plummy voice intoned its temporal litany.

'At the third stroke, the time sponsored by Accurist will be eight-nineteen and forty seconds . . . '

Sonny spread out a hand to silence Del.

'You,' he said to Elaine. 'Find the kitchen. Nice large bowl full of water. Bring it in here.' He turned to the Pruens whose faces now watched him with unconcealed earnestness, as if terrified to miss a word of their instructions. 'Now then. This is what is going to happen. I got questions. I want answers. I'll keep you till last, Pruen. I want you to watch the old woman and the horsey first. That way you won't be inclined to mess us about when your turn comes.'

'Whatever it is . . . ' Pruen began but Del cut him short.

'Shut it, Pruen, and listen.'

'I ask questions,' Sonny said. 'Each time I don't hear an answer, Ma Pruen goes under the water. You act stupid and she goes under till the bubbles stop. See? It don't matter if you're telling the truth, Pruen. If I so much as think you're holding out, it's just the same for your old lady.'

'Tell me what you want!'

'Shut it!' Del said indignantly.

'I'll tell you when I'm ready,' Sonny Hassan said quietly. 'Now listen. You got to convince me, Pruen. If the water don't work with Ma Pruen, we'll start on the horsey. Few minutes with a box of matches is all it takes. A kid could do it. And if we don't get satisfaction there, we'll come asking you. You play stupid with us, Pruen, and the horrors is really going to come true for you tonight.'

He came closer to Pruen, took out a lipstick-shaped lighter and broke out the flame with his thumb.

'So let's not have any heroes. All right? Got that, 'ave you? You're rubbish, Pruen. The world don't need you.'

Pruen nodded, silently and urgently promising anything. Elaine came in with a washbowl. Sonny indicated the table and watched her set it down. He and Del lifted the woman's chair and carried her tied in it so that she sat at the table like a baby to be fed. Mrs Pruen uttered a faint shivering sound.

Sonny turned to Elaine.

'Out in the garden. Keep an eye on the gates. Anyone comes near, ring the doorbell.'

Elaine combed back her hair with her fingers, bestowing a look of adolescent contempt on the Pruens as she went out.

Del and Sonny moved close to Pruen.

'Before I ask questions,' Sonny said, 'she goes down once. That way you won't none of you act up. Save us all a lot of time. Save you a bit of grief.'

'For God's sake!' Pruen said. 'Whatever it is . . . '

Del's hand moved lazily, the fogged brass of the rings like chilblains under the woollen glove. Pruen recoiled from the impact, sitting white-faced and marked. He made no sound.

Del stroked the older man's head.

'Shut it,' he said with mocking kindness, 'there's a good boy.'

He turned away to where the woman was sitting in her chair.

'You're mad!' Pruen said, as if he had stumbled upon the truth at last. 'Listen . . . '

Del was holding Mrs Pruen by her grey hair.

'You want fisting,' he said humorously over his shoulder to Pruen. 'I'll see to you in a minute.'

Sonny nodded at Del. Their hands pressed down easily and firmly. Pruen stared as if he felt nothing. Noreen with her ankles pinioned and her wrists tied behind her still lay curled on the floor. The light from the standard lamp imparted a worn shine to the tightened jeans on her hips and buttocks.

From the next room the well-upholstered telephone voice consigned time to eternity.

'At the third stroke, the time sponsored by Accurist will be eight thirty-two and twenty seconds . . . '

'That's handy,' Del said with a breathless giggle. 'They must have known we was going to time Ma Pruen.'

'At the third stroke, the time sponsored by Accurist . . . '

'Please!' It was Pruen's cry. 'Whatever you want— '

'Shut it!' said Del, squealing with indignation. 'She's hardly started yet.'

At last they moved their hands and hauled her up.

'There,' said Del, beaming at Pruen through the distortion of the stocking-mask, 'she's just as good as new.'

Sonny Hassan stood before Pruen's chair.

'Now the questions,' he said softly. 'Only ask once. After that she goes under for twice as long.'

'Tell me!' Pruen howled. 'Take what you want and leave us!'

'I want to know where the cash is in this house,' Sonny said quietly. 'The cash and the old bag's jewels. And when I say cash, I don't want to hear about anything that can't be counted in thousands. All right?'

'There isn't— '

But Del interrupted him with a voice of mock-disappointment.

'You don't care much for your old lady, Pruen. We got you wrong. It's the horsey we ought to be working on.' He crossed to Pruen's chair and rattled the box of matches.

'There's money,' Pruen said, his voice suddenly and uncannily calm. 'There's money in the floor-safe. I don't know how much. Four or five thousand maybe. She's never had a lot of jewels. What there is, they're there as well.'

'Where?' Sonny's question was like a sneer.

'Under the hall carpet.'

'Alarm?'

Pruen shook his head.

'There's a pressure pad over it. Anyone who steps on it or tries to move it sets off a bell. But it's all turned off.'

'All right,' Sonny said reluctantly. 'Still, if it rings now, you can guess what happens to you and these two before anyone gets here. Can't you?'

Pruen nodded. The blood drawn by Del's knuckles had trickled half-way down his cheek and dried.

'Untie his hands,' Sonny said to Del.

A moment later, he led Pruen into the hall. Sonny watched him kneel and turn back the beige carpet, moving aside the thin cover of the pressure mat with its length of wire. The safe was like a round steel drum set in the tiling of the original floor of the house. Pruen turned its dial to and fro. There was a click and the six-inch armoured-steel disc of the door opened upwards.

'Leave it!' Sonny said. 'You could have a gun in there for all anyone knows. You might hurt yourself, if it was to go off.'

He took Pruen back and tied him in the chair again. The safe was about twelve inches deep. Sonny reached in and felt the packed wad of banknotes. They were fifties and he guessed that there must be well over a hundred. Much more than five thousand pounds then. The rings and brooches were rubbish, not worth taking. But as he reached deeper, there was a metal shape that made him smile. Pruen, the old clown, had a gun there after all.

He hooked his fingers round it, drawing it out. At that moment, like the blast of an alarm klaxon, the front doorbell rang. Sonny Hassan's heart leapt with fright. He dropped the snub-barrelled revolver into his pocket. Elaine was at the doorway.

'There's kids at the gate,' she said, 'asking about Pruen's tart.'

'Tell 'em she's out till later and everyone else is busy. Who are they?'

'Next door, I think.'

'Tell 'em that and keep looking. We'll be finished in a minute.'

He turned to the drawing-room. Del handed him a can of red spray paint from the utility cupboard. The Pruens bowed their heads as if it might be aimed at them. Sonny squirted a thin drift of it at the ceiling and the walls, inscribing playground obscenities of the casual housebreaker. Del's knife rent the cushions and the chairs, carving the walnut and mahogany veneer deeply. Still the Pruens hid their faces. But however hard they tried to conceal their defeat, this was visible and blatant. By next day, the whole of Ocean Beach would know that Pruen had been turned over. The 1950s King of Greyhound Track and Pinball Arcades, the greatest 'firm' ever tolerated by Carmel Cooney in Ocean Beach, had been shafted as easily as the mug punter that morning.

Del went up the stairs, wrenching out the spokes of the banisters and snapping them. With a hammer from the kitchen, he smashed a crack in the sunken bath and broke through the front of the lavatory bowl. His knife scoured the bedroom walls, ripping and rucking the paper. With a window pole he broke upwards through the ceiling plaster. Then he came back down the stairs. Sonny with the remainder of the red paint had inscribed 'PRUEN THE PUNTER DIED HERE!' across the front door. He dropped the can. Their pockets fat with banknotes, he and Del let themselves out.

The dusk had deepened. They made for the wall, the gates still locked. Sonny went up and saw the road was clear. He helped Elaine over and dropped down to wait for Del. They crossed Highlands Avenue. The shimmering boiled-sweet neon of the Cakewalk lay spread out below them against the evening tide.

'You was quiet,' Sonny said to Elaine. 'You could have done some smashing.'

Del grinned on her behalf.

'She was in the garden, wasn't she?' he said waggishly. 'Time for a little present in the swimming-pool.'

Sonny stopped and looked at him. Then all three of them began to laugh.

'Like to see the cleaning-lady's face tomorrow morning,' Sonny said. 'Pruen won't be able to hush this one up. It'll be round the clubs in no time.'

'The horsey lying there with her bum in the air . . . '

'Pruen with it all on show . . . '

'Could we teach old bastards like him how to run this town! All it takes is a bit of ambition. Didn't I tell you?'

They laughed again, almost unnerved by the extent of their success, walking quickly down between the trees towards the first lights of the promenade.

'Seeing that we come into real money this time,' said Del good-naturedly, 'what we ought to have is a bit of a celebration.'

6

While the Luxor was screening its Sunday matinée of *September Song*, the tea-time sunlight fell in yellow shafts, the colour of a peach, on stone and sand. Sam Hoskins sat on the low sea-wall and surveyed the length of beach allotted to him. With his greying hair and round eyes behind tinted spectacles, his slightly paunched singlet and slacks, few promenaders gave him a glance. To the scornful young, he was prat-trousered lumber with punch-bag possibilities. To the middle-aged, there was a certain sceptical irony in the eyes behind the tinted lenses. His look was best avoided. Those who guessed he might be a policeman imagined him as an administrator of some kind. Chief Inspector Hoskins had been many things. An administrator was not one of them.

'Calm before the storm, Mr Hoskins,' said Patrolman Scott

philosophically. 'There could be aggravation round here tonight. Be all right while the groups are on stage. After that you can reckon on fist and puke.'

Hoskins grunted to himself. He stared across the parkland and the boating lake towards the square 1930s lines of the Blue Moon Club. The preliminary thump and jangle of percussion was testing the amplifiers with sounds of a thumbscrew shrillness. Scott had parked his patrol car discreetly by the houses. He stood at the sea-wall, eyes hooded by the black slashed peak of his uniform cap. With his Latin moustache and half-hidden eyes, this soft-bellied under-exercised twenty five year old combined the air of an SS interrogator and a Mexican bandit.

'I'll be off watch before the gig gets going,' he said cheerfully, 'soon as the kiddies and the families are off the beach.'

'Nothing new down the busy end of the prom?' Hoskins asked.

Scott pulled a face.

'Nope,' he said dismissively, opening his notepad and flipping through its pages. 'Couple of wilful obstructions. Soon moved on. Two giddy turns and a heart attack in the deck-chairs. A whacker on the pier by the name of Jonas thinks he lost a wallet from his hip pocket. Glad to have it back, if found. Someone needs to tell him wallets don't fall out of hip pockets, unless you're holding your trousers upside down. They get lifted by thieving fingers. Either he's innocent or having us on. Seen the last of his wallet, anyway. Quiet Sunday, really. So far.'

Hoskins turned a little. He gazed out above the heat-shimmer of the long sands and the glitter of slack water. A sweet and creamy odour of suntan oil hung in the stagnant air of hot afternoon, thickened here and there by the heavier scents of ice-cream and candy floss.

'Family life,' he said glumly, glancing away from the sands and the glitter of the ebbing tide. 'Look at it. Nasty little housefuls out to screw the rest of the world. And in the end to screw each other. If you want real viciousness and perversion and crime, Scottie, you look up the statistics on domestic bliss. Makes the Mafia seem like amateurs. And some of the worst of it isn't even illegal. Next time you hear some wiseacre on the telly yakking on about the values of family life, have a close look and imagine waking up with that face on the pillow next to you for the rest of your days.'

Scott opened his mouth to say something. Just in time, he remembered Hoskins's long-dead wife and baby. The motorway miscalculation after eighteen months of marriage. He scraped a gum-sticky blemish from his shoe on the promenade paving that was stained pink and yellow from dropped confectionery.

'I'll just take a walk up and down, Mr Hoskins,' he said cheerfully, 'then back to the car and call in before it's nicked. Some little smart-arse had the radios out of two patrol cars in Ocean Beach last week. The crews get called to so-called incidents in the Boot Hill flats. Only there aren't any incidents. A couple of young villains wait there and watch. Rip out the radios while Dave and Jimmy are up the top floors trying to find the bother.'

Hoskins sighed and did not seem to care.

'They're getting cheeky, my son. No two ways. Try locking the cars.'

He watched Scott in his police-blue shirt sleeves walking quietly towards the end of the Cakewalk promenade, past the open green of The Vale. On that Sunday afternoon, The Vale was the quietest part of Ocean Beach. It was a secluded area at sea-level, below the beginning of the western overcliff. Bay Drive skirted it, leaving it as an enclave of calm and prosperity. Laid out in the 1930s, the crisp lines of its white stucco houses stood well apart behind dark hedges of laurel and yew. The angular flat-roofed modernism formed a semicircle, looking out on to the wide public garden and boating lake. It had been known as The Vale long before the houses and the concrete-edged lake. At the seaward end, two flights of steps led up to the raised promenade and the gleam of Channel waves reflected in a wash of sky.

Near the garden entrance was a row of single-storey neighbourhood shops. A post office and an ice-cream parlour, a greengrocer's and a bungalow with 'Tea Rooms' painted in white on its roof had been built at the same time as the houses. The fruit on the pavement trestles looked fresher, the white or yellow awnings seemed newly laundered. The assistants in the little shops smiled and said 'Thank you'. The Vale was quiet and select as it had been in the years before Hitler's war. Looking at it from where Hoskins sat, it seemed like a residential Eden, unblemished by death, or doctors, or crime.

Along the sands, the family trippers were packing up to go. They slung their baskets and canvas bags, trudging up the beach towards the car parks or the black scar of the Canton metro-rail that ferried them home to the little streets of Barrier or Orient, the high-rise blocks of Peninsula or Mount Pleasant. For Hoskins and the rest of the Beach Patrol, it had been a quiet Sunday at The Vale. A thin pale girl had removed the top half of her black bikini and revealed a pair of meagre white breasts to the sun. Following instructions, WPC Cummings had been despatched from the deck-chair office to have a quiet word. The girl had blushed a little, her female companion had giggled, and the black bikini-top had gone back on. The cause of law and order had triumphed.

Hoskins glanced up and down his length of the beach. Supervision of the Ocean Beach 'Pervert Patrol' was intended by Superintendent Maxwell Ripley as a clear indication that the Chief Inspector was being punished. Hoskins had got the message. 'Someone has to do the job,' the Ripper had said cheerfully.

Folding his tinted glasses away in his top pocket, Hoskins stood up and began to walk slowly towards the little promontory that marked the seaward extreme of The Vale. The square white lines of the Blue Moon Club still stood there. But the trees behind it had gone and even on Sunday mechanical diggers were munching up brown sandy soil by the ton. The first of the Ocean Front apartment blocks was being woven on its girders in bruise-coloured stone.

The Blue Moon Club had the modernistic look of all the buildings in The Vale, as if Malibu or Las Palmas had come to the coastal strip of industrial Canton. It had been built in the last years of peace before 1939 as a dance-floor and cocktail club for the sons and daughters of coal-owners and shippers, their managers and their managers' wives. Everything about the Blue Moon Club suggested the rhythms of the tango and the samba, whose notes had been dead for fifty years.

The posters of that golden age had been copied as mosaics on the terrace. Young men in dark suits and white shirts, with glinting blue eyes and hair that looked as if it had been set in a jelly-mould, smiled quizzically at girls in white fur wraps and silk gowns whose promise was soft and fragrant as blossom. In the pictures, the handsome couples looked out from the portico of the Blue Moon Club across a driveway where a silver Rolls-Royce stood waiting, beyond gardens of tropical suggestion to a midnight-blue sea where a white steam-yacht rode at anchor. The reality of the hourly car park, the municipal boating lake, the black coastal tankers on a cold and blustery night-tide, had been transformed into an Arabian Nights dream.

But the Blue Moon Club was still a going concern. Two pantechnicons were unloading amplifiers and arc-lamps. There were instrument-cases and lengths of cable, tubular scaffolding and planking. By evening, the Blue Moon terrace would be an open stage and the public garden its rowdy auditorium. Tickets had been changing hands for the past week or two at a premium. Star attraction was Canton's own chart-topper, the Hangman's Children, and more specifically their leader. Here and there the hoardings carried his simple message: 'The Hangman Sings To-Nite!'

The voices on the radio and the promotion from Coastal Television spoke with frenzied enthusiasm of the fun to come. Sam Hoskins was apt to see the occasion in another perspective. Fun and noise, exuberance and self-assertion, usually ended as chronicles of booting and knifing and vomit in the long wearisome routine of charges and statements.

Canton's chart-topper . . . SUNDAY LOVE! There was an electronic screech from the public address system along the promenade. Then the tone dropped to that of a man telling a ghost story. *All you mummies and daddies lock away your little girls when the dark comes. Keep them safe from harm. Bolt the doors and fasten all the windows! Pull the sheet above your head and scream into the pillow, when you hear those footsteps coming up the stairs! You daddies lock yourselves in the bathroom. Tell the judge you never heard what the Hangman's Children did to the mummies in the bedroom. And all you kids giggle when the bathroom door goes in and the rope creaks and the knots slip tighter and the daddies sing, 'Don't do it to me! Not to me!' Because – THE HANGMAN SINGS TO-NITE! Come and hear him. Or he may come to you!*

Snarling and blasting in its anger, the voice of 'Sunday Love' whanged and shrilled from the speakers the length of the Cakewalk.

> *Monday is for Susie*
> *And Tuesday we sleep late*
> *Wednesday does for Julie*
> *And Thursday got no date.*
> *On Friday I'm in training*
> *And Saturday I rest,*
> *Ready for that Sunday Love*
> *That's gonna be the best . . .*

As Hoskins walked in the same direction as Scott the jangle and snarl faded a little, only to be renewed as he got nearer to the next lamp-post amplifier. The concert promoters had commandeered the public address system whose speakers hung from every light along the Cakewalk.

> *My Sunday Love, I'll take you*
> *And put you on your back,*
> *And twist and roll and squeeze you*
> *And hear your pips go crack!*
> *And every Monday morning,*
> *You'll hate what you have done,*
> *An icy little maiden*
> *That's melted by the sun . . .*

A few bikes had arrived. Their riders and passengers sprawled by the boating lake in the late warmth, indifferent or mesmerised by the din that now made the quiet residential air of The Vale shimmer with sound like a heat-haze.

Hoskins stopped between two of the public address speakers and looked down at the beach again where two girls, recognisably sisters of about fifteen and sixteen, were sitting with a younger boy. He glanced from the group to a man with a camera, standing some distance away. The voice from the speakers gave the summer tea-time no respite.

My Sunday Love I'll take you,
And stretch you on your back . . .
If you're the virgin martyr,
I'm gonna be your rack.
I'll pluck your little fiddle
Till every string hangs loose,
And weave that glossy golden hair
Into a silky noose . . .

The man's camera had its telephoto lens attached. It was, Hoskins judged, aimed at the younger of the two girls.

Hooooo, Sunday Love I'll grab you,
And take you all the way . . .

A sharp and shrewd little face, Hoskins would have said, looking at the younger sister. A hard lascivious slant to the brown eyes, a mouth prim and tight. Confidence, perhaps. Adolescent independence of the adult world. The hair cut straight and short, in the restrained punk of a middle-class daughter, with a bang of it on the forehead. A pair of close-fitting black pants showed the slim thighs of a nymph, hips and buttocks that suggested fledgling womanhood. Anyone who doubted the male appetite for such marginally under-age figures need only glance through the files of Canton City Police 'A' Division. The two girls and the boy were getting ready to go. As they stood and turned, knelt and stooped, the black arc of the lens came repeatedly to rest on them.

As if conspiring with her voyeur, the younger sister turned to face him and brushed the hair aside on her forehead.

'Take a proper photograph, then,' she called out, hands on hips.

She must have thought, Hoskins supposed, that he would hesitate in his guilt and slink away. It was a mistake made by women much older than she.

'Don't, Victoria!' the elder sister said sharply.

The man had raised the camera and taken his shot of her with her hands on her hips. Now, in his sun-hat and glasses, he was coming across to them, his mouth curved in a smile. Hoskins watched the group begin a curiously intent conversation. Perhaps the camera had been just the means of getting introduced. The elder sister and the boy turned away. Urged and coaxed by the photographer, Victoria was posing self-consciously, facing the sea and looking back over her shoulder a little at the man with his camera. The posture had a slight suggestive quality, but even from his own distance, Hoskins could see the uncertainty and strain in her young face.

'What's this then, Mr Hoskins?'

Scott in his patrolman's 'shirt-sleeve order' had come back.

'Probably nothing. A fancier chatting up a girl. Taking her picture. Nothing illegal just now.'

'There wouldn't be,' Scott said, 'would there? That comes later, out of sight. Could just be a hand in her knickers round the other side of the beach-huts. Could be the complete menu in the back of his car, in exchange for a banknote or two.'

Hoskins shook his head.

'She acts like the wrong class, Scottie. Two sisters, daughters of the bourgeoisie. To judge by the voice and even more by the manner, could be one of the private day-schools out towards Sandbar.'

Scott's bandit face grinned under his uniform peak.

'You want to do a bit of time on the cars, Mr Hoskins. It's the private school girls of sixteen or seventeen that drop 'em first and quickest. Dads in business or the professions. And they do it for free. At least the little girls down Peninsula and Barrier got the sense to put a price on it.'

'Romance,' said Hoskins sourly, 'is what it must be.'

Victoria was still in the photographer's clutches as he changed the lens and took her from close up. But she was looking round towards her elder sister and the boy, as if seeking a way of escape.

'Biting off more than she can chew is how it looks,' Scott said. 'You want me to take a walk along the sands, Mr Hoskins? Have a quiet word with our cameraman? Move him on? I could say hello to her. Ask her how many of her gentlemen-friends' balls her dad's guard-dogs have had for dinner this week.'

'Just subtle, Scottie,' Hoskins said, 'nod and a smile. A bit of interest in sir's camera and what it can do, and how much it costs. Nothing too heavy.'

'Right,' Scott said. 'Watch me.'

Hoskins shook his head.

'I'm going for a leak while I've got the chance. With all this bongo music and the yobs on the rampage, it could get to be a busy night. I'll be down the deck-chair store if I'm wanted.'

Even with the doors closed in the storeroom that overlooked the boating lake, there was no escape from the Hangman's angry and sardonic snarl.

> *Nah, Sunday Love I'll spread you*
> *And fill you full of fright*
> *And make you see the stars burst*
> *And turn your day to night . . .*

'Mind,' Hoskins said presently to PC Aspinwall in the deck-chair store, 'you've got to hand it to old Wadman. There he was, forty-five, dead-beat actor. Last proper engagement was playing the arse-end of a pantomime-horse at the pier pavilion one Christmas. Then a summer on the sands as a kids' entertainment. Uncle Willie: Punch and Judy, Conjuring, and Pederasty.'

'And what, Mr Hoskins?'

Hoskins waved away the objection.

'Then the poor old bugger suddenly gets it. Buys a wig that might be a long-haired girl of sixteen. Smooths out his wrinkles and takes in a tuck or two. A loan from his brother staked him to that. Then he works up his act. Young Revolution. Best performance he ever gave. Dam' sight better than when he was doing Ben Travers farces and Agatha Christie in local repertory. Got himself up all young and angry and snarling. Electric guitar and pre-recorded backing. Screw all the mummies and pig-stick the daddies and Let Young Revolution Rule the World. The best bit of make-up and acting he ever did.'

'Old Wadman?'

Hoskins nodded.

'And then he really hit it. Called himself the Hangman. Got a group called the Hangman's Children – scoutmasters from the *Gang Show* got up to look nasty. And four girl-dancers, made up vicious and sexy. The Toppers. Says he actually wants a volunteer to get hanged on stage during a concert. Anyone that's got nothing to live for but wants to leave a bit.'

'He can't!'

'Of course he can't!' Hoskins said. 'But asking for someone on the dole to volunteer in exchange for seeing his family all right is worth a fortune in publicity. And he'll get a few names. Headline stuff. All over the *Sun* and the *Mirror*. Unemployed miner to hang for money. The world might hear about Wadman. Then, best of all, he gets a juicy lyric like "Sunday Love" and makes the bloody charts. Young Revolution! He can't be that far off fifty. And all RADA and BBC repertory with it. He played Julius Caesar in a broadcast once.'

The door opened and Sergeant Rogers came in, track-suited from a patrol of the Ocean Park district.

'You been with that silly young bugger Scott, Sam?'

Hoskins braced himself for bad news.

'A while back. Why?'

'There's a punter on the beach with a bust camera and a fat lip. That stupid fucker Scott hit him.'

'Hit him?'

Rogers sat down and pulled off a canvas shoe, inspecting a small blister on the heel of his foot. He frowned at what he saw.

'Exchange of words, Sam. The bloke's got Scott's number and he's putting the matter in the hands of his solicitor. That's what comes of fat-arsed and jelly-bellied young clowns riding round in macho cars. Act like the sodding Gestapo. Land us all in the shit. And will you look at my bloody foot! Hand us a wet towel, young Aspinwall. I reckon I may never walk again.'

'Where's Scott?'

'Driven off in his fairy coach to hit someone else I expect. Bloody clown.'

Hoskins shook his head, as if fuddled by information.

'One thing,' he said presently, 'that punter's going to have to explain to his solicitor and the inquiry – and probably his missus – what he was doing taking friendly photographs of an under-age girl that he hadn't known from Adam two minutes before. I shouldn't think we'd hear from him again.'

'No thanks to the boys on wheels,' Rogers said.

Hoskins went to wash and then to eat his sandwiches in the rest room. As he prepared for the Hangman's concert, he guessed that it would be a long night. For him, the aggravation of that long night had already begun.

7

Until just before ten o'clock the performance was what the *Western World* and Coastal Television liked to call 'good-natured'. Hoskins stood with Sergeant Rogers at the side of the packed gardens, by a screen of laurel. The warm-up groups had finished. Out to sea, the lightning of blue and red lasers danced, describing arabesques in the sky above the cold Channel. Arcs of white brilliance lanced the late dusk and the jangle of strings from the amplifier gathered to a thumping and ear-aching din as Blitzkrieg finished its warm-up in a red burst of stage-fire.

Hoskins looked warily across the packed bodies in the space of the public garden, but the audience was collectively quiet and content as a baby with a bottle. From the Blue Moon terrace, a thunderflash lit the white lines of the surrounding houses and shook their windows.

The voice from the speakers keened and warped with excitement.

And now, all you mummies and daddies, pull them sheets up high! Push your faces into the pillow and scream quietly! Plug them fingers in your ears so you don't hear your little girls shriek with joy! Because now . . . Because now, it's the Hangman's Children that's coming up the stairs!

The din burst like a hailstorm on the public park. The Toppers swirled on to the stage, four young women in thigh-high snakeskin boots, waist-length cloaks of black silk, masks, and black hot-pants that were cut as brief and tight as the stitching would allow.

'That's Sharon Rees,' Hoskins said for Rogers's benefit, as the leader of the girls stepped forward. 'About a year ago, she was a trainee drama teacher out at Mount Pleasant Junior School. Never looked back.'

The din subsided to an electronic jingle as the pale, sleekly plump young woman came forward, long-haired and pudding-faced with green and red scrolling painted on her upper thighs and cheeks. She held the microphone like an ice-cream cone, her voice a husky murmur to begin with.

And tonight . . . we dedicate tonight to the mummies and daddies and their favourite toys. We're gonna take those toys away. We're going to take them all away . . . Nothing to play with any more . . . So tonight is dedicated to the destruction of cars . . .

She swirled round the terrace in the brilliant white-fire, trailing the flex, smacking herself on the thighs and hips as if in a promise of violence to come. Then she was back again.

Last year, the mummies and the daddies in their cars killed six thousand people. The Hangman adopts those that the pigs in their cars hate and hurt. Six thousand of the Hangman's Children. The Hang-man is angry. And the Hangman's Children want justice. Rough justice . . . So tonight is sacred to the destruction of cars . . .

She did another turn of the stage, came back, smacked herself, braced her sleekly booted legs and began again in a simple little-girl voice. The three other Toppers jigged and smacked and finger-clicked behind her.

I was so poor . . . I was so poor I had nothing but one little penny. I took my penny for a walk, down the street they park their cars . . . My penny made a silver flash down the side of every car . . . My penny cost a million pennies more . . .

She turned her back, bent over, and pulled a grimace at them through the arch of her own legs.

The face that sits in the driving-seat of a car is a pig's face. . . . Tonight is dedicated to the destruction of cars . . . And of pigs that make the air smell and kill the Hangman's Children . . . All of you – the Hangman's Children. Young Revolution is the Hang-man's Children . . . The Hangman's Children are everywhere . . . Waiting . . .

A sudden female ululating began on the far side of the gardens and ended with laughter.

The young woman on the stage grinned quickly and returned to her theme.

Tonight is sacred to the destruction of cars ... And pigs ... Whole families of piggies ... If you can't stick a pig with your point ... Stick his tyres ... All you little girls hear the sigh of the tyre go down when you stick it ... Like a pig's belly going down ... And the way a girl is made, it takes a boy to fill the piggies' petrol-tank with no-go fuel ...

Rogers turned to Hoskins while Sharon Rees cooed and sneered on the stage.

'What's old Wadman got against motors?'

'Nothing. He's got four limos parked in his palace grounds out on Hawks Hill. One's a Bentley. That and half a million quid of house, a heated swimming pool and a clean change of teenage girls every Friday.'

By now the Toppers were leading the fans in a familiar ritual chorus.

Bored and blue? Nothing to do? Kill the pigs and smash their cars!

Wadman, the Hangman himself, had appeared with his four masked 'children' behind him. He was dressed in black leather riding-breeches and singlet, stitched with red spangles. He wore welder's goggles in place of a mask and a Ned Kelly hat.

What do the Hangman's Children say?

The fans chanted back in a gathering howl.

Bored and blue! Nothing to do! Kill the pigs! And smash their cars!

Wadman grinned. He shook the long hair of his teenager wig and began to snarl into the microphone again.

It takes the Hangman's Children to drive the mummies wild! More than one at a time – and more than one way at a time ... Yeah, it takes the Hangman's Children to do it the way the mummies like so much that they don't mind the curtain-call – only please don't leave me! Yeah! It takes the Hangman's Children to drive the mummies wild ... The mummies squeak with fright and wanting it, when they hear the Hangman's Children on the stairs ...

One of the masked quartet leant forward and breathed into the microphone.

The mummies with their legs crossed tight ... And the daddies that can't get it up ... They love their cars ... Meaning, LOVE THEIR CARS! ...

Wadman intervened in a low sardonic whisper.

And when the Hangman kicks the stool away, the daddies get it up ... Die smiling ... And the mummies squeak with two at a time ... Yeah! ...

The leader of the Toppers was twirling round him, smacking her thighs and hips to lend emphasis to his words.

Hurting the daddies is smashing their cars ... And hurting the mummies is smashing their cars ...

'This could get nasty,' Rogers said, shifting foot to foot.

Next time a pig in a car horns you off the road, take his number and go looking for him ... Next time a prat at the wheel runs you aside, go looking ... Go looking ...

Wadman was there again, the Hangman grinning against a background of jangle and drum-beat.

When the mummies in their car break down ... The Hangman's Children wheel them away ... The Railway Dock ... Lock them in ... Wheel them over and down they go ... See them twenty feet below the tide ... The mummies at the window making faces ... Real good faces ... When the water creeps in and rises ... Good to see them making faces ... Pressing harder at the glass ... Saying ARRRRRGH! Tonight is sacred to the destruction of cars ...

'The whole thing's sick,' Rogers said. 'See if I'd let my kids near it!'

Young Revolution! Let's hear it for the Hangman's Children!

The fans roared back at him.

Bored and blue! Nothing to do! Kill the pigs! Smash their cars!

The night sky above the waters of the Channel danced again with lasers, yellow and purple. White shafts divided the darkness, like a city under aerial attack. At last, with a thump and a growl, the Hangman gave them what they were waiting for. The Finale.

> *Oh, Monday is for Susie,*
> *And Tuesday we sleep late.*
> *Wednesday does for Julie*
> *And Thursday got no date ...*

Hoskins turned away and walked towards the road that circled the park. A white transit van was parked in one of the residential closes with a dozen uniformed men from

Ocean Beach Division. There were four patrol cars and an unmarked Fiesta. No more than five or six uniformed men were in position. He doubted that there could be more than thirty all told. He turned and walked back.

'If this gets rough,' he said to Rogers above the din, 'we could find ourselves a bit lonely.'

But Wadman was giving his admirers value for their money. The Toppers in the hot-pants and masks, their bare thighs and cheeks painted in the tribal swirls of red and green, were trailing long whips, cracking them at random with a report that made the air sing.

> *My Sunday Love I'll take you,*
> *And stretch you on your back,*
> *If you're the virgin martyr,*
> *I'm gonna be your rack . . .*

'Mobile Four to Chief Inspector Hoskins. Sergeant Lucas. We might have trouble down the Ocean Front end. A couple of bottles being thrown and a lot of jostling by the lake.'

Hoskins lowered his mouth to his lapel.

'Keep an eye on it, Harry. Don't get in too fast. This lot's breaking up in a minute. We'll need everyone in place to get them all away.'

'I'll just watch then, Mr Hoskins.'

> *I'll pluck your little fiddle,*
> *Till every string hangs loose . . .*

'What I don't understand,' Rogers said wistfully, 'is girls liking this sort of thing.'

Hoskins grunted. The spotlights were flashing in time to the thumping beat of the music.

> *And weave that glossy golden hair*
> *Into a silky noose . . .*
> *Ho, Sunday Love you'll walk on air*
> *And high-kick can-can style . . .*

'There ought to be a law,' Rogers said.

At last the applause died away and the Blue Moon terrace went dark. In the pause before the bemused fans began to shuffle away, the young woman's voice breathed through the amplifiers again.

Six thousand of the Hangman's Children killed last year . . . Young Revolution is angry . . . Tonight is sacred to the destruction of cars . . .

Like a sudden downpour of cold rain, the system went dead. Hoskins turned towards the half-built Ocean Front apartments. The crowd at that end was sitting tight, shouting and laughing. In the park lights he could see bottles being passed round and cans ripped open. All the same, there was no sign of a disturbance.

'We'd best get these little bastards on their feet and out of here,' Rogers said, nodding at the squatters by the boating-lake. 'Supposed to be a residential area, not a sit-out for yobs.'

Hoskins looked again.

'Give 'em a minute. They can't get through yet. Not the way the road's swarming with people. Let most of 'em start and we can deal with the rest.'

The slow press of bodies moved down The Vale towards the main sweep of Bay Drive, tossing its cans and wrappers over garden walls. Hoskins guessed that the residents would be grateful for their reprieve. On occasion, it had been worse than litter. Much, much worse. Somewhere he heard glass break. It was probably a bottle rather than a window. Probably. The voice from the lapel radio squawked at him.

'Mobile Four to Leader. Bit of high spirits by the Ocean Front part of the boating lake. Someone might end up going in. Want us to move, Mr Hoskins?'

'I'll come down,' Hoskins said quietly. 'Keep clear if you can. Respond but don't start anything. There's half a dozen press cameras still wandering about. I don't want to see police punching up fans on the front page of the *Western World* tomorrow morning.'

'Right-oh, Mr Hoskins,' said the disembodied voice of Sergeant Lucas.

Hoskins followed the path round the dark space of the boating lake, past the lit windows of the deck-chair store and the flights of steps leading up to the Cakewalk promenade. The fans at the Ocean Front end of the lake were standing up now, forming a semicircular human arena round a group of several young women who sat near the concrete edge. On the far side of the crowd Hoskins could make out Sergeant Lucas and a constable in the lamplight.

He began to shoulder his way through the tight press of grinning onlookers. One of the young women was arguing with the front row of the crowd. She was sharp-eyed and prim-mouthed, hair tousled and cropped. Her knee-boots were of the sleekest and tightest tan, the jeans above them fitting like a second skin.

There was a silence in the crowd, and then a jeer.

'You want to get them wet things off,' a voice said, 'before you catch a cold or worse.'

'Less you're so shy you'd rather swim the lake to the bushes,' someone else said. 'Fancy that, would you?'

'P'raps she's only thirteen . . . '

'Who cares? I'm not superstitious.'

There was a snort of laughter from several of them.

Hoskins began to push through harder. He heard a muted argument, a splash, and a cry from one of the other girls. He shoved the last intervening body out of the way as a photographer's flash split the lamplight at the lake's edge. The young woman was being helped from shallow depth. Her boots had filled with water, her jeans were soaked above the knees. Before he could reach her, she turned in the arms of her male supporters and screamed back, 'You bastards! I hope you're satisfied!'

With a feeling of unease, Hoskins knew that she was looking towards him. Sergeant Lucas was at his shoulder.

'All too quick, Mr Hoskins. Never saw what was happening through the crowd. Any case, she should've had more sense than to parade in front of this lot wearing pants that must have took a shoe-horn to get into. Still, no real harm done.'

'I hope you're right,' Hoskins said glumly.

The last of the crowd were beginning to drift away from the concrete shore of the lake. Shouting and laughter faded towards Bay Drive and the Cakewalk. Hoskins walked back slowly to the deck-chair store. Another two months, he supposed, and the season would be over. The holiday beach

'Pervert Patrol' would be wound up for another year. His punishment would be at an end. The Ripper would allow him back to Canton 'A' Division and some real work.

Someone was waiting for him by the door of the deck-chair store. It was Rogers.

'You'd better not get too comfy, Sam,' Rogers said.

'Why's that?'

'Old Clitheroe, Duty Superintendent down the Beach. He wants the lot of us. Now.'

'Now!' Hoskins glared at the Sergeant. 'What for?'

'There's hell let loose down Ocean Park funfair. Some of this lot, I suppose. There's fisting everywhere and the yobs on the rampage. Smashing up stalls. And bloody Wadman ought to be done for incitement.'

'Wadman?'

'Yes,' said Rogers savagely. 'Seems his admirers set the first car on fire down there. About ten minutes ago.'

8

The unmarked Fiesta with Hoskins, Aspinwall and Rogers cut the curve of Bay Drive. A light sea-mist of the summer night dampened the Cakewalk. Reflected neon lozenges of green and red shimmered and melted in the movement of the tide. Wet and wrinkled, the last of the torn posters with their angry long-haired hero still promised that the Hangman would sing to-nite.

Ocean Park was the run-down eastern end of Ocean Beach. It was hidden only by a headland of scrub and the tall whispering grass of waste land from Harbour Bar and Canton Railway Dock. Its concrete fairground, a railed-in metro-track to the Ocean Park platform, and a dilapidated row of cafés, souvenir shops and bingo parlours made up the area. Bay Drive circled the raised stretch of Ocean Park and came back on its tracks. With a swish of tyres on the damp tarmac, the Fiesta skirted the iron railings and tall grass of the railway bank. The driver pulled in by the kitchen yards of the cafés, at the back of the old Dunes Cinema that now housed the 'Family Fun' Amusements of gaming machines. At the rear of the buildings, the white rendering had decayed to the grime of trodden chalk or the piebald look of rancid cream.

Three of Clitheroe's patrol cars were drawn across to block Bay Drive between the bulb-lit entrance arch of Ocean Park and the lawn of the promenade. But the blue light flashing over the pay-box at the park entrance belonged to the County Fire Service. The hydrants were open and the blocked end of the sea-front was crossed by a network of hoses. Half a dozen unlit cars had been parked along the grass strip of the promenade, one of them hidden from view by the number of people round it. Hoskins guessed that it must have been the one set on fire. And, in that case, the fire was out.

He found Martin, the uniformed Inspector whose drivers had blocked off the road and the entrance arch of the concrete park.

'What's the score so far, Ken?'

'Damage,' Martin said grimly, nodding at the cars. 'Bloody great scratches down every set of doors. Wings kicked in on three of them. Two windscreens gone. Tyres slashed. And a can of paint-stripper splashed about. You can smell it from here. Don't tell me the little bastards didn't come prepared! Not a sign of who did it, by the time we got here. All the same, we've got a mob of them boxed in. In the amusement park. Only thing is, we're short-handed to put a cordon round it. There's some of 'em fisting the stall-keepers and park security men already. And there's two lots of black and white yobboes slaughtering each other. Couple of hundred all told, by the look of it. Not to mention a mob of civilians gaping at 'em. What a bloody mess!'

'And how many of our lot?'

Martin counted Aspinwall and Rogers.

'Fourteen with you three.'

'Sod that for a game of soldiers,' Hoskins said. 'Where's Mr Clitheroe? He was the one that sent for us.'

'Sticking pins in a map on his office wall. Doesn't want

to be provocative, he says. Doesn't want his balls kicked in, more like. I've put in another call to division. We can't handle this alone.'

At that moment there was a shout of warning from beyond the neon-lettered entrance arch of Ocean Park. Hoskins could just see that the 'Horrors of Fantomas', plywood-thin but large as a cinema façade, was swaying to and fro.

'You might have to handle it alone, Ken,' he said bitterly. 'They'll have that lot down in a minute. Someone could get killed in there.'

'I can't put a cordon round all that with fourteen of us, Sam. It's not . . .'

A ten-foot glass-fibre grass-green goblin, with a hatchet and a severed head dangling from one hand, slipped from its high ledge on the 'Horrors of Fantomas' front and crashed down twenty feet among the darts stalls and the shooting galleries. There was a communal roar of approval and a woman's scream. Martin looked about him helplessly.

One of the uniformed men was coming back from the entrance at a brisk stride.

'They've got the rifles from one of the galleries,' he said breathlessly. 'Not much power but they could put out an eye, Mr Barrett says.'

Hoskins stepped in.

'Right. I want three squads of four men each. We go in together. Each squad snatches one ringleader. Two men in each squad hold off the opposition, the other two do the snatch. If we can knock off half a dozen troublemakers, the rest might do a bunk.'

Martin looked at him uneasily.

'You done this before, Sam?'

'I'm doing it now,' Hoskins said grimly. 'Get the others.'

He took his glasses off and folded them away.

They advanced through the park entrance, stooping as the first bottle wheeled through the air and smashed on the ground just behind them.

'That bastard over there in the blue top and red trousers,' Hoskins said to Rogers. 'Get him first.'

'Right, Sam. Come on, you lot!'

The lights were still blazing and the steam-organ music

pumping out 'I Could Love a Million Girls' from the ampli-fiers. But the mob was scragging the gimcrack front of the 'Horrors of Fantomas', determined to bring it down. Two other adolescent gangs seemed to be fighting it out between themselves, over and round the 'Thunderbird' ride with its swivel seats and its blown-up 1950s portraits of Elvis and Marilyn smiling down from the backdrop.

Hoskins led his three uniformed men towards the giant skeletons, the skull-carrying demon and the red-eyed dragon of the 'Horrors of Fantomas'.

'I want that comedian with the rifle from the gallery,' he shouted back. As the four men dashed forward, the crowd of youths turned upon them. Hoskins put himself and Aspinwall between the sneering young faces and the two uniformed men carrying out the snatch. He was distantly aware that beyond the immediate concrete battleground the public had gathered in placid enthusiasm for the display. They stood meek and curious, watching the fight as if it had been an additional spectacle, staged by the management of Ocean Park. He had time only for an instant of incomprehension at the scene before someone hit him.

It was a boot, intended for his genitals but landing too low on his thigh. He and Aspinwall were still holding off the mob while the other two uniformed men grabbed and withdrew the boy at one side. Hoskins's immediate opponent might have been any of twenty in the crowd – the shaven head, the sleeveless black singlet and the heavy boots, the tattoo marks on arms and scalp. At close quarters there was a rank smell of sweat. A few yards away, Aspinwall was struggling with a black youth in a beige suit. The youth broke free. Aspinwall went to grab him.

'Don't!' Hoskins shouted, too late. Aspinwall lunged into the trap and was knocked to the ground by two of the others. He struggled up, bareheaded.

'Fucking Zulus,' he said uncomprehendingly, and then went down again. The two others had grabbed the sallow youth and dragged him off. Hoskins's skinhead aimed another kick, missed, and gave Hoskins time to grab his raised leg and twist it sharply. Thee boy spun and went down with a scream, a kitchen knife falling from his hand and bouncing on the concrete. Perky and undaunted, the steam-organ jollied the evening along. 'I could love a million girls with every girl a twin . . . '

There was a police helmet rolling on the ground as several hands reached for the fallen kitchen-knife. Hoskins knew that he and Aspinwall had left it too late. They should have pulled back as soon as the other two made their snatch. Thanks to Aspinwall's enthusiasm, they were caught alone among the mob. Someone jumped him from behind. He managed not to give way under the dragging weight. Once on the ground, he would get no mercy from the boots of the gangs. As he struggled against the weight on his back, he was distantly aware of other fights going on in the concrete spaces of the bright and noisy fairground. The others watched Hoskins and the assailant who rode him. As yet, no one else interfered. Then there was a splash on his cheek as one of them spat in his face.

A sudden bound, down and forward, threw the attacker off over his head. He looked for Aspinwall and knew that some-one was going to have to come to the rescue of them both. The organ pooped and blasted its encouragement. 'I could love a Chinese girl, an Eskimo, a Finn . . . ' At that moment, like a miracle from the sky, the bulb-lit skeleton on the high ledge of the 'Horrors of Fantomas' came down with a bright electric flash and smashed among the crowd in a shower of sparks. The youths began to scatter. Almost at once, there was an urging heave from the mob behind the sideshow and the entire façade swung to a new and curling angle. Another heave and the front of the horror house came down, rending itself vertically as it did so. There was a brighter electric flash, high above the darts stalls and the shooting galleries. In a split second, the fairground went black and the steam-organ, still rasping out its love of a million girls, failed with an expiring groan. Night and silence descended on the concrete spaces, like the slamming of a door.

While the gangs looked about them, Hoskins dived free in the direction of Aspinwall. The uniformed man was on the ground mumbling to himself, as if in uncertainty of some kind. Hoisting him in a fireman's lift, Hoskins picked his way, unrecognised in the sudden darkness, towards the entrance arch. Ahead of him, he could hear Martin shouting in the blackness, 'Turn the power off! Will you turn that power off! Someone could get injured!'

On the roadway the lamps along the promenade lawn lit the scene with the brassy fire of a sodium glow. Hoskins carried Aspinwall across to the grass.

'Sod it!' said Rogers. 'What's happened to him?'

'Knocked down and hit. Stunned, I think. I just hope to hell he hasn't been kicked in the head. Get on the blower. Ambulance. Quick.'

As Rogers went across to the cars, Aspinwall turned his head this way and that, lying on the grass.

'I'm all right,' he said, as if pleasantly surprised by the discovery. 'I'm fine. You carry on.'

Then he went quiet again.

'Sam?' It was Martin. 'I'm getting Clitheroe down here. Those little bastards in the fairground have bolted down the road to the metro-rail. I'll block off the approach. And we'll have men at every station to catch them as they come off. We've got three handcuffed in the van. What's wrong with him?'

'He got hit,' Hoskins said bitterly. 'I don't know how badly.'

'Ambulance?'

'Sent for. Everyone else OK?'

'Our lot are. There's some smelly little skinhead. He's going to get his dad to sort us out, he says. Leg twisted half out of its socket.'

'I reckon I must have done that one,' Hoskins said more brightly.

'Then I'd keep quiet, if I was you, Sam. Police violence towards the public is bad news nowadays, case you hadn't heard. And by the way there's a bloke looking for you. Sergeant Chance, he's called. Not from round here.'

'Jack Chance? He's my sergeant when I'm home, Canton "A" Division CID. When I'm not stuck on your bloody "Pervert Patrol" down the Beach. All we had today was one poor girl that wanted to show her chest of drawers. Four of us stuck down the deck-chair store all day just for that!'

'Country's got to be cleaned up, Sam. That woman on the telly's always saying so. You wouldn't want your kids seeing all that topless, would you?'

'Don't talk bloody daft, Ken. Topless is what they live on for the first few months. Holds no secrets for them.'

'Well, it does for the one on the telly.'

'Hang on to old Aspinwall for a minute,' Hoskins said. 'I'm going to see what Jack Chance wants.'

'Looking for you by the pay-box, he was.'

In the sodium half-light, Hoskins could identify the Sergeant by his bulk. Jack Chance had the round flushed face and flat black hair of an amiable drinking companion. His interrogations seemed like a chat between old friends. When he carried out an arrest it had the air of two reunited acquaintances going down to the pub together. Criminals were apt to misjudge him. There was still an incomplete internal inquiry as to how Jock the Mug from Martello Square managed to break his elbow while Chance was holding him by the arm.

'You're wanted, Sam,' Chance said cheerily.

'Wanted?'

'Bit of business.'

'Not tonight, my son. I've been on my bloody pins since eight this morning and I'm due off any minute. And I've got all the business I need, right here.'

'The Ripper says so.'

'After you with the Ripper.'

'And Clitheroe says it's all right by him. The party's over down here. Been a break-in at Ocean Beach.'

'Break-ins at Ocean Beach are nothing to do with me. Just topless on the sands.'

'This one's to do with you, Sam. Pruen.'

'Pruen? "Horse-Parlour" Pruen? Who's he done?'

'He's been done, Sam. Tonight. In very unusual circumstances. Neighbours go round. Find all the doors and windows open. Lights blazing. No alarms on. Looks like the SAS just been through it. Wrecked. And not a sign of Pruen, or his old lady, nor of the dolly that he had for Christmas. No one. Work that out. Bit of overtime in the old pay-packet.'

'Tomorrow,' Hoskins said reasonably. But Chance was unimpressed.

'Mr Ripley says tonight. There's two plods in pointed hats on guard there. But you don't really think that some underworld semi-final is going to be handed over to Clitheroe and his parking wardens? Do you, Sam?'

'For all I care,' Hoskins said, tight-lipped but resigned.

'I left the car just round the other side,' Chance suggested helpfully.

9

Chance turned the car on to the main sweep of Ocean Beach. The white pearl-chains of ornamental lamps traced the line of the Cakewalk in the dark, curving away towards the western hill and the overcliff drive of Highlands Avenue. The illuminated clock at the New Pier entrance showed that it was a few minutes past midnight.

'There's this one about Clitheroe and the woodentops in Ocean Beach,' said Chance with a snigger. 'Anyway, one day they're all going down in the lift and it sticks between floors. And it's all these blokes trapped in there with Councillor Eve Ricard and the Women's Committee.'

Hoskins glanced aside. A boy was being sick in the shelter of the pier entrance. Two uniformed men were holding another youth between them. Chance pulled out, round a parked squad car with its blue light revolving lethargically.

'Anyway,' said Chance happily, 'they're stuck there for days. And everyone's hellish hungry and really frustrated. Dying for it. And then Eve Ricard comes up to Clitheroe and says that the Women's Committee have decided to make the big sacrifice. They all want to be casseroled. And Clitheroe says, "Bloody hell," he says. "Whatever happens we couldn't eat human flesh." "I'm not talking about eating," Eve Ricard says. "Casseroled. Done slowly for several hours."'

He snorted again and slapped his knee at the neatness of it.

'Yes,' Hoskins said glumly, 'very humorous. Turn right here, if you want old Pruen's place.'

'Not your day, is it, Sam?'

'Not my night either. I should've been in bed by now. And I was ballsed off even before that. Comes of having your sense of humour to share a car with.'

Chance spun the wheel.

'You could do worse, Sam. You want to hear old Dodd going on about Bradley's feet in their motor. Pong something awful however much the poor devil washes them. Hereditary, they think.'

Hoskins yawned.

'Pull in, over here by the call-box,' he said. 'I want a look round first.'

Chance locked the car and followed him to the open gate in the flintstone wall. One of the uniformed men came up to them.

'Family,' Hoskins said, flipping open the misty green plastic of his warrant-card, 'Hoskins, DCI, Canton "A" Division. What's all this about?'

'Dunno, Chief. Next-door neighbours come round about an hour ago. They find the doors open and lights on, the place done over. Alarm switched off. No sign of Pruen or his missus or the skivvy. Someone made a real pig of themselves in there. The carpet's turned back in the hall and the floor safe's open. There's a few bits of jewellery left in there. Might not be much value. Can't say what might have gone. And the phone's been ripped out, by the way. Torn clean out of the socket.'

Hoskins shook his head and came to the white front door with its red spray-can graffito. PRUEN THE PUNTER DIED HERE!

'That's nice,' he said, 'real class. Wait till Pruen's friends and a few of the hard men start tickling up this comedian with a knife. Plastic surgeons that whistle while they work.'

They stepped into the hall with its disordered carpet and the round, up-ended steel door of the safe.

'Pruen's too old,' Chance said knowledgeably, 'past that sort of aggro.'

Hoskins squatted down and peered into the looted barrel of the safe.

'He may be old, my son. But even if he doesn't call out the razors, Carmel Cooney and the rest aren't going to stand for the brotherhood being hit like this. Pruen could be in a terminal coma and still hand out a spanking second-hand. Whoever did this, I'd say they have strictly limited expectations of life.'

Chance went up the stairs, not touching the rail. A moment later he reappeared on the landing.

'Up here, Sam. Right little slaughterhouse. They've smashed the bog. It's leaking all over the bathroom. The bath's been cracked. There's a bedroom ceiling down and the paper hanging off the wall in strips.'

Hoskins went up, noticing the splintered struts of the banister.

'Might be burglary,' he said. 'Might be civil war, if we're unlucky. Some impatient young bull ready to bust Pruen and Cooney and the rest.'

He looked about him and the two of them went downstairs again. The sweet peardrop smell of spray-paint hung heavy in the air and irritated his throat. He went into the sitting-room and saw the cotton-fluff trail of ripped cushions, the arcs of dribbling paint across ceiling and walls.

'You could almost feel sorry for Pruen,' he said.

An engine roar filled the darkness outside and a white light cut across the uncurtained windows. Chance looked out.

'It's all right,' he said. 'The Martians have landed. That's all.'

Two police motor-cyclists in helmets and boots were crunching across the gravel.

Hoskins turned to Chance.

'We've got a scene-of-crime officer. That's you. And what we need now is forensic, knee-deep. Tell that pair to shove off and arrest someone.'

'Right,' Chance said. 'And, by the way, you're scene-of-crime officer. Mr Ripley says so.'

Fifteen minutes later a sergeant and a constable from Area Forensic arrived and began to dust over the furniture-surfaces with white powder to show up fingerprints. The first camera flashed.

'Don't move that,' Hoskins said, pointing to an enamel bowl of water that stood on the polished table.

Chance looked at it closely.

'You reckon Mrs P liked to wash the old boy's socks on the Chippendale, Sam?'

Hoskins glared.

'What I reckon is that if Pruen or one of the others doesn't show up soon, I'm going to radio in another report. Three missing persons. If there's a civil war breaking out, this might not be burglary. Kidnapping. Even murder. I don't much care for the smell of it.'

One of the uniformed men came in.

'Had a word with the neighbours, Chief. Pruen and his wife and the skivvy were definitely here early this evening. Then about half-past eight the kids saw a girl in the garden. Didn't know her from Adam. They asked her about Noreen, Pruen's bit of extra. This girl says Noreen's out and won't be back till later.'

'Did they give a description of the girl?'

'Bit rough-looking. Fourteen or fifteen. Schoolgirl.'

'*Schoolgirl?*' said Hoskins scornfully. 'You reckon a team of fourteen year olds from Parklands Comprehensive did this?'

'Team of fourteen year olds from Parklands and the house wouldn't be standing at all,' said Chance quietly.

Hoskins glared again at the interruption.

'What I want— '

The second uniformed man appeared in the sitting-room doorway.

'Chief! There's a car turning in at the gate. Reckon it must be them.'

Hoskins strode forward, his head beginning to ache with fatigue. The car ground its way slowly over the gravel and stopped by the garage door. Pruen got out on one side and a girl on the other. This, Hoskins supposed, was Noreen.

'Mr Pruen?'

Pruen looked up, the squat weighty figure with a grey fringe, moustache, and horn-rimmed glasses. He walked slowly and comfortably across, recognising the Chief Inspector as if with relief.

'Mr Hoskins? What you doing here?'

'You've had a break-in. Let's go somewhere and talk about it. Leave the girl here. Where's Mrs Pruen?'

'I know all about the break-in,' Pruen said, shouldering his way into the hall. 'Mrs Pruen's in Canton Infirmary. Intensive care. Heart trouble. Soon as she's well enough, I'm moving her out of that dog-house. Somewhere private, where they listen to what's said to 'em.'

In the light of the hall, a purple swelling and a cut appeared clearly on Pruen's cheekbone. Hoskins ignored this for the moment.

'We'll go in the room opposite, Mr Pruen, if that's all right. Just need a few details. That's all.'

They picked their way over the disordered carpet in the hall. The dining-room had received little of Del's attentions, apart from the ripping out of the telephone lead. The two men sat down at the table with Chance at a discreet distance.

'You knew about this, Mr Pruen?'

'That's right.' Pruen spoke heavily, almost with indifference. Hoskins wondered if he could have been given a sedative at the infirmary. He thought not.

'How's that then, Mr Pruen?'

'I was out with the girl, Noreen. Just for a drive. She drives me sometimes, when I don't feel up to much. Come back about half-past eight or so. And I find this. The dogs that done it had just scarpered, I reckon.'

'Mrs Pruen was here when it happened?'

Pruen raised his head and the watery blue eyes behind their thick lenses stared at Hoskins as if he should have known better.

'Course she was here, Mr Hoskins! That's what all this is about, isn't it? Soon as I stopped the car, I could see what was wrong. I came through that front door at a run and took a fall over the carpet, the way it is. Cut me face open. Into the sitting-room and there she is. Out cold. Collapsed. She got a heart condition, Mr Hoskins. Had one for years. Them dogs got something to answer for, believe you me.'

'You called an ambulance?'

'Case you hadn't noticed, they done the phone in!' said Pruen bitterly. 'And don't ask me did I fuck about raising a neighbour and see if I could borrow theirs. And then find the ambulance lot won't accept a niner unless you're a doctor or something. She was unconscious, Mr Hoskins! We got her to the car and drove like hell for the casualty department. And as soon as we done all we could there, we come back. I sat by the ward a couple of hours. I'm so knackered just now I could lie down in the middle of all this and go to sleep.'

'You weren't anywhere near during the break-in?'

'I told you,' Pruen pleaded. 'I was out with the girl. Out towards Sandbar for an evening drive. If I had been here, it wouldn't ever have happened.'

'And how do you suppose they managed to open your floor-safe?'

Pruen bared his teeth with impatience.

'Because I hadn't bothered to set it, Mr Hoskins. There was nothing in there worth taking.'

'But they found it, all the same.'

'Yes,' said Pruen sarcastically. 'I 'spect they threatened to do something highly original to her if she didn't tell 'em where it was. Thank God she did.'

'We'll have to ask her about it, Mr Pruen.'

'You do anything to upset her recovery, Mr Hoskins, and I'll have so many writs plastered over you, you'll look like a bog-roll on legs. All right?'

Chance sighed and intervened.

'We want to catch these villains, Mr Pruen. See them put away for what they did to you. That's all.'

'Right,' said Pruen, a grudging apology in his voice. 'Only don't you go upsetting her until she's well. And if it's all the same to you, I'm going to bed.'

'You won't find it easy up there, Mr Pruen.'

'I didn't say here. I put through a call to the Garden Royal for rooms for me and the girl. They got twenty-four-hour porter and car-monkey.'

'I dare say we'll still be here in the morning, Mr Pruen.'

A few minutes later, Hoskins and Chance watched Pruen and his girl carry two suitcases out to the car.

'What d'you think, Sam?'

'Ask Muriel Pruen.'

'Load of old tom, that stuff about going for a drive,' Chance said. 'Look at his face. Someone hit him. You think his tart's in it?'

Hoskins stared at Noreen, the lank dark hair fringed on her forehead, the firm fair-skinned features and the contemptuous slant of her brown eyes. In her singlet and jeans, she appeared well-made rather than plump. There was strength in the firm length of her smoothly jeaned thighs, worn tight enough for the seam to be drawn between her buttocks and legs.

'I reckon she can get old Pruen's attention,' he said. 'Still, if she was part of the hit, I don't think she'd be hanging around now. She might really fancy the poor old sod.'

'When I'm his age,' said Chance wistfully, 'what I'd really like— '

'More to the point,' Hoskins said firmly, 'I don't want Pruen feeding us a load of old garbage just so that he can settle accounts with whoever did this.'

The midnight-blue Citröen banged into life and crunched slowly down the drive.

'P'raps he did it for the insurance,' Chance said. 'Knock off the insurance.'

Hoskins turned and stared at his sergeant with a mixture of astonishment and pity.

'You really don't get it, Jack, do you? In this line of business, Pruen *is* the insurance. And the judge and jury. You want a razor in the corner of someone's mouth and a nice neat cut back to the ear? I don't say Pruen would do the job himself. But the man who would is only a phone call away. Whoever turned this place over, their best bet would be to top themselves now, nice and easy with a handful of pills. Might save them more grief than they could even bear to think about without a scream or two.'

He turned away and began to pick his path through the rubble of the Pruens' sitting-room.

10

The cricket-chirrup of the alarm-clock woke Hoskins, light-headed after two hours' sleep. Beyond thin bedroom curtains, early sunlight flooded the empty concrete-banked arena of the Lamb's Acre rugby ground which the Lamb's Chambers apartments overlooked.

It was just after seven o'clock. The Ripper would be off-watch by eight. Catch the Ripper before he left. Report the events at Ocean Beach and hand the whole thing over to some other poor sod. Hoskins pulled on his slippers and shuffled into the little kitchen to heat the coffee. He turned the switch and the radio came on simultaneously. He recognised the voice of Coastal News.

'... in the concert gardens of The Vale last night. The Hangman's first concert on the Blue Moon terrace was a lively but generally ...'

'Good-natured,' said Hoskins sourly before the newsreader could get there.

'... good-natured event. Councillor Eve Ricard ...'

'After you with Eve Ricard.' Hoskins poured milk from the bottle.

'... Chair of the Women's Committee, will move later this morning for an inquiry into reports that young women were intimidated and assaulted by certain groups of fans when the concert was over, in the presence of uniformed and plain clothes police officers. Councillor Ricard told our reporter George Owen that police had stood by and watched while the assaults were carried out. Elsewhere in Ocean Beach last night, three arrests were made after several cars were damaged near Ocean Park. Canton city centre was quiet and the weekend was generally ...'

'Good-natured!'

'... without serious incident.'

'Bollocks!' Hoskins said and turned off the set.

He went into the bathroom and, curiously for a man who had lived alone for fifteen years, bolted the door.

By ten to eight he was driving down the pink-tarmac'd Mall, past the Memorial Gardens and the Exhibition Domes of City Hall towards the bleak cliff-face of the new City Police Headquarters. He took the lift to the fifth floor and went down the corridor to his room. Leaving his case on the desk, he crossed the corridor and tapped at the door of Superintendent Maxwell Ripley.

Ripley looked up, a grey moustached fifty-three year

old, nursing his blood pressure along to retirement and the Bournemouth train.

'How's it going, Sam?'

Even with the most dire decision confronting him, Hoskins had seldom known the Ripper to begin a conversation with any other comment than this.

'It's going too fast for me, Max.'

Ripley stood up and nodded. The gesture conveyed that he understood and was displeased.

'We've got flak coming in about Ocean Beach last night, Sam.'

'Oh?'

Without explanation, Ripley turned and flicked on his television monitor. He slid the tape into the player and pressed a button.

'Watch this,' he said quietly.

The *CN* logo of Coastal Television's early morning news swam into focus.

'Councillor Eve Ricard, Chair of the City Council Women's Committee, interviewed by George Owen, explained her accusation of police inaction . . . '

'I had an earful of this on the radio,' Hoskins said.

'Then you can have it with pictures as well, Sam.'

Pictures. Eve Ricard, in her nondescript twenties, hoisted to prominence on Canton City Council over the heads of long-serving party members, the steady and despised old buffaloes of the Labour political team. She was blinking in the camera-light, blue eye-shadow and black hair in a little-boy shortie.

'When the hell was this done, Max?'

'Just before seven this morning, Sam.'

Eve Ricard, perhaps not realising she was on camera, gave a quick self-confident smile over her shoulder. Behind her, several of her supporters' voices were chanting, 'Whatever we wear, wherever we go, "Yes" means "Yes" and "No" means "No!"'

Eve Ricard froze them to silence by her smile. The camera moved in so that the rest were excluded, except for a cross-looking girl with a freshly scrawled placard. 'Dead Men Don't Rape', it said.

George Owen's voice assumed the earnest curiosity of the dedicated student.

'Councillor Ricard, we heard the police view, a moment ago, of events at the Blue Moon concert last night. In what way does your account differ?'

The eyelashes blinked with anger or excitement.

'In almost every way . . . ' Hoskins recognised the twang and whine of the cultivated 'classless' accent, the voice of a new ruling class in town hall and council committee.

'But the allegations specifically, Miss Ricard . . . '

'Specifically, the police were there to keep order during the concert. Right? And afterwards, it was their job to protect people from attack or molestation. Our information says that a group of men in Fascist gear deliberately set out to provoke trouble. Assaults were made on women. In front of witnesses. Deliberate assaults, right? And the police stood on the edges of the crowd and did nothing. In fact, they packed up and left during the attacks. And we want to know, how dare they turn away when women were being attacked, when . . . '

Behind her the steps of City Hall seemed a forest of disembodied legs in the early morning sun. George Owen got in again.

'According to the police this morning, some of the officers were called away because of the trouble at Ocean Park and— '

'Most of the police were called away,' she said with gentle anger, 'because, in this city, damage to a few cars is thought to be more important than violence against women . . . '

The reply brought a burst of clapping and an ululating that was quickly hushed.

'I understand,' Owen said obligingly, 'that you have details of a young woman who fell into the boating lake – or was pushed . . . '

'And several cases of assault on women by gangs of men, while other men in police uniforms stood and did nothing. Right? All men together there, against women! And we've got independent witnesses to that.'

'If that's so . . . '

'It is so. No question. And it's coming before the Police Committee of this city in a few hours, to see justice is done to the women who were the victims.'

Eve Ricard's eyes were bright with the zeal of a martyred ecstatic. Then, as if at the moment of release, the energy went and she seemed to sink into a calm post-coital contemplation. It crossed Hoskins's mind that this was how she got off, on the excitement of her own rhetoric. Ripley turned off the video.

'That's it, Sam.'

'Bollocks,' Hoskins said for the second time that morning. 'There was a girl fell in the boating lake, at least she got wet up to the knees. She might have stepped in, for that matter. That's the lot, except for a bit of language. As for walking out on it, old Clitheroe sent word. Yobs fisting the public down Ocean Park and the cars being set on fire. What would you have done? Told your superior officer to get stuffed?'

Ripley stared at him and cleared his throat.

'You can remember a bit of law from your inspector's exams, can you, Sam?'

'Meaning?'

'Meaning, that assault does not require physical contact. Assault is an act which puts the victim in reasonable fear of such contact. Ricard says so in another part of that interview. And she talked to a lawyer first. Assault, in that sense, is said to have occurred in your presence.'

'Come off it, Max.'

'No, Sam. You come off it – in short order. You may like to think of Ricard as a stupid ladder-climbing little dyke. But that woman's going to the Police Committee, with the full backing of the Women's Committee. And they've got a tame lawyer – Lobo. Remember him? He must still love you for telling him in cross-examination that he's not really black!'

'Look, Max— '

'No, Sam! You look! They have witnesses to assault in the strict legal sense, even if no one was touched. Even if that girl fell into the pond because she was tight, you'll still get screwed. I dare say the *Western World* may put up two fingers to Ricard and her gay friends. But Coastal News and the telly is running scared witless of her attack on media bias. You could see how even George Owen wouldn't tackle her. And she's got a couple of her lady friends vetting the news output. I wouldn't like to be wearing your skin when the broadcast coverage of those committees starts. Just a minute.'

He switched on the video and wound the picture fast. It steadied and the sound came on.

' . . . evidence of assault, apart from allegations?' Owen inquired.

'Assault,' said Eve Ricard with grinding insistence, 'is being put in reasonable fear of attack. Right? These women were victims of sexist assaults by a gang of men. Probably intending rapists. Take their words for it, not mine. "Get those things off!" Things, of course, being the woman's clothes. We know if we're put in fear or not. We're the ones who can say. We're not having other people decide our feelings for us. Right? If women were put in fear, that's legally assault. The police stood by and did nothing. Just watched the assaults taking place – crime taking place – and did nothing. They weren't interested, until they heard that a car or two had been damaged.'

'How many of you here at the moment have evidence— '

'No!' An angry voice from somewhere in the crowd cut the interviewer short. 'They know if they were put in fear by these men. We're not having Tory media misrepresenting the victims of sexist violence! Never again! Never again! . . .'

The chant spread. A disproportionately-sized hand, evidently not Eve Ricard's, descended and blacked out the image. Ripley turned the machine off.

'In case you still don't get the point, Sam, there it is. In simple words and pictures.'

Hoskins felt like a man caught in the middle of a tornado. There was no safety in any direction.

'What happened,' he said doggedly, 'was that this girl starts parading up and down in skin-tight jeans and high boots. Some comedian shouts out, asks her to give the assembled company a flash. A few more witty remarks like that and then she probably steps, not falls, into the water. She was wet to the top of her legs at most. If she did it of her own accord, by accident, or got nudged, I can't say. And that's all there was. Finish. The lot.'

'Her name is Miss Wood,' Ripley said quietly, 'and she's a management trainee, twenty-six years old with a BA degree. Articulate and respectable.'

'Then she should have more sense than to go squirming her backside about in front of a load of half-pissed yobboes,' said Hoskins furiously.

The Ripper shook his head.

'Try that tack in front of the committees, Sam, and you'll be lucky to have a job this time next month.'

There was a pause. Behind Ripley's head the window showed a northern prospect of Canton, summer heat gathering over the leafy gardens and red tiles of Hawks Hill, shimmering on the Stalinist tower-blocks of the Mount Pleasant estates.

'I left on Clitheroe's orders,' Hoskins said simply, 'so that I could enjoy myself down Ocean Park, where a sweaty little skinhead was trying to kick my appendages clean past my Adam's apple.'

The Ripper picked up a sheet of paper.

'We've got a threat of a complaint about that, Sam. Overreaction towards a civilian. His dad was called.'

'As for that!' said Hoskins bleakly. 'I was the one who nearly got the reaction, Max! With the toe of his boot! For God's sake! Some smelly little tearaway from down Peninsula or Barrier . . . '

'You're behind the times, Sam. They don't all come from back-to-back and high-rise any more. His dad is senior partner in Ramsay and Braden, the city accountants. All the best skinheads nowadays come from families that vote Tory or SDP. They know their rights and they can afford a bit of law.'

Hoskins sat down, uninvited.

'I've had two hours sleep in the last twenty-four, Max. I don't think I really care about much at the moment. Sod the lot of 'em!'

The Ripper sat down too, behind his desk with the personal ruler and the framed photograph.

'On the other hand, Sam,' he said pleasantly, 'there's Pruen. A nice juicy one, that.'

'I dare say.'

'I had a word with Mr Clitheroe. I think – and he agrees with me – as things stand you might be better employed on that investigation than on the beach surveillance. We'll have to run the Pruen case from city CID, of course.'

'That's something,' Hoskins said, reserving his gratitude.

'You'll be brought back to Canton "A" Division from secondment. My suggestion, Sam. What I thought was, when the council committees start roasting you, it'd be more convenient to have you on hand in the city centre than stuck all the way out at Ocean Beach. It makes better operational sense. Wastes less man-hours with unnecessary travel.'

Half an hour later, Hoskins faced Sergeant Chance in his own office.

'I never felt more like handing in my papers in my life.'

'Oh, yes,' said Chance heavily, 'very clever. So you could start being a brave front-line store-detective down M & S or C & A, grappling with hardened female criminals that's helped themselves to an extra pair of tights. Real step-up that'd be.'

Hoskins screwed up a sheet of paper and threw it at the basket. It missed and bounced away, as he knew it would on this particular morning.

'Oh, what the hell,' he said wearily.

'You'll be around here a long time, Sam. Same reason as the rest of us. Bugger-all else to do for a living in this poxy town.'

Left alone, Hoskins stared moodily from the windows of his room. Like the Ripper, he had a northern panorama of leafy Hawks Hill, the beginning of the long green valley and the other extreme of the fortress-like Mount Pleasant estates. It was the far window that showed him the southern scene, the flat alluvial foreshore on which the city of Canton proper had been built.

Immediately below him lay the pink tarmac of the Mall and the public gardens, the cherry trees and the domes of City Hall in hot August sunlight. Beyond that the department stores of Great Western Street led down to the railway bank dividing the shops and hotels of Atlantic Wharf from the dockland cranes. To the east of the centre lay the old back-to-back streets of Barrier. To the west was the dockland Peninsula across the river bridge, and the nearer spread of Orient with its narrow terraces, clubs, Tandoori restaurants and Chinese takeaways.

For all his experience, it was the only place he had ever known – except the jungle during two years of National Service in the Malayan Emergency. Chance was right, of course. There was nowhere else and nothing else for him. The grimy dockland or the lush-gardened cocktail-belt of Hawks Hill, the concrete roofs of Mount Pleasant or the sweet stench of suntan oil in the warm air of Ocean Beach. It was, as Sinatra sang of Chicago, his kind of town.

The phone on his desk rang. It was Charlie Blades from Forensic Area One. Dr Blades with the haggard face at forty-five and the cancerous stomach removed. Charlie Blades who had married a sexually eager divorced nurse, half his age, encumbered with the two resentful children from her first marriage.

'You busy, Sam?'

'No, Charlie,' Hoskins said brightly. 'Not busy at all. How's life down the constabulary funeral parlour?'

'Not so dusty, Sam. Got her two little bleeders in for private school, hundred miles away. They can take 'em at seven. And what I didn't know, her old man has to pay half the fees. The thought of having her on her own over that sofa! The beast I'm making of myself, Sam. It doesn't bear repeating.'

'That's nice, Charlie. What's in all this for me?'

'You alone, Sam?'

'As a hermit, Charlie.'

'It's down to this Pruen business,' Blades said. 'You've inherited that, I hear.'

'Indeed I have, Charles.'

'Then I got some early news for you,' Blades said, 'hot off the scalpel. Mrs Pruen croaked last night. About seven this morning, actually. There was a preliminary examination, as per usual.'

'I knew she was bad. In Intensive. What about the examination?'

'You think she was kinky, Sam?'

'Muriel Pruen? Darby and Joan Wear Leather Together? Doesn't bear thinking of, Charlie.'

'You're going to have to start thinking about it, Sam.'

'Certainly can't ask her now, Charlie. Pruen just said she'd got a dodgy pump.'

'Oh, she died of that all right, Sam. Just like it says on the certificate.'

'Should be enough for an inquest, Charlie.'

'Only thing is, Sam, this bit of paper in front of me says something else as well. When she was admitted to the get-well-soon ward last night, Muriel Pruen had some rather nasty rope-burns on her wrists.'

'Wrists?'

'And ankles, come to that. So she wasn't kinky. You think old Ma Pruen could put up much fight against the thugs who did what they did to the house? Why'd they need to truss her up like that? Could lock her in a cupboard or frighten her senseless. Unless she wasn't alone in the house. Unless the chancers found too many to handle without tying them all up. If I'm right, I'd say Pruen must have been there. So they screwed him as well. In which case, Samuel, you can reckon on Pruen and Cooney restoring capital punishment. Single-handed.'

11

Hoskins sat in an amber twilight of expensive linen blinds drawn against the marine brilliance of afternoon sun. Through an archway to the other area of Pruen's suite at the Garden Royal Hotel lay rich Persian runners, leading to a rounded window-arch and a flash of blue water.

'I want to know who did it, Mr Pruen. That's all.'

'You think I don't?' Pruen's ample face in its trimming of grey-white sideburns and moustache creased with an effort of sincerity. 'You think I don't want to see them dogs put where they belong? If there was a law they could be hosed down with petrol and then lit up, I'd strike the first match.'

Hoskins shifted in his silver-leather chair.

'Whatever happens, I'll need your help.'

Across the central patio of the hotel two elderly women were sitting in their verandah doorway. Despite the heat, their mohair stoles lay close to hand. They talked directly into the bright stillness of sky beyond the white-painted rail, neither looking at the other. One of them touched the front of her permanent wave, the face-powder dry as brick-dust among the roots of hair. Even at a distance, Hoskins noticed, her fingernails were varnished vermilion as a barmaid's.

'What I need in the first place, Mr Pruen,' he said gently, 'is some elimination. Fingerprints we've done. But then there's your story.'

'Story?' Pruen swung round from the window where he had been looking down at the midsummer crowds on the Cake-walk and the trippers winding their way along the paths of the central gardens between tall camellia and rhododendron. A woman's voice came from the shell-contoured bandstand among the shrubs.

> *Beautiful dreamer, wake unto me . . .*
> *Mermaids are chanting, the wild Lorelei . . .*

'Until I get corroboration,' Hoskins said firmly, 'until I get evidence, your version is a story, an assertion.'

'You got the girl's word for it. We was out in the motor.'

'It'll be evidence after I put a question or two to her, Mr Pruen. Be out long, will she?'

The first movement of a smile touched Pruen's lips and was gone again.

'Quite a little while, Mr Hoskins.'

Hoskins waited for the explanation. In the fierce azure of the sky a seabird circled with the patience of a vulture. Among the click of plates and knives, the girl's voice surged and trembled.

> *Gone are the cares of life's busy throng,*
> *Beautiful dreamer, awake unto me . . .*

'If you've been stupid enough, Mr Pruen, to pack her off to some villa in Spain, she'll have to be fetched back.'

Pruen held his hand up, praying silence.

'Do I look like the kind of skate-arse that'd grudge her a proper holiday after what the poor little girl's been through? Do I, Mr Hoskins? You want to see our Noreen, all you got to do is hop a plane to West Palm Beach. Cousins of Mrs Pruen's out there. Florida, Mr Hoskins, in case it don't ring a bell with you right away.'

Hoskins let out a long breath as if that simplified matters.

'All right, Mr Pruen. I'll be back in a little while with my sergeant. In his presence, I shall give you a formal caution. Unless, by then, you can show me some very good reason why I might not. There's a case against you for obstructing this investigation. The rate you're going on, you could face something a bit heavier.'

'What's that, then?' Pruen said, as if he scarcely cared.

'Being concerned in the murder of Mrs Muriel Pruen,' Hoskins said coolly. 'The way you're going on, you could be the prime suspect.'

Pruen turned to the window again, his back to Hoskins.

'We'll just have this straight, Mr Hoskins. My wife, that I been married to thirty years and hardly had a cross word with, is beaten up and left for dead by some team of yobboes. Me and the girl is out at the time. We come back, find the place smashed up and her unconscious. We rush her to hospital and she dies there. I dare say I could find a dozen people that saw us out in the car. Supposing I had to. And as for the girl! Noreen tells her story to the law. Then she's due a holiday and she takes one. She's over eighteen, able to decide for herself.'

'And so?'

'And so,' said Pruen, turning to Hoskins again, 'if you want to come round here with a load of fucking cautions and the rest of it, you do it any time. And my brief, Jack Cam, he'll be waiting. And I dare say it might be him that cautions you.'

'I know Mr Cam,' Hoskins said equably.

'That must be nice for him.'

'And I'd like you to give me the names. Just the witnesses that might have seen you and the girl in the car, Mr Pruen. Just at the time in question.'

But he knew it was pointless. Pruen went across to the table, poured some orange juice into a glass and squirted soda on top.

'Any more conversation you want with me, Mr Hoskins, you have it when Jack Cam's here.'

And that was it, Hoskins thought. He was about to get up from the silver-leather chair when he heard a sound from the bedroom of the suite.

'Not staying here alone, then, Mr Pruen?'

'For what it matters to you, Mr Hoskins, I'm alone. That's my servant. I get him to valet the suits once or twice a week.'

'Keep a dog and bark yourself, Mr Pruen?'

'What's that supposed to mean?'

'Hotels like this have all the servants you need.'

'And I've had all of you that I bloody need, Hoskins . . .'

The bedroom door opened and closed. In the little passage-way Pruen's valet appeared. He was a muscular young man but not tall. His suit of grey flannel had the smooth and expensive nap of well-groomed billiard-cloth. He was square and unsmiling. His hair had the close razor-trimmed neatness of a toy soldier. The clipped moustache seemed like a badge of office.

'It's Mr Raymond,' Pruen said, looking suddenly older and more untidy by contrast with his minder. 'He's my man.'

Raymond gave a short nod towards Hoskins but said nothing.

Hoskins stared at the burly figure.

'Mr Raymond and I must have met before somewhere. It seems to me. Would he be able to place you in the car with Noreen that evening?'

Pruen waved his finger to and fro slowly, like the needle of a piano-top metronome.

'You know as well as I do, Mr Hoskins, that's a matter for you and me and Jack Cam when he's here.'

'I'd prefer Mr Raymond to answer on his own account.'

'Not without I tell him, Mr Hoskins.' Pruen went across and manipulated Raymond's shoulder affectionately while the man stared down at his own shoes. 'One of the best, he is. Pure gold.'

'Right,' Hoskins said. 'Then I'll leave you to it. Just for the moment.'

He went down to the lobby, a wide concourse of caramel and white marble paving with a central dome of coloured glass. The Garden Royal was an hotel in the grand manner of the 1920s, its vestibule a cross between a conservatory and a shopping arcade. Behind the dwarf palms in brass urns edging its semicircle, there was a barber's shop, a jeweller's display-window, a florist and a tobacconist. It was a place of cigars and orchids, perfumed pomade and diamond clusters set in gold. Hoskins turned and crossed to the wide mahogany sweep of the reception desk.

'Chief Inspector Hoskins, Canton "A" Division,' he said to the girl. 'You got Percy Rawson hidden away somewhere?'

She looked up, the lacquered face suggesting the Rue de Rivoli or Bond Street, but the eyes betraying high-rise Canton.

'Hotel security?'

'That's the ticket,' he said encouragingly.

As the girl turned, a door at one end of the counter opened and a half-bald, dark-haired man looked out. Protuberant eyes gave his face an air of preposterous humour, like an entertainer at a children's party.

'Hello, Sam,' he said. 'Don't tell me you've got a client in the Garden Royal.'

'Just visiting, Percy. You free for five minutes?'

Rawson gestured him in. He sat down behind his desk while Hoskins took the visitor's chair. Rawson pressed the speaker-button on the house-phone.

'Two light ales,' he said, 'special brew. Mr Rawson. Right away.'

'I'm on duty, Percy,' Hoskins said gently.

'So am I, Sam. So what?'

'You're not on the force any more, my son. That's what!'

Rawson grinned.

'Best day's work I ever did, Sam. You want to think about the hotels along the beach. Security officer. Just like being on holiday most of the time. Guests pay by credit card, nine out of ten. Accounts does the checking on that. So, no moonlight flits to chase up. Cooking melts in your mouth. And there's more chuffy around here than you'll ever see down Canton nick. Foreign girls working their way through men. Not to mention one or two lonely ladies booked in the top-floor suites. It's the foreign waitresses this time of year. Scandinavians. I tell you, Sam, how they manage to get such a silky toasty-brown tan all over, that far north, I will never understand.'

Presently there was a knock and a monkey-suited waiter served them beer with a flourish.

'See?' said Rawson cheerily as Hoskins took a sip. 'I told you you was wasting time down the Mall with the Ripper. That's special brew, that is. Family concern in Shropshire. We buy their complete output.'

'Nice, Percy. Just nice. Did you know you've got Pruen staying here?'

'Old "Horse-Parlour" Pruen? Yes, Samuel. I know. I run the eyes down the register once in a while. Part of the job. He used to stop here quite a bit. One-night stands with ladies of his acquaintance. Didn't like to take them home to Mrs "Horse-Parlour". Poor old devil. Someone kicked the shit out of him this time, by all accounts.'

Hoskins studied his glass.

'There was a girl with him, when he moved here that Sunday.'

'Personal assistant was how it was put to me, Sam. She pushed on after three or four days. He's got a valet now. Fine big boy.'

'I know him, Percy. Raymond. Former SAS or something. Given the nudge by his regiment. Used to break necks for Carmel Cooney. Bouncing stroppy teenage punters out of clubs on their shaven heads. Keeping order in the Realito down the Peninsula.'

'Law and order, Sam. Can't have too much of it.'

'Cooney been visiting Pruen much, has he?'

Rawson grinned.

'That's his business – or Pruen's. I don't keep tabs, Sam. That's bad news. Pruen's retired. Cooney's on the council. I'm not sticking my neck out.'

Hoskins sighed and put down the glass.

'If a fly on the ceiling in this hotel so much as scratched its backside, you'd know about it, Percy. So what's the SP?'

Rawson shrugged.

'Cooney's been in a couple of times. But then he's here, on and off, anyway. He's got money to spend, Sam, and in Ocean Beach you can spend it faster at the Garden Royal than anywhere else.'

'And what else?' Hoskins asked gently.

'Only what you know already. A lot of the local choirboys drink here. There's gossip that Pruen was knocked over by some young chancer with his eye on promotion. Someone that thinks Cooney might be impressed and give him Pruen's place. The view in the parish is that whoever it is doesn't know Cooney. Pruen's been a good boy all these years. He's entitled to moral support and Cooney's going to give it to him. It's just talk, Sam. But that's what the boys are saying.'

Hoskins grunted.

'Cooney's supposed to keep his nose clean. He's Councillor Cooney now. Chamber of Commerce and Police Committee. He's the Royal Peninsular Emporium and Mount Carmel Coastal Ground Rents. Not to mention Canton Coastal Construction and Peninsular Trucking. Captain of industry. The rake-off from the Petshop and the Blue Moon or the Realito is just bus fares to him. There's something in Cooney that likes the clubs, seeing the punters ripped off, putting the girls through the hoops. Getting other names to do his carving and pimping. It's in his blood. But you couldn't fault him. You couldn't even prove that Mr Raymond upstairs was a present from Cooney to Pruen.'

Rawson smiled over his glass.

'Sam, I don't have to prove it. Cooney and Pruen is down to you. What I've got on is young Grete from Norway. Chambermaid. Blonde as they come and silky gold all over. I'm close to knocking off a slice, Sam. You could do worse than that.'

'I am doing worse, my friend. A lot, lot worse at the moment.'

Rawson raised his glass.

'Got time for another, Sam?'

'I didn't have time for the first one, Percy.' Hoskins stood up and looked round him. 'I was due out the front to be picked up by Sergeant Chance.'

Rawson shook his head, as if it was all beyond him.

'And how's Jack Chance doing these days?'

'Well,' Hoskins said. 'At least he hasn't got the Women's Committee after his arse. And he's not being hunted by the got-rich-quick dad of a smelly little skinhead that tried to kick me in the pills and fell on his back. He's ahead on that. But he did grab hold of Jock the Mug's arm down Orient Parade a week or two back. And Jock's elbow suddenly came apart in two bits. He's got his little troubles. All in all, Percy, you could say the political guano is pretty evenly spread over "A" Division just now.'

Rawson clucked his tongue and paused with his hand on the door.

'You really want to think about it now, Sam, not when it's too late. Might be time for you to come in where it's dry and warm.'

12

Sergeant Chance steered the Fiesta round the taxis that were waiting at the palm-flanked portico of the Garden Royal. Between the evergreens that concealed the ground-floor windows from the traffic of Bay Drive, the sea was as blue as Biarritz or Cap Ferrat in the breezy sunlight.

'Pruen knocking off the old lady so as to give Noreen a time of it without interference,' Chance said. 'That's what I'd like. Better than civil war breaking out between the young bulls and the old studs. Take-over time in clubland! England's very own South Side Chicago in Canton and Ocean Beach! You fancy that, Sam?'

'Nope,' Hoskins said. 'Not with me still on the force. I want to see Cooney next, though. A word in his flap. Just in case he's thinking of a little private justice. He's got an office out here.'

'Blue Moon or Petshop?'

'Petshop,' Hoskins said wearily. 'There's not much back-stage at the Blue Moon.'

The Fiesta drew into the slow line of seashore traffic, drivers and families staring sideways at the water, all day and nowhere to go.

'Scott's in the shit,' Chance said cheerfully. 'Business of the girl-fancier that he punched on the Beach. Day you were down at The Vale.'

'How's that, then?'

Chance sniggered.

'Bloke's solicitor wrote in. Bringing an action in the civil court. Scott's got the wind up. All red in the face and per-spiring. Fragrant as a vulture's armpit. Huffing and puffing. The chap he hit got the number off his tunic and off the patrol car. And good old Scottie's also sweating on an inter-nal inquiry. Clitheroe doesn't want to do it, but now he can't avoid it.'

'Stupid bastard!' said Hoskins savagely.

'Who's that, Sam?'

'Bloody Scott, of course. Flat hat with a peak slashed to make him look like the Gestapo! Moustache off a Mexican bandit! Same as the rest of his lot! Swaggering and fat-arsed from riding round in cars all day! Arrogant and quick-fisted with it!'

'A civilian couldn't put it better,' Chance said reproachfully.

Hoskins glared at the wavering heat above the crowded sands, the half-naked bodies sprawling like victims of an aerial attack.

'Civilians get off light, my son. He just hits them, from time to time. They don't have to work with him.'

Chance braked at the lights by the New Pier, where the elderly trippers from a tour bus had begun to file across in a condemned man's shuffle.

Just beyond the entrance arch and turnstiles of the pier, Chance turned up from the sea-front to the car park of the Petshop. With its angular 1930s look, the tall windows and a dance-hall like the saloon of an ocean liner, it had been the

Winter Garden of Hoskins's boyhood. But the tea-dances and the white shirt-fronts, the beat of the tango in summer twilight and the celebrity piano recitals on Sunday evenings had long since passed away. The city council had sold off the buildings to Cooney's Coastal Ground Rents ten years ago. After a judicious interval, Carmel Cooney took back CGR from his 'nominee'. The little waitress-skirts and frilly knickers of sin and skin now accompanied scampi and 'house wine' in the new Paradise Lounge.

'Not here, Chief! We're closed till seven! Park outside!'

A hefty attendant was signalling an about-turn with one hand. Chance put his head out of the car window.

'Don't be a prat, Jimmy. It's us.'

'Oh, sorry, Mr Chance. Not any bother, is there?'

'If there is,' Chance said, 'we'll keep some for you.'

He parked at the club entrance. The reception desk lacked its usual young woman in hip-length swallowtail and fishnet stockings. The door of the stairs that led up to the offices was locked by a computer-dial system. To one side were the double doors of the old dance-floor, heavy and with windows like cinema portholes. A man in shirt-sleeves came out. There was a sound of voices and hammering before the doors closed again.

'Mr Cooney in his office?' Hoskins asked.

'Who wants him?'

'Chief Inspector Hoskins and Sergeant Chance, Canton CID.'

Without answering, the man took the wall-phone off its hook and spoke to someone. He put the phone back.

'Mr Cooney's in the balcony. I'm to take you up.'

He played a little tune on the numbers of the computer-lock and pushed open the door to the stairs. They went up and through another doorway on to the balcony that ran round the four sides of the old Winter Garden dance-floor.

Carmel Cooney, large and smooth at fifty-five, turned towards them. The melon-head split in a grin. He was wearing a pale grey suit with a tight waistcoat that made his stomach swell. With the size of his paunch and his thin-legged trousers he looked, as always to Hoskins, like a large blunt-headed tadpole walking on its tail.

'Mr Hoskins!' The hand went out and Hoskins took it uneasily. 'I won't keep you one minute. Just refresh your tired old eyes on this!'

Below them, on the little stage where the Squadronaires, Joe Loss, Ambrose, Felix Mendelssohn and his Hawaiian Serenaders had kept time for the dinner dancers, there was a spread tarpaulin. It was about eight feet square and covered thickly with a black viscous liquid like sump-oil. Two girls in white leotards, the unblemished nylon and flesh all the whiter by contrast with the splashed blackness, were struggling and snatching at one another.

'That's nice,' Chance said heavily.

Cooney turned to Hoskins.

'Next week's show. Michelle and Melanie. Sisters. Not actual twins but they look it. Having a little argument. Wrestling and slogging. These days of equality, Mr Hoskins, the ladies got the right to join in all the sports. It keeps saying so on one of those pouftah television programmes.'

One of the sisters struggled up, dragging the other with her. She threw a punch below the belt that made Hoskins wince with the sound of the impact.

'That's faked, of course.' Cooney puffed on his cigar. 'The mud and the wet makes it sound worse than it is.'

There was another impact. One of the girls slipped and they both went down, sprawling in the black liquid so that their bodies and faces, limbs and hair were soaked in it. They might have been any race or sex, Hoskins thought, except for the way in which the wet mud made the leotards cling suggestively tight and sleek.

'Mind you,' Cooney said reassuringly, 'it's not the real thing. Just washes off with plain water afterwards. You can't see it now but Michelle and Melanie got a little touch of the tar-brush in 'em. Makes it seem more mean and savage when they start. We sold out every night next week. What with this and the bicycle capers and the gee-gee games. Erotic Circus. Saves all this cruelty to animals that's upsetting people nowadays.'

The round face opened again in its melon-smile as he beamed down at his two struggling and panting protégées.

'I'm not here for a ticket, Mr Cooney,' Hoskins said. 'I've just been to see Mr Pruen.'

As if the sadness of life suddenly overcame him, Cooney turned his back to the balcony parapet and lodged his ample buttocks against its plush rim. He shook his head slowly.

'That got to me, Mr Hoskins. I can tell you that got to me. Muriel Pruen that I'd known all these years. We was kids together down Jamaica Street Elementary School. And then Pruen too. Poor old devil. "Horse-Parlour" Pruen! He wasn't even that. Did most of his business out the old Ocean Park dog-track. Works all his life for what? So some snotty yobs can come and smash it all in an hour or two!'

He looked at his feet, shook his head again and then met Hoskins's look with a level stare.

'And to think, Mr Hoskins, that I saw poor old Pruen and his girl Noreen on the overcliff above Sandbar the very time that them young villains must have been turning his place over.'

'Really,' said Hoskins coldly.

'Not to speak to, of course,' Cooney said reassuringly. 'Me and the young lady with me just had time for a wave and a smile to them as we drove past. They'd parked the motor and got out. Taking the air on the grass-walk, just where the road turns and starts going down. I'd like an hour alone with whoever did it to Muriel Pruen, Mr Hoskins. I could be highly original with scum like that.'

'The investigation's under control, Mr Cooney.'

Cooney raised a hand to forestall criticism.

'I'm well conscious of it, Mr Hoskins. I wouldn't quarrel with that. I just wish there was one extra law. A law that said me and Pruen could find them scumbags. Take our little bats and play an hour or two of table-tennis with 'em.'

Hoskins eased forward and perched on the edge of a table.

'The only one we know of is a girl, Mr Cooney.'

Cooney made a mouth, as if it were all the same to him.

'I could make her wish she wasn't, Mr Hoskins. If the law allowed, of course.'

'Thing is,' Chance interrupted, 'we all have to remember what the law is. Don't we, Mr Cooney?'

Cooney put his hand up again for peace.

'I don't quarrel with that, Mr Chance.'

Hoskins nodded.

'So long as that's agreed.'

Cooney grinned at him, as if he might poke the Chief Inspector in the ribs for fun.

'You're trying to rile me again. Ain't you, Mr Hoskins? Now, play fair. You and I might not always have seen eye to eye. But you know as well as I do that I don't break the law and I've got a clean sheet that shows it. Not so much as a parking-ticket. I haven't a mark against me.'

'Not of late, Mr Cooney.'

'You mean when I was a lad for Queen and Country in the army? Mr Hoskins! A man could be on a charge for not having his buttons shined! I don't call that a criminal record!'

'And a man could be found with army supplies that he shouldn't have, Mr Cooney. And he might leave a couple of squaddies with their mouth-openings cut wider an inch or two.'

But Cooney smiled peaceably again.

'You won't rile me, Mr Hoskins. So don't try it. Still, I'll tell you something. What I like to think of these days is all them young lieutenants with their squeaky voices and shiny shoes and little sticks under their arms. They thought they were one-hundred-and-one per cent! I got them working for me now. Calling me "sir" and holding the door open. All them captains and majors. I could have them shovelling shit for me now, Mr Hoskins, and thanking me for letting 'em do it! I actually got one. Poor retired old bloke that was a major in the war. He's working behind the bun counter down the Emporium. Part-time and grateful for the money. Good as gold. See?'

'Right, then,' Hoskins said quietly. 'So what's the news about Pruen?'

'Nothing I've heard.' Cooney's eyes were wide with sincerity. 'No one's got a clue.'

'And who gave him Raymond as a toy soldier?'

'He's a big boy, Raymond is. He can pick jobs for himself.'

'And Pruen's girl, Noreen?'

Cooney flashed a smile of apologetic schoolboy honesty.

'Now there I plead guilty, Mr Hoskins. I promised I'd see the poor little thing all right for a job in the shop and a roof over her head if things got rough for old Pruen. That's all. Something in the storeroom down the Royal Emporium.'

Hoskins straightened up from the table.

'Just so long as we understand, Mr Cooney. If I was to hear that scores were being settled privately . . . '

'Then I'd jump on the parties harder than anyone, Mr Hoskins. On the council and the police committee I support my officers. That includes you, Mr Hoskins. That most certainly includes you. I spoke up for you the other day, when that brainless little dyke Ricard was trying to cause trouble.'

The girl-wrestlers fell with a wet thump in the mud and there was a cry.

'All acted, Mr Hoskins,' Cooney said reassuringly. 'Rehearsed to perfection. A couple of little treasures they are.'

There was no more to be got out of Cooney. The three of them walked along the balcony towards the doors. Cooney paused.

'If I was to stray from the straight and narrow, Mr Hoskins, this'd be the worst time. I might as well let you into the secret. You'll know in a few days anyhow. I'm on the short-list.'

Hoskins stared at him.

'What short-list?'

A shadow of displeasure crossed Cooney's face at such ignorance.

'Canton Peninsula, of course. Parliamentary constituency. Been Labour for years. Old Trubshawe. Bunch of their young pansies got him deselected. Equal rights for nancies and dykes, all that crap. Lot of local resentment, Trubshawe being a good man and some lesbo likely to be put in over his head. He's going to stand on his own as Parliamentary Labour. Split the vote. First hope the Tories have ever had down the docks. They seem to think I might be the chap for an area like that.'

'Yes,' Hoskins said, 'well, that's politics, I suppose. I wouldn't know.'

Cooney chortled.

'I'll tell you both something,' he said. 'Lot of people moan about all these new ideas. About Ricard and her kind. But I have a lot more fun with them about. All their college education and poufy talk! And you could sell 'em water while they was drowning for all the sense they got. It's a real bit of sport, shafting that lot.'

'I imagine it must be,' Hoskins said coolly, nodding at Michelle and Melanie slithering and scrabbling. 'How does the selection committee feel about all this?'

Cooney chuckled again and wagged a finger.

'You can't rile me, Mr Hoskins. There's not a girl I've asked that ain't willing and eager to be in the show. Real sports, every one. We've had to turn away a dozen or two. And if you took the trouble to read the programme, you'd see why. It's a charity show. Spina bifida and handicapped babies. They take a cut from every ticket that's sold. We got the Mayor of Ocean Beach and his chaplain coming to the first performance.'

'That's nice,' Hoskins said flatly. 'I'll keep in touch about Mr Pruen.'

At the doorway, Cooney looked back affectionately at the refurbished dance-floor. He turned to Chance.

'Me and Mr Hoskins go back a long way,' he said gently. 'We was kids together here. Not even out of short trousers.'

'Really,' Chance said, defeated by it all. 'I never knew.'

A few minutes later, Hoskins and Chance sat together in the car, staring at the posters for the 'show'. The credits were bold and clear. 'Sponsored for Spina Bifida and the Canton Baby Unit by Mount Carmel Coastal Ground Rents and the Royal Peninsular Emporium.'

Chance started the engine.

'What a bastard that man is,' he said thoughtfully.

'One of the finest. Ten per cent to charity and the rest to Cooney. Prices raised so that he doesn't lose a penny. You try and prove that Michelle and Melanie doing it together isn't just clean muddy fun by good-hearted girls.'

'Real sports, he said they were. Doing it of their own choice.'

Hoskins yawned.

83

'Yes, my son. Simple choice. Either a punch-up in the mud-bath or they never work the pavements and houses round Martello Square again. That means being hungry. And it probably means a worse thumping from their ponce than anything that might happen on the stage.'

'Can't be as bad as that, Sam.'

'It's worse, Jack. Believe me. I know Cooney.'

The families and the swimsuited couples were wandering back to tea through the central gardens, away from the beach where the sun cut lower across the waves, towards the tile-hung department stores and the cool shopping arcades. Chance turned on to Osborne Hill with its franchise garages and little hotels, making for the main roundabout and the Canton link-road.

'What's this about you and Cooney being kids together?'

Hoskins chuckled.

'Culture,' he said. 'When I was a nipper I used to be taken to the celebrity piano recitals in the old Winter Garden. Pouishnoff, Mark Hambourg, Moiseiwitsch. All Chopin and Schumann and Rachmaninoff. Ma Cooney had the same idea. Young Carmel sitting there in his velvet suit and his hair brushed, good as gold. He's still got a Steinway out at Hawks Hill. Model A. A concert grand. Pays some girl that can't get concert work to go out and play for him. That's his real indulgence.'

'Cooney? After Melanie and Michelle belting each other with mud on?'

They were halted by the traffic queue on the hill, a thin petrol-haze rising in the early evening light along the ice-cream parlours and the little hotels with sun-coloured door-blinds.

'A simple mind, Jack Chance,' Hoskins said helpfully. 'That's your problem. Cooney's not a Dyce Street villain with pretensions. He's a very bright boy whose chosen profession happens to be crime. He likes it. He enjoys shafting the opposition. He gets a kick from making people do things they hate. He loves every minute. You saw the way he gave Pruen his alibi about being out for a drive when the house was burgled. Cooney was lying. He knew I knew he was lying. And he was as good as saying there's fuck-all I can do about it.'

Chance persisted through the clogged traffic of the round-about. He let out a sibilant breath of exasperation between his teeth.

'Bloody stroll on!' he said helplessly.

13

If anyone had asked The Man how he felt, he would have said, 'Invisible'. And he would have smiled at the thought. It pleased him and it was true. In the streets that he walked, by the shops that he passed, over the sweeps of terraced housing on Lantern Hill, he saw a landscape in which he had no more part than a ghost. He could not imagine what he looked like in such places, or how he might appear to others. Nor did he care. In the most important way of all, he was entirely concealed. That ended the matter.

It was his thoughts that were truly invisible. Never betrayed by a look or a glance, except to his prey. The Man thought of his brain as a top-security information system. The girls who had attracted his attention were on file there, in the bombproof armoured vault of his head. He had given such care to them that in many cases he knew their dates of birth, as well as their names and homes, their families and schools or jobs. Most of them had no idea that he existed. Some noticed him and, as a rule, dismissed him with a stare or a glance. The Man smiled again, comfortable in his security. If only they knew! If only they could imagine! But it was their inability to imagine that made the whole thing so easy.

And then there was the inner vault of the brain, behind guards and checks, combinations and intricate locks. Compared with it, Fort Knox was a child's piggy-bank. It was here that The Man's desires and ambitions, lusts and satisfactions were coded and kept. It was utterly impenetrable. Its very existence was unknown to the rest of the world. Best of all, it boasted the total integral security of a single mind. Absolute and undivided allegiance, like the most fanatical regime. The crowds roared, the banners flew, and one raised fist symbolised such undivided purpose. There was no risk of remorse, contrition, compromise or confession. To have shared such a secret would mean disaster. Misgivings by the partner. Betrayal. Not this way. It lay in the sole possession of The Man. There was no higher authority in his universe. He knelt to no one and prayed to no one. His decisions were absolute and unchallenged.

To be sure, there were those whom he was 'up against', as he liked to think of it. They had systems of great sophistication. They could press a button and calculate, retrieve, compare. But they had nothing to match the inviolate unity of a single resolute mind. They finished work and went off duty. The Man was never off duty. His opponents grew weary or speculated on the pointlessness of it all. The Man was never weary and the point at which he aimed was not for an instant in doubt.

All the computer banks and instant recall, communication at the speed of light, all of it was useless against one human brain, unknown and unsuspected, resolute for pleasure or murder.

It had been a day of final summer heat across Canton city centre. The grey blue sky of the warm morning seemed hung with veils of lavender gauze as the last haze burnt away. Then, beyond Atlantic Wharf, the dome of Channel sky turned a distant pale blue with a few drifts of thin cumulus, reflecting the sunlit waters of the September ocean. A fuzz of yellowed light gathered on the horizon line.

The Man had been patient, postponing the time when he would take the metro-rail to Lantern Hill, as if increasing his pleasure by delay. He waited until almost tea-time, when a hot wind blew dust and scraps of paper through commercial streets between the glare and shine of office towers and department stores. It turned Canton briefly into a dry autumn city of the Middle West or southern Spain. There came a time of afternoon when it was not to be noticed whether The Man was at work or not. He went out into the Memorial Gardens of the civic centre, where a sky of hot nude pearl formed the backdrop of the Mall. Against it the City Hall clock-tower rose like a ship-owner's vision of Old Vienna, cupids and arabesques in a finger of pale Edwardian stone. The metallic strike of the hour at half-past three gave out a dry and curt reverberation behind the disc of golden numerals.

The Man walked quickly from Great Western Street into the wide square of Atlantic Wharf. By the Paris Hotel, he noticed the chic little blinds and elegant windows of Madame Jolly, Modes, the figure of the girl with the golden skin, odalisque eyes and sharp young profile. He smiled again at the thought that she already had her place in the impregnable vault of his mind and in his plans. No one, not even she, was aware that The Man so much as knew of her existence. And yet, from one public record and another, he had his invisible dossier upon her.

Half an hour later, a fresher wind blew from the Channel across the high sunlit streets of Lantern Hill. The Man had not allowed himself an excursion of this sort for some time and he felt the more entitled to it now. He stepped out on the metro-rail platform above the esplanade of Harbour Bar, its steamer jetty and the turrets of its little Edwardian shops and snack-bars. He walked past the newsagents and the Cloud Seven Arcade, from whose open doorways the clash and bleep of gaming-machines carried through the hot tea-time air. As always on these occasions, The Man walked with a sense of effortless vigour, jaunty and light-footed, ripe for pleasure and adventure. It was out there, somewhere, waiting for him to find it. In this mood, he could walk for miles after his quarry without noticing the effect. Once or twice, reliving the scenes of a day, he was astonished and even sceptical at the distance he must have walked.

Today he was a little late, but not much.

The long hill of Shackleton Road with its semi-detached houses in cherry-red brick and sour-cream gables lay stunned in the heat. Fruit trees in the exposed front gardens wilted and the hydrangea heads were shrivelled. The first of the bicycles were coming out past the open double gates of the school grounds. It was the boys who rode them, seldom the girls, their coats flying and feet racing on the pedals, down the long wide sweep of the road towards the shops and cafés of the town. The rest of them, on foot, formed an untidy army of motley and dark-clad adolescents. Like a trail of variously clad refugees. With a smile, The Man mourned the passing of proper uniforms. In his own schooldays there had been something particularly exciting about the girls in their white blouses and striped ties. The uniform. It hinted, The Man supposed, at neatness and obedience, commands given and obeyed. Schoolgirls and air hostesses, nurses and even female traffic wardens. There was a lot of that in the magazines and the videos.

One of the red buses was loading by the gates and The Man slowed down as he approached, casually noting which of them was getting on it and which was not. Then he saw her and smiled. There was a nice irony in finding that Elaine, the most wayward of all the girls, a thief and a bully to his certain knowledge, was the one who still wore a uniform. The pleated skirt was shorter than a tennis-girl's, drawn almost to the tops of her thighs. That, of course, made it all the more exciting.

The Man noticed that she was not alone. There was another girl with her, dark-haired and about the same age. They walked together, Elaine shaking her lank hair into place from time to time, her admirer about twenty feet behind her or sometimes a little less. Though she strode out in her short skirt and sturdy bare legs, her movements were slower in the moist heat, like everyone else's. She turned her head to exchange raucous laughter and banter with the other girl, but she avoided looking right round at him. All the same, The Man could see that she knew he was there. That was the important thing. She was laughing and sneering for him to hear. It was all part of her character.

The presence of the other girl decided the matter, or probably so. This would not be the day when The Man fulfilled his ambition with her. But, then, he could never be quite sure. It depended on events. The other girl might turn in through a gate at any moment. The concrete path between the railings and tall hedges might be deserted as Elaine walked along it. It was impossible to say. Part of the excitement lay in the unpredictability of these little dramas. It was like watching a thriller on the screen and not knowing the ending until the last minutes. The Man never knew, when he set out, whether he would merely come back with his imagination more richly stored or from a secret act whose details must be held securely in the deepest vault of the mind.

They were walking up the hump-back of Arkell Street, the doors of brick terrace houses opening on the pavements. The Man had a theory and a belief that what was shown and offered him belonged to him by moral right. At least, the image of it belonged to him to do with as he pleased in imagination. And by giving away the image, the objects of his attention gave him part of themselves. That was how he understood it and, if he had needed justification for his pleasures, that would have been sufficient. But what he saw was more than sufficient. His eyes bestowed an invisible caress on the rather heavy pallor of Elaine's bare thighs. It was easy enough for him to establish a superiority to her kind, loud-mouthed and rough, vulgar and dishonest, blatant in flaunting themselves during a so-called age of innocence. He felt his most vindictive resolve, a surge in the brain that was like being confidently drunk. His scorn was roused against such wantonness and his heart was more profoundly excited than by mere erotic pleasure.

The Man was dangerous. He knew it and was fired by a fierce secret pride. The girl mistook it for simple lechery and he exulted in her stupidity. But then stupidity was the characteristic of all her kind and their protectors. He heard one of the girls say 'Pathetic!' to the other and knew that it was said about him deliberately for him to hear. The dark-haired one looked round and The Man was careful to let her see his caressing gaze on her companion before he met her eyes with what he hoped was a sardonic smile of conquest.

At the foot of the hill they crossed the road bridge over the metro-rail and he guessed they were going down to the little esplanade. Elaine stopped and The Man stopped too, lighting a cigarette to avoid the interest of passers-by. It was not intended to deceive the two girls. That would have spoilt the afternoon for him. As if in defiance, Elaine unhooked her skirt and drew it off, revealing that she was wearing a swimming costume under her clothes. It covered her almost as completely as the skirt had done, but to The Man it was preposterously suggestive.

He followed more closely, the dark-haired girl looking round uneasily from time to time. But The Man chose with care. He knew as well as anyone that Elaine was a thief. The last person she wanted to speak to was a policeman. There was no law between them now but the law of nature.

The Man exercised his imagination as he watched the bare adolescent legs and the somewhat heavy movements of her buttocks in the nylon swimsuit. There was a fantasy which had excited him all the more for its combination of moral righteousness and the infliction of his most cherished desires. She, the adolescent thief, was caught by him burgling his house. The thief became the prisoner, unable to appeal to the law. As the price of a promise that he would set her free again, she submitted in the fantasy to a catalogue of his inescapable demands.

The Man rested his arms on the duck-egg-blue promenade rail and watched the two girls on the muddy little beach of Harbour Bar, across the water from the dockland of the Peninsula. Elaine behaved with the same indifference and disdain. Her companion sat tense and fully dressed. The Man felt a warm satisfaction. Today was not to be the day of the apocalypse, after all. But it was a day the dark-haired companion would never forget. The view that the world held of her and her kind was something The Man felt sure she would remember.

When the dark-haired girl looked again, he was nowhere to be seen. By then he was somewhere above them, in one of the new spartan carriages of the metro-rail, travelling against the tide of commuters who flocked home to Lantern Hill from the city stations at Atlantic Wharf and Balance Street, Colenso Road and King Edward Square. The centre of Canton itself was quiet in the day's declining heat. The Man felt a great tranquillity as he walked back past the closed department stores and the shuttered entrances. It had not been the apocalypse, after all. But he thought of the dark-haired girl and smiled. To judge from her conduct on the muddy beach, it seemed to him that he had made his point.

2
AUTUMN

14

'Two months,' the Ripper said with gentle logic, 'August till October. ACC Crime can't understand why we haven't more to offer him about Mrs Pruen by now. And there's Pruen as well. Wants his wife's body released for burial. Much as I hate to say it, Sam, you can't help seeing his point of view.'

'Pruen's the star of the whole show,' said Hoskins bleakly. 'He's the one that could tell us who turned his place over and topped Muriel Pruen. Of course he won't. He and Cooney want them, especially Cooney. Make a real example. See that no other snotty little tearaway so much as thinks of knocking off one of Cooney's clients. If ACC Crime feels that badly about it, perhaps he'd like to add an inch or two to Pruen's height on the old constabulary rack.'

The autumn's acid leaf-decay had touched the trees with dark pink in the distant gardens of Hawks Hill, seen from the Superintendent's window. Ripley nodded, as if he understood.

'I know, Sam. If it was less than murder, I'd put the case on the back-burner. I really would. But Muriel Pruen's dead. We can't sit on our hands.'

Hoskins pulled a face.

'That's another little gem I've got for you, Max.'

The Ripper scowled uneasily.

'Little gem?'

'Yes, Max. So far we've got a dozen witnesses, Cooney's lot, saying on instructions that they saw Pruen and his girl out for a drive at the time the house was turned over. Pruen's saying it. So's his girl. It's such a simple story, they can't go wrong on it. Even if we could slip the old thumbscrews on and wind them up a notch, we've lost the most important liar of all.'

'Who's that?' There was no mistaking the Ripper's unease or Hoskins's bitter satisfaction.

'Muriel Pruen was conscious when they got her to the infirmary. In fact, she didn't seem that bad at the time. She talked to a couple of the nurses in the ward, on and off. Then about three in the morning she had another attack and died about seven.'

'Talked about what, Sam?'

'She told at least two of them that she was in the house alone when it happened. There were two thieves, both men. Both in stocking-masks. That was all. So if we go any further with this, we've got to be prepared to say that the murder victim lied before she pegged out. And Pruen and his girl lied. And a dozen witnesses lied about where Pruen and the girl were. How do you fancy going to court with a case like that, Max? Admitting in advance that all your witnesses are bloody liars?'

Ripley let out a long breath of exasperation.

'We can't pack it up, Sam. We daren't. If Muriel Pruen said she was there alone, how do we know she was lying?'

'Because,' said Hoskins doggedly, 'someone hit Pruen that night. Hit him hard. Knuckles like flintstones. It was up on his face, where you might punch someone, not where you bang your head if you fall over. I saw him, remember.'

'And Mrs Pruen?'

'Gave the nurses the story she was told to give. Told by Pruen on the way to the hospital, probably on instructions from Cooney. Pruen said to me that he didn't waste time trying to call an ambulance, his own phone having been ripped out. But there's a call-box opposite his gate and I don't suppose it gets much use that time of a Sunday night in that area.'

'So?'

'I may be daft, Max, but I'm not bloody daft. I had the fingerprint lads on it. Someone wearing gloves had used that phone not long before. But the last prints on the phone itself were Pruen's. We checked with the ones he gave us for elimination. Charlie Blades made the match. Now Pruen didn't phone the ambulance and he certainly didn't phone us. Who else would he phone in a hurry before they wheeled Mrs Pruen off to Intensive? His insurance company.'

'His insurance company?'

'Yes, Max. The best in the business, so far as he was concerned. Carmel Cooney. I'd bet my pension on it. Pruen asking for instructions. That safe of his must have been knee-deep in undeclared income. Who else would he phone that he couldn't tell us about?'

The Ripper sighed.

'It's not evidence, Sam. At least not evidence of that. You think that Pruen was there and knew the yobboes that did it?'

Hoskins shook his head.

'They'd be dead by now if he did. And I don't think they are. Cooney makes examples of that sort. Skinned and gutted and hung up in the market-place, not just given a nudge into the Railway Dock done up in a sack.'

Ripley adjusted a silver-framed photograph on his desk and set his cylindrical ruler straight. Then he stood up, turned his back, and stared out at the trees of Hawks Hill and the high-rise blocks of Mount Pleasant.

'Forget whether Pruen was at home or not, Sam,' he said gently. 'Find the little bastards who were there and do 'em for manslaughter, if that's all we can manage. At least it prevents civil war between Cooney and the young bucks.'

Hoskins stood up as well.

'Right,' he said. 'I'll go on looking. Just so long as we can stand the cost in time and effort. So far we've got almost nothing. Except this nonsense about a girl of fourteen or fifteen in Pruen's garden while the house was being turned over. If we catch these merchants, it's probably going to be because they come to us. Chucking money around or telling big he-man stories in pubs or to their girls. Watch and wait is what it has to be, Max. And we could still be bloody well waiting this time next year.'

Ripley turned round.

'If that's what it takes, Sam.'

'And if Cooney or one of his colleagues doesn't get to our clients first. You want me, personally, to go on with it?'

'Unless there's a good reason to hand it to someone else.'

'Yes,' said Hoskins firmly, 'there's the best reason of the lot. I've got two weeks' leave coming up in ten days' time. It's well planned-out. And the plans don't include Pruen, Cooney, or Ocean Beach.'

Ripley looked at him with the faintest suggestion of distaste.

'If you feel happy about going off just like that, Sam.'

'I'll be singing and laughing all the way to the car park, Max.'

The Ripper opened his desk diary and frowned at what he saw.

'Wallace Dudden could hold the ring for two weeks, I suppose. You'd better brief him. I'll speak to him tomorrow. Chance can continue as back-up.'

'Right,' said Hoskins briskly. 'I'll see to it.'

Ten minutes later in Hoskins's own room, Chance's florid, well-fleshed face crumpled with incredulity.

'Wallace Dudden? For fuck's sake, Sam! He's waiting on a transfer to traffic division.'

'That's nice,' Hoskins said, sitting down behind the desk with a sigh. 'Should be a dab-hand navigating round Ocean Beach.'

'Why can't Clitheroe's lot handle it?' Chance said miserably. 'They're paid for being the police down the Beach!'

'You seen their handiwork, Jack? That merry little punch-up down Ocean Park funfair Bank Holiday Sunday? Cars on fire and mobs running riot? Half a building demolished? Clitheroe sticking pins in a map on his office wall, not knowing that half the squad cars he thought he was moving about were still parked in the yard under his window. That's why for a start.'

'Even so, Sam! Dudden!'

Hoskins grinned. He drew open a drawer, took out a bottle and two glasses, and did some pouring.

'It's only for a couple of weeks, my son. I feel as if I'm on holiday already. Old Ripley telling me how important it is to catch these yobboes or else there might be a gang war between Cooney and the youngsters? What's he think we've been on about since the end of August? He sits on his brains in his office and talks as if he's the one that's made the great discovery.'

Chance sat down on one chair, put his feet on another, and raised his glass.

'There's a memo in your tray, Sam, incidentally. Ties another name into this mess. The chap who reported losing his wallet on the pier that Sunday. Jonas. Court records. He stood bail a couple of times for names that were prosecuted on illegal gaming charges. Nothing heavy. All the same, we reckon they were Cooney's nominees. I don't suppose Jonas knew them from Adam till Cooney's boys gave him a wedge of banknotes and told him what to do.'

Hoskins yawned.

'Stuff Jonas,' he said casually. 'Half this town works for Cooney, one way or another. The only thing that could put Cooney away for a long stretch is what he's doing for Pruen. Perjury to start with. Accessory to murder as the main course. Conspiracy to pervert the course of justice as an extra. Try nicking him for those, Jack, while I'm on my fortnight of fun in the sun.'

'You think Cooney chanced all that for a daft old bugger like Pruen, Sam? He wouldn't risk it now. Not after this long. Not with everything he's got.'

Hoskins relaxed, as if the cares of the investigation were sliding from him.

'There's no risk to Cooney, Jack,' he said reassuringly. 'He knows he won't get caught. Only in my dreams. He's had well-paid mugs to stand in the dock for him, when anything goes wrong. If Cooney had the Cakewalk machine-gunned at the height of the season, he'd be in church at the time with a dozen bishops as character-witnesses. Each one a Cooney charity-chief. I've been in this game too long, my son. I don't reckon you catch villains of Cooney's sort any longer. Once upon a time, perhaps, but not now. What you do is let 'em get rich, elect 'em for Parliament. In the end, they're making so much money they don't need crime any more. Then you give 'em a life peerage.'

Chance snorted with laughter at the incorrigible cynicism of Sam Hoskins.

'All right, Sam,' he said reasonably. 'So where're you going on this holiday?'

15

In the quiet yellow sunshine of the late October afternoon, Hoskins parked his own car in the little streets of workmen's terraces on the height of Lantern Hill. Despite the uneven pavements and the patched roadways, the red-brick streets had been newly gentrified. Teachers and social workers had replaced the charge-hands of the docks, the dredger crews and their women who worked and died there fifty years before. The narrow pubs at the street corners, named after Victorian royal dukes and Edwardian landowners, still had an air of gaslit Saturday nights, squandered paypackets, fighting and vomiting on the noisy pavements. Here and there a small Nonconformist chapel was squeezed in between the pubs and workshops, its stone-facing now brightly painted. Posters for play-groups and senior citizens' lunches hung over the severe biblical script of the lintels.

It was still as well to be prudent. He parked the car above Arran Street, where the grass sloped down beyond iron railings to the motionless water of the docks. Half a mile across mudflats and channels that dwindled at low tide to a muddy stream, the cranes and concrete dry-dock basins were sealed behind their wide steel lock-gates. Everywhere the afternoon lay silent, as if the year had run its course to exhaustion.

Locking the car, he turned and walked back to Arran Street. There was no reason why it should always be her place rather than his. The risk seemed about equal. It was as if she left Hoskins to take the initiative. At the top of the street he paused and smiled. Lesley was as he had first seen her, taking evidence from her in an earlier case. In a sweater and trousers of thin black nylon she had been tidying up the narrow area of low-walled garden that separated the door of the house from the pavement. The short cut of straight fair hair, the rather sulky look to the fair-skinned young face, reflected her character accurately enough. But effort and persistence paid off. There were times when Hoskins got through to this self-absorbed young woman, twenty years his junior, and found softness and desire strong in her. The desire was deep-rooted, he thought, to judge from the restless changing of partners. To identify and encourage it was easy enough. To satisfy it in the long term seemed more difficult.

She picked up a trowel from the path, the gesture emphasising the firm maturity of her thighs and hips, the suggestive curve of her hips and buttocks. Coming close enough, Hoskins murmured, 'You'll cause a traffic accident one day, bending over like that.'

Her smile went on and off like a light. She made no attempt to kiss him until they were in the house. When the time came for their friendship to end, Hoskins supposed that she would settle the matter in a sentence or two. After rinsing her hands in the kitchen, Lesley went upstairs without saying anything and waited for him. It was the ritual, the invitation. On the days when she stayed downstairs, the signal was equally clear.

He put down the paper he had been reading, went up, and found her unhooking a pair of black briefs from one ankle, steadying herself with a hand on the bedpost as she did so. Hoskins thought of his fortnight's leave and decided to postpone the discussion until afterwards. Whether Lesley was at the peak of her attractiveness depended, he supposed, on one's point of view. Enthusiasm for the slim, half-developed adolescent girl was a taste he had never shared. Making conversation with a bored and half-smart sixteen or eighteen year old was, in any case, more trouble than it was worth. He stared at the firm sleekness of Lesley's figure, the mature swell of breasts and buttocks and thought, as he had once said to her, what a lucky old bugger he was.

She stretched out on the bed.

'Come on, for goodness' sake,' she said, wide-eyed and chiding. 'Stop fantasising.'

Hoskins grinned and took off his shoes.

'I keep having this fantasy. Muzz Eve Ricard comes to see me secretly one day, saying that she's got this terrible guilty urge. Daren't tell her friends. She has to get gone over by a bloke in a police uniform and . . .'

Lesley turned away on her side.

'You really are a pig!' she said.

Hoskins undid the other shoe.

'Fantasies are all right,' he said reassuringly. 'I asked about it at my last medical board. "You keep right on having your fantasies, Hoskins," the surgeon said. "You'll feel all the better for them."'

Lesley turned back and put her arms up to draw him down.

'You might at least have the decency to fantasise about me,' she said.

Later on, as they lay relaxed and lazily together, Hoskins took the plunge.

'I ought to do something about this fortnight,' he said. 'My leave.'

'Why do anything?'

He tickled her bottom and she flinched away from him.

'Because I don't want to spend the time at home, decorating the bathroom or whatever the punters do. We could go somewhere, together. Bucket shops have a lot of flights going spare this time of year.'

'What if it doesn't work?' she said. 'You know.'

Hoskins propped himself on his elbow and kissed her ear.

'Best way to find out. Nothing like holidays and Christmas for bringing out the worst in people. Families stuck together, realising they can't stand the sight of one another. Divorce rate goes up like a rocket in January and the end of the summer. If we could stand a holiday, we could stand just about anything.'

'Where would we go?'

Hoskins turned on his back.

'I hadn't got that far. When I was a sprog DC, years ago, we'd got this really acid old chief. Inspector. Wizened like a prune from the booze. Liver waving the white flag and kidneys like pickled walnuts. Always going on about Dino Marina. Italy. If only he was in Dino Marina, he used to say about three times a day. Going to retire there and keep a bar. Only thing was, he went to stop a car down the Peninsula one night. Reported stolen. And the bloke went right at him. Never caught the driver. So poor old McGuire goes out to Dino Marina in an ash-can and they scatter him somewhere. He liked the place so much, he put that in his will.'

Lesley shivered and pressed naked against him for warmth.

'Not Dino Marina, under the circumstances,' she said.

'There's a lot of other places.'

'I'm not sure it's a good idea at all.'

'All right.' This time Hoskins stroked instead of tickling and she relaxed. 'But I'd rather go somewhere and try it than stay at home wondering if it's a good idea. I'll go round the shops tomorrow, see what I can find, and give you a ring in the evening.'

He felt her stiffen a little.

'Not the evening,' she said. 'I've got someone coming round.'

'Oh?'

'A woman.'

'Oh.'

'Yes,' she said, sitting up. 'And if I want to go to bed with her, I will.'

'Fair enough.'

'It doesn't matter if it's a woman? Women don't count?'

Hoskins sighed. They were back on familiar but dangerous ground.

'I don't shock,' he said gently. 'You forget where I've been the last twenty years. Raids down the Peninsula. City father in one of them that couldn't get anywhere unless he was done up with a nappy and a dummy. Another that had to have twin sisters going hammer and tongs. Big girls and little girls. Black and white. Contraptions I thought only doctors used. I don't get into a state of shock that easy.'

Lesley stood up and pulled on the black cotton briefs again. She turned, stooped and kissed him.

'I was just making a point,' she said gently. 'See what you can find out.'

16

The Man felt calmer. Calm and safe was how he thought of himself now. He walked through the mild sunlight of the late autumn afternoon. To either side of him, Saturday crowds moved slowly under the shopblinds of Great Western Street and Atlantic Wharf. The sales had ended and the girls were preparing the window displays for Christmas, an extravagance of red swathes and white snow, dark bottles and polished leather, shot silk and tortoiseshell. The autumn was almost done. After this the canvas shopblinds would be drawn in until summer came again.

The Man smiled at the people as he passed them. He liked them with a sudden welling up of gentleness and affection. The usual hatred of them for impeding him by their indecision or infirmity, their stupidity and brutishness, had quite gone. It was a feeling of infinite peace. Few of them returned his smile but here and there he saw the hard self-obsession of their greedy features soften at the encounter with his gentle eyes.

This, he supposed, was what it felt like to be good. Perhaps it was something of what it felt like to be a saint.

He crossed the traffic of the wide street where it opened into the sea-wind coolness of Atlantic Wharf. Though the docks were hidden by the high railway bank at one side, he could almost smell tar and rigging in the late yellow sun, the crisp scent of marine paint and the thick mineral richness of oiled engines.

His present state of mind would not last. The Man was too experienced in his own moods to believe that such a relief was possible. But while he was calm and safe, like this, he found it possible to believe that there would come a time when old age might bring him to permanent serenity. It was useless to hope for this before its time. It would happen then – or it would not. As a young man, he expected that it would have happened by his present age. But, if anything, he was now more confirmed in his 'rages', as he thought of those other moods. Even when he was not possessed by them, he could justify them to himself absolutely, as he had never been able to at twenty-five or thirty. It was partly a matter of chemistry. And why, after all, should he not feel scorn and vindictiveness for a grasping and malevolent society that deserved them? If the girls of the day chose to talk and act and look like whores at fourteen or fifteen, why should they not be treated accordingly?

All the same, while the present remission persisted, it was agreeable to be at peace with those who passed him. And there was another thing, in this benevolent phase. He noticed everything about him with great clarity and liked what he saw. It was as if the lenses of his eyes had somehow been washed over. He had made no effort towards this. The mood had come as unpredictably as the mild autumn Saturday in a season of fogs and chill. And there it was, for a few hours. He wished no harm to the world nor to anyone in it.

Passing the chic little windows of Madame Jolly Modes by the brasserie of the Paris Hotel, he saw the girl who stood with a tray of brooches in her hands just beyond the glass. She was going to set them out among the draped blue silk and the gold lamé. He liked her, the brown slant of almond eyes and the high arch of pencilled brows, the profile that might be oriental or grecian with its sharp young nose and the slope of the brow. He smiled at her, not with his former sardonic contempt but in an attempt to assure her that he meant no harm after all. She was a good girl, probably, concerned about her home and family, the salvation of her soul. Perhaps, for the future, he ought to think of that, redeeming her from being a mere caricature of his lust and scorn. To be sure, he meant no harm to her now. He would not have hurt a fly.

She turned, the narrow waist and trim hips moving in a lascivious swagger, and caught his smile. But she looked quickly away. The Man smiled again, to himself this time, and forgave her. The memory of previous meetings of eyes had made her cautious. That was all. He would have to show her that he meant nothing by them. Perhaps he would buy some flowers, walk in and hand them to her. What would she say to that? He almost laughed out loud at the thought.

All the same, he was going to have to watch his step from now on. No mistake about that. It had been a silly business with the schoolgirl from Shackleton Road. Silly. This afternoon, he had done his best to put it all behind him. It was like the episodes of childhood when he had been naughty and forgiven. 'He's a good boy now,' his mother would say, cuddling him for reassurance. 'He's a good boy now.' And seeing that it was over, half a lifetime later, he felt the truth of her reassurance. He could hear her voice as clearly as if she looked down and saw him. He was a good boy now. He was indeed.

But how astonishing that he should see familiar places and the people in them with such new clarity during his benign moods. Someone ought to investigate it scientifically. It was like the year when he had decided that they needed to have central heating installed. A holiday had been out of the question. And so they had decided to holiday at home, seeing the city as if they were tourists there. Going to museums they had never entered. Taking bus-rides to remote and windy destinations on the concrete fringes of the town. Seeing the familiar world from the tops of towers or through unsuspected archways. Visiting the city art gallery as if it had been the Louvre or the Prado. Even lying in the sun on Ocean Beach, a thing he had never done before. That was how it seemed now. The Man was on holiday from his habitual preoccupations. He smiled again at the passers-by. They stared back at him, unblinking and suspicious.

St Luke's church on the corner of Albany Street was the only building in the riverside cul-de-sac that was not occupied by commerce. There were clearing banks and merchant banks, temples to life insurance and the dome of the Victorian corn exchange. St Luke's itself, with its wide flight of steps and columns at the top, had a suggestion of Italy or Spain under its sooty gritstone. The Man walked up and opened the smaller door at one end.

There was no one inside, except a grey-haired woman who looked as if she had been polishing the altar brass. Each sound rippled up against bare stonework to the dim light of the barrel-vault. Stale incense, a sweetish smell of boiled washing, touched the air. A few dim electric lamps like clouded moons rivalled the little stars of the candles. The Man walked slowly down the nearer side-aisle and began to read the wall tablets, like an earnest student of such things seeing them for the first time. He paid his respects to each Victorian obituary incised on the stained white marble. Virtue and piety, certainly a lot of that about, to judge by the carved inscriptions. And what good had it done them? Dust and ashes! Dust and ashes! The Man felt a sneer beginning to gather on his lips. But he pulled himself together and passed the grey-haired woman with a nod.

'Wonderful old place,' he said.

She smiled and went on with her cleaning in the wide stone space of the darkened chancel. The Man walked down the other side-aisle, still reading the tablets. Dust and ashes! The moral of which was to make hay while the sun shone. Smoke 'em if you got 'em! He repressed a snigger. Pious memory! If the truth were known, the dust and ashes had done its fair share of sinning and copulating. Whorehouses with girls in red garters down the Peninsula. Young governesses seduced and set up in rented rooms. Children who never knew their fathers, only the fat top-hatted 'uncle' with his rare but expensive presents. Bloody hypocrisy!

By the time The Man came out on to the steps again, the sodium glow of the street lamps lit the deserted banks and exchanges of Albany Street. At the far end, open to the Town River, a fierce and frosty sunset assured him that the day had been only a respite before bitter weather to come. The Man took a deep breath and was glad, after all, to be out of the place. It held no comfort and no certainty for him. Dust and ashes. Make hay while the sun shone. Better to do it and regret it than regret too late you never tried it.

After the dark candle-lit interior of St Luke's, Great Western Street was bracing and exhilarating in the cold lamplight. The shops were closing now. Shutters came down on the stalls of the Saturday market, leaving the pavement treacherous with squashed fruit and abandoned boxes.

The mood passed by that evening, as all such moods pass. In the bare unfinished brick of the garage, The Man opened the free-standing cupboard and took out the lower shelf. In the space underneath it the full-plate photographs were safe from casual discovery. Black and white but none the worse for that. Easy enough to develop and print out here. And the little notebook with its ruled pages. Several hundred entries. Names. Addresses. Dates of birth. Places of birth. Schools and jobs. Names of brothers or sisters. None of it had much use, except as a talisman, except in the sense of power it gave The Man to know so much about the objects of his enthusiasm. Best of all, to the uninstructed reader the notebook contained only lists of numbers. A code whose simple key was locked in the bombproof vault of the skull.

The Man shivered and saw his breath mist the air. Despite the paraffin heater, frost struck upwards through the cement floor of the garage. Beyond the brick partition, he heard Annie's movements, hesitantly on the other side of the door that led straight to the utility room. He stood with the first package in his hand. The movements stopped. The Man watched the handle of the door. The movements began and then stopped again, as if she might be listening.

'Stop mousing about, you stupid bitch!' The Man said under his breath. Then he clenched his teeth in exasperation. 'Stop bloody well mousing about!'

He made sure that she did not hear. Then he heard her moving off and the door of the utility room being closed, as if she understood. The Man opened the car door and sat behind the wheel. No one would come out now. The light in the utility room had gone off and he could hear the rumbling and tumbling of the washing-machine.

One by one, The Man opened a score of the envelopes and drew out the glossy monochrome prints. They represented a small part of his mental harem, several pictures of each as she walked, or turned, or stretched at her work, some in swimsuits and some in jeans and singlets, some in uniform and one naked in a garden, not knowing that she was spied on as she changed from her sunsuit into her other clothes. There had been ten times that number of prints over the past year or two, a thousand rather than a hundred, but the rubbish had been burnt. The Man kept only the best. For half an hour, while the purr and rumble of the washing-machine assured his privacy, he sat in the car and browsed through them. One of the pictures caught the brazen amusement of a girl on the beach. Another showed puzzlement and unease as a young woman looked over her shoulder at him. Here and there he found scorn or indifference and his thoughts returned that with interest, sneering at the monochrome image as if it were flesh and blood.

The girl from Shackleton Comprehensive. A couple of dozen prints had been worth keeping. One showed her walking past with hard-faced indifference. In another her teeth were pulling at her lip as if with instinctive nervousness. The school tie was carelessly knotted and had slipped down an inch or so. These and the others taken from behind her showed the bare pallor of thighs almost to the tops of her legs. The Man studied the sight, the swell of the calves, the hollows behind the knees, the pale weight of the upper legs. His mouth tightened, as if what he saw displeased him.

In his mind The Man berated the girl, censure and lechery firing one another to hotter passion. The gem of the collection had been taken on a hot August afternoon, by walking along the alley at the backs of the houses, raising the camera above the eye-level brick wall and shooting blind. To his delight, it had produced half a dozen prints of Elaine lying on the grass in a pink bikini. By sheer luck they were astonishingly good, and the almost childish slovenliness of her undress and her awkward poses as she knelt or sprawled were extremely suggestive by The Man's valuation. This strip of half a dozen prints was quite good enough to put in a magazine, he thought. When he first printed them, the thought had attracted him. Send them in as a reader's contribution. Glamour on the grass. If they printed them, leave a copy where she could hardly miss it. Watch her face. It was like the excitement of childish naughtiness even to think of it.

Sitting there with the prints before him, he looked at those of Elaine's scornful young face and then the uneasy pulling at her lip with her teeth. He turned on the car engine to drown the sound of his own voice and gave way to the luxury of rage. Addressing the photograph of her face, as if it could hear and respond, The Man cursed and sneered, promised and exulted. He sat back at last, breathless and calm again, and turned the engine off. Before he got out to open the garage door and clear the air outside the car, The Man sorted through the photographs and put them away.

At the bottom of the last pile was a small poster. A young and unfamiliar face looked out from it. It was an unsmiling face, the hair worn in a sharp or spiky cockscomb. The girl from Moxon's College who had been found stabbed to death on the pavement early one Sunday morning. The police had worked on the case for months. Door-to-door inquiries were announced, though he could never find anyone at whose door a single inquiry had been made. In the end, they had given up. The killer might have been a foreign student, gone home before the inquiry began. There was talk of a motorist from a distant city turning off the motorway and being two hundred miles away again before the body was found.

The Man had not approved of the murder. He did not share the lecheries of others. Stabbing was something that he did not understand and found repulsive. All the same, from the moment the inquiry began his hopes were with the fugitive rather than the hunters. He wanted the perpetrator to escape. And so he felt a small triumph each time a police spokesman admitted a setback. At the same time, he nourished a secret scorn and scepticism at every televised promise of clearing up the crime. Had there been any small way of helping to prevent the murderer being caught, it would have pleased him to exploit it.

There had been excitement in that. Being one of the few, perhaps the only one, secretly on the side of the killer. It was the private exhilaration of being a member of the resistance during an enemy occupation. No one even guessing at the truth.

He opened the car door and held his breath in the fume-laden air until the garage door had swung up and over. If he was ever trapped, cornered by them, that was what he would do. Run the engine and keep the garage door closed. Simple as that. He stood and looked out into the late November darkness. The washing-machine was spinning through its last cycle as his breath hung damp and pale in the frosty air of the garden. He went back and sat in the car again, staring at the poster. By now, he supposed, the men investigating the case must have packed up and gone. After a year or two. Failure. Unannounced. Not that the actual murder of the girl from Moxon's College held any charm for him at all. It was certainly not how he would have done it.

17

Three weeks later, Dr Blades said, 'How was Dino Marina, Sam?'

'Wasn't Dino Marina, Charlie. Viareggio. Bed and brek for two.'

They went up the stairs to Blades's office in the Forensic Area One building, at the rear of Ocean Beach police headquarters.

'Sounds all right, Sam.' Blades sounded smoothly envious. 'Got in a bit of exercise, then?'

'I try, Charlie. I keep trying.'

Blades opened the door of a room on the top floor that looked across the tiles of the little hotels on Osborne Hill and the flat roofs of the department stores to the cold November sea. Whatever his mood, Blades's saturnine face always presented the same intent and concerned expression, thin and lined. It was the consequence, Hoskins understood, of the removal of a cancerous stomach. Blades liked to boast that it was caused by the sexual demands of the new Mrs Blades.

'I'm always glad to get back from two weeks of sun and fun, Sam. Be all right if it wasn't for her two little bleeders. Belly-aching every minute. They're back at boarding school now. I can't tell you the time I'm having with her! How was Viareggio?'

'Much the same as Ocean Beach, Charlie, to tell you the truth.'

Blades sat down and winced as a nerve plagued the phantom stomach.

'That's nice, Sam,' he said without listening as he opened

his desk and took out a bottle and two glasses. 'And how's the Ripper doing?'

Hoskins took his glass.

'It's the Pruen business, Charlie. They let old Wallace Dudden take charge while I was away.'

'Must have produced sighs of relief and smiles all round in the criminal fraternity,' Blades said cheerfully.

'You sure there's nothing more in it from your angle, Charlie?'

Blades shook his head.

'What there is, Sam, you've got. We went over it twice. But the mess it was in didn't make it any easier. Not a sign of a fingerprint. Could be we found fluff from woollen gloves, but it's stuff that's sold in millions of articles every year. Littlewoods. Marks and Spencers. You name it. We found a footprint. Tallish bloke. But they'd had window-cleaners, decorators, builders in the place. And it was Mrs Pruen that dealt with a lot of that. If Pruen was on our side, we might get somewhere. As long as he plays dumb, it's useless.'

Hoskins put his glass down.

'We asked Pruen about his prints on the phone in the public call-box. Says he stopped to ring Mrs Pruen's cousins on the way back. Then remembered he hadn't got enough change. International call, it was.'

'Handy,' Blades said sceptically. 'So that about winds it up. No one else saw anything that night?'

Hoskins shook his head.

'Only the neighbours' kids that spoke to some girl in Pruen's garden. While I was on leave, Jack Chance went round just about every house in The Links. The old door-to-door. Complete waste of time. Entire neighbourhood seems to have had its head up its backside that Sunday night. No one saw a thing.'

Blades winced and held out the bottle to refill Hoskins's glass.

'Dare say Cooney solved the case and handed out a bit of swift justice.'

'Thanks,' Hoskins said. 'No, Charlie. I think he'd want an example made. No sense doing it on the quiet. He'd want a body or two found.'

Blades thought about this.

'It could've been just one bloke, Sam, if Cooney was telling the truth. One bloke that knew Mrs Pruen was alone and knocked her over. But he also had to shove her face in that water. Human saliva in it.'

'Pruen's lying, Charlie. No two ways. But if we went to court, you'd have to be our star witness. Probably our only one. As it stands, I could only charge Pruen with being concerned in his wife's murder. No evidence who the others were. And he's got a dozen tame monkeys to say he was somewhere else. Including Councillor Cooney. You think a jury would send him down?'

'Nope,' Blades said, 'you'd get a thumb-in-the-eye from the Ripper and that'd be it. Face it, Sam. This has got to be one of that great majority of crimes. The ones that never get cleared up.'

Hoskins stood up and stared at the cold green sea beyond the rooftops.

'I don't like murders that aren't cleared up, Charlie. That's bad news.'

Blades winced again, the whisky turning acid.

'Cooney's got someone who was with him when he's supposed to have seen Pruen that night?'

Hoskins nodded.

'Dolly. Sarah Thorne or some such name. Tight jeans, high heels and make-up like a car paint-spray. One of his club girls, I suppose.'

Blades cheered up again, as if that seemed to put the matter to rest.

'I hate to say it, Sam, but in that case you've been screwed. Good and proper. You go to court with this lot and the best you'll get is a long speech from the judge about police forcing through a case that should never have come up. And you might be stopped before that by some young pansy in the prosecution service.'

Hoskins growled assent. Presently, they went back down to the car park.

'I dare say you're right, Charlie. I'll have a word with the Ripper and see where we go from here. I suppose if we can't find who did it, there's just a chance that Cooney can't either.

Whoever it was wouldn't be daft enough to stand forward and take a bow after Muriel Pruen snuffed it.'

'That's the idea, Sam.'

'There's been no news of any scrubby little yob throwing money around,' Hoskins said. 'I've had an ear open for that. Whoever did the Pruens must be pretty well-fleshed. There was a good wedge in that floor-safe, Charlie, there had to be. Five or ten grand, probably.'

'There again,' Blades said, 'Pruen's not going to start yelling. Not without the Inland Revenue and the VAT come nosing up his bum.'

'In his case, Charlie, more likely to be the Horserace Betting Levy Board. He must have ripped them off something cruel, since the Ocean Park dog-track closed.'

'Remember me to the Ripper,' Blades said.

Hoskins got into the car and Blades leaned in at the window.

'You come across a book about the story of O, Sam?'

'Can't say I have, Charlie.'

'She's reading it aloud to me in the evenings. Sort of book at bedtime. There's some quite original ideas in that. I suppose she thinks it's good for the old muscle-tone.'

'Dare say it is, Charlie. What you want to watch is your blood pressure. At your age. We don't want to read about you in the papers with one of those misadventure verdicts.'

Blades stood back and waved him off. The wind was cutting the wavetops as Hoskins took Bay Drive towards Ocean Park. Along the pier-approach the summer posters were wrinkled by mist and rain. Only the Petshop and the Blue Moon Club seemed busy in preparation for the winter season.

Chance was waiting for him when he came out of the lift at Canton divisional headquarters.

'You get anything from Charlie Blades?'

'Sod all,' Hoskins said. 'Not his fault. Sod all is what any of us have got just now.'

He opened the door of his room and went in with Chance following.

'There's another thing,' Chance said, 'if you want to look after it. Phone call from a chap called Harold Moyle. About twenty minutes ago. Says he knows you.'

Hoskins shifted some papers across his desk.

'Went to school with him, Jack. Bright lad. He's a teacher. Headmaster. Out at Shackleton Comprehensive. Did he say what he wanted?'

'Yes,' Chance said. 'He wants you to phone him back. There's one of his girls gone missing. Name of Elaine Harris, about fifteen years old. The way he put it, the whole thing sounds a bit rum.'

18

'Shut up! Settle down!' Superintendent Ripley's voice came in a weary monotonous bray across the hubbub. 'This is a briefing room, not the leisure centre. Thank you.'

They moved towards the metal chairs, shifting anoraks and crash-helmets.

'Who won the draw for Lamb's Acre duty, then?' Chance asked Hoskins.

'Dudden, as usual. South Stand for the Barbarians and London Welsh. North Enclosure for the Harlequins. So he says.'

Chance gave a look of jaded envy.

'Jammy sod!'

'When you're ready, Sergeant Chance,' said the Ripper smoothly across the dying murmurs.

Hoskins sat in the front row, the seat ahead of Chance. It was like school again, the restless class of a dozen burly men called in from their canteen-break. And there was Ripley at the classroom table with his billiard cue to act as a pointer, the white screen on its metal stand beside him. His grey moustache looked freshly combed, though the raspberry glow of his cheeks suggested a bad afternoon for his blood pressure.

'Right, people!' he began crisply. 'What I have to say can be said quite succinctly. Each of you represents a CID team and I look to you to brief your colleagues in short order.

You are all of you familiar with the case in general terms. Elaine Harris, fifteen years old, has been missing for the last fortnight. A missing person file has been opened but, so far as we know, no harm has come to her. We can't divert much full-time manpower to a search like that. It's just a little something extra for the menu. On the other hand, make no mistake, we want her found. I won't pretend we're looking for an innocent child. You'll find something about that in the hand-out. Additionally, there is a particular urgency over this one. Some months ago we were warned by Shackleton School that she was attracting rather sinister attention from men on the prowl. We kept a watch and saw nothing. Perhaps the school got it wrong. Perhaps some of us took a few short cuts and didn't look long enough or hard enough . . . '

'Stuff that!' said Chance from the corner of his mouth, loud enough for Hoskins to hear. The Ripper frowned briefly, catching a murmur but not its origin.

'All the more important, then, that we find her now. Right, Sergeant Truman. When you're ready, we'll have the first slide. Yes, Mr Nicholls?'

DCI Nicholls shifted on a chair too small for him.

'If she's been missing for a fortnight, sir, how come we only just heard about it?'

'No one knew,' the Ripper said sourly. 'The girl was living with her mother and stepfather in the Coronation estate on Lantern Hill. There seems to have been a quarrel between them. The mother went to her sister in Luton, the stepfather stayed put. The stepfather claims he understood the girl was going with her mother. The mother insists she told her to stay put and get on with her schooling.'

'Left her with the stepfather?' asked Dudden sceptically.

'So she says. The story of the mother's trip to Luton is one thing we'll be looking at closely. The point is, since the day of the mother's departure, the girl hasn't been seen.'

'If she's done a runner, sir,' said Chance hopefully, 'why can't the Social Services round her up?'

There were one or two derisive hoots at this and Ripley scarcely concealed his pleasure.

'Principally, Sergeant Chance, because the Social Services can't find their own backsides in the dark without a navigational beacon, let alone trace a missing girl. We'll have the first slide, if you please, Sergeant Truman.'

The lights went out. Beyond the uncurtained windows, a dull mist of the December afternoon veiled the cold phosphorescence of ornamental lamps among the trees of the Mall. Hoskins watched the familiar snapshots of Elaine Harris, blurred by magnification on the screen. There were crisp police photographs of the shabby cement-rendered council house and the CID draughtsman's maps of the area. He listened with half his mind to Ripley's explanation of the case. Closer attention was superfluous. He had, after all, fed the material to Ripley in the first place.

When it was over and the lights went on, they waited expectantly for Ripley's verdict. He did not disappoint them.

'There is, of course, one other reason why we don't want the Social Services crawling all over this case.' He looked round and paused, like a teacher prompting one of his pupils to anticipate the answer. No one gave it. 'We are asked to look for a missing child. There is, however, the obvious possibility that we may be in the first stages of a murder inquiry or at least a case of abduction. A photograph of Elaine Harris with an appeal for information will go out after the local news on Coastal Network at half-past six and half-past ten tonight. The same picture will be in the *Western World* tomorrow morning. To that extent, the case is going to have a high public profile in the hope we can wind it up quickly and happily. For that reason also, a senior officer will be in command to co-ordinate both the structure of the investigation and public response. A good deal will depend on the image we can put across through the media. The Chief Constable feels, and I agree with him, that we should call upon one of our more experienced diplomats. To that end, Superintendent Clitheroe will lead the inquiry.'

Even the cramped shifting of bottoms on the little metal chairs was stilled by this announcement. Hoskins just caught Sergeant McArthur's awe-stricken gasp: 'I'm having a bloody nightmare!'

'I know', said Ripley smoothly, 'that you will show Mr Clitheroe the same co-operation and diligence as you would if I were leading the inquiry myself. Anything less than that would, I'm sure we all agree, be unacceptable. Mr Clitheroe is in conference at the moment with the ACC Crime. You will all be good enough to remain here, so that he can have a brief word with you presently.'

The Ripper picked up his folder, walked slowly across the room, went out and closed the door after him. Chance put his mouth to within a few inches of the back of Hoskins's neck.

'Key-ripes!' he said grimly. 'Fucking Clitheroe!'

Sergeant McArthur swung round in his chair and grinned at Sergeant Truman by the projector.

'Come on, Jim! Give us a flash of the vice squad in action!'

There was a growling chuckle from the row behind Hoskins and someone turned the lights out. The first slide flicked on to the screen. There was a yelp of approval at the projected image of a tan-skinned girl naked with her partner.

'That's Tooty Fruity,' said Sergeant McArthur knowledgeably. 'The Mouse's old place down Martello Square. Nice girl. Make someone a good husband.'

'Who's that underneath?'

'Old Clitheroe in his frillies.'

This produced a cackle as the slide carrier clicked across and changed the picture.

'What's this one? . . . Who's been a naughty girl, then?'

'That's Councillor Ricard in the gas-mask,' Sergeant McArthur said. 'Know her anywhere.'

'Seen her distinguishing features often, have you, Sid?'

'It's her feet,' McArthur said. 'Cruel toenails.'

The carrier clicked across again.

'Where'd this rubbish come from, Jim?'

'The Squire's place down Monmouth Terrace. Dawson and his panty-raiders turned it over last week. The Squire hadn't been paying his respects to the dirty squad, I suppose.'

The carrier clicked again.

'That's disgusting . . . They're both blokes . . . That is really revolting . . . Get it off the screen, Truman. Go on!'

The door moved. Truman hit the switch. At once the screen went blank and the lights came on. Ripley was back again, this time with Clitheroe and a young man of about twenty-five.

'Mr Clitheroe needs no introduction from me,' Ripley said, suddenly more amiable and with the foolish half-smile of a man felled by treading on a garden rake. 'I know I can leave him to your mercy while I make my own peace with ACC Crime.'

The young man, with curly hair and an ill-fitting tweed suit, stared at his toecaps. He swallowed several times and his face coloured a little, as if he was disconcerted at being ignored. Ripley dredged up a few more pleasantries for Clitheroe. Then he withdrew. Clitheroe, whose black moustache and rimless glasses gave him something of the air of an Edwardian poisoner, looked about him.

'I don't want to begin by imposing rules of my own on procedures here. I should like to say, however, that I do not encourage smoking at my briefings.'

There was a moment of shock. Then someone mumbled, 'Sorry,' and Hoskins heard the scuffing sound of Sergeant McArthur stubbing out a cigarette on an upturned boot-sole.

'This afternoon,' Clitheroe resumed, 'is in the nature of a preliminary recapitulation. It will not take long. We are, however, fortunate to have with us Mr Hallam. At my request, he will be on hand to assist the investigation in the roles of consultant and intermediary with DHSS.'

Without raising his eyes too far, the curly-headed young man gave a quick smile of acknowledgement and Clitheroe continued.

'Most of you, I imagine, will already know Mr Hallam as senior community welfare officer for the Social Services in Lantern Hill. I know that you will be glad to have him as a colleague during the course of this inquiry.'

Sergeant Dudden said something under his breath. Hoskins did not quite catch what it was.

Half an hour later in Hoskins's blank-walled office, Sergeant Chance said, 'Clitheroe! What the hell is all this about, Sam?'

Hoskins walked across and made sure the door was properly shut.

'Senior officer, my son. Need a face that fits the television screen. Important case. At least, it will be if they don't find her soon.'

'Then why not you?'

Hoskins shrugged.

'Ask Ripley. Or ACC Crime. Or the Chief Constable.'

'All right,' said Chance reasonably, 'why not Ripley, if it's got to be a super?'

Hoskins pulled a face.

'Two years to go for his gold watch, Jack. Ripley's demob-happy and his blood pressure's up again. His pump could go before he catches the Bournemouth train. He doesn't want to go tramping through marshes in gumboots or be called out of bed to see bodies. Once he's had his Ovaltine and biscuits, he's tucked up until early morning tea.'

'So we get Clitheroe!' said Chance bitterly. 'And he brings that limp dick Hallam in with him! A young prat with a fat salary because he had the right political smell at his interview. And we'll all have to carry the useless little bugger on our backs!'

Hoskins sat down, looked at his watch and yawned.

'When I joined the force, my son, being a mason was what counted. Unless you wanted to stay sergeant for ever. Now it's kissing the welfare services' trouser-seat. Always something. No point griping, Jack. Clitheroe it is.'

Chance grabbed two handfuls of air.

'Clitheroe and Ocean Beach! It's all parking tickets and lollipop ladies over there. Even old Pruen, they have to send for us.'

Before Hoskins could reply there was a peremptory rap at the door and Ripley came in.

'Give us a minute, Jack,' he said amiably to Chance and then turned to Hoskins as the Sergeant went out. 'We thought you'd be best off out of the Elaine Harris business, Sam. As things are. Not that you couldn't handle it, I know, but we need a senior man who can put on a front with the media-boys.'

'Meaning Clitheroe?'

Ripley sighed and sat down.

'This may be nothing, Sam. The girl could walk in at any minute. In that case, you'd have wasted your time.'

'Clitheroe, Max!'

The Ripper's face hardened.

'You've got the Muriel Pruen case, Sam. If I'd put your name up to the Commander for the Harris case, that would be as good as saying we'd come to an end over the Pruen business.'

Like a double string of white pearls, the rush-hour car headlights queued patiently down the Mall, across King Edward Square, down the shop-lined avenue of Great Western Street towards the cold sea air of the December night.

'I'd say we're about at an end, Max. Not a single witness, except the ones that tell Pruen's version of the story. Bugger-all from Charlie Blades and the Nobel Prize winners out at Forensic. I might as well be back on holiday for all the good I'm doing.'

The Ripper stood up.

'Yes,' he said. 'My point exactly. I'd rather not go to the Commander and ask him to put you in charge of the Elaine Harris business. What do I tell him? You can't sort out the case you've got, so you want us to give you one more to your liking?'

'I don't want . . . ' Hoskins began, but the Ripper was not to be deflected.

'You've done well, Sam. I'd be the first to say it. That business of catching Weekes for the murder of poor old Stoodley was smart as new paint. But you can't be a prima donna here.'

'I don't want, Max—'

'Just try and see how others have to cope. Including me.'

'Right.'

Ripley stood up.

'I don't mean to lay it on you, Sam. There's a slackness in the whole division. ACC Crime has a bit to answer for. But some of the people in your area carry on like clowns in a three-ring circus. That seizure from the shop in Monmouth Terrace. There's fifteen slides missing from the stuff that Dawson brought back. It is not a joke, Sam! Those things are on inventory and they're missing, Dawson says. One official check or audit and there's trouble. Jack

Chance and the sergeants' room treat this place like the Hawks Hill Golf Club. You can tell him I'll run an official check tomorrow.'

'I'll mention it,' said Hoskins solemnly.

'It takes one strait-laced female DC to walk in when they're making free with stuff like that. That's all. We could face one hell of a row.'

'I'll mention it to some of them,' Hoskins reassured him.

'Her Majesty's Inspectors of Constabulary,' Ripley said with bitter satisfaction. 'They'll be here sooner or later. The ritual visitation. After my time, I hope. They'll put this entire division through the mincer. A bunch of real assassins. Jack Chance and his lot won't know what's hit them. It's going to take a monkey-wrench to get the boot-toes out of some of the backsides round here . . . '

'All right,' said Hoskins pacifically, 'I'll say something.'

In the excitement, the Ripper's face was turning a light mauve. That worried Hoskins a good deal.

That evening, he parked the car and went up the cement steps to his apartment in Lamb's Chambers, closing the door on the world with relief. Lamb's Chambers in St Vincent Street, the first shabby side-avenue across the Town River bridge from Canton city centre, had been built as red-brick Queen Anne in the early 1930s. Doctors and barristers who first occupied the apartments had long gone. Lamb's Chambers was marooned in the traffic-din of St Vincent Street, the shouting and vomiting of two commercial pubs. Hoskins withdrew to the rear of the flat, the sitting-room that looked out across the turf of Lamb's Acre, stands and enclosures silent now, until the rugger match on Saturday.

He stirred food into a saucepan, and thought of Ripley. Inconceivable to Ripley that he had not wanted the Elaine Harris investigation as a matter of personal advancement. Still, it would have been undiplomatic to explain the truth. He knew he could do the job better than Clitheroe. With his eyes shut. Anyone would do it better than Clitheroe. He wanted it himself to prevent the carnage that an idiot like Clitheroe might cause. He wanted it now, so that he and others would not have to clear up the mess left by Clitheroe later on. He stirred his meal with one hand and tried to read the Swedish instructions on the tin which he held in his other. It was the nearest he had come to self-improvement lately. He did not, it seemed to him, feel much better for it.

19

Like a belligerent cricket, the phone filled his sleep with its persistent chirrup. Hoskins, light-headed, disentangled his arm from the sheet and fumbled the handset towards him in the dark. Far off, he could hear the quack of an impatient voice.

'Sam? . . . That you, Sam? . . . Hello? . . . Anyone there?'

'I'm here,' he mumbled morosely, finding the light switch by the bed and turning it on. Without his glasses, he was not sure whether the alarm clock said quarter-past five or nearly half-past three.

'Gerald Foster, *Western World* night-desk. You there, Sam?'

'Of course I'm bloody well here,' Hoskins said, finding his glasses with one hand. 'Where else would I be?'

'Got something for you, Sam.'

'What's the right time?'

'Gone five,' said Foster cheerfully. 'Time you were up.'

'I feel as if I've only been in bed about ten minutes.'

'There's a woman wants to talk to you, about that picture of Elaine Harris. She saw it on the telly last night. Couldn't sleep for thinking of it. Came in with her kids about ten minutes ago to have a good look at our copy.'

'You woke me up for that?' said Hoskins incredulously.

'She recognises the girl, Sam.'

'Then bloody well wake up Clitheroe and tell him. It's his case now.'

'Clitheroe's a shithead,' said Foster dismissively. 'This is for you, Sam.'

'I don't care what he is, my son. It's his case. I'm going back to bed.'

Even before Foster replied, an uneasy stirring in Hoskins's spine told him otherwise.

'I think you'll find this one's down to you, Sam. Mrs Levens brought her two kids in. She and they recognised the girl in the picture. They're next-door neighbours to old "Horse-Parlour" Pruen. Your Elaine Harris is the girl they saw waiting in the garden while the place was turned over that Sunday evening. No question. Absolute cert. Even down to the school clothes and striped tie.'

'Right,' said Hoskins crisply. 'I'll be with you in about fifteen minutes.'

'I hoped there might be a drink for the press in all this, Sam.'

'There most certainly will be, Gerald, if there's a result. Might even let you hold the bottle while you pour.'

He rang off and dialled Chance's number.

'Get up,' he said. 'I need some company.'

Chance coughed and caught his breath. There was a pause. Then he said, 'It's half-past five, Sam!'

'I didn't ring you up to ask the time, my son,' said Hoskins bleakly. 'See me down the *Western World* office. Gerald Foster. Night-desk. Fifteen minutes.'

'What for?'

'You could end up famous, Jack. On the telly. Like Mr Clitheroe.'

Dressed and shaved but hungry, he felt the intense cold of the December morning as he went out into the shabby lamplit dereliction of St Vincent Street. There was a clout of icy air as he pushed open the door and went down the steps to the glittering pavement. The city was empty and silent. Opening his garage in the yard at one side of Lamb's Chambers, Hoskins reversed the Vauxhall Cavalier and turned into the street. The garage door remained open. Enterprising burglars of twelve or thirteen could help themselves as far as he was concerned.

The Town River bridge and Longwall Street between the Victorian-mediaeval Keep and the first shops was as clear as a grand prix circuit under the orange sodium glow of street lights. It was like the aftermath of a nuclear winter. The lamps caught the twinkle of crystal-ice on the mudflats at low water, where the black river mingled in the tidal channel of the docks.

The *Western World* offices occupied a concrete fortress on King Edward Square built in the advent of new printing technology. It sat sullen and brutish across the empty bus terminal from the Edwardian domes and pillars of City Hall. Hoskins saw a family group standing in the fluorescence of the lobby behind a front of armoured glass. He recognised Foster and his protégées.

The woman was in her mid-thirties, dressed in gumboots and jeans as if fresh from the plough. She had short dark curls, a neat and rather pretty face. Beside her was a boy with the air of a ten year old captain of industry, and his younger sister.

'I'm Trish Levens,' the woman said, hardly waiting for Foster to finish the introductions. 'It's the girl in the photograph. She's the same one. The one that was in Mr Pruen's garden.'

Hoskins calmed her. They sat down in the squealing plastic of lobby chairs.

'First of all, who saw her?'

'I did,' said the infant captain of industry, frowning as if Hoskins should have known better. 'And so did Phoebe. And mum as well. I spoke to her. She had a common voice. Definitely common.'

'You all gave your descriptions to Sergeant Chance at the time.'

'Yes,' said the boy, a ring of command in the prep school voice, 'but that's not the same as seeing her in the photograph. She's definitely the one. The tie was yellow and blue stripes, I think. And she was wearing this pale grey skirt very short. You could almost see her knickers underneath.'

He sniggered involuntarily and blushed, the future captain of industry reverting to a furtive child again.

'And Phoebe saw her too?'

'Yes,' said Phoebe scornfully. 'Only I never spoke to her. Tristan did.'

'And she had a common voice,' the boy insisted. 'The tie was definitely yellow and blue. It might have had a black stripe too. She wasn't really tall but she seemed a bit big and rather rough.'

123

'Good,' Hoskins said. 'Well done.' He looked up at Mrs Levens.

'It is the girl,' she said reassuringly. 'I think I told the Sergeant that her eyes had a funny look. Like in the photo. Slightly hooded and somehow a bit slanted. I can't quite find the word for it.'

'Did you speak to her?'

'Oh, no,' said Trish Levens hastily. 'I walked as far as the gate with the children. I waited while they went in and asked about Mrs Pruen's companion. Noreen. But I saw her as plain as I can see you now.'

Even the pale marble lobby of the *Western World* building was bitter cold that morning. Hoskins repressed a shiver. He walked aside with Gerald Foster, leaving Trish Levens and her children in the chairs of brown buttoned plastic.

'What d'you think, Sam?'

'It's bound to be a starter, Gerald. The photograph only shows her face. But this lot have got the rest right as well. Description of clothes and build. Even the right colour stripes on the tie.'

'And they're positive.'

'Yes, well, witnesses generally are positive at this stage. I'll have to take them down the constabulary rest-home and get proper statements. Then run the old interrogation routine. Show 'em different photos of her and a few of girls like her that aren't her. See if we get consistent answers.'

'It's bloody well got to be her, Sam!'

'Dare say you're right, Gerald. Still, it's not going to make much odds to you at the moment.'

'How's that, then?'

'Because so far as you are concerned, Gerald, none of this ever happened.'

'Sod that,' said Foster from the corner of his mouth. 'It's our story, Sam.'

'You fallen out of your tree again, Gerald? Elaine Harris is missing, still alive, we hope. You print a story about her being one of the yobs that turned over Pruen and what happens? Pruen's friends will be looking for her even harder than old Clitheroe. And being brighter than Clitheroe, they'll probably find her first. Then it's pulling out finger-nails and the rest until she tells 'em a story they believe. And then, from a crowd of eager volunteers, they pick the expert that's going to polish her off. Not subtle, Gerald, not original, but highly effective. Clitheroe may be looking for her, but she's now a witness in my case. I want her found alive.'

'I understood there was a drink in this for the press,' Foster muttered.

'In good time, Gerald. For the moment, Elaine Harris was never near old Pruen's place. Right? And anyone who was to print a story on the subject could expect more grief than a month of funerals.'

Foster was about to say something else when the swing door flew open and Sergeant Chance hurried in. His normally florid plump face was pale and the black hair was inexpertly combed. He came up to Hoskins and Foster.

'Where's the fire, then?'

Hoskins looked him up and down.

'If you'd joined the brigade, my son, we'd have our work cut out keeping the blaze going till you got there. You call this fifteen minutes?'

'Flexed her muscles. Wouldn't let him go,' Foster suggested sympathetically.

'He's a martyr to it,' Hoskins said. 'Come on, let's get this lot sorted out.'

Just after nine o'clock, Superintendent Ripley began to see the bright side of it all.

'Depends which way you look at it, Sam. Having the Muriel Pruen murder and the Elaine Harris case cross like this saves manpower. A bit messy administratively. But that needn't be too bad so long as you don't rub Mr Clitheroe up the wrong way.'

'Suppose he was to rub me up the wrong way, Max?'

'Privilege of his rank, Sam. Senior man. Catch his act on the telly last night, did you?'

'No.'

'He was rather good actually. Put it well. Frightened child of fifteen in need of protection. Prepared to understand anyone's perversion so long as we get her back all right. No hint of I'd-like-to-string-up-the-bugger-who-did-it-with-my-own-hands. Cool. Laid-back. Did Elaine Harris proud. Home-loving girl, worried parents, Clarendon Street Bible Class . . . '

'What?'

'Not lately, of course. There's no point giving the other story, Sam. You go on television and tell 'em we're looking for some hard-faced young scrubber who's into robbery, sex, and probably blackmail of middle-aged men. Turns the public right off. Deserves all she gets. End of co-operation. We have to project a positive image, Sam. That's what Clitheroe is good at.'

'As it stands, Max, she's a likely accomplice in the murder of Muriel Pruen.'

'Only between these four walls, Sam. One whisper of that outside and I'll come down on Gerald Foster like the wrath of God.'

'Not to mention those two smart-arsed Levens kids. You can bet the news is all round the school playgrounds by now. Still they did their stuff. Passed every test with the pictures here. Pound to a penny it was the lovely Miss Harris in old Pruen's garden.'

The Ripper smiled. Behind him the bare trees of expensive gardens on Hawks Hill were almost obscured by the cold mist. The Stalinist tower blocks of Mount Pleasant rose grey on grey through the chill vapour.

'Anything else?' the Ripper asked.

'First anonymous phone call. Chap anxious to tell us in detail how he made off with Elaine Harris, where he took her and what he did to her before dumping the body in the Railway Dock. We've got him on tape. Sounded as if he'd just run up four flights of stairs. Apart from loonies, we've got half a dozen other witnesses with possible sightings. They're coming in to look at pictures.'

'Nothing about possible associates in the Pruen business?'

'Not yet,' Hoskins said. He noticed, on top of the papers in the Ripper's in-tray, a brochure from a Bournemouth estate agent.

'Right,' Ripley said. 'I won't keep you, then.'

Ten minutes later, in Hoskins's room, Chance said, 'I've got Wallace Dudden in charge of the six people coming to look at photographs. You still want to go out to Lantern Hill this afternoon?'

'I'll need to riffle through the home-life of the lovely Harris family,' Hoskins said. 'I want anything that connects her to Pruen or to anyone who might have done Pruen. And I don't intend to hang about. If Pruen hears that she was there, it won't just be a matter of vengeance. He knows that if we get Elaine Harris, she could blow his story about being out in the car when the robbery happened. And that lands Carmel Cooney and a dozen others in the shit. Possible conspiracy charges. Reason enough to wipe her out.'

Chance shifted and clasped his hands behind his back.

'Bit unfortunate, Sam, us needing to go out there this afternoon.'

Hoskins opened an internal memo.

'Why's that?'

'Clitheroe's lot are out there already, this morning. Turning the place over. Sergeant McArthur says old man Harris is playing the grief-stricken parent and going on something dreadful about being treated like a criminal.'

Hoskins sighed and put the memo down.

'Why in hell can't someone get this lot organised, Jack? Not a word from Clitheroe or Ripley! Clitheroe's lot are looking for evidence of where she is. I'm looking for evidence of whether she's accomplice in murder. So the house has to be turned over twice in one day. With another warrant if necessary.'

'Clitheroe might do it for us, Sam.'

Hoskins looked up at him from behind his desk.

'You think I'd trust Clitheroe and his meter-maids, do you, Jack? And there's Ripley can't get me out of the room fast enough because his in-tray is full of pictures of Eventide Homes in Bournemouth and Boscombe. I'm going out to Lantern Hill this afternoon, my son. And I'll be on a short fuse.'

Chance sat down.

'According to Dudden, Clitheroe's got it worked out. He's read that when you get chopped, it's usually by someone in the family. It says so in the police handbook on how to solve your first murder. Keeps it simple. If you believe old Dudden, Clitheroe's got his scenario. The Harris couple have a real ding-dong. Ma Harris does a bunk to her sister in Luton. Elaine gets left behind with stepfather. Harris reckons that if he can't have his bedroom workout with his wife, he's entitled to her daughter. There's a fight, during which he either does or doesn't get his wicked way with Elaine. Whichever it is, he somehow snuffs her during the course of the discussion and gets rid of the body. Probably about two weeks ago.'

'Clitheroe thinks that?'

'So Dudden says.'

'In that case,' said Hoskins firmly, 'I'm going out to Lantern Hill now, before anything worse happens.'

20

Hoskins went down to the car and waited for Chance, his driver. Frost still rimed the walls of the motor-pool yard. The disc of the December morning sun was thin as a fogged image of the moon. Sergeant Chance appeared in a fur-lined anorak. He looked cheerful, as he always did when there was news to impart.

'Need to be back here sharpish tonight, Sam,' he said as he slammed the car door. 'Seems Clitheroe's giving a press conference at six.'

'Who says?'

'Word's just going out from the press office. There's an urn of tea laid on. Cables for the cameras all down the second-floor corridor. By the way, Browne and Eveleigh are following us to Lantern Hill in the mini-van. Just in case there's a lot to bring away.'

Hoskins grunted and stared unappreciatively at the bare almond trees of the Memorial Gardens as Chance drove down the pink-tarmac'd Mall, past City Hall and across the grey spaces of King Edward Square, the custard-yellow buses unpatronised in their bays.

'When there are grey skies . . . ' Chance crooned.

'Across the Town River and out through Orient,' Hoskins said quietly.

'Right-oh.' Chance made a change of lane past the Victorian gothic of the Keep with its painted Florentine watch-tower. 'I don't mind grey skies . . . You make them blue, Sonny Boy . . . Doo-dah-dee-doo-dah . . . '

'Bloody press conference!' Hoskins said. 'What for? He's got nothing to tell them.'

They passed the City Tabernacle, gateway to working-class Orient, its grim Pentecostal stone adorned by funeral-blue neon. The drab little shopfronts of Osborne Road began. Even in the cold, the worn secondhand furniture of house clearances stood on the pavements outside the cave-like show-rooms of the dealers. Twenty minutes later, the suburb of Lantern Hill, extending downwards to Harbour Bar, seemed almost as deserted as Canton before dawn. The streets were quiet, the children at school, only a few shoppers struggled home along the hilltop avenues of redbrick houses in low-walled gardens.

'Snow!' said Hoskins miserably. 'Will you look at that sky! It's going to snow. Not even Christmas.'

As they reached the hump of Arkell Street, the view across to Peninsula and the docks was bleak as Murmansk. Nothing moved in the dry-dock basins or the anchorages. Even the slow tide had a frozen look. Coronation estate had been built at one side of the Bellevue as a hope-ful post-war experiment. The houses in rows of four were rendered in ash-coloured cement with access lanes and high-walled gardens at the rear. Shelved on the hillside, they had terraced grass and steep paths between the levels. The Harris family lived at the end of a terrace. A police car, two unmarked Fiestas and a Land-rover were parked out-side.

A man in plain clothes came down the narrow concrete path from the front door. Hoskins recognised him as Alan Willis, one of Clitheroe's inspectors in Ocean Beach Division, the head youthfully bald with a look of shiny virility.

'Hello, Sam. What brings you out here?'
Hoskins slammed the car door.

129

'An interest in the Harris family. I want to look the place over. I've got Jack Chance with me. DC Browne and DC Eveleigh on the way in the mini-van. Jack and the other two can turn the place over. I want a quiet talk with Harris and his missus.'

Willis barred the way on the narrow path.

'Bit difficult at the moment, Sam. You can have a word with Harris, if you want. But our lot's in the middle of rummaging. With a warrant. Mr Clitheroe's instructions.'

'I'm after evidence, Alan. If that's all right with everyone else.'

'Taken care of, Sam. We're doing the lot, down to the last pair of dirty socks and souvenir wedding-cake. Old man Harris is going spare. Victim of tragic circumstances now persecuted by the police. That sort of thing.'

'I'd as soon see for myself, Alan.'

'Not necessary, Sam. All under control. Usual missing person routine.'

Their breath was steaming in the dank air of the front garden.

'I'm not interested in missing persons,' Hoskins said firmly. 'In case news hasn't reached Ocean Beach, there's a murder inquiry in progress. That's why I'm here.'

Willis remained unimpressed.

'We know about that, Sam. It's all in hand. There's Forensic in there. The lot.'

'You know what precisely?'

'Elaine Harris being in Pruen's garden. Isn't that it?' Willis looked surprised and a little uneasy.

'And how come you know about it?'

'Clitheroe,' said Willis cautiously. 'Not a state secret, is it.'

'Not any more it isn't.' Hoskins gestured Chance forward.

They shouldered their way into the narrow hall with its steep staircase. Anstey from Ocean Beach Forensic was coming down the stairs.

'Morning, Sam,' he said, preoccupied. Hoskins glared at him.

'When the other two get here,' he told Willis, 'I'll want them to start all over again with Jack Chance. Understood?'

'Mr Clitheroe never said anything about that.'

130

'I'm saying it, Alan. What Clitheroe's looking for and what I'm looking for are two quite different things. And if anyone else breathes a suggestion about Pruen's garden, they can look forward to a month or two of uniform. Late-night punch and sick down the fish and chipperies in Rundle Street.'

'You're the senior officer here, Sam,' said Willis help-lessly.

'Too right.' Hoskins turned to Chance. 'Soon as the van arrives with Browne and Eveleigh, sort this lot through. Room by room. Now, where's Mr Harris?'

'They're both in the front room.'

'Right. I'll go in and have a chat.'

He tapped on the door and pushed it open. The heat from a powerful three-bar fire hit him like a blast furnace. They sat there, either side of the fireplace in cheap-print armchairs. Thick carpet, wide curtains and stuffed cushioning gave a musty air to the concrete shell of the room. The television, its sound turned off, flickered in a corner under holiday souvenirs in polished wood. Neither of them was watching it. On the screen, an American policeman with the air of a stunned gorilla was driving through a landscape that seemed made of cardboard.

'Mr Harris?'

The man looked up as Hoskins spoke. Pug-faced. For the first time the term truly meant something to Hoskins. Squashed, dog-like, aggressive and fawning simultaneously. Ironically, stepfather Harris looked more like Elaine than her natural mother. Mrs Harris, hair frizzed orange-brown, was forty-five in white boots, short skirt, and black stockings with a playing-card pattern.

Harris shifted in his chair.

'What's it now?'

'I'm Chief Inspector Hoskins. I'd like to apologise for the disturbance that's been caused here. I promise you it's necessary. We'll get it done and everything put tidy again as soon as we can.'

He sat down uninvited. Harris stared at him.

'First time anyone's apologised,' he said, suspiciously. 'Treated like criminals, we've been. I asked why the place was being searched. One of 'em tells me I'll find out.

The other says to button my lip. Evans, the one from Lantern Hill.'

'I'll have a word with Mr Evans. I don't allow witnesses to be talked to in that manner.'

Harris puffed out his chest a little. He was impressed.

'I should think not, Mr Hoskins. On the same side, after all, aren't we?'

'Even so,' said Hoskins equably, 'the search was necessary. You see, we know the kind of things we're looking for. You might not. Anything that would give us a clue as to where she went or where she might be now.'

Mrs Harris sniffed and touched a handkerchief to her eye.

'We did everything for her, Mr Hoskins. We never had any trouble with our other two. Grown up, moved away. Married. She's not been near them.'

Hoskins shook his head, as if at the difficulty of it all.

'I can imagine what you've been through. Both of you. I know you've had enough questions from people like me.'

'Oh, no,' said Mrs Harris quickly, pulling the hem of the white leatherette skirt to cover her knees again. 'If there's anything else, Mr Hoskins, we'd be only too glad.'

Hoskins acknowledged her willingness with a smile.

'It's just one thing, Mrs Harris. We know Elaine hasn't gone to anyone else in the family. Not yet, anyway. Not to her brother or sister. But when a youngster of her age goes missing, it's quite often with a friend. Or, at least a friend knows about it. A sort of prank or adventure. Was there anyone of her own age or a little older, perhaps? Boy or girl?'

'We told Mr Clitheroe,' Harris said. 'We gave him a list. There's two or three girls at the school. They've been seen already.'

'Boy friends?'

'Not that we know of.'

'Anyone mentioned, just as a name?'

'Not to us.'

'But she presumably had a boy friend?'

'Not that we knew. Seemed to go round with this group of girls. They been asked about it. Didn't seem to mention a boy.'

'Was Elaine ever out at unusual times? Very late at night or even all night?'

'Not that we noticed.'

'And a fortnight yesterday was the last time you saw her?'

'Yes.'

Several minutes later, in the hall, Alan Willis said, 'It's not on, Sam. We can't have our lot crawling over the house and your lot crawling over our lot.'

'If Clitheroe had bothered to mention to anyone what his plans were, we could have had one lot doing it for us both. Organise it room by room.'

'Forensic can't do it that way.'

'Bollocks,' Hoskins said. 'I'll go and have a word with Anstey.'

Presently he came back down the stairs and went out into the garden at the back. By the kitchen door a constable in rubber gloves was sifting through the contents of the dust-bin.

'That'll have been emptied twice since she went missing.'

'Mr Clitheroe thinks it's worth a try, sir.'

In the garden itself there were four burly men in waterproof trousers, gumboots, and yellow sou'wester jackets. They were digging in parallel lines along the meagre vegetable-plot.

'Winter cabbage?' Hoskins inquired sceptically of Willis.

'Mr Clitheroe reckons it's most likely down to Harris. In cases like this, one of the first things is search the house and dig the garden.'

'I know,' Hoskins said. 'I read the Teach-Yourself book about it.'

'She could be under there.'

'Not with the soil in that state. Not exactly freshly dug. I shouldn't think it's seen a hand's turn from Harris for a year or two. Not so long as there's films about American dumbo-cops for him to watch on the telly.'

Willis sighed.

'It's all there is, Sam. Elaine Harris as a victim of family life. Not a bloody clue to anything else. Not as Clitheroe sees it. If we don't get any further here, I reckon that's the lot. Elaine Harris is officially selling her beautiful body in some other city. File stays open but investigation ends.'

'And Clitheroe winds up as a lollipop man.'

Willis shook his head.

'Dunno, Sam. You lot in Canton Division reckon he's a no-hoper. Actually, when you work with him, you realise he's quite clever. Shitty but shrewd.'

A spade struck flint and the mound of heavy clay shone wet in the chill morning. The kitchen door opened and Hallam appeared, the Social Services welfare officer who had accompanied Clitheroe at his briefing. The young man's glasses glinted in the grey outdoors.

'I wonder,' he said to Hoskins and Willis, 'I wonder if you'd mind keeping your voices down. Mr and Mrs Harris do have feelings, you know. And there are two sergeants, Chance and Strachey, arguing in the front bedroom. Perhaps you'd care to do something about that.'

Without waiting for a reply, he went back inside and closed the door. Willis looked away from Hoskins and stared across the garden wall.

'Little prick,' he said quietly.

In company with Jack Chance, Hoskins drove back to Canton through the murk of mid-afternoon.

'Thing is, Sam,' Chance said cheerfully as they passed the take-aways and betting-shops, funeral-home and laundrettes of Osborne Road, 'no one got anything out of it. Nothing there for us and nothing there for Clitheroe. Either it was a rub-out at home or else she's up and away with the mob that shafted Pruen.'

'Maybe.'

Chance sniggered and changed lanes for the Town River bridge.

'Ken Martin reckons old Clitheroe's going down to her school next. Question two thousand kids. Should keep him out of the way till after Christmas.'

Hoskins ignored this.

'Let me out at the King Edward Square crossing,' he said. 'I want to get a haircut before his press conference this evening.'

As Chance slowed the car, Hoskins took from his pocket a handwritten list.

'What's this?' Chance asked.

'When you get back, phone this lot. Banks. All of 'em.'

Chance looked quickly.

'Bit of trouble with the old overdraft, Sam?'

Hoskins handed him a second sheet of paper.

'And ask them just one question in these words.'

'Videos?'

'Just do it.'

'Right,' said Chance. 'Can't be any worse than a day with old Harris's last week's socks. I shouldn't think their washing machine's seen action the past month or two.'

The press conference, when it began, packed the second-floor briefing room at the headquarters building. The *Western World*, Coastal TV News and the BBC were represented, as well as stringers for the national tabloids and qualities. Clitheroe stood in a shaft of floodlit brilliance, Ripley sitting beside him and ACC Crime in the shadows. Hoskins stood with Chance, Martin, and several other CID officers at the back of the room. From the rows of chairs, Gerald Foster was doing his responsible best.

'We understand that detectives involved in the London and Bristol abduction cases of young women may travel to Canton in the next few days.'

'It's obviously under consideration,' Clitheroe said. 'Nothing definite.'

'And that your officers are actively seeking a connection with a local case last year in which a schoolgirl, Rachel Lloyd, was found stabbed to death.'

Clitheroe made a helpless little gesture.

'Clearly, Mr Foster, we must compare and analyse. But this remains a missing person case and not a murder inquiry. We hope to find her alive and well.'

There was a lull. It was ended by a bright fluffy-haired blonde from the Rockwell chain. She raised a hand.

'Miss Amanda Rayner,' Clitheroe said graciously.

'Can you comment on the report, Mr Clitheroe, that a girl now identified as Elaine Harris was seen in the garden of the house where Muriel Pruen was murdered in August, at the time the murder was committed?'

'It's news to me,' Clitheroe said amiably. 'As usual, Miss Rayner, you are a step or two ahead of our investigation.'

The tight mean face with its Edwardian-poisoner moustache broke into a smile of sheer good-nature.

21

'For goodness' sake, Sam!' The Ripper rested his buttocks on the rim of his desk, legs braced at an angle. 'Be your age!'

Another morning mist over Hawks Hill and Mount Pleasant filled the view behind him.

'Clitheroe leaked it!' Hoskins said bitterly. 'He must have done, for Rayner to ask if she was in Pruen's garden. He's deliberately put the Harris girl in the firing-line. Every villain in Canton and Ocean Beach must know she was part of the Pruen business by now. Cooney. Pruen himself. They'll have their runners and tarts out on the streets, looking for her already. Not just a dozen of them like us. Every tearaway and grafter that wants to do a favour to the big men. You have any idea the kind of money that Cooney or even Pruen might offer? Have you, Max? And that stone-face that is minding Pruen on Cooney's orders. Raymond. They hand Elaine Harris over and tell him to get the truth out of her. He'd be like a kid on Christmas morning.'

'Leave Clitheroe out of it.'

Hoskins looked at him for a moment without saying anything, as if Ripley had still not taken the point.

'In words and pictures, Max. Clitheroe was leaking yesterday by the bucketful. In every direction. Elaine Harris being on hand when someone did Muriel Pruen. He told his entire crew out at Lantern Hill, for a start! You think he didn't tell his pet journalist as well? Miss Cuddles with the teasy curls. When she spoke up at that press conference, he looked as pleased as if her hand was half-way down his trousers. You saw him, Max!'

Ripley sighed, like a man who has done his best.

'All right, Sam. You want to make a formal complaint against Clitheroe. Divulging classified information to a member of the public. Official Secrets Act and all the rest. Right the way to the Crown Court. You've got rock-solid witnesses, have you? Times, places, details? And if you even want to get to an internal inquiry, you'd better have something that Clitheroe put in writing. You can provide all that, can you?'

'Of course I bloody can't, Max! He didn't need to write it. He told his entire crew . . . '

'Which he was entitled to do. They are working on the case, Sam. You told Jack Chance, didn't you? He could be the leak, for all you know.'

'No.'

'Why not?'

'I know Jack Chance and I know Clitheroe. In any case, the senior officer takes responsibility. This is down to Clitheroe.'

'And your friend Gerald Foster? He's so public-spirited he wouldn't breathe a word of it?'

'I trust him,' said Hoskins more calmly. 'In any case, he'd hardly go and blab the whole thing to the opposition, to bloody little Rayner. It started with someone in this building, Max. It had to. You saw Clitheroe, when that girl asked her question. He didn't even look surprised. He was practically grinning all over his face. He didn't even ask the press not to speculate on whether the girl was in that garden or not. Nothing.'

Ripley shrugged.

'Then prove your charges, Sam. Put up or shut up.'

'I don't have to prove them, Max. If this story leaked from Clitheroe's case, then he's not fit to be in charge of the inquiry. Thanks to him, we could have civil war on our hands, if the old pros and the young bulls start killing each other off.'

'This isn't Sicily or Chicago, Sam.'

'It doesn't need to be, Max. If that girl dies, as a result of Clitheroe, no one knows what the end might be. I'd like him moved over.'

The Ripper straightened up, went round his desk and sat down. He fenced a little with his cylindrical ruler.

'Clitheroe's being moved over,' he said. 'It was decided last night. Chief Constable and ACC Crime. The girl's disappearance and the death of Muriel Pruen can't be separated any longer. Stupid to run two inquiries in isolation. Look at that cock-up over the two searches at Lantern Hill yesterday. The Harris house. We're not having that again.'

'So?'

'So, Sam. You remain in charge of your particular inquiry for the Muriel Pruen case. But Clitheroe moves over in command of the joint investigation. That's the decision. We'll have chaos otherwise.'

'In other words,' Hoskins said slowly, 'he's effectively running the murder inquiry as well. In charge. In charge of me.'

'At a distance,' the Ripper said dismissively, 'in general terms. Come to that, he always has been in charge, as the senior officer. The internal memo on the new inquiry structure has been done. It's going round this morning.'

Hoskins leant his knuckles on the desk, as he stood before the Superintendent.

'The first time, Max, I've actually had a case taken from me.'

'Don't be such an ass, Sam! You're still running the actual inquiry. For God's sake, we can't go on pretending there's no connection between Muriel Pruen and Elaine Harris. You're responsible to Clitheroe. That's all. No one's a free agent in this business. Not you. Not me.'

'Evidently not.'

'And if I may say so, Sam, you won't cut much ice talking about "your" case.'

'A manner of speaking, Max.'

'Well, leave it alone. You've got a future here, Sam. A great future. Don't ruin it all by being a prima donna.'

There was, Hoskins noticed, a fresh brochure from an estate agent in the Ripper's in-tray. It was Eastbourne this time.

Later that morning he sat in one of the dark wooden booths of the Porter's Lodge, a mock-gothic pub of the 1890s in the heart of Canton's banking and insurance district between Great Western Street and the Town River. A hundred years before, it had been just what its name suggested, a lodge where the dock porters waited in a sawdust bar to unload the sailing barques that came upstream to a riverside quay in the very centre of the city. The Lodge offered Hoskins anonymity. Policy salesmen and bank clerks packed it with a rumble of lunch-time conversation. No one else from 'A' Division ever set foot there so far as he knew. Its interior was dark mahogany brought from Brazil with the old coffee trade on the river wharf. The gloss on the polished wood had the satiny sheen of a thoroughbred racehorse. Hoskins felt at home with the frosted leads of the windows and the coloured glass of bottles lining the mirrored bar. The white stucco of the dado with its Tudor roses had long since darkened to a creamy brown under the pall of tobacco smoke which never seemed to clear. It suited him. There was comfort in the warm tobacco-fogged air.

Gerald Foster returned from the bar, navigating with difficulty through the packed room with two glasses and two plates bearing sausage and mash.

'There you go, Sam,' he said boisterously through the din. 'Canton's very finest.'

Hoskins took the paper napkin, spread it on his lap, and helped himself to mustard.

'Thanks,' he said, cutting into his sausage. 'So who told the lovely Miss Rayner?'

Foster shrugged.

'Not me, Sam. I don't make presents like that to the opposition.'

'I told Ripley so.'

'It's Clitheroe, Sam. If you were anywhere but on the force, you wouldn't even have to ask.'

Hoskins reached for his beer.

'Meaning what?'

Gerald Foster leant forward, safe from eavesdroppers in the background din.

'Meaning that the bloody lot of you in Canton make the same mistake. Just because you think Clitheroe's a shit – which he is – you also think he's a clown. He's not, Sam. Anything but a clown.'

'Alan Willis said something of the sort to me yesterday, when we were going fifteen rounds together to see who turned over Harris's place first.'

'He's right. You know what the whisper was when Clitheroe was first sent down here to Ocean Beach?'

'Nope.'

'Politburo. Special Branch. Listening post. They reckoned with the long-haul crossings from Belfast and Cork we might have shady figures slipping through the docks here. The boyos. Bottles of Guinness in one hand and rocket-launchers in the other. Queue here for the mainland campaign. See?'

Hoskins put his glass down and pulled a face.

'A prat like Clitheroe as the nation's first line of defence? Should have the other side giggling.'

Foster studied a sausage on a fork.

'You know why he leaked, Sam?'

'Probably.'

'To shaft you,' Foster said. 'Once that tale about Elaine Harris in Pruen's garden was out, the two cases had to be co-ordinated. And that put Clitheroe in charge and Canton "A" Division nowhere. He may be a shit but he upstaged the lot of you. That's how it looks from outside.'

'Does it?' Hoskins said, as if to show how little he cared.

'And you know the rest?'

Someone leant down and borrowed the mustard.

'Not at the top of your voice, Gerald, if you don't mind,' Hoskins said.

Foster looked surprised.

'It's no secret, Sam. The entire world knows except you and the lads. Two years from now, ACC Crime retires. Canton "A" Division would likely provide a successor. But then old Ripley's on the out at the same time.'

'Clitheroe?'

Foster screwed up his napkin and sat back.

'Figure it out, Sam. He's got Elaine Harris and Muriel Pruen. If he sorts that lot – even if you do it for him – he's on the way. If he gets someone for the Harris girl, that's an excuse to close the file on the killing of Rachel Lloyd and anything else they can pin on the bugger they get. You heard them last night, Sam. Detectives travelling from London and Bristol. All this sex crime that's plagued Canton for years cleared up at a stroke – by Clitheroe.'

'It's the form nowadays,' Hoskins said sardonically. 'Lumbering someone with other people's previous. Helps the clear-up rate.'

'And by the same token, Sam, he almost certainly gets someone for Muriel Pruen's murder. And the truth about that lands Cooney and the whole bloody lot for conspiracy over Pruen's story. Shuts down the gangs and cleans up the town. Fuck it, Sam, he's more or less found a cure for cancer and the elixir of life. He'll be able to write his own ticket.'

Hoskins put his knife and fork together on the empty plate.

'Dare say you're right, Gerald,' he said philosophically. 'Anyway, I'm off back to the factory. Get the paperwork cleared up today. We've got the lot coming from London and Bristol tomorrow. Television cameras outside the main entrance to film 'em striding in. They could just as easily write a letter or make a phone call. Thing is, pictures on the telly make the punters feel they're really getting something for their rates and taxes. Stern-faced men putting best foot forward in Austin Reed suits and carrying executive briefcases. Fighting crime the modern way. Keen, vigilant.'

They walked together from the pub above the brown flow of the silted river, past the banks and insurance offices of Victoria Quay and into the wider avenue of Great Western Street with its shop-lit pavements and the department store windows full of Christmas. Hoskins left Foster at the *Western World* building in King Edward Square and began the long walk down the Mall to the headquarters building at its far end.

Chance was waiting for him in the open door of the sergeants' room.

'At last!' he said. 'Where the hell were you, Sam? I've rung everyone the past hour. Home. Lantern Hill. Even The Harp.'

Hoskins got out a key and opened his door. Chance followed him in.

'Practising my interrogation technique on Gerald Foster. Why?'

Chance's face seemed ruby-red and larger with excitement.

'We got a result, Sam. A real beauty. Thing is, if you hadn't shown up, I couldn't have held it much longer. Have to go to Clitheroe or one of his Ocean Beach bumboys.'

Hoskins hung up his coat.

'Oh, yes?' he said sceptically.

'Midland Bank,' Chance said. 'Riverside branch.'

'Just walked past it with old Gerald Foster.'

'Last night I got the same answer from them as the rest. They keep the video cameras over the counters rolling, but they don't hang on to the tapes for more than three months. Not without reason. So naturally they hadn't got anything with possible friends of Elaine Harris depositing a lot of stolen "Horse-Parlour" money back in the summer.'

'Naturally.'

'Then this morning old McArthur has another witness in. Mr East. Elderly chap. Saw the photo in the *Western World*. Swears he saw the same girl on the metro-rail between Lantern Hill and Ocean Park about three weeks ago.'

'We know she was around three weeks ago. Still at home.'

'Hang on,' said Chance. 'She was with a bloke of about nineteen. Tall and large. Fair hair. Looked like a thug. Big rings on his fingers.'

'Pick anyone out of the files, did he?'

Chance shook his head.

'Then comes the call from the Midland in Riverside. About twelve o'clock. One of their girls on the counter reckons she saw Elaine Harris in there about ten days ago. She and two men came in. One of 'em tall and fair. Elaine and the tall fair bloke stand back. Not on the video. The other comes to the counter and draws money out of a deposit account. You were at lunch when I came to tell you. I went down for a quick look at their tape. No two ways, Sam. Sonny Hassan putting away a bit for his old age.'

'Hassan? That half-smart little bugger? If it's him, Jack, your fair-haired thug is Del Warren. Has to be.'

'I did manage to get that far on my own, Sam.'

'Right!' said Hoskins enthusiastically. 'Right! Show lovely young Del Warren's photo to Mr East. See if it starts bells ringing.'

'Tried it, Sam. He says he can't be sure.'

Hoskins put his coat back on.

'Hassan had an address to go with his account, did he?'

'Prince of Wales Road. Flat at the far end, on the edge of the park.'

'Bit above his class, isn't it, Jack? Be interesting to know how he came into money like that, if it wasn't from Pruen's floor-safe. Get Dudden and McArthur off their backsides.'

'You just going to do it, Sam? Without saying anything to Clitheroe?'

'You bet I am, Jack. Any case, Clitheroe's out at Shackleton Comprehensive today, asking two thousand kids if anyone can still remember what Elaine Harris looked like. He's not here to be told, let alone asked.'

'Warrant?'

'I'm not arresting anyone yet, Jack. They're being brought in for questioning. Friendly little discussion in the basement with their local Gestapo. That's all. Get the team together. Four mobiles. Three unmarked cars and a van. And I want a couple of non-smokers who can sprint, if necessary. Sonny Hassan's got a fair turn of speed.'

22

Sergeant Chance shuddered and wiped the condensation from the car windscreen with the back of his glove.

'I am bloody freezing,' he said. 'I cannot tell you how cold I am. Let's turn the engine on again and have a bit of heater.'

'No,' said Hoskins firmly. 'Keep doing that and you'll get too much attention. We're a parked car. Empty, so far as they're concerned.'

'There's a light on downstairs,' McArthur said from a back seat. 'They've got to be there. What do you think, Sam?'

'I'd rather have them all, Mac, if that's just the same to you.'

'It's half-past three, Sam,' Chance said reproachfully. 'We can't wait all night. With two cars parked out here, one on the cruise and a van round the back, they could rumble us any minute. Can't someone have a word with Dudden? He keeps coming round the same way, regular as a bloody bus service. Half the street's probably on crimewatch round here.

Someone's going to dial three nines and report him as a suspicious vehicle. Then we'll have blue flashing lights and flat-heads. Marvellous.'

Hoskins said nothing. He stared at the tree-lined length of Prince of Wales Road, fading in the distant vapour of an early winter twilight. Until 1914, it had been the city's most fashionable residential avenue. The tall houses stood singly or semi-detached, solidly built in coal-darkened stone, the handsome bay windows now picked out in cream or white paint. Several of the wrought-iron gothic conservatories still survived. Here and there a ship-owner's vision in stained glass filled a landing window. Some of the buildings were flats and some were private hotels. The rest housed dental surgeries and architects' offices, shirt-sleeved insurance clerks and solicitors. The pavements were wide in Prince of Wales Road, their worn York stone and chestnut trees evoking a vision of Edwardian nannies and prams.

'All right,' said Hoskins reluctantly. 'Let's do something before it gets dark.'

The traffic had begun to build up down the length of the road as the first cars turned homewards to Hawks Hill and Clearwater. He put the condenser microphone to his mouth and called DS Venning whose men were in the access lane at the rear of the houses, blocking it at one end with the van.

'Blue Leader to Zebra One. Move to standby. Then wait till I give you the signal.'

'Zebra One,' said Venning's voice. 'We've got four in the lane here. Nothing but a wooden door in the garden wall. Should go in at the first shove!'

'Do it when I tell you.'

'Where's Dudden?' Chance asked.

'Probably stuck in the traffic somewhere.' Hoskins put the microphone disc to his lips again. 'Blue Leader to Zebra Two. Report position.'

There was a sense of strain in Dudden's reply.

'Zebra Two. We're at the traffic lights, junction of Connaught Road and Clive Street, boss. Had to make a stop for personal reasons.'

'Bloody Dudden,' said Chance grimly. 'Pints of lager at lunchtime with a prostate like his!'

'Zebra Two rendezvous with Blue Leader. Urgent. Curtain up in five minutes.'

'Right-oh, Blue Leader. Sorry.'

'Sorry!' said McArthur scathingly, as Hoskins pressed another button. The third car was in sight, facing them, parked the far side of the house outside the Chestnuts Private Hotel.

'Blue Leader to Zebra Three. When you see Zebra Two park, we'll be going in. Leave the entry to us. Stand by to intercept any fugitives who get past us. Zebra Two will follow any vehicle that they may have.'

'Zebra Three to Blue Leader. Right-oh, boss. When you're ready.'

'More like it,' Chance said. 'That's a pretty flash carload. Burden's having a try at the Three A's championship. And Tranter had a try-out as wing three-quarter for Canton B Team last month. Even WPC Morris and Shirley Jones are pretty fit, come to that.'

McArthur muttered something to Constable Marchant beside him. Hoskins let out a long breath, releasing tension.

'There's Dudden's lot!' said Chance suddenly.

'Where?'

'In the mirror. Coming up behind us on the other side of the road.'

'Stupid bugger's going past,' McArthur said.

'No he's not. He's seen Burden.'

'You sure he's not pissed?'

'Shut up!' said Hoskins irritably. 'Blue Leader to all mobiles. Remember, we want target one and target two. Target three, if she's there, is a bonus. In any case, she won't get far on her own. I want the others. We'll go in one minute from – now.'

There was a scrambling in the back of the car as Marchant and McArthur got out. Hoskins and Chance followed, locking the doors of the Fiesta. The December twilight had deepened, nothing but a plum-coloured flush left in the western sky, the tree-lined avenue a harsh metallic gold in the street light.

The four men in their anoraks, McArthur trying to carry a sledgehammer inconspicuously, strode down the pavement to the street gate in the low-walled garden. The seconds ticked away on Hoskins's watch. There were twenty to go.

145

He turned up the short garden path. Adjoining the Chest-nuts, the semi-detached house was in multiple occupancy, converted to three flats on separate floors with a communal staircase. He glanced at his watch again, put the radio to his mouth and said, 'Remember. Ground-floor flat. Let's go!'

Nothing seemed to change. Venning's vanload were presumably forcing open the garden door at the back. Burden and the others were peering from their car windows. Dudden had parked on the far side of the road.

'Ground-floor flat,' Hoskins said. But he rang the bell of the flat above.

There was a pause and then the front door was opened by a middle-aged woman in a house-coat. Hoskins flicked open the green plastic of his warrant card.

'City police,' he said quietly. 'Sorry to bring you downstairs. Report of disturbance in one of the other flats. We need to get in there without too much fuss. Nothing to worry you. Go back. Lock your door. We'll let you know if we need any more assistance.'

He walked into the hallway. The stairway went up on the left. The right-hand side was blocked in by the door of the ground-floor flat. Hoskins tapped on it politely. There was a pause, then the rattle of a chain. The door opened a couple of inches. It showed a blond kiss-curl and a slightly deformed upper lip.

Hoskins took a chance.

'Mr Hassan,' he said courteously. 'Mr Hassan is expecting me on a matter of life insurance.'

The lip moved a little and a voice said, 'Fuck you, Hoskins!'

Before he could prevent it, the door was slammed and locked. He heard the shrill friction of a sash window thrown up and a shout from outside. Drawing back, Hoskins was just in time to see Del leap the low wall of the front garden and set off down the road in a lumbering sprint and a flapping of canvas shoes. It was almost too easy. Tranter was after him like a greyhound. The young constable's feet left the pavement with the skill of a ballet dancer's and he brought Del to earth in a flying tackle. Burden, from a few feet behind them, dived on the fugitive and handcuffed his wrists behind his back.

'Nice one,' said Chance appreciatively. 'Where's the rest?'

They waited. McArthur, having gone in through the open window, opened the door of the flat from the inside.

'No one else here, Sam. No Hassan and no girl.'

Hoskins, going through the hall inside the flat, looked over his shoulder.

'They won't have got out this way, Jack. I can see Venning and the others in the back yard.'

In the kitchen that overlooked the yard he was about to open the back door when a seismic roar tore at his ears. It was like a blow to the head in the confined space of the ground-floor flat. Turning, he saw McArthur spin and fall to the floor, just inside the front door of the house. Then McArthur scrambled clear, stunned but not hit. From somewhere out there, Chance shouted, 'The bastard's on the stairs with a gun, Sam.'

There was a second roar and the frosted glass of the front door disappeared in a shattered cascade, leaving an open view of Prince of Wales Road.

'Chief Inspector Hoskins to all officers. Warren apprehended. Hassan is on the stairs of the house, armed with a gun. No one is to approach him.'

There was an eerie silence in the aftermath of the second shot. No one moved or spoke. Not a sound. Hoskins waited, motionless. He thought he had never felt such silence in his life. It was as if the hunters and their prey had somehow moved off without warning. He eased forward a step, trusting the carpet to prevent him being heard. He stood in the doorway of the flat, able to see the square of communal hall just inside the main door of the house but nothing of the staircase. Hassan's voice came suddenly from just above his head. It was a shriek, rather than a shout, of defiance.

'You want me, you fucking well come and get me!'

There was another blasting discharge from the gun, the bullet singing away somewhere beyond the open door. Hoskins saw the spent cartridge case land in the hall by a little table with unclaimed mail on it. He thought Hassan could not see him but he was not sure. Drawing breath, he took the biggest risk of his career.

'Don't be stupid, Sonny,' he said. 'We're not even interested in you. Elaine Harris. She's missing from home. Her parents are half-crazy with worry. That's all.'

'She says fuck them and fuck you.'

'Let her talk to us, Sonny. Just let her tell us. Don't dig yourself in deeper.'

'I'll dig you in, you bastard!' Sonny Hassan's voice was sawing in his throat now, as if in fury or delirium. 'I'll dig you deep.'

Hoskins heard him move down the stairs. He tried the only bluff possible.

'I've got a gun too, Sonny. Don't make me use it.'

The footsteps paused. Hoskins thought he was standing almost underneath Hassan, though neither could see the other. The gun roared again, aimed downwards. Hoskins saw the wooden partition of the stairs split. There was a smell of burnt wood.

'Don't be a bloody fool, Sonny!'

There was a click of the hammer and then nothing. The fifth was a dud.

Hoskins drew a deep breath. Then, without a sound, Sonny Hassan appeared before him, ten feet away, round the end of the partition. The dark eyes glittered and the sharp nose with the tight mouth suggested a fury of unreason.

'Where's your gun?' he said, suspicious and yet sounding uneasy on Hoskins's behalf. 'Where is it?'

'Gun or no gun, Sonny, you can't get out,' Hoskins said simply.

Hassan raised the gun. Hoskins, looking beyond Hassan's shoulder, waited for Chance or one of the rest to jump from behind. No one appeared. The weapon was an old .455 Eley service revolver, its barrel sawn short. It pointed at the centre of Hoskins's chest. Hoskins looked into the dark angry eyes.

'Life, Sonny,' he said quietly, 'until the day you die. Forty years banged up in a piss-stinking maximum-security cell. Not worth it.'

Chance was there now beyond the open door of the house. Moving slowly forward towards Hassan's back, trying not to make a sound on the garden path.

Before Hoskins could say anything else, Hassan turned and Chance dived aside. Weak and perspiring, Hoskins moved too late. Hassan was back up the stairs.

'Leave it, Sam!' Chance shouted. 'He can't get out!'

Hoskins moved forward cautiously with Chance and the others behind him. There was a crash from above them.

'I reckon he's got one left,' Hoskins said quietly.

McArthur looked up.

'That was the trap! He's got the trap off! The little bastard's in the roof.'

Looking up through the stair-well, Hoskins saw the extension ladder that had given Hassan access to the loft.

'Someone go back and get a torch from the car.'

Marchant went back. Chance, McArthur and Hoskins moved cautiously up the stairs. By the time Marchant came back they had reached the metal ladder. Hoskins took the torch and began to climb. As he did so there was a hammering and cracking, then a heavy thump.

'He could be over the hotel next door,' Chance said. 'These two probably used to be one house. Only lath and plaster between them up there.'

Hoskins raised his head carefully into the darkness of the loft. There was a crash and a showering of plaster fragments as Sonny Hassan smashed through the ceiling somewhere in the Chestnuts Hotel.

'Watch it!' Hoskins said to Chance. 'I'm coming back down. He's somewhere in next door. There's probably still one bullet in that gun. He might even have time to reload.'

Down on the landing, his hands free again, he fumbled for his radio. There was a shout below them. From the landing window, Hoskins saw the fiasco as leisurely as if in action replay. Burden's carload and Dudden's crew had converged on the front of the house. Sonny Hassan, partly concealed by a bay hedge at ground level, stepped casually out of the doorway of the private hotel. Then a woman screamed and there was another shout, somewhere in the hotel entrance.

Even before Burden or the others turned in his direction, Hassan had dodged out into the road. Avoiding the first flow of traffic, he ran down the middle as a cyclist came towards him. In a split second, it seemed, Hassan knocked the aston-ished man from the saddle with a punch to the face, grabbed the cycle and began to ride off. Burden took off at a sprint. Dudden, his car facing the wrong way, began desperately to try a U-turn in the busy traffic. There was a blaring of horns and a flashing of lights. Hoskins leaping down the stairs with a speed that astonished him felt a stoical gloom. He had been right, of course. The arrest of Del Warren had been far too easy.

But Burden was hanging on, sometimes almost in reach of the bicycle as Hassan sped down the length of the road. Tranter, in Zebra Three, was starting up as Hoskins dived into the back of the car. Dudden's instant traffic-jam gave a clear road in the direction of Hassan and Burden. Tranter drove after them, lights flashing and siren braying. Burden was flagging but the car was almost level with Hassan.

'Take him!' Hoskins snapped at Tranter. And then Hassan turned, skidding between two stationary cars in the blocked traffic of the opposite lane. Pedals going like pistons, the bike flew into a side turning at the end of which the railway line ran parallel with Prince of Wales Road.

Tranter and Hoskins abandoned their car. Burden had stopped running and was doubled up, hands on thighs, heaving in lungfuls of air. For Hoskins, the pursuit on foot was a token gesture. But Tranter was fresh, his face set in surging determination. To Hoskins's astonishment, the wing three-quarter was gaining on Hassan. Hassan looked back. Then he rode straight for the footbridge and began to carry the bicycle up the steps.   Tranter was going to do it. He was on the steps. Taking them two at a time. At the top, Hassan leapt on the saddle again and rode furiously over the wooden boards. And still Tranter was gaining. Hassan, half-riding and half-pushing the bike down the far steps, was in a frenzy of fear at impending capture. Hoskins saw Tranter rise in the air as if in another balletic rugger tackle and then come down with a muffled thump on the planking of the bridge. Hassan, down the far side, pedalled out of sight. He was lost somewhere in the narrow terraced streets of Orient.

As Hoskins went up the steps, he saw that Tranter had pulled himself up and was hanging on to the grey plate-iron of the bridge wall. His face was white with sudden pain and drawn into a mask of exasperation.

'My ankle, boss,' he gasped. 'I think I've bust the bloody thing.'

Hopping between Hoskins and Burden, an arm round each, Tranter was brought back to the abandoned police car. The length of Prince of Wales Road and as far as the eye could see into Canton centre, the rush-hour traffic was blocked. The first patrol-cars and flat-hats had appeared from traffic division. A motor-cycle patrolman was arguing with Dudden. Hoskins's own car, with Del Warren handcuffed to McArthur in the back, was surrounded by uniformed men. He was talking to Chance when a figure in plain clothes stepped forward from another car. The rimless glasses and narrow moustache of the Edwardian poisoner. Clitheroe looked up and down the road at the stranded traffic, drivers standing outside their cars and talking together.

'Next time, Mr Hoskins, that you allow a prisoner like Hassan to escape from your custody, you might consider doing it without quite this degree of public advertisement. And, indeed, the next time you think you have the answer to Elaine Harris at your fingertips, I should like to be informed. Briefly and without delay.'

Chance came up as Clitheroe turned away.

'What was all that, Sam?'

'Clitheroe,' Hoskins said. 'He can't stand seeing cars snarled up like this. Must be the traffic warden in him. Come on. Let's get our friend Del down the old torture-chamber. See what he's got to tell us.'

23

'Nice bit of page one yesterday then, Sam?' said Charlie Blades cheerfully, opening his office door and leading the way. 'Bit of the old intrepid.'

In the lamplit room on the top floor of Forensic Area One at Ocean Beach, he gestured at the morning's copies of the *Western World* and the evening's *Canton Globe*. By now, Hoskins knew the headlines like a school poem. 'GUNMAN FLEES POLICE IN TRAFFIC CHAOS' that morning, and by the first evening edition, 'COMMUTERS IN CITY GUN-BATTLE: MAN HELD, COMPANION BREAKS FREE ON PUSH-BIKE'. Alongside, as if the two stories had no connection, there was a familiar face and a single column headed, 'HAVE YOU SEEN THIS GIRL?'

'Rough with the smooth, I suppose, Charlie,' Hoskins said, taking the chair by the desk.

'Ah!' said Blades disparagingly. 'Bit naughty that rubbish about breaking free when you never had him in the first place. That's Rayner, for a bet. Stirring the pot on Clitheroe's instructions.'

Ocean Beach, beyond the window, lay in winter darkness. Even the cinema neon and the lights along the Cakewalk had a frosted glare.

'Depends how you look at it, I suppose, Charlie. Clitheroe and Miss Teasy.'

Blades poured Famous Grouse into two glasses and sniggered. He handed one to Hoskins.

'Tell you what, Sam, talking of such things. We've moved on a bit since her two little bleeders went back to their boarding school. You never knew she was one of twins, did you? Not quite identical. We got her sister coming to stop a week or so. The ideas that keep going through my mind. How would you feel about it, Sam? Suppose you were offered? Two-to-one. I mean, suppose they were both really keen?'

Hoskins clicked his tongue.

'Hard to say, Charles. Not exactly a decision I've ever had to make. I reckon you'd do better with advice from Jack Chance.'

Blades pulled a face.

'Not without him wanting to get his sticky fingers on the merchandise.'

He put down his glass, opened the drawer of his desk and took out a folder.

'You get anything clever on Del Warren or Hassan, did you, Charlie?'

Blades shook his head despairingly at the mention of the names.

'Bloody amateurs. All that money spent on their education. And they pull a stroke that'd make an old smash-and-grab thick-head die of shame.'

'That's nice, Charlie,' Hoskins said brightly. 'What've we got exactly?'

'They hadn't even bothered', Blades said, 'to get rid of the clothes they were wearing. They hadn't had them cleaned. They didn't even throw away the woollen gloves. You think they were that sure they wouldn't be caught?'

'Probably.' Hoskins held out his glass for the proffered refill. 'Pruen wasn't going to co-operate with us over money that he'd filched from the Horserace Betting Levy Board or whoever. And he hadn't got a licence for a gun. That revolver that Sonny Hassan was good enough to show me the other day has a distinctly Pruen look about it. Nicked from the safe by Hassan, I dare say. Not what a modern young gentleman like Sonny would pay money for. I'd swear it was a .455 Eley. Wartime service revolver. Almost antique.'

'Bloody lucky not to get your head blown off with it, Sam.'

'Dunno, Charlie. He stood there pointing it at me, about as close as you are now. He must have had one round left. Why he didn't fire, I will never know. Perhaps he wanted to keep one up the spout for his breakout. Perhaps he thought it might not go off properly in which case I'd jump him.'

'All your past life go through your mind, did it, Sam?'

Hoskins shook his head.

'Funny thing is, Charlie, I guessed he was going to shoot. All I could think of was how bloody silly it all was. Get nobody anywhere. I told him so.'

Blades frowned at the folder in his hand, indicating a return to business.

'The gloves, Sam. Littlewoods. Pale grey wool. Matching flecks in the water of that basin on the sitting-room table. Where they dunked Ma Pruen. Specks of red paint on gloves. Exact spectroscope match for the spray-paint that they wrote their message with. That's just circumstantial, of course.'

'Anything better, Charlie? More personal?'

'Much better, Sam.' Blades handed him a sheet of paper. 'A few grey hairs on the gloves. We got Ma Pruen's nut out of the fridge. They're hers, all right. And there's a fleck or two of grey wool in her perm. As for footprints, our young friend flooded the bathroom floor when he smashed out the front of the bog. He left quite a few prints behind. Mind you, his shoes have had a bit of wear since then. All the same, there's enough marks on them now that were on them then. There's even a fleck or two of porcelain well trodden in on the heels from the broken bog itself. There's tiny splinters in the gloves from the banister rails. You want me to go on?'

'Not really, Charles. Only thing is, he'll swear the gloves were Sonny Hassan's or that he was just minding 'em for a friend. Likewise the shoes.'

'Her hair's on his jacket as well, Sam. And if you want icing on the cake, someone had a good spit on the way out. I think when Aldermaston analyse it, we'll come up with his genetic fingerprints as they say.'

'No sign of Pruen's hair anywhere?'

'Can't tell you, Sam. Ma Pruen's hair's on call any time we want. The old boy's we haven't got. I don't want it either, my friend. Juries aren't that keen on forensic. You take Pruen into court with twenty witnesses that say he was somewhere else. But you say he must have been there because forensic tests on the hair show it. They're likely to say in that case the forensic tests can't be right. And that shafts your case against Del Warren for doing Muriel Pruen. If you want Pruen and Cooney by the shorts, Sam, I'd approach it some other way. This could definitely be grief.'

'Dare say you're right, Charlie. That folder for me to keep, is it?'

Blades handed it over.

'Who else? You going back to Canton now?'

'Confront the little bugger with this, Charlie. See if we can't get everything he knows about Elaine Harris and the Pruens. When this lot goes off under him, he won't know salt from sugar.'

Blades walked out with him.

'She finished reading out that story of O, Sam. On to something else now.'

'That's nice, Charlie. Keeping you fit, is she?'

Blades clicked his tongue.

'Way I see it, Sam, it does as much good as jogging. More, probably. And you don't have to go hoofing round in the dark in dangerous streets, breathing in traffic fumes and probably wrecking your spine with all that plod.'

'I'll remember that, Charles,' Hoskins said as the lift doors closed.

He drove down Clifton Hill and on to Bay Drive beside the Cakewalk. The broad promenade was deserted and shining wet. The New Pier stretched out to sea in darkness, except for the navigation warning-lights at its far end. There was a mist coming down over Ocean Beach. The groan and thump of the Deep Water light vessel came precisely at every minute. Even the bell from the Lantern Point buoy was audible in the dank stillness.

It was as if the summer had never existed. A few cafés were lit and open, serving coffee and soup to two or three locals. But the posters by the pier were torn and wrinkled. Only here and there had they been pasted over with furred and booted figures, offering *Little Red Riding Hood* at the Pavilion from Christmas Eve for eight weeks. Benny Wadman and Sharon Rees were the stars. Even the Hangman and his Children had assumed their winter charade.

Chance was waiting for him when Hoskins got back to the headquarters building. Hoskins hung up his coat.

'Tell the custody officer to stand by, Jack. I want our young friend Del in the interview room again. And see they've got the charge room nicely warmed for about half an hour's time.'

'Good as that, was it?' Chance said hopefully.

'It was good enough, my son. Good enough to put Del Warren out of circulation the next ten or fifteen years. I'd say the judge is going to see this as a rather serious case of murder. Supposing you think death by slow torture is serious any longer.'

The bleak concrete space of the interview room, its regulation tubular steel chairs and stained table, the single ashtray in brown plastic, was lit by a pale fluorescent tube. As Hoskins came in, the uniformed policeman by the door stood up.

155

Chance put two chairs opposite Del. Del, his elbows on the table, was an image of hunched and flabby defiance.

'Right,' said Hoskins to the uniformed man. 'You can leave us to it.'

'Mr Clitheroe . . . '

'Had your canteen-break?'

'No, sir.'

'You're having it now. Here or in the canteen.'

'Right, boss,' the man said.

Hoskins sat down next to Chance. He looked at Del. The blond head was lowered, the broad face and deformed mouth hardly visible.

'Anything you want that you haven't got?' Hoskins asked his prisoner.

There was no reply, though the flabby shoulders hunched a little more.

'Anything you want us to do for you? Anyone you want notified?'

Del raised his face and, to Hoskins's surprise, there was a glint of moisture in the eyes.

'Get me out of this poxy place! Stop asking questions! I told you before, I got nothing to say about anything!'

Chance leant forward.

'You'll only get in deeper, not saying anything. Makes people think the worst.'

'I got nothing to say. I talked to the duty brief, didn't I? He said to say nothing. That's it.'

Hoskins sighed.

'Right,' he said sadly. 'I'll tell you what's what, then. I'm not holding anything back. You or your lawyer will be entitled to all the details in due course. In fact we have to give them to you. That's the law.'

Del shook his kiss-curl.

'What's that supposed to mean?'

'Forensic evidence,' Hoskins said. 'Scientific tests. We don't need you to say anything. We know the lot. Grey woollen gloves found in your flat. Worn by you. Traces of them – the actual fibres – in Mr Pruen's house. In the bowl of water that Mrs Pruen's face was pushed into. In her hair. Several of Mrs Pruen's hairs in the wool of those gloves. Flecks of red paint from the very can you used to spray the sitting-room. Splinters from broken banister rails. Not just any rail. A match right down to the tree and the grain pattern.'

'I don't know anything about fucking gloves,' Del said miserably. 'I got nothing to say.'

'Not just gloves,' Hoskins said reassuringly. 'The water in the bathroom. You stepped in it. Left prints of your shoe outside. A ringer for your brown shoes in the flat, even to the marks of wear and stitching. Shoes only worn by you, my son. No one else's fingerprints on them. Fair enough?'

'I got nothing to say! I told you! I'm not answering any questions!'

Hoskins sighed again.

'And what tops it off, for you, is that nasty habit of spitting in other people's houses. Funny thing, spit. Once upon a time it only told you which saliva group people belonged to. But everyone's spit is different. Nowadays Forensic gets very clever with that sort of thing. Show 'em a blob of it and they'll tell you who it belongs to. We'll want a sample off you tomorrow.'

Del looked at his hands and said nothing.

'Listen,' Chance said, 'there's no point acting silly. As it is, you'll go down for Muriel Pruen. Life. Ten or fifteen years. Anything you say can't make that worse. Might make it better for you.'

'Parole,' Hoskins added. 'I don't say you'd be out after five years, but you could be. On the other hand, with this sort of carry-on there's no one likely to put in a good word.'

Del looked up and the deformed lip moved in its old scornful grimace.

'Don't waste your fucking time!' he said.

'Meaning?' Hoskins asked.

'You all think you're so fucking clever! Gloves! Footprints! Spit! You're a pair of real bloody clowns.'

'How's that, then?' Chance inquired.

Del broadened his scorn into a sneer.

'Because I'm pleading guilty. And I'm not saying anything nor answering any questions. Not here. Not in court. Not nowhere. Finish. Got that, have you?'

He bowed his head again. Hoskins looked quickly at Chance and shared a glimmer of dismay.

'Not that easy, my son,' Hoskins said quickly.

'Not for you, maybe. Just don't waste my time.'

'The girl. Elaine Harris. What about her? Where is she?'

'I don't know about any girl. I don't know where she is.'

'You were with her three weeks ago. You were seen.'

'I was with a lot of people three weeks ago.'

'Where is she?' Chance intervened. 'She could be in a lot of trouble. Real, actual, fatal, trouble.'

'I'm not answering any more questions.'

This time the head was not even raised.

'That could be murder number two on the charge sheet,' Hoskins said quietly. 'If anything's happened to Elaine, you were the last person seen with her.'

But he saw Del closing up. Like a depressive in a psychiatric ward.

'I'm not saying nothing. Fuck off.'

'Don't be a fool, Del,' said Chance gently. 'We only want to find her before she gets hurt.'

'Fuck off. I want my brief. Put that in them notes. Whatever the time is, put it down that I said I want my brief. Go on.'

'Go on,' Hoskins said aside to Chance. 'Then put your head out of the door and ask someone to whistle up Mr Harvey if he's still duty solicitor.'

Later that night in Hoskins's office, Chance unwrapped the sandwiches fetched from the Harp and took the tops off two bottles of Jupp's Special Brew.

'That lot could have gone better,' he said, glancing at the copy of the charge sheet on Hoskins's desk. 'I've never known a case in such a mess as this. One pleads guilty. The other's vanished into the stews of Orient on a push-bike carrying a loaded gun. Probably never to be seen again. As for Elaine Harris, she could be alive or dead or neither or both, as they say. I reckon we've seen the last of her. As for your friend Gerald Foster and the *Western World*, will you look at those bloody headlines!'

'There's worse,' Hoskins said, 'and it's not about Warren or Hassan.'

He opened the *Canton Globe* at a centre page. The headlines were in thick black type, unlike the more decorous morning editions. RAPIST GOES FREE AFTER PROMISE ... SCHOOLGIRL ATTACKED IN CONNAUGHT PARK: BEARDED MAN SOUGHT ... KIDS IN AGONY: CHILD-ABUSE SHOCK FIGURES ... SHOWFOLK DEMAND PERVERT REGISTER ... OCEAN BEACH MAN BURNT WIFE WITH CIGARETTE, COURT TOLD ... RACHEL LLOYD: CASE RE-OPENED ... WHERE IS ELAINE HARRIS? ... POLICE CRITICISED AT CHILD INQUIRY ...

'A whole bloody page,' Chance said helplessly. 'You wouldn't think ninety-nine per cent of crime was about something else.'

Hoskins helped himself to a sandwich.

'What the punters want, my son,' he said indistinctly through a mouthful of bread. 'All the juicy details but able to feel self-righteous about it at the same time. Shock figures! Says here they're estimates. In other words, make it up as you go along. Pages like this sell more copies than all the girlie magazines. No wonder Gerald Foster started wearing handmade suits.'

Chance handed the paper back.

'Find Elaine Harris, Sam. Otherwise you could have a lynch mob downstairs.'

Hoskins checked a belch.

'Object of their exercise, my son. Rapist goes free after promise. In other words, telling the readers to get out there and string the bugger up. Hang on, there's another thing. It didn't even happen in Canton. America, it says here, bloody San Diego! Gets off gaol so long as he takes pills for it.'

Chance shook his head and drank beer from his bottle.

'What's our plan tomorrow?'

'First thing,' Hoskins said, 'we'll have all the available strength looking for Hassan. I fancy Peninsula rather than Orient. We'll have to issue guns. That narrows it down to blokes who can get a gun out of its holster without shooting themselves and several passers-by. Small team, in other words.'

'He could be anywhere with a wedge of Pruen's money,' Chance said glumly.

'We'll go looking anyway, Jack. And so far as we're concerned, Elaine Harris now takes a back seat. She may be alive

RICHARD DACRE

or she may be dead, but at least she's not shooting up Prince
of Wales Road with a .455. Hassan's our target.'

He crumpled his sandwich-wrapping and threw it in the
basket. Then he reached for his coat.

'You going out Lantern Hill, Sam?'

'Why?'

'Just wondered if she was still keeping your feet warm
out there. How things were going after Viareggio.'

'If there's anything to report, my son,' Hoskins said gently,
'I promise that you'll be the last to know.'

160

3
WINTER

24

At the end of the first week in December, after ten days of fruitless door-to-door questions round houses and clubs in Orient and Peninsula, Hoskins rode the metro-rail through the snow from Lantern Hill to Canton. He had been with Lesley when Chance's phone call came, lying in the pink light of curtains drawn against the wintry afternoon. Hoskins had been right about the weather. It was not even Christmas and the first freak blizzard had obliterated familiar streets.

As usual it caught the city authorities, their gritting-lorries and snow-ploughs, unprepared. Only the metro-rail still functioned on its embankment, riding at roof-level past the shabby terraces of Orient. Cars stood like igloos in the whitened spaces of little streets. A few were abandoned on the urban-clearway lanes. The congested and rumbling ring road of the day before now lay vast and still as Antarctica. Not a school was open. Children, black against snow-light, honed their pavement-slides to ankle-fracturing sleekness.

It had been after midday when the first yellow ploughs and diggers appeared, munching a slow complaining path through two feet of sponge-like snow. They had left it too late. With the fading of afternoon light, a Siberian cold was gathering in the air. In an hour or two the spongy depth of snow would be hard as concrete.

Hoskins got off at Atlantic Wharf, picking his way across the shining waste of the square towards Great Western Street. One or two of the department stores had made a brave attempt to stay open. The salesgirls were muffled in furs. The lavish displays of the Royal Peninsular Emporium had only a handful of customers. King Edward Square and the domes of City Hall looked like a snapshot of Prague or Budapest. Here and there rose the bronchial whine of a car engine, the trapped tyres slithering and swerving on the packed ice. The snow was untrodden down the Mall. Hoskins cursed as it came over his trousers and seeped into his shoes. At last, stamping and dripping, he pushed open the glass door of the headquarters lobby and walked across the puddled marble to the lift.

The fifth-floor corridor was deserted. He opened the door of the sergeants' room. It was almost empty. Chance sat at his desk and McArthur was staring out of the window at the winter scene. Chance came out to him.

'I didn't know what the hell else to do, Sam,' he said under his breath. 'I wasn't even sure it was her number. I went through the phone book and took a chance.'

'That's all right, Jack,' Hoskins said, wiping his nose on the back of his hand. 'Come on in. Where did they find her?'

'Out on the levels. Between Eastern Causeway and the sluice. I got it wrong at first. Some story about a pensioner clearing snow from his path. Turns out it was some old boy shovelling a way in for the managers by the side of Atlantic Factors.'

Hoskins drew off his gloves. He stamped and shivered, half-melted snow falling from his coat-hem.

'Talk about sod's law!' he said bitterly. 'Clitheroe out there, is he?'

'He was going. With chains on the wheels. Only the Land-rovers can get through down there.'

'Got one left, have we?'

'There's one in the motor-pool. Jock and Dave have got it loaded up with tarpaulins and arc-lamps. Just about squeeze us in, I should think.'

Hoskins nodded.

'Not my idea of how to spend a rest day. All the same, I'm going.'

'She's dead anyway, Sam.'

'That's why I'm going, Jack. Paying respects, you might say.'

No one spoke much during the drive. The whine and grind of the Land-rover's gears rose and fell like the chant of an urban requiem, the wheel-chains rattling on the frozen tarmac of the snow-plough's furrow. A single track had been cleared to the outer ring road, chosen by the driver to avoid the obstruction of abandoned cars in the city streets. Hoskins shivered. At last they turned off on the spur that ran down to the workshops and muddy coastline of the levels.

The Eastern Causeway was a four-lane feeder road for the city and the outer docks, a changing and weaving network of tarmac now concealed by the shadowed snow. There was a roll-top concrete wall blocking out the view on either side of the clearway. It had been built after the first fatalities among schoolchildren who found a sprint or dash between the traffic the shortest way from classrooms to shops at lunchtime. At the best of times, the smoke-grey hardtop and sea-grey walls made Eastern Causeway as anonymous as Detroit or Glasgow or Berlin.

The East Sluice was a dribbling cocoa-coloured stream, almost without movement. Its steep mud-banks sloped down from the wild unkempt grassland of the levels. The river currents were dissipated far out, among sand-flats that lay to one side of the dock wall. A few anglers' huts along the bank and poles embedded in the silt were all that suggested habitation.

The driver followed the road a little further and then pulled up. Hoskins got out. He could see a group of men standing in the wild grass about a hundred yards away. The snow was thinner on the fringe of the levels. Perhaps it was a freak of wind that had blown it the other way. Perhaps it was the salt in the air and the earth this close to the sea. There was only about six inches of it, he guessed. That presumably was why they had found her.

With a bite like a razor, the icy wind caught his face and he pulled the collar of his driving-coat higher. The movement of the air stirred the tops of tall grasses and scattered the snow-particles with a dry electric hiss like the movement of a silk evening gown. From this deserted fringe of coast, the city appeared through the gloom as finger-towers of black and grey, dwarfing the older spires and municipal belfries. A square stone-built loading-granary rose distantly on the quay of Connaught Dock. Closer at hand, the corrugated sheds of Atlantic Factors stood vast and gaunt as airship hangars. Beyond the sidings and the long supply pipes, the rolling-shed in blue corrugated steel with a grey roof had the bulk of a severely functional cathedral.

'One thing,' Chance said at his elbow, teeth chattering slightly, 'I don't suppose we'll be bothered by sightseers in weather like this.'

Hoskins grunted and felt the crisp frozen grass compressed underfoot.

Most of the others were there already, it seemed to him. Clitheroe and Ken Martin. Mosley, the police surgeon, and ACC Crime. Of Ripley there was no sign.

'Hello, Sam,' Martin said. 'I understood it was your rest day.'

'Not any more it isn't, Ken. What's the news exactly?'

'Some old boy that sweeps up for Atlantic Factors. Takes the alsatian guard-dogs for a walk at lunch-time. Brought 'em this way. One of them came straight to her.'

'Meaning she wasn't here yesterday?'

'Not necessarily, Sam. The old chap didn't bring the dogs this way yesterday. Can't ask him much at the moment. He got back to the gate-house at Atlantic Factors, told 'em the bad news and then collapsed. There's a nurse with him. He could have had a slight coronary. Poor old sod.'

Hoskins glanced across at the others. Two uniformed men in gumboots and black waterproof clothes were trying to drive the poles of the green tarpaulin screens into the frozen earth. Partly sunk in the snow, he saw the white length of bare legs and the moisture-darkened hair of a head whose face was turned in the other direction. It looked as if Elaine Harris had taken off her skirt in order not to crease it and then lain down for a nap. The peaceful look of so many murder victims haunted him most of all. Dumb and uncomplaining, Elaine Harris was curled on her side in a blouse and a pair of white elasticated briefs, the garments still in place. He turned away.

Mosley, the police surgeon, came up to him.

'Not your case, is it, Sam?'

'Might be, John. Depends on how she got here.'

Mosley shook his head.

'We're whistling up Saville and his entire path lab. Might not be able to say which day she died, let alone what

166

time. Lying out here in this weather is like being in a deep-freeze.'

'How did it happen?'

Mosley shrugged.

'Someone beat the living daylights out of her and then strangled her. There's a post-mortem flush on her wrists. Hands tied, in other words. Not usual in crimes of passion, probably something planned. No sign of the school tie she was wearing in the photograph. And her skirt's gone. Might have come off in a struggle or when she was brought here.'

'She was dumped here, then?' Hoskins asked forlornly.

'Ten to one, Sam. I don't see a rumpus like that happening out in the open.'

'Bloke who put her here might have left a tyre track or a footprint.'

'Not much of a footprint with the earth this hard, Sam. Probably parked on the road and dragged her through the grass.'

'Still dressed,' Hoskins said. 'Not another homicidal rapist by the look of it.'

'Not as yet, Sam. She's still wearing all her underclothes and blouse. The injuries look as if someone set about her with a rolling-pin. Legs, arms, shoulders, hips. Whether that's killing for sexual kicks depends on what the bloke's idea of a thrill might be.'

'Could have been a woman?'

'Could have been, Sam. Except the dumping of the body here doesn't sound right for that.'

The first line of tarpaulin screens was in place and a generator was being run from a tracked transporter. Two of the gumbooted detail began to set up the first arc-lamp on its stand in the gathering dusk. Chance came up to Hoskins and Mosley.

'What's needed here is a caravan and heating. No one's going to work all night in this temperature.'

Mosley shook his head.

'They'll move her. Soon as Saville's done his preliminary and the photographer's finished. It's sub-zero out here now. Just leave a guard on the site and begin again tomorrow. There's nothing here that won't keep.'

Behind the green canvas, the camera began to flash as Sergeant Hardy photographed the body where it lay.

'You fancy young Del Warren for this, Sam?' Chance inquired. 'She could have been dead a week in this weather.'

Hoskins shook his head.

'No idea, Jack. He's mean enough but it's too much of a coincidence. He knocks off Elaine Harris one day and we just so happen to arrest him for another murder the next afternoon? Not likely. Anyway, if he had words with Elaine, he'd be more likely to black her eye and kick her out. Where's the point in murder?'

'If she threatened to tell us about Muriel Pruen in revenge.'

Hoskins stared sceptically at the darkening line of sea and marsh.

'Thereby landing herself in it as well? Doesn't ring bells, Jack. More likely to be one of your straight-up-and-down-the-wicket maniacs.'

'Or there's Sonny Hassan?'

'Yes,' Hoskins said. 'If we ever see the little sod again, I'll make sure to ask him about it.'

Professor Saville and his two assistants arrived. Clitheroe came across to the group. Hoskins thought there was a jauntiness in his step and a glimmer of excitement in the dark eyes.

'Not on duty this afternoon, Sam?'

'Rest day,' Hoskins said. 'Jack kindly gave me a ring.'

'And your thoughts on all this, Sam?' The careful voice was like a razor in a velvet sheath.

'I'd fancy a word with young Hassan. As for Pruen and his minder, I'd need to be told more. Once they knew Elaine Harris was part of the break-in, she was bound to be on their list for attention.'

Clitheroe's mouth tightened perceptibly. He looked away, not rising to Hoskins's bait.

'Hardly Mafia territory this, Sam,' he said.

'Quiet shed down a disused part of the docks,' Hoskins suggested. 'A thumping to make sure she's told the whole truth and nothing but. Then the grand finale.'

Clitheroe turned back again.

'Ten out of ten for imagination, Sam. Unfortunately for your hypothesis, professional killers of that kind would hardly have dumped her body for us to find. Chopped up and through the mincer. Burnt to ashes in a casting-shop furnace. Covered with concrete in-fill somewhere down the foundations of the Ocean Front apartments. But not dumped on the levels like this. What we've got here, Sam, is a punter in a fright.'

Hoskins pushed his hands deeper in his coat pockets.

'They want her found,' he said firmly. 'Where's the point of setting the young bulls an example if you never let them see what you did to the culprit?'

Clitheroe was no longer listening. An ambulance with a tracked van as its escort had drawn up. Professor Saville and his assistants approached. Clitheroe walked away to greet them, Hoskins's question still unanswered.

That evening, just before half-past ten, Hoskins sat in an armchair in the front room at Lantern Hill. Lesley was curled on the carpet with her back against his knees. Figures moved in dumb-show on the television screen.

'It wouldn't make the national news,' Hoskins said, stroking the high crown of her fair-haired crop. 'Just Clitheroe on *Coastal Round-Up*. So I heard.'

He felt the shiver down her spine.

'I can't imagine anyone who'd do it to that girl,' she said. 'I can't imagine being inside their head.'

'Nor can I,' Hoskins said. 'Wish I could. Make this job a lot easier.'

'I'm glad you can't.' She reached back over her shoulder and took his hand.

They watched the alphabetical fish of *Coastal Round-Up* swim about the screen and form the opening title. Lesley turned the sound on. Clitheroe was in his chair to begin with, while the news items were read. Then the youthfully grey-haired presenter turned to the Superintendent. Hoskins listened to the expected questions. At last the presenter said, 'You have no doubt, Mr Clitheroe, that Elaine Harris was murdered?'

'Subject to what an inquest or a trial jury may determine, Mr Howells. My inquiry is a murder inquiry. Possibly linked to earlier investigations.'

'And if that's so, isn't there an epidemic of crimes of this seriousness? Not always murder but sexual attacks that sometimes end in murder, sometimes in rape or assault? Day after day, week after week, month after month?'

Neat as his moustache and sharp collar, Clitheroe parried him.

'We've had a disturbing increase. Perhaps the work of a handful of men. We believe the murder cases, at least, may be linked. Perhaps by just one man. Epidemic suggests something out of control and spreading . . . '

'Which attacks of this sort surely are? And which sexually-motivated murders surely are?'

'It also suggests something that must get worse before it gets better.'

'Most people, Mr Clitheroe, would say it has got much worse with no sign of getting better. Girls of this age, fifteen, sixteen, seventeen, have proved the most vulnerable. They are being attacked, raped, assaulted, even killed, day after day, night after night. In Canton itself. In Ocean Beach. Most we forget, but we remember the murders. Jane Page. Rachel Lloyd. And now Elaine Harris. Those who committed murder are, in these cases, still at large.'

Clitheroe nodded, as if he accepted this and agreed.

'As yet they are.'

The presenter's face contracted with well-practised concern.

'So can you understand that some people wonder, rightly or wrongly, if the police are doing their job? What can you say to reassure them, Mr Clitheroe? The parents whose daughter is out tonight and not yet back home? The young married woman going out on night-shift in a hospital? The mother out late-night shopping or the baby-sitter alone in a house with small children?'

The question had been prepared and the answer rehearsed. Hoskins would have bet his pension on it. Clitheroe composed his narrow bony face like a preacher about to pray.

'We shall catch the man – or men – who committed this crime, Mr Howells. That is my assurance to you and the people watching this programme. No matter what it takes – no matter how long it takes. We shall catch him.'

The presenter leant forward a little more.

'And to those who say that the killers of Jane Page and Rachel Lloyd are still unknown after two years, that the abductors and possibly the murderers of Heather Mills and Karen Roberts have escaped the net – what will you say?'

'The files remain open.' Clitheroe's face showed the same ecstatic calm. 'Whether it is one man or several men. In each case we shall go on until the man is caught. If he is sitting out there now, watching this programme and thinking he has got away with it, let me assure him otherwise. In each of these cases, we continue to gather evidence. In one case, we are very close. We know the sort of man we are looking for. We know a good deal about him.'

'But not enough to arrest him?'

The merest quirk of irritation marred Clitheroe's serenity.

'We need one more thing. In each case we think there is a person who knows the identity of the man we would like to speak to. Probably a wife or a girl friend, perhaps some other member of the family. That person, we believe, knows or suspects what a husband or boy friend, even a son or a brother, has done. The unexplained absences, the soiled clothes, the abnormal behaviour. That witness has been reluctant to come forward. We can understand that. But I would ask that person to picture the beaten and broken body of a fifteen year old child found on the levels today. If we do not catch him, that man will kill again and again. To the person shielding him, I put this question. Can you bear to have so many deaths of the innocent upon your conscience? If you cannot, I beg you – I beg you for the sake of your loved one as well as for the victims – to contact me in confidence. Anonymously, if you like. We shall have a telephone line manned day and night. Anything you say will be confidential. I will talk to you myself. You need not even give me your name. It is not a matter of vengeance but preventing another death of this kind with all the heartbreak it brings to parents and children.'

'And what do you say to those in fear after the death of Elaine Harris?'

'We shall catch this man, Mr Howells.' Studio light flashed black on the rimless glasses. 'We shall catch him and put him where he belongs. In the only place where the rest of society

171

can be safe from him. Make no mistake about that. Better for him and for others that we should catch him quickly.'

'Thank you very much, Superintendent Clitheroe.'

The studio went black except for a pool of light on the presenter's leather chair. Solemnity slid from his face. He became the perky youthful uncle.

'After the break we look ahead to showtime. How did a public executioner become Red Riding Hood's mother? Why did Sharon Rees forget about creeping up your stairs at night in black leather and decide to be a good little girl in this year's Pavilion pantomime? For those of you who can bear the dark, the Hangman will be here – to-nite – to tell us about his last gig before the panto opens on Christmas Eve. With his children, including the mean leather-loving Sharon, he'll chill your blood a little with a number from his new album – *Only One Lip*. They say you can manage with only one of most things that you have two of. But only one lip? Stay tuned, folks, and he will show you how.'

Lesley switched the set off. She stood barefoot in short cotton nightdress.

'Your Clitheroe sounds as if he's about to make an arrest.'

Hoskins stroked the pearly sleekness of her bare thigh appreciatively.

'My Clitheroe hasn't got a clue. So far there's nothing on Elaine Harris. They'll have a job even deciding when she died. Lying out in this weather, it's like being in a deep-freeze. Hardly able to tell if the processes of decay were held up by the cold or if she just hadn't been there that long.'

'Will anyone use the confidential phone line?'

Hoskins's hand moved under the hem, sliding over the cool smoothness of Lesley's bottom.

'Oh, yes,' he said. 'A few well-known nuisances who want to tell us how they did it to her and what fun it was. A few others with grudges to pay off. Framing their local tax inspector or VAT man. Won't get him arrested, of course. Just wreck his reputation round the office. Personal stuff as well. Family scores being settled.'

She stood thoughtfully for a moment.

'All the same,' she said presently, 'he seems like the sort of man you could talk to in confidence. Clitheroe. Even I might trust him.'

A snorting laugh escaped Hoskins.

'You think there wouldn't be three other pairs of ears listening to the call?'

'Would there?' She pulled away startled, as if he might have pinched her. His hand soothed her again.

'Of course there would.'

'Three?'

'For tracing the call while Clitheroe keeps the witness talking.'

'You're making it up.' Lesley turned and put her hands on his shoulders.

Hoskins shook his head in despair at her.

'You don't really imagine they're going to have a phone call from a witness that could prevent another murder – even from a multiple murderer himself – and let the person just ring off and vanish? Do you?'

'I suppose not.' Lesley sat on his knee. 'Not after that poor girl.'

Hoskins nodded.

'How about a bit of sleep?' he suggested hopefully.

25

Christmas morning in Ocean Beach was cold but crisp. Invigorated by the keen chill of the air, the scattered promenaders on the Cakewalk strode against the light breeze and felt the good it was doing them. The car parks of the Garden Royal and the other grand hotels were busy with Christmas visitors. Fit grey-haired men strolled about in camel-hair coats trailing a cold scent of cigars and astringent. The ice-grey sea moved in quiet ripples and a watery sun slanted across the sands from under a shelf of winter cloud. Red-berried holly and imitation snow edged a few of the café windows in Rundle Street. The New Pier was open but unlit. A few children played the fruit machines and the video games. Nothing more. The dancers and waitresses of the Petshop, the doormen and hostesses of the Blue Moon Club, were at home with their feet up. Even the pantomime was closed today.

Gary Fielder and his gang, guns still hidden in their pockets, trotted on to the sands. They loped forward to the dark nave of the pier ironwork, looking for aggression. Trigger fingers itched and hearts beat faster. They were almost under the pier, the crusted piles and girders, the decking that never ceased to drip in any weather. Then they saw the young man.

He sat with his back against one of the pier uprights. Because the action of the tide scoured out the sand at the foot of the iron, he was sitting in a shallow pool. Gary Fielder motioned the others to silence and walked more slowly towards the young man, about to speak to him. The young man took no notice. His head was turned aside a little. He was looking at his hand. His hand and arm were extended, pointing out and down towards the grey rim of an incoming tide. He looked funny, as if he had been drunk and fooling about, like the man at the circus who has just had the clown's third or fourth bucket of water emptied over him.

Gary Fielder stood over the young man. The others began to gather behind him. His sister Karen, who had been allowed to act as second-in-command of the gang for that morning, began to cry.

'Cripes,' said someone else. 'Is he dead?'

'I should think he must be.'

'He doesn't really look dead.'

'How d'you know about that, Billy Franks?' said Gary Fielder with the scornful authority of a twelve year old. 'I bet you never saw anyone dead before. He's been shot. Anyone can see that.'

'Then why's there a rope round his neck?'

'Perhaps he was going to hang himself and then thought he'd use the gun instead.'

'I can't see any gun,' Billy Franks said. 'Perhaps someone else shot him.'

'Stupid!' said Gary Fielder impatiently. 'Where's the sense in that? They wouldn't shoot him and hang him as well, would they?'

Karen Fielder emitted a whimper of fear.

'Stop blubbing,' said her brother severely. 'I suppose we'd better tell someone.'

'We could go to the police station,' said Karen Fielder with a sniff.

Billy Franks, the hard man of the gang, turned on her.

'They'd keep you there all day. No Christmas dinner and no presents for you. If you go to the police, you're the first suspect. They take you down to a cell and ask you questions. They know how to hit you so it doesn't leave a mark. In the stomach mainly. And they take all your clothes off.'

Having led Karen Fielder this far, his imagination failed him.

'What then?' Gary Fielder asked.

'They do things to you. Like they do to terrorists.'

'What things?'

'I don't know, do I? Just things.'

Gary Fielder resumed command of the other two.

'I'm going back and tell my dad. He's been in the army. He'll go down and sort out the police. I'd just like to see them try it on with him.'

In the aftermath of Christmas lunch, the phone rang in the hall at Lantern Hill. Lesley picked it up, listened, and handed it to Hoskins with a tightening of the mouth in mimic fury.

'Sam? It's Jack Chance.'

'First Christmas I haven't volunteered for duty in about the last ten years, Jack.'

'I know,' Chance said. 'Look, I'm sorry about this, Sam. No one wants you to come pelting in here. I just thought you'd better know. We've found Sonny Hassan.'

'Hiding on the top of someone's Christmas tree, was he, in a tutu and carrying a wand?'

'He's dead, Sam.'

'One way of celebrating Christmas, Jack. Sorry. I've just had a smashing lunch and a quart or two of vinho tinto. A bit detached. Still, that just about tidies away the Muriel Pruen case.'

'Does it, hell!' said Chance sceptically. 'Hassan was found

under the New Pier this morning, at low tide. He'd been shot through the head. No sign of the gun but the bullet looks like a match for the ones he was handing out in Prince of Wales Road.'

Hoskins felt buoyant.

'Slight case of suicide, Jack?'

'Sam, his hands were tied behind him. There was a rope round his neck loosely attached to one of the pier girders above him. He had bruises from neck to knee. A hell of a bash on the head. It might come from being knocked against the pier ironwork by the tide. Saville thinks it's more likely to have happened before anything else.'

Hoskins yawned, sleepy from food.

'One way or another, Jack, that's the end of the Muriel Pruen case. Hassan and Elaine Harris dead. Del Warren about to plead guilty and go down for life at the Crown Court next month.'

'What this is, old friend,' said Chance quietly, 'isn't the end of anything. More like the beginning of the Sonny Hassan case. Seems he was beaten up very professionally. Then he was shot dead with his own gun. Close range. Gun muzzle touching the back of the neck to judge by the burn. Then he was going to be hung by the neck under the New Pier. To be found on Christmas morning as a warning to any other young buck who thinks he can tangle with the likes of Pruen and Cooney. This could be worse than Muriel Pruen, Sam. In spades.'

'Day after tomorrow, Jack, it shall have my full and undivided attention. Until then, I'm a civilian. I don't want to know.'

'Right,' said Chance. 'Day after tomorrow. Keeping your feet warm for you, is she?'

'As toast, my son.'

'This whole bloody building is like a refrigerator. The Ripper suggested turning off part of the heating to economise during the holiday. Result is, the cold part froze and sprang a leak. They've had to turn off the lot.'

'Try and have it back on by the day after tomorrow, there's a good chap.'

'Ha-bloody-ha,' Chance said. 'Watch your feet don't scorch. Oh, yes, and Happy Christmas.'

*

In the early darkness, the bedroom lamps threw back a warm glow from the pink curtains. Hoskins unlaced his shoes and considered the improbable image of Lesley. She was wearing the Christmas present he had bought her, black diaphanous nightwear consisting of a short black top and tight pants. The sleek pallor of her hips and torso showed mistily through it. He supposed she considered herself too old for such frivolities. Yet there was a piquancy in the contrast of the glamorous nightwear and the plain crop of her fair hair, the cool, self-possessed look of her face. Hoskins felt a sense of triumph at seeing her in this bedroom costume, not of sexual conquest but at having rescued her from earnest solemnity in such matters.

'I wonder why men like you want to see women dressed up,' she said thoughtfully, 'made objects of desire.'

He turned and caressed her.

'I'll be your sex object, if you will be mine,' he promised happily. 'Can't say fairer than that. You look absolutely smashing. Made my Christmas.'

'Come on,' she said, feeling for the elastic waistband. 'I want to see Swan Lake on the television at seven o'clock.'

Hoskins pulled a face and unbuttoned his shirt.

'Right,' he said. 'I'll race you.'

Presently they lay warm and expansive in the reflected glow of the curtains.

'If I could get my Christmas and New Year leave in one,' Hoskins said, 'I wonder how often we could do this in a week? Just out of curiosity.'

Lesley shook her fringe into place and turned towards him. Hoskins stroked her breasts.

'You've never grown up,' she said. 'It must be the police force. You're still a randy-minded little boy.'

'And happy with it,' he said quietly. 'I see a lot of these grown-up and responsible types. Miserable buggers they always seem.'

She turned a little further.

'Yes,' she said. 'Well, I suppose no one could call the Boy Hoskins miserable or a bugger.'

He brought his hand down in a brisk slap on her bottom.

'Come on,' he said. 'You'll miss Swan Lake.'

Lesley sighed.

'I don't know. I've seen it before. It can't have altered much.'

'In that case,' he said quickly, 'let's try something you haven't seen before.'

26

In the cold January morning, the sky above the tall hedges of Challoner Road had the intense blue of a desert noon. Until Hoskins stepped out of the car's warmth, it was almost possible to imagine that summer had come to the foreshore of Canton, spread out below Hawks Hill, and the tidal anchorages that glittered in the distance. Even in winter, Carmel Cooney's lawn had a billiard table perfection. The calm of the swimming pool quivered in California blue.

Hoskins heard distantly the fluttering notes of a Chopin *ballade* from the Steinway concert grand in the room that Cooney called his saloon. He saw a movement beyond the Moorish arches of the conservatory and Cooney himself appeared. He showed the same tadpole-shape in the same tight suiting.

'Mr Hoskins!' He lurched across with hand outstretched. 'Pleasure to have you up here. All on your own today?'

'Jack Chance caught 'flu last week. Half the division's off sick with it.'

'Never mind. You come on in just the same, Mr Hoskins.'

Hoskins followed him into the room with its dove-grey silks and silver hangings. The winter light shivered and split in lozenges of warm colour from the crystal chandelier. But his heart sank with a long-familiar feeling of having let Cooney win the first round. The boisterous hospitality. The confident bonhomie. The municipal gangster on the Police Committee. Councillor Cooney of Hawks Hill and the Blue Moon Club.

Ignoring the young woman who sat at the piano, Cooney motioned him to a deep-cushioned chair.

'You'll have a drink, Mr Hoskins, not being on duty?'

'Official visit, Mr Cooney.'

'Shame,' Cooney said in a tone that was not quite a jeer. 'I'll ring the girl for coffee, then. I thought you'd took up my offer to come and hear this young lady that plays my piano to me. You run along, my dear. Get yourself something nice on the Emporium account. Mr Hoskins and me is going to have a little chat. Shame, Mr Hoskins. Hang on, I'll get Maggie in here.'

'Don't bother with coffee,' Hoskins said. 'This is still official.'

Cooney pressed the bell. He lowered himself into his chair and held up his hand.

'No bother, Mr Hoskins. I got that young tart, Maggie from the Petshop, helping out. Stocky one with blonde hair worn loose and fringed like a little girl. Used to dance there in school uniform. You know, all lollipop and knickers. Ten years or more since she saw a school. Still, if it's what our lords and masters wants, Mr Hoskins, who are we to say 'em nay? Not quite the same league as young Sarah Thorne. She's class, my Sarah is. Real class.'

The door opened and a young woman of twenty-five or so came in. Hoskins recognised the figure, the straight blonde hair fringed and framing a face whose features were firm and rather crude. He remembered her as one of Cooney's shopgirls before her moment of fame on the bandstand of the Petshop.

'Coffee for three, Mag, there's a good girl. And just ask Mr Cam if he'd be good enough to step in and join us.'

Hoskins's heart sank further. Jack Cam's considerable skill as a lawyer was portioned out between three or four clients. Carmel Cooney was one of them.

'Mr Cam just happened to be here, did he?'

'Oh no, Mr Hoskins. He comes up Monday mornings. Business to do with the clubs and the Emporium. But you wanting an appointment, it seemed handy just now. Me on my own, Mr Hoskins? No knowing what you might have me saying!'

The door opened and Jack Cam entered. A gold watch-chain was looped across the waistcoat of his trimly cut fawn suit. He had a languid, dandyish air, a floral tie and two-tone shoes. With slim build and neat grey hair, he looked like a stage-door hunter of can-can dancers. His voice suggested a sharp mind trained in a world of commercial schools and the shabby courts of Canton's petty crime.

'Morning, Mr Hoskins. Don't get up,' he said, coming across and shaking Hoskins's hand. 'How's life in the division?'

'Cold at present, Mr Cam. Three weeks the engineers have been trying to put the heating right. Economy over Christmas, it was supposed to be. Leaks like Niagara ever since. Costing someone a fortune now.'

'Local government!' said Cam scornfully. 'Want hanging up by their knackers. Understand you wanted to put a question or two to Mr Cooney? About Hassan.'

'Just a few, Mr Cam. I hope he'll feel able to answer for himself.'

'I'm sure he will if I tell him to, Mr Hoskins. And I'm more likely to tell him if I know exactly what this song and dance is in aid of.'

'Muriel Pruen,' Hoskins said.

Cooney shook his head at the sadness of it all.

'What about her?' Cam asked.

'The break-in at Mr Pruen's involved three people. Elaine Harris. Sonny Hassan. Del Warren. Elaine Harris was the first to be named. A few days later she was found dead by the East Sluice.'

Cooney bowed his head and shook it.

'Shocking, Mr Hoskins. Makes you despair of the world.'

'Before she was strangled,' Hoskins said, 'someone gave her the kind of hiding she couldn't be allowed to talk about. Her hands were tied during it and a rag was probably shoved in her mouth. We found a thread of it.'

'They ought to bring back the rope,' Cooney said earnestly. 'They really ought. Or kill them vermin the same way they kill their victims.'

'Del Warren,' Hoskins said, 'was arrested. Sonny Hassan was named. Warren was scared so witless he pleaded guilty. Won't say a word to us. Can't get him to verify or deny Mr Pruen's story that Mrs Pruen was alone in the house.'

'What's it matter?' Cooney demanded. 'You going to take the word of scum like Warren against Mr Pruen and me and a dozen other proper witnesses? Are you?'

'On Christmas Day,' Hoskins persisted, 'the body of Sonny Hassan was found under the New Pier at Ocean Beach. He'd been savagely beaten. Marks showed that he'd had his hands tied as well. There was fluff from a gag in his upper throat. Judging by the abrasions to his knees, he was made to kneel while he was shot in the back of the neck. Russian-style execution. His own gun. The body was taken down the Beach and an attempt made to hang him by the neck from the pier girders. As an example.'

Cooney pulled a face.

'Comedians,' he said.

'Forensic evidence suggests that Hassan was killed on Christmas Eve, between noon and about four o'clock. Where were you then, Mr Cooney?'

'Me? What the hell's it got to do with me?'

Jack Cam intervened.

'Before we go further, Mr Hoskins, what is the purpose of this question?'

'Mr Pruen expressed to me his wish that he could put to death with his own hands the murderers of his wife. When I spoke to Mr Cooney to confirm Mr Pruen's story, he said much the same. In the presence of my sergeant, he said, talking of the killers, "I could be highly original with scum like that." He said he wished there was a law that he and Mr Pruen could "find them scumbags, take our little bats and play an hour or two of table-tennis with them". When told that one of the suspects was a girl, Mr Cooney said, "I could make her wish she wasn't."'

'So what?' Cam asked.

'So, Mr Cam, I need an answer from anyone who could be connected with Hassan's death. Mr Pruen tells me that he was at a special Christmas Eve lunch given by Mr Cooney in a private upstairs dining-room at the Paris Hotel on Atlantic Wharf.'

'And what if he was?' Cooney demanded. 'I have one every year. Staff of the Petshop and the Blue Moon. A few from the Emporium, across the Wharf, and Jolly Modes. I treat my people right, Mr Hoskins. Give 'em a party. Give 'em each a little present. Where's the harm in that? We was there all lunchtime until about five o'clock. And from five till seven I was at a little staff do in the Emporium itself. Fifty witnesses. I don't suppose there was a minute in all that time when a dozen people weren't looking at me. Unless when I was taking a leak, perhaps.'

'Mr Pruen was there, was he?'

'Course he was, Mr Hoskins. I invited the poor old chap to join us, so as to cheer him up. Bloody miserable Christmas he was going to have otherwise. First one without his Muriel. And his man Raymond was with him and that girl of his. Noreen. But that ain't the same as his Muriel, Mr Hoskins. Hortop and Spencer from the Blue Moon was there. And Jackie and Sue from the Petshop, and a few other girls. Claire and Viv from the Modes. Benny Stevens from Peninsular Trucking. And Sarah Thorne did the honours for me, in the absence of Mrs Cooney abroad. There was a few other people I invited because they'd done me favours. Was you there, Mr Cam?'

Jack Cam shook his head slowly.

'You did invite me, Mr Cooney. I'd got a previous, though.'

'What we didn't have,' Cooney said, 'was garbage like Hassan. This was a respectable do, Mr Hoskins.'

'How was the homemade pâté?' Hoskins asked.

Jack Cam intervened, the voice smooth and assured but with just an edge of Saturday-night Peninsula.

'Mr Cooney's not going to answer that, Mr Hoskins. Unless you can give me a very good reason why he should. You're well out of order there. And you know it. And I know it too.'

'Might not be too important,' Hoskins said. 'They do a nice pâté with the bar snacks, though. Serve it in the Brasserie Magenta too. Being homemade, you can tell from the ingredients that it's the Paris Hotel's. Their red house wine's an exclusive too. Bordeaux. Cahors black label. Quite a bit of both in Sonny Hassan's digestive tract. Seems the condemned man was eating a hearty lunch just below Mr Cooney. Finished by two. They don't serve after that. Dead by about four. Even you, Mr Cam, have to see possibilities. Someone notices

Hassan there. When he steps outside after lunch, he's picked up. Taken somewhere. Beaten and topped with his own gun between two and four o'clock or thereabouts.'

'If you say so,' Cam conceded.

'And in the room above is Mr Pruen, who knows Hassan is wanted for the murder of Muriel Pruen. And there's Mr Pruen's man, Raymond. There's Mr Cooney as well, come to that. Both Mr Pruen and Mr Cooney told me months ago just how they'd like to deal with the killers of Muriel Pruen. Now, Mr Cam, do you imagine I'd be allowed to overlook a little coincidence of that sort?'

Cam shook his head.

'Of course not, Mr Hoskins. But Mr Cooney's been frank and open with you. You've had all the answers from him that you need. To be fair, you and I know I've been rather on the lenient side, seeing that you were here on your own without a witness. But from now on, Mr Cooney says not another word. On my instructions. In fact, you don't even come asking questions without my being here.'

'And if that's not acceptable, Mr Cam?'

Jack Cam sighed and looked at his watch.

'Then I'll see you in court, Mr Hoskins. My client is a city councillor and very likely to be a parliamentary candidate. We can't stand for anything that looks like an attempt to destroy his character by innuendo. Mr Cooney naturally felt strongly about the brutal murder of a lady he'd known all his life. His language, in the first instance, may have been a little intemperate. Who shall blame him? But if there is one man who cannot have laid a hand on Hassan, it is he. The fact that he was unknowingly in the same hotel as the deceased a few hours before the murder is neither here nor there.'

'And Elaine Harris?'

Cam clicked his tongue.

'Mr Hoskins, as I understand it, you can't tell within two or three days when she died. You can't expect a witness to account for every minute of that time. Mr Cooney or anyone else was bound to be alone somewhen. During the night. Taking a bath. I'll not stand for innuendo over that. It's not on, Mr Hoskins. And you know it.'

Carmel Cooney's face split in the familiar melon-grin.

'Course he does, Mr Cam. Mr Hoskins is all right. As a member of the Police Committee, I'm proud to have officers like him on my force. And he knows I don't take offence if he asks questions, so long as he doesn't mind the answers.'

He looked about him and reached for the bell.

'Where's our coffee?' he said, pressing the button again. 'Sometimes I think our Maggie needs waking up with a good kick in the pants, poetically speaking.'

It was an hour later when Hoskins got back to his office. He dialled Chance's number and sensed, even over the phone, the congested warmth of the sick-room.

'Bloody useless,' he said. 'He'd got old Cam out there already.'

'But he admitted he was at the Paris Hotel on Christmas Eve?'

'Him and fifty witnesses.'

'Did he know Hassan was in the bar downstairs?'

'He must have done,' said Hoskins glumly. 'I don't believe in coincidences like that. Only question is, was it just accident that they saw Hassan there and then arranged to knock him off? Or did someone tempt him there somehow so that he could be set up for it?'

'I'd settle for temptation,' Chance said.

'Me too. Not that it's going to do much good. The Ripper's all for closing the case down. We've run into the sand, he says. Underworld's not talking. Public doesn't care about Hassan anyway. Well rid of.'

'Balls to that,' Chance said indistinctly through a tissue.

'Unfortunately he's right, Jack. I could question fifty people who were at Cooney's lunch and much good would it do. Short of the killer walking in here and bursting into tears of shame, that's as far as we get.'

'What's Ripley's notion?'

'He's caught Clitheroe's complaint. Sees sex-maniacs jumping out of every bush in Connaught Park each time one of the High School damsels trips by. Whenever they line up for deep breathing exercises, a titter runs along the row. What Ripley wants is a "Pervert Patrol" twelve months of the year. Don't know what the idea does to the sex-maniacs but it's struck terror in the sergeants' room.'

'What about Elaine Harris?' Chance inquired.

'Four of 'em, house-to-housing in Clearwater. After that it's Mount Pleasant and Hawks Hill. Two women on the confidential line this week, saying their old men did it. Another says she did it herself because her son was ruining himself with girls like Elaine Harris. A bloke who's rung four or five times before had to tell us all over again how he did it in a designer-dungeon. All of them rang off giggling. And Clitheroe's got an early morning spot on Coastal Network on Thursday. Progress report to the nation. We'll get this man if it takes another hundred years.'

'And that's it?'

'That's it, Jack. Get well soon.'

Chance sneezed and rang off.

27

Clitheroe's head jerked and quivered as if in a sudden cardiac spasm. The mouth twitched and quirked, the hands describing convulsive and restricted arcs. The Man took his finger off the fast-forward button of the video remote control and the electronic puppet settled down to a calmer display. The Man had found the bit he wanted, where Clitheroe was talking about a confidential phone line. It showed how far removed from modern life the old-fashioned values of the authorities had become. Members of families protected their own. The Man had seen it. They looked inward to their warm homes with the bright flicker of enchantment on a glass screen. They feasted on frozen luxury that had been only a name on the menu of the rich fifty years before. Those who might once have been servants themselves now commanded service from gadgets that scrubbed and rinsed and dried. Their backs were turned upon the cold and threatening streets outside. Who could blame them? They were gentle but self-indulgent creatures. They wished no actual harm to others. But if the policeman on the screen really thought that people would betray one another and bring ruin on their warm little homes as he was suggesting . . .

The Man checked his thoughts and listened. He listened again to the part where Clitheroe was talking about the confidential phone line. The Man smiled. It might be possible to have a bit of fun with that. Nothing too risky. Just a bit of fun.

He had put all the news items on to one tape in the past month or so. It ran for more than an hour. The Man played it through from time to time, late at night when only he was still up or when he was in the house alone. Annie was out tonight. At her sister's. Watching the tape, he thought the official pictures of Elaine were poor quality. Fuzzy and stilted, compared with some of his own. Now the film was showing the scene on the levels. Tall winter grass moving in the wind. The Man had driven along there once or twice lately. Strange what an effect the television camera could have. The East Sluice and the Causeway, the corrugated hangars of Atlantic Factors, looked more dramatic, more poetic than in reality.

Then came the most enjoyable bit of all. Clitheroe on the first night promising, 'We are going to catch this man.' Clitheroe a couple of weeks later, still saying, 'We are going to catch this man.' A month. Two months. Still the same. The interviewer's tone sympathetic and encouraging, because people were scared when another girl, Alison Shaw, had gone missing after Elaine. The Man had always thought of himself as clever, without particular arrogance, but it seemed to him that a killer hardly needed to be clever. So long as he worked alone. The police and their friends on television spent so much time falling over one another's feet. And events were always handing the killer a bonus. Another girl would go missing for quite different reasons. And that disappearance would entwine itself in the existing case, like a rope caught in a donkey-engine.

The Man switched off the recording, wound it back, and took it through to the garage. He was extra careful nowadays. The photograph album and the cassette were concealed in the garage wall itself. The flimsy back of the hardboard cupboard in the garage could be lifted off. He had loosened two bricks in the wall behind it, so that the hole could be reached through the cupboard itself. When the bricks were taken out, there was a cavity between the inner and outer walls. A plastic liner for a wastebin contained his souvenirs in this hiding place.

The Man drew the plastic bag out. How careful, it seemed to him, he was being at present. He was most definitely a good boy now. There were longings he might have indulged at any other time. But not as things were. He opened the album and looked at the familiar full-plate prints of Elaine Harris. She was walking towards him, looking a little away, as if aware that her picture was being taken. Walking in front of him after school. Then in her pink bikini. Lying and kneeling, stretching and stooping in the garden.

The Man was determined upon one thing. He wanted people to know about these photographs. Not, of course, to know that he had taken them. Just to know that they had been taken. To know what it was that he – and he suspected most other people – privately thought about the girl. For the photographs revealed his thoughts. No doubt of that. He had intended to leave copies of them here and there. On the seat by the school bus-stop. Or left to be found on buses or the metro-rail. Sharing his enjoyment with others. But not as things were. That would be silly. One thing The Man had never been was silly.

He turned the pages of the photo-album. Neat and tidy, the press cuttings of the Elaine Harris case lay between clear plastic. Everything was there, from the first missing person report to the latest promise by Clitheroe on television last week. Only a single line in the *Western World* betrayed the truth that the number of police officers working on the case had been scaled down from twelve to four. A few weeks more, The Man thought, and four would be nil. As had happened with Rachel Lloyd. And Jane Page. And the rest.

He turned the pages, content and affectionate. There were photographs of his own. A girl with a shock of raven black hair and saucer eyes, as if she might be intensely angry. Maybury's department store in the shopping precinct. A job of some kind there. Seen in high heels and tight jeans, agile hips in a vigorous bouncing walk. Somewhere in the bombproof vault of the skull, a file was opened. Name, age, occupation, status. Description and usual movements. Times and routes. Resources were allocated. The Man frowned at the monochrome image of Kim. He was going to be busy this coming summer. Busier than he had ever known.

As The Man flipped the pages back, he saw on the rear of a press cutting a fragment of another case. GUILTY PLEA IN PRUEN MURDER. The Man could never understand that. Never guilty. Never surrender. Rather the capital in flames. Mongol invaders fighting street by street towards the chancery. Gush of flame-throwers and crash of masonry. The leader at his post until the end. Falling at last before the barbarian hordes. One bullet left to avoid the ignominy of capture, the circus of the victors. There was another tape on which he had collected old newsreel footage of his heroes. Setting the bricks back in the garage wall, he felt in the mood to play a little of it through.

28

Rain drifted thick as veils of smoke across the city sky. Chic hair salons and delicatessens, warmly lit little restaurants and estate agencies, lined the final descent of Park Drive as it joined the promenade of shopping-centre chain stores. The hill curved into the eastern end of Longwall past the open green and a distant view of the docks. The beginning of Canton centre was a pedestrian parade of newly built department stores and hotels. Among survivals of old Canton were the façade of the Palace Theatre and the French Gothic shape of the Catholic cathedral, built by Butterworth in Victorian cherry-coloured brick with bands of drab yellow and slate-grey.

The storm came on. Hoskins, having left the Coastal Network Television studios on foot, dodged under the curved yellow street-blind of the Trattoria Venezia. A warm lunchtime smell of Italian food, a perfume of spiced tomatoes, blew with the draught from the extractor fan. The rain fell with the increased ferocity of a tap being opened. Its drops struck and bounced on the flooded tarmac like the surface of a lake being machine-gunned. Traffic moved slowly, throwing up a wake behind it. Running downhill, round the corner and into Longwall, the gutter was like a mountain torrent, apples and cigarette packets, chocolate wrappings and newspaper swept clear with an efficiency unmatched by the mechanised brushes of the municipal cleansing cart.

In a rare moment of enthusiasm for exercise, Hoskins had decided to walk. It was not an urgent visit, more a matter of routine. The 'community affairs' unit of Coastal Network Television had lately decided to imitate others in scolding its viewers for anti-social conduct. For several weeks, the names and addresses of those convicted of drink-and-drive offences appeared like a list of credits at the end of the Thursday night programme. They were introduced by a presenter whose face had the air of a disappointed but resolute schoolmistress waiting for a malefactor to own up.

Hoskins shifted his feet and tried to get nearer the extractor fan for warmth. Senior police officers, including Ripley, had responded enthusiastically to the CNT suggestion. The courts had fallen over themselves to provide names and addresses to the television company. The drink-and-drivers were to be shamed into compliance with social policy.

It might have worked elsewhere. The culture of the young Canton male was made of stronger stuff. The po-faced presenters of 'community television' were variously dismissed as 'cream puffs' and 'interfering old cows'. Then, ten days after the first list of drink-and-drivers had appeared, a programme secretary was attacked in the CNT car park, in the evening darkness at six o'clock. She had been thrown to the ground, her arm broken, the contents of her purse tipped down the drain. Two well-built men in balaclavas were sought. A week later, at about 3 a.m., fire-lighters were lowered through the letter-box of the programme's producer. Petrol was poured and burning paper dropped in. The blaze had gutted the ground floor of the house but its sudden ferocity had drawn attention and saved the occupants. At present, programme policy was under consideration. For the time being, Thursday's *Week On The Coast* appeared without credits, protecting its makers by anonymity.

189

CNT had taken on extra security men to patrol its car park and accompany its crews. But in the end, Hoskins thought glumly, it would mean a police guard on all the management and producers. Hours of police time had already been taken up interviewing every person convicted of a drink-and-drive offence in the past few months, checking movements and stories. Not a single case could be proved against any of them. A good many, however, had assured the police of the satisfaction they felt at what had happened to CNT personnel.

The rain stopped. Hoskins stepped out from under the dripping canvas blind and began to walk quickly down Longwall before the next downpour. The troubles of CNT's community affairs unit were a symptom of a more alarming malaise. Through CB radio and makeshift pirate broadcasts, Canton's very own 'Hit-Back' campaign had begun. Detector vans and squad cars had so far failed to track down the mobile offenders. The broadcasts had begun several months before, late at night, offering innocuous advice to those faced with problems by the police or the courts, the social services, the inland revenue, even customs and excise. Since then the tone had changed. Names and addresses of magistrates and police officers, social workers and tax inspectors were read out during the broadcasts. Those who felt injustice had been done them were urged to 'go looking' for those towards whom they bore a grudge. Methods were suggested for causing embarrassment, alarm, even damage to officials and their families. Some of these were both simple and vicious. Compared with the *Hit Back Radio Show*, the Hangman's exhortation to smash up cars seemed a forgivable little eccentricity.

Here and there, the pavement of the Mall swam with water, the gutters blocked and the road flooded. Hoskins stepped round the shallow pools. Hit Back. It was, he supposed, inevitable as the power of authority increased and the television companies allied themselves indistinguishably with public policy. In the great divide of Them and Us, Coastal Network tried to insinuate that it was part of Us. In a city like Canton, it was regarded irredeemably as a representative of Them. The Fifth Column of authority. With the glum satisfaction of one who had seen it all coming, Hoskins rode the lift to the fifth floor of the headquarters building. He pushed open the door of the sergeants' room.

'Anything for me, Jack?' he asked Chance.

Chance came out with a folder under his arm.

'Bit of news, Sam,' he said quietly. 'Somewhere in private. Been saving it just for you.'

They went into Hoskins's office.

'What's it about?'

Chance sat down with his folder.

'Remember old Dawson and his lads raiding the Squire's sex-shop in November? The bollocking because we borrowed a few pin-ups of Tooty Fruity for the slide show? Looks like the case is closed. Items to be returned. Magistrates only granted a destruction on a couple of American imports. The rest goes back to the shop.'

Hoskins shed his coat.

'That's nice,' he said. 'Old Dawson over the moon, is he?'

'This morning,' Chance persisted, 'McArthur and I were just thumbing through the exhibits. In the line of duty, that is. I borrowed one for you to read.'

Hoskins looked up.

'Any trouble with Ripley, my son, and this time it is definitely your turn in the barrel.'

Chance was unperturbed. He took a magazine from the folder and handed it to Hoskins.

'I signed for it, Sam. Try page sixty-two. Tell me if I'm right.'

Hoskins looked at the magazine. It was called *Velvet*. The cover showed a girl in a leotard touching her toes, sideways on, smiling with gymnastic enthusiasm.

'What's this, then?'

'Local talent,' Chance said. 'The Squire's very own publication. When I was a nipper, the local stuff was turned out on an old roneo machine by hand. Marvellous how science has moved on. With desk-top publishing, he can paste up a magazine down Monmouth Terrace and have it looking like *Vogue* or *Harper's Bazaar*.'

'Not quite,' Hoskins said, searching for page sixty-two. 'They've moved on a bit since then as well.'

It was a feature called 'Readers Right'. The letters column. Cheap copy. The Squire's punters even providing him with photographs and stories. Several pictures were posed by allegedly willing wives and girl friends. Hoskins glanced down the page and his heart jumped with something akin to fright. In the centre was a crudely reproduced photograph of Elaine Harris. He looked at the heading of the letter, 'Wayward Pupil'. There was nothing obscene or erotic about the picture. At the most, it seemed to him suggestively vulgar in its pose. The black-and-white picture showed her in a light-coloured bikini. Kneeling on all fours, she had just spread a towel upon the grass. The photograph had been taken from behind her and to one side. She was looking back but not at the camera. Her eyes were directed to one side with a slight frown of annoyance, as if she had mislaid something. The picture had every appearance of a photograph taken without her knowledge.

Hoskins closed the magazine and put it down.

'What date was this?'

'Back last summer he printed it,' Chance said, 'before she went missing. I checked it out. That was taken over the wall of the Harris back garden in Lantern Hill. Someone that had a real interest in her, I'd say.'

'You reckon many people read this magazine?'

'Locally?' Chance thought about it. 'A few hundred. The rest must get dumped on the London market. Limited circulation for enthusiasts. Whoever took that photo has a local smell about him. Don't see him coming all the way from London for a snapshot of Elaine Harris in her bathing suit.'

'I hope not,' said Hoskins, piously. 'Let's see what the Squire has to say about it all. A punter that's keen enough to send in a photo and a little story about a wayward pupil is more than likely on the subscription list.'

'Could be a hundred on it,' Chance said uneasily. 'Thousands even.'

But Hoskins was more cheerful now.

'Sooner we get started the better, then,' he said, waving the magazine at Chance. 'Booked this rubbish out properly on the inventory, did you?'

*

192

A recent 'slim-down' in the equipment grant had brought chaos to headquarters transport. The last Fiesta in the Division was on the motor-pool ramp with its exhaust unit dismantled. Taking his own car, Hoskins drove with Chance down the Mall and Great Western Street, across Atlantic Wharf and the Balance Street river bridge to the beginning of Peninsula dockland. Peninsula proper was divided by the long bleak artery of Dyce Street, running down to the pier head a mile or so distant. It began where the road dipped under the plate-iron grey of the old railway bridge, pavements running high on either side. Just beyond the bridge, an Edwardian pub in amber and green tiling stood on a corner. Monmouth Street went one way and Monmouth Terrace the other.

Though lying in the Peninsula district, Monmouth Terrace was no more than ten minutes' walk from the banking and commercial district of Canton across the Balance Street river bridge. The Squire and his competitors were well-placed for lunch-time custom from punters in pin-stripe. It was a narrow street, an old dockland terrace whose houses with their stone-lintelled street doors had stood for a hundred and twenty years. At the centre of the terrace, many years previously, half a dozen front parlours had been turned into little shops. For the past ten years or so, they had been occupied by a betting-shop, a dockland discothèque popular with middle-class students, a Lebanese restaurant, a delicatessen, and the Squire's 'Books 'n Pics'.

Hoskins slammed the car door and stood on the worn uneven paving of the terrace. Nothing, so far as he could see, had received a coat of paint in living memory. The windows of 'Books 'n Pics' had been curtained over, ostensibly to comply with provisions on indecent display, in practice to give privacy to the Squire's browsers. This curtaining gave his shop the look of a funeral parlour. There was a sign in neon script above the door, dead and unlit since the day it was installed. Those who sought the Squire found him without its assistance.

Hoskins hitched his trousers up a notch and stared at the windows. The contents were yellowed and curled by sunlight, unchanged for months. Among dead flies and dust, there were several men's magazines that could have been bought at most newsagents. A thumbed and cheaply produced copy of *The Road to Buenos Aires* with a lurid cover in red and blue stood next to a life of Sacher-Masoch, *The Dreadful Disclosures of Maria Monk*, and – for reasons not evident to Hoskins – a book on embroidery. These and the covers for videos of *Emmanuelle*, *Red Nights of the Gestapo* and *War at Sea* made up the window display. The Squire was taking no chances with the law.

Hoskins pushed open the door. Beyond the ranks of magazine racks, divided according to obsession, the Squire sat at a table beside his till. He stood up and nodded at them, a seventy year old with unkempt hair and shabby tweeds. He had the air of an officer too old for his rank, a senior captain or a major. The lines and pouches in the sad face always suggested to Hoskins a story of conduct unbecoming an officer and gentleman, embezzlement of mess funds, a proud name humbled. But the Squire's voice and manner were those of a public-school housemaster with a twinkle in his eye. Summer camp-fires and ghost stories in the dark. It was easy to see why he had been known for more than twenty years down the Peninsula as the Squire. Easy to imagine him reading the first lesson from the brass eagle lectern in the parish church.

When confronted by the obscene publications squad, the Squire was apt to sigh over the contents of the magazines and remember fondly how much better things had been 'in my day'. He talked of himself as a man already dead. In whatever form the moral vigilantes presented the wraith of a hard-core pornographer, it bore little resemblance to the Squire in reality.

'Afternoon, Mr Hoskins. Mr Chance. They telephoned me the good news this morning. Those American things I don't care much about. It's the being without stock for months that seems to me all wrong. But I said to Mr Dawson – I said straight – it's never right. The law lets him come here any time and take away my entire stock. Including what you could buy at Smith's or any of those places. He knows he'll have to bring it back because the magistrates won't give him a destruction order. So back it comes. And by then the magazines are all six months out of date. And I've had capital tied up in what's been confiscated. If that's not harassment, Mr Hoskins, I'd like to know what is. This time, I'm asking the court for costs against the police.'

'I should just about think you are, sir. Still, I'm not here about that. I'm interested in Elaine Harris.'

'What's she?'

Chance intervened.

'The girl whose body was found near the East Sluice. In the snow.'

'Oh,' said the Squire, straightening up. He braced the small of his back with his palms and raised his eyebrows. 'Her! Well, gentlemen, you won't find anything under-age here. She was only a schoolgirl, wasn't she? One rule I have for the stock we carry and the magazine we do, minimum age eighteen. They're adult then. We wouldn't so much as mention an age less than that. And schoolgirls never. Absolutely not. Not with all this child abuse hysteria. You know me, Mr Hoskins. Play the ball where it lies. As I said to Mr Dawson, I don't want to fall foul of the law. Trouble is, there aren't any guidelines. I asked Dawson. All the silly fool tells me is that he can't say.'

Hoskins looked sympathetically at the Squire. He held up his copy of *Velvet*.

'Elaine Harris was in one of your magazines. A magazine produced by you.'

The old man's voice grew quieter.

'Oh dear, oh lor',' he said. 'Oh dear, oh dear. You'd both better come in the other room. Just a minute.'

He went across to the street door, closed and locked it, then pulled down a dark green canvas blind. With Hoskins and Chance following, he led the way into the room behind the shop.

'Sit down,' he said.

The back parlour of the Victorian terrace with its walls plainly distempered in a grimy cream showed no evidence of the desk-top technology that had produced *Velvet*. A warm mineral odour from a cheap oil-stove filled the air. The floor was bare-boarded at the skirting, the centre carpeted by a worn covering the colour of sacking and smelling of dust. An old gate-legged table, several kitchen chairs and a stained oak bureau made up the furniture. Behind the Squire, on the bureau, was a framed school photograph of boys in grey flannels standing on tiers of benches, the chairs in front occupied by masters in gowns and mortarboards. A creeper-covered building with a square collegiate tower rose in the background. Beside this was a photograph of a young man in Royal Flying Corps uniform of 1918, set in the polished fragment of a wooden aircraft wing.

Hoskins laid his copy of *Velvet* on the table, open at page sixty-two.

'This one,' he said gently.

The Squire looked at it. The hanging flesh of the elderly face coloured a little with self-consciousness.

'Oh dear,' he said again. 'Well, gentlemen, I can only plead good faith. You're positive it's her, are you?'

'Quite positive,' Hoskins said. 'That's the garden of the house she lived in. And as a matter of information, when it comes to court the plea is either guilty or not guilty. You can't plead good faith. The rules don't allow it.'

But the Squire was off the ropes again now, boxing back.

'Looking at that photograph, Mr Hoskins, could you honestly say she was fifteen or eighteen for certain? I take it you couldn't object on grounds other than her age? In itself that picture's entirely innocent. If you saw it in a family album, for example.'

Hoskins took the magazine back.

'But then, my friend, this isn't exactly a family album, is it? Look at the other pages. Young ladies two at a time and all the rest of it. In any case, it's not for Mr Chance or me to say about her age. That's your responsibility.'

'Just a minute.' The Squire pulled open one of the drawers in the bureau and continued to talk as he rummaged in it. 'The policy is this, Mr Hoskins. In each magazine we include a model release form. Before any picture can be printed, even professional, the model has to sign a form agreeing. Any reader whose wife or young lady poses – and he sends us a copy – she has to sign that form. Among other things, it says she's over eighteen.'

He showed them the page with the form on it. Chance shook his head.

'Thing is, sir, you don't know who fills in the form and posts it to you. Could be the girl in the photograph or anyone else.'

The Squire sighed and shrugged.

'I can't travel round and call on 'em all, Mr Chance, if that's what you mean.'

'Or write for confirmation?' Hoskins asked.

The Squire shook his head, still rummaging in the drawer.

'If it went back to whoever signed it in the girl's name without asking her, Mr Hoskins, the chap would just confirm it, wouldn't he?'

Hoskins nodded, as if he understood the Squire's difficulty.

'We'll just have this straight, though,' he said. 'I'm looking for a man who killed Elaine Harris. I don't care about your magazines or what's in them. Mr Dawson may do, I don't. For all I care, you can have two girls or two hundred in each photo. If your readers want to beat each other black and blue, that's fine by me. But I want the bloke that took the picture of Elaine Harris. I mean to have him. If I don't, Mr Dawson is going to spend so much time in this back parlour, you'll think you've got him for a lodger. Fair enough?'

'A moment,' the Squire said. He drew out a folder with the name of the magazine and the number of its issue written across it. 'I'm not sure we had the photo back from the typesetter. We haven't room to keep all that stuff. But as a firm we always keep the forms signed by models, for legal reasons.'

Hoskins tried to imagine the Squire's 'firm' and failed to do so. The Squire gave a sigh of contentment. He drew a form out of the folder and handed it over. Hoskins and Chance examined it.

'Polly Perkins?' said Chance incredulously. 'You take signatures like that, do you?'

'A young lady is entitled to a *nom de guerre*, Mr Chance.'

'And an address to match?' Hoskins inquired. 'Look at this rubbish. A hundred and eighty-four, White Horse Lane, London W1. White Horse Lane's about the length of Monmouth Terrace. I don't imagine its numbers go half that high.'

The Squire let his breath out in a long whistling sigh, as if to show he had had enough. Those who had ragged the good-natured housemaster were about to see the steel of the ex-subaltern trench-raider.

'The law requires such forms to be provided and signed, Mr Hoskins. It does not require the publisher to employ private detectives to check names and addresses. I've played the game by you, gentlemen. If I can help you catch the man you want, I will. But upon your conduct and attitude now depends whether I phone my attorney and say no more. And that, gentlemen, is that.'

Hoskins relaxed.

'All I want', he said, 'is information. I'd like the original copy of that photograph, if it can be found. More important, I want a list of all the subscribers to this magazine.'

The Squire turned back to the bureau.

'It won't do the circulation much good, Mr Hoskins, if you go knocking at their doors.'

'How many are there?'

'Between four and five hundred. It's a contact mag mainly. We sell about twice that over the counter. Here and elsewhere.'

'I shouldn't think we'd need to knock at many doors,' Hoskins said reassuringly. 'We'll just run the list through the Criminal Records Office central computer. See if any names start lights flashing and bells ringing.'

The Squire turned round again, a wad of perforated print-out in his hand.

'That's it, Mr Hoskins. The list.'

'Thanks. Who does the sticking and stamping for this lot?'

'I do,' said the Squire wanly, 'and my daughter.'

'Your daughter?'

'Yes, Mr Hoskins. Ladies now are a bit different to what they were in my young days. Not liable to the vapours at a naughty picture. She's a treasure, Suzanne is. I don't think I could keep this going without her. Not at my age.'

Presently they walked out together to the front of the shop. The Squire pulled up the blind on the door and turned the key in the lock to open it.

'Thanks,' Hoskins said. 'We'll be in touch. I'd like that photo if the typesetters can find it.' He paused and made a friendly gesture at the window display. 'I didn't know you had a line in books about embroidery.'

The Squire smiled self-consciously.

'I do a little of it myself, Mr Hoskins. Sit for hours at the counter in case a customer should happen by. Often they don't, but I have to stay put. Something to do. I'm on a tablecloth just now. Willow-pattern on Irish linen. Rather pleased with it, actually.'

Chance exchanged a look with Hoskins.

'You could always pass the time checking your stock,' he said sardonically.

The Squire shook his head, as if the Sergeant should have known better.

'They pay you to solve crime, Mr Chance. But you don't go round committing robbery and murder. And I don't read the magazines. *Ce n'est pas mon métier*, as they say.'

Hoskins drove back across Balance Street river bridge.

'Take that list, my son. Through the CRO computer. Every name and address. And bring the results straight back to me. If the line's busy, I'll wait until there's space for us. But I want an answer tonight.'

29

While he waited, a recorded voice spoke to Hoskins in tones of quiet promise. There was a vindictive logic in the careful phrases that suggested to him the kingdom of the truly mad. He watched the tape turn, trying to concentrate on the words while still thinking of the Squire and his punters.

'Our spotlight for the second night is on Brown the Builder. Brown, you may recall, has an easy way of getting tenants out of tower blocks bought from the council for demolition and redevelopment. The water and electricity fail. The lifts stop working. When the tenants come down the stairs, they find Brown's alsatians on guard in the lobby. Brown's solicitor tells each tenant, though never in front of witnesses, that failure to move will mean harassment. So let's try a little harassment –

on Brown and his lawyer. John Appleby Lyot-King practises in Great Western Chambers. Aged forty-five, he is short and bald. Lyot-King is married but also screws his typist, Miss Worth of Five, Paget Street, Orient. He lives at Thirty-eight, Godwin Road, near Connaught Park Lake. His telephone number is Canton 634818. His wife is Shirley Lyot-King, tall and dark-haired, late thirties. Their kids, Dominic and Angela, go to Connaught Drive School. We on the Hit-Back team will be looking for Lyot-King. So we hope will some of you. We think it would be nice if Lyot-King came home soon to a real fire. He drives a grey BMW, number LRK 175C. Shirley Lyot-King uses a metallic-gold Passat, number JCY 1498B . . .'

Hoskins got up and stared from his window at the darkening sky. Somewhere in the streets below was a lunatic with a transmitter. Several lunatics with transmitters, perhaps. And how many of Canton's street-fighters waiting to join in the fun?

'Presently,' the voice assured him, 'we shall be giving you names and addresses of social workers in the Ocean Beach area and of several customs officers at Canton airport. But first here are one or two things that those of you suffering harassment might like to do to Brown the Builder and the Lyon-Kings. Remember, you don't have to stand for garbage like them. No one can protect all of your oppressors from you all the time. So, don't stand for them. Hit back! The *Hit-Back Show* will tell you how . . .'

Hoskins turned off the recorder as Chance came in.

'Bloody rubbish, Jack,' he said. 'One nutter sitting in his car with a CB rig. We fall for this and we've got to provide a twenty-four-hour guard for any name that's mentioned. There could be a hundred. Two hundred. The entire division tied up for nothing. And meanwhile, our friend at the microphone does what he really means to do. Sees the police force chasing its own backside. Then he sets off with his mates and robs the city blind.'

'Maybe,' Chance said. 'Anyway, there's nothing from CRO on any of the Squire's punters.'

'Sod's law on the march again,' Hoskins said dismally, pushing the recorder aside.

Chance grinned.

'But I did run names through records here and Ocean Beach.'

'And?'

'Patrolman Scott, out at Ocean Beach.'

'On that list of punters?'

Chance shook his head.

'Mr Walker, the chap that brought the complaint against Scott for hitting him on the beach. The day of the Hangman's Blue Moon concert. The day Muriel Pruen was snuffed. He's down here. Name and address. Seems he never went any further with the complaint about Scott hitting him and busting the camera, not after shouting the odds at first. No proper witnesses. His brief must have warned him off.'

'Camera!' Hoskins said.

'Right, Sam. Snapshotting adolescent girls.'

'It's got to be a runner, Jack. Where's this merchant live?'

'Out Clearwater, supposing the address on the list is right.'

'That's it, Jack. I'm ballsed off with this "Hit-Back" rubbish. Let's go out there and shake him gently by the throat.'

'And Clitheroe?'

'So far as I'm concerned, my son, I looked for Clitheroe and couldn't find him. Let the bugger read about it in the papers.'

30

Like a child staring with wonder into the bright mirrored pattern of a new kaleidoscope, The Man gazed at his dream city. He felt calm and yet uplifted by the very sight and sound of it, as he always did when playing this tape. There was the avenue of the Unter den Linden, a rare piece of colour film showing the buses and trams. It was spliced with the marching battalions, eight or ten abreast, turning to the Roman salute of their leader. They were in the long-vanished Potsdamer Platz now, the massive fronts of hotels and department stores, the traffic tower at its centre. Another clip followed this. He watched the cafés of the Friedrichstrasse, the busy Anhalter station, the cabaret girls of the Kurfürstendamm in black silk and leather, a sense of power and the perverse.

Calm and yet exalted, The Man occasionally let himself dwell for an hour in that dream city, lost as Babylon or Thebes, visionary as the Lost Atlantis or the New Jerusalem. He did not do it too often, fearing that familiarity with the film would destroy his enjoyment. A good deal of his pleasure came from secret worship of the place, while all around him its memory was reviled and feared. And still more pleasure came from despising the revilers for their feebleness and stupidity.

Those who made the film had done so with condemnation and even scorn. The Man had gone through the tape carefully. Where the commentary had been, he had superimposed upon it the great hymn-like glory of the overture to Wagner's *Tannhäuser*. Elsewhere, his doomed heroes spoke for themselves. The banners with their emblem hung red and black and white over the vast arenas. Across the silent crowds, the hoarse rhetoric rang on modern concrete and steel. The street-fighter on his podium rose to glory. Then the loyal crowd rocked the stadium with a massed roar while they offered their new Caesar his crown. The Man felt his heart swell with pride as the engines of the planes overhead drowned even the mass chanting. Now they were in the fields of Pomerania. The tanks burst through frontier barriers and farmhouse walls, the sirens of the dive-bomber squadrons screamed and it seemed to him he was among them as they soared again to glory.

It was through the thump of the bombs that he heard another sound, no more than a disturbance on the periphery of his attention. The Man got up and went into the hall. Annie was standing out there, of course. She had opened the door to someone. A stranger whose neat lank hair was turning from fair to grey. A tall, carefully dressed figure. The face full and smooth but unlined. A pair of glasses that had a tint of blue. There was a second man behind him. Younger. Plump and florid with flattened black hair.

'Mr Walker?' the first stranger said. 'Detective Chief Inspector Hoskins, Canton CID. This is DS Chance. I wonder if we might come in and have a word?'

They were in already, of course. Across the step and standing in the hall. As if on the tape that still ran in the other room, The Man saw in his mind the spring sky above the doomed capital veiled by a dust of plaster from the ruined city shell. The siege was closer. Rockets from the invaders' batteries in the suburbs now landing at the heart of the city. The last two-seat fighter taking off down the long arterial avenue. Everywhere there were ruined walls and fire-blackened stone. But the locks on the bombproof vault of the mind had begun to close. The armoured steel doors of the bunker slammed into airtight seals. Deep in its heart, far from the sight of those who sought him, the hero was at his post. Leading the fight until the last bullet but one had been fired.

'Mr Walker?'

'You'd better come in, Mr Hoskins,' the woman's voice said. 'You can talk in here.'

There were two more men now. The one with the blue-tinted glasses was saying something about a search.

'It's probably nothing, Mr Walker. A matter of your sub-scription to a magazine. We've got to check with everyone on the list. Several hundred all told. A matter of routine.'

The Man saw that the second pair were looking about them. They must be wondering where to begin in their ransacking of the house. Annie stood there, as if none of it were her business. She made no protest. It had nothing to do with her. And yet it had everything to do with her. They were one another's business. A mutual creation.

'Mr Walker?'

The first one touched The Man's arm and he pulled away instinctively. They made no attempt to touch him again. Three of them stood there looking at him as if he were some kind of curiosity. The woman was beyond them, looking over their shoulders as if in the crowd at a zoo. For the first time, The Man felt how completely he detested womankind. With utter incongruity, the words of his philosopher and teacher began to run through his mind. He heard them even while he listened and answered mechanically the first words of the stranger in the blue-tinted glasses. 'For the woman, the man is a means, but what is the woman for the man? . . . The true man wants danger and play. So he wants woman as his most dangerous plaything . . . '

'It's just a matter of a magazine subscription that you made, Mr Walker.'

Two of them were talking to her now. He was back in the room with the first pair. The bright screen flickering in silence. The hope that it was about the policeman on the beach, the official complaint, had flickered and died at their first words. He sat and listened to the routine questions. Question and answer. Nothing that mattered. Ten minutes, The Man thought, certainly no longer. One of the others came in and said, 'We've done it, boss!' in a significant tone to their leader. The oldest of them got up and went out. There was whispering in the hall. A younger one in uniform came in to join the red-faced Sergeant. They both sat there, sometimes looking at him. No one spoke. No more questions.

The Man watched the silent images on the screen, clinging to his faith. The film had reached the part now where he had blotted out the sanctimonious voice of the commentary with the only accompaniment fit for such grand tragedy. *Götterdämmerung. The Twilight of the Gods.* At last the oldest of the policemen with the tinted glasses came back. He was carrying an ordinary photograph album. But it was not ordinary after all. If they had that, then they had gone straight to the cavity in the garage wall. The grey plastic of the waste-bin liner. And if they had gone straight there, it could not have been coincidence. Someone had led them. Someone who had found out despite all his care. Annie had led them. It could only be she. She had betrayed him. 'Let man fear woman when she hates,' his philosopher had taught him, 'for man is at the bottom of his soul only wicked, but woman is base.' The iron guard had relaxed its vigilance once, in a fearful miscalculation. But now he was alone and there would be no more betrayal.

He felt no further bitterness just then, not even surprise. There were always traitors at the end who made their peace with the foe, opening the gates softly from within. But all that was over now.

The policeman who was holding the album leant down to The Man as he sat in his chair. The voice was gentle.

But it was the quietness of the executioner who seeks not to make his own job more difficult by terrifying the culprit without need.

'I think we'd better go down to my office, Mr Walker,' Hoskins said calmly. 'We'll be able to talk in peace there. I dare say we can have this whole thing sorted out in no time at all.'

31

'Photographs,' Hoskins said quietly, 'that's what needs to be explained, Mr Walker. The rest I can understand. The photographs of her — and of some of these other young ladies. I'm afraid you're going to have to tell me about those.'

The prisoner shook his head slowly without taking his eyes off the Chief Inspector. He sat in clean white overalls, like a nuclear scientist or a space-walker without a helmet. His own clothes had been taken for forensic tests. In the stuffiness of the closed room late at night, a line of sweat-beads dotted his hairline. The repaired central heating of the headquarters building was surging out of control. In the blank-walled interview room the atmosphere was like midnight in Cairo or Tangier.

'I don't have to tell you anything,' The Man said. 'If you think I've committed a crime, you prove it. I'll have another of my cigarettes, if you don't mind.'

WPC Gillian Simmonds was taking shorthand notes at the far end of the table. A leather-cased recorder lay near her. She handed the cigarettes to Chance on one side of Hoskins, who in turn handed them to Walker. On the other side of Hoskins, Clitheroe said, 'As it stands, Mr Walker, you have nothing to lose by explaining those photographs. They could only have been taken by a man with an interest in the girl. A man who followed and intimidated her. A man who kept every newspaper cutting and recorded all the television coverage of the inquiry.'

'That's my business,' said Walker through the flare of a match. 'You think there's a crime in any of that, you prove it. I've got nothing else to say.'

Clitheroe sat back and Hoskins took over. Above the stained table, the fluorescent strip cast a bleak glare through a ceiling haze of cigarette smoke.

'It won't do, Mr Walker,' Hoskins said gently. 'What do you want us to think? You spend days out at Lantern Hill or Ocean Beach, not able to take your eyes off this girl. The photos show that you followed her up hill and down dale. Not just once, either. Some of these pictures were taken when there were no leaves on the trees. Back last January or February. Then there's this one in her bikini. Probably about May. And there's a few choice comments jotted on the backs of some of 'em. There's photographs of the place where we found her and some scribble about it that even you ought to be ashamed of.'

'It doesn't say I killed her,' said Walker simply. 'I just happened to see her. I'm allowed to think what I like about her. No law against that.'

Hoskins shook his head and glanced at his watch. It was almost half-past one in the morning. Beyond the metal slats of the blinds covering the window, a cold breeze from the anchorages stirred the trees in the Memorial Gardens. A large fly knocked and fussed round the white fitting of the fluorescent strip in the blue spirals of cigarette smoke. Hoskins studied his notes.

'I don't think you just happened to see her, did you, Mr Walker? What's written down here, in a code that would take a schoolboy five minutes to work out, is all about her. Name, age, place of birth, school, the lot. Have some reason for this, did you?'

Walker stared at him.

'Prove it,' he said. 'That's only the way you make it out. To suit yourself.'

'You work for an insurance company, Mr Walker,' Clitheroe said. 'At least you did until today. You know something about methods of investigation. So you know quite well it's not Mr Hoskins's way of looking at things. You collected information on a number of girls. Including Elaine Harris. And including

Rachel Lloyd. There's a shop assistant at the Royal Peninsular Emporium and a clerk in the Canton Deposit Bank. Photos of the first one. Press clippings and video tapes of everything to do with the two girls that were murdered.'

The bluebottle swooped, soared, and attacked the light-fitting again. Chance nudged Hoskins under the table at Clitheroe's ill-judged suggestion of Walker losing his job with the company in consequence of being questioned. Immobility sealed the culprit's features like the lowering of a portcullis.

'I like reading about crime,' Walker said. 'What's wrong with that?'

'Nothing wrong, Mr Walker,' Hoskins said sympathetically. 'Lots of people do. But that's not quite the whole truth, is it? You liked a certain sort of crime. Murders of young women mainly. Most of all Elaine Harris and Rachel Lloyd. A great album of press cuttings and reports, as well as your own personal interest in them. A guilty secret hidden in the garage cavity.'

'Not by me.'

Hoskins felt like a man stepping forward confidently and feeling infinite space beneath his foot. He drew back.

'Not by you? Never hid it away there, did you?'

'No,' said Walker. 'I never bothered. That stuff's been missing a while. She must have found it and put it there. How else do you suppose she could tell you it was there right away?'

Clitheroe came to life.

'And why would she do that, Mr Walker?'

'Ask her. Perhaps she wanted to hide it away from me.'

'Including the photographs, the negatives and the rest?'

The fly landed at the table's centre, nosing into the saucer of an empty cup. No one disturbed it. Walker looked at his hands.

'Never occurred to you, I suppose, that she might have been the one that kept those press-cuttings.'

'Your wife?' Clitheroe asked sharply. 'You want us to believe that your wife had a hand in this?'

But he had gone too far now. Walker looked at them.

'I don't care what you believe. So far as I'm concerned you can think anything you want. If I've committed a crime, you prove it.'

Hoskins intervened.

'Mr Walker, no one wants to make out a case against you for something you didn't do. But even you must see that your photographic hobby and your interest in these girls and young women doesn't look good. Does it, now? Be sensible. After all, you've got your alibi. The three days in December when Elaine Harris could have been murdered – Monday to Wednesday – you were at work all day. You went straight home from work each evening. Right? Monday evening and all night you were home with your wife as witness. Tuesday evening at a sales reception where twenty people saw you, then home again. Wednesday evening and night home with your wife and her sister as witnesses.'

'I told you that. So did she,' Walker said. 'So why am I being kept here?'

'Because,' said Hoskins, 'you want us to think she was somehow part of your hobby. She was the one that collected cuttings about the murders and hid them in the cavity. In that case, she won't be much use as an alibi, will she?'

There was a flicker of dismay in the dark eyes, extinguished at once by another glare.

'She must have put that stuff in the cavity, if I didn't. How do I know why?'

Sergeant Chance leant forward.

'Find her fingerprints on it, will we, Mr Walker? We know there's yours.'

'She might have worn gloves,' Walker said quickly, 'for all I know.'

Hoskins sounded disappointed in the suspect.

'You tell me, Mr Walker. Why on earth should your wife have worn gloves, if she was just hiding the album and the other things away from you? Why would she wear them, if she never thought anyone would look for her finger-prints?'

'If she was trying to set me up,' he said, impatient of their stupidity.

'But, Mr Walker,' said Hoskins quietly, 'she's given you your alibi. How's that going to set you up?'

Walker looked away from them, staring at the window-slats. He was pale and hot from the exhaustion of the interrogation.

Presently he looked back at the three men sitting on the other side of the table.

'You all think you're so clever,' he said with a casual sneer. 'Don't you?'

'We're trying to help you, Mr Walker,' Clitheroe said, 'so far as we can.'

'I don't need your help. Either charge me or let me go. I'm not answering any more questions.'

Clitheroe was unflurried.

'I'm afraid the law has changed since that formula applied, Mr Walker. We can hold you without charge or formal arrest for another day or so. If we proceed beyond that, you'll be brought before a magistrate for a remand.'

'I've answered all the questions I'm going to.'

'You want a solicitor?'

'No,' said Walker indifferently, 'I won't need one. I'm not saying any more. I've done nothing. You can't arrest me for taking photographs or keeping press cuttings. You can't arrest me for what I think of people. Doesn't matter if I think she was rubbish or not. I've proved I couldn't have killed her. That's it. Keep me here as long as you like, you won't get any more.'

'That's silly,' Hoskins said. 'If you were to co-operate, Mr Walker, you could be home for breakfast.'

It failed, as he thought it would. Walker turned in his chair, sideways on to them. He stared at the window-slats.

'I don't want a solicitor,' he said. 'What I want is a doctor. I've been questioned until I can't think straight. Done to confuse me. I want him to see that I get proper rest. And I want to complain to him about it.'

Clitheroe stood up. Hoskins and Chance pushed back their chairs.

'Very well, Mr Walker,' Clitheroe said. 'I'll have the duty police surgeon called. And we'll talk again tomorrow.'

Walker, with his back to them, made no attempt to respond to this.

They waited until the Custody Officer had taken the prisoner to the cells. Then the three interrogators withdrew to Hoskins's room. Hoskins plugged in the electric coffee-pot, his Christmas present from Lesley. The phone rang.

'Sam? Gerald Foster, *Western World* night-desk. Man being held for questioning in the Elaine Harris case. Any more news?'

'Not now, Gerald. We're having a meeting in here.'

'Oh,' Foster said, 'all right. Only I rang a few times, Sam. And some bugger's feeding Coastal News like a baby from a bottle. I don't want to end up reporting their morning newscast rather than the real thing.'

'I'll do what I can later,' Hoskins said and put the phone down.

Clitheroe frowned.

'If our friend Walker didn't kill her, he's giving a bloody good imitation.'

'If it is him,' Hoskins said, 'we could be a bit unlucky. Unless we get more than press-cuttings and photographs of her, flavoured with spicy comments of his own, he'll be home in time for tea.'

Clitheroe sat down and shook his head.

'If he did it, Sam, we'll have him now. Anything more on the search, Jack?'

'Only more of the same, sir,' Chance said. 'Magazines. Heavy stuff but not illegal. And stuff about the Nazis. Oh, yes, and a book of witty comments by some bloke.'

He handed his list to Clitheroe.

'Nietzsche,' Clitheroe said. 'Not exactly complimentary to the fair sex. What we may have here is our local sado-fascist. One of them, anyway. Does that tally with the magazines and the other stuff he had tucked away?'

'Pretty well, sir,' Chance said. 'Fairly heavy on that, it was.'

'But not illegal,' Hoskins suggested. 'Not enough for the prosecution service to find a prima facie case.'

The scorn was visible in Clitheroe's face.

'Walker's mind is a mess, Sam. Any case of this kind now has to have the senior investigating officer's opinion as to the suspect's likely fate in court. Don't waste public money putting a half-smart lawyer up against a bright defendant with a good story. The powers that be want a result, not a fiasco. Our Mr Walker thinks he's one of the master-race. I reckon he'd be easy meat.'

'And you think on the evidence of these photos and press cuttings and the rest that we ought to wheel him forward?' Hoskins asked sceptically.

Clitheroe shook his head.

'Not my decision, Sam. The prosecution service rules are nice and simple. More than fifty-fifty chance of a conviction, go ahead. Less than that, forget it. Just now, with the public anxiety there is to find the man, we might just tip the scales with a jury. But I can't say I'd like to underwrite it.'

Beyond the window Hoskins could see the trees standing black against a flush of starlight. The first pink blossom of late winter always appeared in the Memorial Gardens, sheltered from the north and east.

Clitheroe stood up and stretched.

'There's enough to hold him on suspicion, Sam. We've got a man here with a violent obsession about the murdered girl. An obsession that dates back long before she was killed. Some of the things he suggests in his little book would have done for her anyway. He wanted to murder her, wouldn't you say?'

'He might want to rob the Bank of England,' Hoskins said. 'I'd still want something that Forensic could get hold of.'

'So would I, Sam. Your friend Charlie Blades and his crew are going through that house with a fine comb. All I'm saying is that we've got enough to keep this merchant under lock and key until Blades and his people do their stuff.'

'Wouldn't argue with that,' Hoskins said.

Clitheroe looked at his watch.

'I'd like everyone to get some sleep for the next few hours. I'll want to start again with Walker at ten o'clock. Before he changes his mind and decides to have a brief after all.'

The other two went out. Hoskins saw that someone had put an audio cassette on his desk, next to the recorder. He pushed it into the slot, pressed the button and listened.

' . . . living in Clive Street,' a voice said, 'were informed that the child would be taken into care by the social services, following the case-worker's report. The parents were told that they had no right of appeal. Their request for an independent examination was refused. Mrs Downey, expecting another child, afterwards attempted suicide. The case-worker had arranged to take the child from her as soon as it was born. The case-worker's name is John Kairn Lewis of Eighteen, St Stephen's Road, Harbour Bar. He is twenty-eight years old, married with two children. His telephone number is Canton 668844. His car registration on a pale blue Saab is LNO 937V. Slim-built, he has dark hair, sharp features and rabbit teeth. Over the past year John Kairn Lewis has sexually molested two children in council care, under pretext of assisting in a physical examination. Hit-Back will be going looking for him. So, we hope, will you. We might even consider taking his children into our care . . . '

Hoskins turned off the recorder. He drew the other chair closer, put his feet on it, settled back and closed his eyes. Sleep was impossible, of course. On the other hand, there was something to be gained from putting the feet up and closing the eyes. He treated himself to a re-run of Lesley in her black nightwear and smiled contentedly. This summer was definitely going to be different. He was really going to follow up the results so far. If they could survive a holiday and Christmas together, anything was possible. Lantern Hill was going to see a lot of him. No two ways about that.

In some surprise, he woke with the room full of daylight and the phone ringing.

'Sam? Gerald Foster. Look, have you seen the early CN newscast? No? Well, someone's spilt everything to the buggers. Man in custody. House in Clearwater searched. Items taken away. Man being questioned by officers from the Elaine Harris, Rachel Lloyd and Alison Shaw cases. It's not on, Sam. It's really not on.'

'That's rubbish,' Hoskins said. 'There's only three of us here. Jack Chance and I aren't on any of those inquiries. Just Clitheroe.'

'I think the *Western World* could have had a bone tossed its way, Sam.'

'He's forty-one years old and he works for insurance, Gerald. That any help? He's a keen amateur photographer. Admirer of Uncle Adolf and dancing in leather knickers. He keeps all your crime reports about sex-murders. The house is in Ashley Drive. And I never said any of this. Right?'

He put the phone down. It rang again.

'Sam? Charlie Blades. Haven't been to bed tonight. Haven't done much with the exhibits either. But there's a pair of shoes with commando soles. Earth well trodden in the grooves. There's a layer that's got a definite look of the levels and the East Sluice about it. Salt content high and grass seeds dormant. I'd say we'll get a perfect match on the electron-beam. He was definitely on foot somewhere round where you found her.'

'We know he was round there, Charlie. Snapshots in his album.'

'On foot, Sam. Not recently. There's other layers of earth – clay mostly – on top. This must be a few months back. Might even date it from the state of development of the grass. Round about December. I'm looking again at the soil sample from where she was found. Looks like a result on his footwear.'

'That's nice, Charlie. Anything on his clothes?'

'Not yet, Sam. We'll get it, if there is. Have to bear in mind that he might have ditched what he was wearing or burnt it. Solid-fuel boiler. We're going through the residue. Got an alibi, hadn't he?'

'Not if there's bits of her in his clothes, Charlie. Not so much an alibi. More a matter of perjury for his missus, if she doesn't watch her step.'

'That's nice,' Blades said. 'I'm going home for a sleep and a shave, Sam. I'll keep you posted.'

'Thanks, Charlie. I'd say you've earned another read from the book at bedtime.'

Blades chuckled and put down the phone.

32

Hoskins turned his key and opened the door of the grey metal locker. He took out his razor, pushed through to the communal row of washbasins, and plugged it in. His face in the mirror looked to him surprisingly well-rested. Beyond the buzzing of the blades, he noticed a face reflected behind his own.

'A word, Sam,' Ripley said, as Hoskins turned off the switch. 'Clitheroe's gone to see the Harris family and a couple of the kids at Shackleton School. Wants to put Mr Walker on an ID parade.'

Hoskins turned round.

'That should keep everyone quiet for a day or two, Max.'

Ripley glanced at the row of stalls and made sure there were no feet under the closed doors.

'Not quite, Sam. Walker has changed his tune this morning. Wants a brief. Not his own. Not the family lawyer. A criminal lawyer. He's prepared to face it out over the photographs and press cuttings. No law broken. Entitled to be interested in the Nazis and sex crimes if he wants to be. Most people are, he says. No case to answer. He's right, of course. This one wouldn't get to court on what we've got so far. Charge him or release him, he says.'

'Tell him to pick Jack Cam as his brief,' Hoskins said facetiously. 'It's about all we need.'

'That's not the issue, Sam. If he keeps this up, you and Clitheroe could find yourselves lumbered.'

Hoskins grunted and folded the razor away.

'Nothing else in his house that the rummage-crew found?'

The Ripper shook his head.

'They've been taking it apart, Sam. No sign of anything. Crime is his hobby, he says. He likes reading about it and going to places where it happened. To judge by the family cars and the sightseers, so does half Canton.'

'But they don't take photographs of a girl before she's murdered,' Hoskins said sceptically. 'That's Walker's speciality.'

Ripley shook his head. The tight curls looked more grey in the harsh washroom light, the face yellow and taut.

'He took hundreds of photos, Sam. Scores of girls among them. One happened to get murdered. A hundred others didn't. That's his answer.'

'You spoke to him this morning?'

'I had to, Sam. With Clitheroe being off the premises, Walker's welfare is down to me. But if you and Clitheroe can't come up with something clever very quickly, then he could be home on police bail within twenty-four hours. And, what's more, we could have an injunction slapped on us for the return of his property. He's also had a complaint in against the police, don't forget. His face punched by that young fool Scott on the sands last summer. Camera smashed. We don't want this to sound as if we're getting our own back on him by hanging a murder round his neck.'

Hoskins rinsed his hands.

'Depends on his brief, Max.'

'He's talking about Claude Roberts, Sam. With him around, you'd better kick your hat well clear before stooping down to pick it up. Suffers from an itchy boot, does Claude Roberts, where the police are concerned.'

Hoskins felt his face for stubble.

'I've known Claude Roberts professionally for twenty years, Max. He's not a bad old stick. At least you can do business with him. Might even make Mr Walker see a bit of sense.'

It was just after eleven when Claude Roberts was shown into Ripley's office, where Clitheroe, Hoskins and the Ripper himself were waiting. Tall, spruce and white-haired, he exuded an air of the senior squash court and the Turkish baths on Victoria Quay. His thin face was pink from the cut-throat razor and his hair springy from a stiff-bristled brush.

'Good morning, gentlemen. Mr Ripley. Mr Hoskins. Any progress on my client's release?'

Clitheroe almost sniggered at the bluff.

'I think you know that's unrealistic, Mr Roberts. Your client has yet to give a satisfactory account of himself.'

Claude Roberts looked surprised and sat down.

'My client won't be adding a word to anything he's said, Mr Clitheroe. He won't be making or signing statements either. In fact he won't be talking to you at all. My instructions, those are. I'd like his lunch brought in from outside today. Proper food. And after that I want him released. This afternoon. On police bail, if necessary.'

'You know that's impossible, Mr Roberts,' Clitheroe said quietly.

Claude Roberts crossed his slimly tailored legs, took out a silver case and chose a cigarette.

'Impossible?' he asked derisively. 'Unrealistic? Mr Walker looks like a hardened criminal to you, does he? Escape artist?

Master of a thousand disguises? I want him out on police bail, subject to agreed conditions.'

Clitheroe shook his head. The enamelled lighter flared as Roberts lit his cigarette.

'Right then, gentlemen. Under the Police and Criminal Evidence Act you have till three o'clock tomorrow morning to bring Mr Walker before a magistrate. By then your evidence against him had better be stronger than the rubbish so far produced. I've been in touch with Rossiter Road. Barristers' chambers. You can look forward to the pleasure of Toby Raven as Mr Walker's counsel.'

'The items found constitute prima facie evidence!' said Clitheroe hotly.

Claude Roberts leant back, but he blew his smoke in Clitheroe's direction.

'Those items, Mr Clitheroe, constitute prima facie tosh. And you know it. Or if you don't know it, someone should have you off this inquiry. A first-year law student could put this case of yours through the mincer. You don't really think that Josh Black and the prosecution service are going to go to court with a stone-cold loser. Do you? It's their reputations on the line, Mr Clitheroe. Not yours.'

It seemed to Hoskins that the room had got warmer and much smaller with the four men in there.

'If you will excuse me,' Clitheroe said breathlessly, 'I have more pressing business than to exchange insults with Mr Roberts.'

'Your privilege, Mr Clitheroe,' said Claude Roberts coolly. 'If we don't talk here, we'll be talking in court. And if you think I'm discourteous, wait till Toby Raven starts. A murder charge is first division stuff, Mr Clitheroe. If that's too rough for you, now's the time to stop.'

Clitheroe was half out of his chair when Ripley intervened, raising a hand to restore order.

'You're suggesting, Mr Roberts, that if a compromise could be reached on the matter of police bail, when the first stage of the inquiry is over, we might let that stand when we come before the magistrates?'

Claude Roberts gave a weary smile and shook his head at their obtuseness.

'What I'm saying, Mr Ripley, is that I won't have my client languishing in a cell because "A" Division can't get its act together. If you spin it out till tomorrow morning, you'll have had thirty-six hours to ransack the house. Thirty-six hours to examine clothing and other items. If my client is still detained then, we shall seek his liberty.'

'For God's sake!' Clitheroe snapped. 'This is a murder inquiry.'

Claude Roberts raised his eyebrows.

'A public relations exercise, yes. Reassuring the ratepayers that the force is still alive and well. But a murder inquiry? You have not a single item of conclusive evidence to show that Mr Walker had anything to do with the young lady's death. With any young lady's death. I'll deal with you over police bail. I won't deal after that.'

The assured insolence of his manner silenced even Clitheroe. Ripley seemed to be hauling up a compromise from somewhere under his desk. His face looked suddenly haggard.

'If we complete the first stage of the inquiry before tonight and if no charge is brought against Mr Walker, you suggest that we might release him on police bail. On stringent conditions. If that were done, you would not oppose such an arrangement again when we came before the magistrates?'

'That's it,' Roberts said brightly. 'In a nutshell. If we can't agree on that, then you know what to expect. You'll have had your thirty-six hours. We'll want him out unconditionally.'

He stood up, smiled at them all, and withdrew. Presently Hoskins went out, leaving Ripley and Clitheroe to discuss terms. Claude Roberts was coming back down the corridor after a visit to the Custody Officer.

'Keeping you busy, Sam?'

'Just coasting along, Claude. I thought you were going for Playmate of the Month award back in there.'

Roberts chuckled.

'Exercise, Sam. Bit of a work-out. Keeps the muscle-tone supple. By the way, I didn't know old Ripley was coming up for his gold watch. He was telling me on the way in. Him and ACC Crime together. Won't seem the same.'

They turned towards the lift.

'Comes to us all, Claude.'

'Not to me,' said Roberts quietly. 'I want to pop off in mid-stream. Right in front of the stipendiary on a bright summer morning. The only way to go.'

'Dare say you're right, Claude.'

'You bet I am, Sam. Drive carefully.'

The lift doors closed and Claude Roberts was borne to the ground floor. Hoskins looked round and then took the stairs towards the car park. Just for a few hours he fancied a little retirement of his own.

It lasted until he reached the lobby. Sergeant Lucas on the desk waved him over.

'Sam! Any chance of Mr Ripley or Mr Clitheroe being free? Official line is that they're in conference.'

'And likely to be, Stan. Why? Who wants them?'

There was no reply. The movement of Lucas's eyes made Hoskins aware that someone was standing behind him. He turned round and saw Mrs Walker.

'Lady wanted to ask about her husband,' Lucas explained.

Mrs Walker was grey and untidy at forty. Her hair looked uncombed and she was pale from lack of sleep. Hoskins could see that she had been crying.

'You were one of them,' she said softly and urgingly. 'You tell me if it's true. He's going to be let out on bail, isn't he? Mr Roberts said so.'

'I don't know, Mrs Walker,' Hoskins said gently. 'Mr Roberts will probably suggest it. The decision won't be mine. It's up to the magistrates.'

She began to cry and he led her aside, like one mourner consoling another.

'Little reception room's empty, Sam,' Lucas called after him.

Hoskins led her in there. They sat down on two chairs, side by side, like patients in a surgery waiting-room. There were several police recruiting posters round the walls and a table with copies of *Police Review* for the past six months.

'Mrs Walker,' he said quietly, 'it's not a decision for anyone in this building. An application for bail can be made to the magistrates by your husband's lawyer. The police may oppose it or they may not. It depends how things stand at the time. But the magistrates make the final decision. Not us.'

She looked up at him quickly.

'If he was on bail, he'd come home?'

'Yes, Mrs Walker. His permanent address. That would probably be a condition. Isn't that what you want?'

She shook her head.

'But why not?' he asked.

She lowered her face into her hands. There was a pause and then a sob.

'I couldn't,' she said indistinctly. 'The same house as him . . . the same bed.'

'He's innocent until someone proves him guilty,' Hoskins said in the same quiet voice. 'In any case, there's nothing to stop you staying with a relative or a friend if you prefer.'

She blinked and stared at him.

'Don't you see?' she whispered. 'Don't you understand? He killed her! I've lived with it for months! I've tried to pretend I was wrong about it. But I'm not. I haven't slept all night. I don't think I'll ever sleep again. Not until this is over. You only *think* he killed that girl. But I *know* he did. And I can't go on any longer. I can't lie for him any more.'

She hid her face again in a splutter of sobs. Hoskins touched her shoulder in an instinctive gesture of sympathy. She shook herself away.

'Don't say anything else unless you mean to, Mrs Walker. And remember that no wife can be made to give evidence against her husband.'

She looked at him again.

'He's not my husband. Not any more. Not after that. The man I married died the same time as that girl. You don't understand, do you? I've lived with this for months. Pretending, shielding. When they came to all the houses, I said I was with him that first night of the three. I wasn't. I was with my sister all evening. I thought he must have been at home on his own. He used to have a pair of these dark blue trousers and he had a sort of donkey-jacket for lying under the car. I saw them next day, clearing out the wardrobe. They were filthy, crumpled up at the back. Of course, no one knew then that the girl was dead. I haven't seen them since. He burnt them in the stove, I think.'

'But all that,' said Hoskins gently, 'isn't evidence of murder.'

219

Mrs Walker shook her head to silence him.

'Next morning, Tuesday, they come for the bin. He went down early to put it out in the back lane. I'd just dressed. I was in the bedroom at the back, looking down. He just stood there. I couldn't understand why he didn't take the bin out. Just stood with it as if he wouldn't trust leaving it outside. Then the cart came. The one that has a destructor in the back. He waited until it was almost there. Then I saw him take something from under his coat and push it down into the bin. It was a tie. Not one of his. Striped like a school tie. And there was a skirt. A child's skirt, it was. Grey with pleats. Before I could do anything else, he'd carried the bin out. Handed it to the dustmen. And they tipped it into the back of the destructor in the van. Everything burnt and ground to powder. And that was the end of that.'

Hoskins let her compose herself.

'You never told anyone, Mrs Walker? You never confronted him with any of this?'

She shook her head again.

'At first I didn't realise. Then I supposed the skirt and tie must be hers. Only two items missing, they said on the television. I didn't know what to do. Suppose I went to the police and they couldn't prove anything else against him. If he killed her, he might do the same to me. In any case, I still hoped it might not be him. I thought perhaps he'd bought the skirt and tie for some funny business of his own. You read of men doing funny things nowadays. I didn't know. Then one day he must have taken his photographs and things out of the hiding-place in the garage wall. He went out into the garden for something. I came in from the house and I was there a couple of minutes. I saw what those things were. He never knew I'd seen them. I ran back into the utility room. But I watched through the crack in the door. And I saw where he put them back. When he was out and I was alone in the house, I went and took them out and looked at them properly. She was wearing the same skirt and tie in some of those photographs that I'd seen him put in the bin that next morning. I felt so sick because I knew the truth. I've felt ill with it ever since. To be able to tell someone! You can't know what a relief it is!'

Hoskins stood up.

'Before we go on, Mrs Walker, I'd suggest you see your solicitor. It's no crime to lie to the police. But you've been less than truthful, haven't you?'

'Because I was frightened!' she wailed. 'Suppose I'd told you and he'd still been set free! He killed her for much less, the poor child!'

Hoskins sat down again, like a teacher coaching a fretful infant.

'Will you tell Mr Clitheroe what you've just told me?'

She nodded without speaking.

'Will you swear to it in court? To being with your sister and seeing the girl's clothes?'

'I don't want to,' she said quietly, 'but I suppose I must. Mustn't I?'

Hoskins left her for a moment. He went across the lobby to Sergeant Lucas.

'Mr Ripley and Mr Clitheroe. To be disturbed, if necessary. Mrs Walker would like a word with them. And you might send a signal to the custody officer. Anything he's heard about bail for Mr Walker is to be scrubbed until further notice. And that's priority.'

'Right,' said Lucas, his tone impressed. 'Right, then. Sounds like someone's got the show on the road at last.'

That night's appearance by Clitheroe on Coastal Network was cancelled. Gerald Foster had the news first this time. Not that it did him much good. Only on the following morning did the *Western World* hit the streets and doormats of Canton with its banner headline. 'MAN CHARGED IN ELAINE HARRIS MURDER: 3 A.M. COURT APPEARANCE'.

Dog-tired, Hoskins drove back to Lamb's Chambers. Catnaps and dozes had left him as disorientated as a jet-lagged traveller. All he wanted to do was to sleep for a week. He lay down on the bed. An hour and a half later he was still awake. The restlessness and foreboding were not precisely linked to any cause. Or, rather, it was a cause just beyond his reach. It lurked and shimmered and hovered on the rim of perception. It was like the nag or the twitch of a nerve that seemed everywhere and nowhere at once. But the juggernaut was on its way. The press and the stern-faced newscasters had the murdering pervert where they wanted him. The magistrates' hearings of the case were reported alongside national alarm about reported rapes and estimated child abuse. In Ocean Beach and Lantern Hill, parents had begun to form playground patrols, guarding the young against the covetous eyes and sinister propositions of strangers. Things, it was suggested, were going to be different in future.

33

The Man felt better now. Much better. He closed his eyes upon the blank, harshly lit walls and withdrew deep into the safety of the redoubt. They were talking to him but they did not sound as if they expected a reply. In any case, the lawyer had told him to ignore their questions. Their words fell like distant artillery fire, inaccurate and harmless above the bomb proof vault.

He was stronger now. The last possible betrayal had occurred. She had betrayed him, as she thought. The truth was that she had conferred upon him a strength that almost frightened him at first by its intensity. It was as if the genius and power of Napoleon or Caesar or one of his own heroes had been conferred upon him by the fire of the gods. His resolve was intact and indivisible. Now there was utter unity, loyalty, purpose. That was something his enemies could not even understand, let alone defeat.

Their mild, hesitant questions were about clothes and journeys. He scorned them in silence without even opening his eyes. He was invincible. All the stronger because they were on his territory, where he knew better than they how to fight. In the west the newsreel armies were massing. Flat-cars and wagons rumbled to railheads in frontier forests with their burdens of armour. Staff officers conferred in manor-houses beyond the range of forward guns. The warlord was at his post. The iron guard flanked its leader. Hard and indivisible. Nothing would defeat him now.

Strategy. The chequered board. Logic and situation. Precise moves. The rules in black and white. He had only to maintain the line and he would win. There could be no other outcome. They would fling themselves against the ramparts and fall back, shaken and scattered. It was as easy as that, once the traitors had been weeded out.

They were talking about the girl again. The Man cursed her to himself for the trouble she had caused. He felt a sudden surge of resentment against her and sensed his mouth tightening in a derisive line. In the secret depths of the skull's armoured vault, The Man rejoiced that she was dead. It was better than she deserved.

'What you don't want, Mr Walker,' one of them was saying quietly, 'is to be found unfit to plead. You don't want to be locked up somewhere as a madman for the rest of your life. Especially if you could show us that you were innocent after all. We only want the truth. That's all.'

The Man opened his eyes a little and saw a watery image of their three earnest faces. He felt an impulse of laughter, that they should talk about him as if he might be mad. His intelligence would match the three of them put together and still have ample left over. It was preposterous to hear them talk and yet it was also very funny. The impulse to laugh grew stronger, like a pain that had to be relieved. It stuttered against his teeth and then burst out. He heard himself laughing, behind the apricot light of his closed eyelids. One of the men spoke his name, as if alarmed by a shrill edge to such mirth. But The Man himself heard nothing of that kind.

He laughed until the moisture gathered under his eyelids and he wiped it away on the back of his hand. Like indigestion, the spasm dwindled and ceased. He sat with his eyes closed. He was prepared now. He was invincible. But in the interim, he returned to Elaine Harris, that other figure of his personal history. The warlord needed a little relaxation from his heavy responsibility. For a little while he would enjoy the luxury of vindictive rage against her for what she had done to him by her death. Suppose she was produced before him now. How would he settle accounts with her? The Man smiled and drifted contentedly back into his own thoughts.

4

SPRING

4

SPRING

34

'GIRL'S SKIRT BURNT IN DUST-CART; WIFE SOBS IN WITNESS-BOX'. Hoskins folded the *Western World* under his arm and walked down from the car park towards Bay Drive. The sea glittered, calm and cold. Off the dead and deserted Ocean Park funfair, the heartbeat of a coaster's engines throbbed, faded and then throbbed again. The sunlight was deceptive enough to have brought the first day-trippers of the year. But the air was cold as March could be and the breeze had an edge of ice. The couples sat in their cars along the length of the Cakewalk curb, the windows wound up, drinking coffee out of flasks with the morose look of the cheated.

Hoskins stood by the pier and stared out across the tide towards Sandbar. As a child, he had been assured that one could stand at a certain angle here and know that the next landfall was Bermuda or the Bahamas. Buttoning his coat, he could believe it. The sunlight of the day, the blue ocean sky, promised him that someone somewhere – on another continent – was enjoying the first blossom and fragrance of spring. Not in Ocean Beach, but somewhere else. And that meant that it would come to Ocean Beach, sooner or later.

Walker could hardly complain of justice delayed, Hoskins thought. They had trundled him to the Crown Court in the shortest possible time. Not that business was ever slack in the Canton division of the prosecution service. Most of its lawyers complained at the groaning burden of work. But in Walker's case, they sensed the chance of a neat presentation and a quick result. And that, Hoskins had no doubt, would be feathers in hats and a drink on the house. All was not well with the service in the Canton area just then. Too many of nature's office boys with bright new law degrees had been shafted publicly by the street-learnt expertise of Jack Cam, Claude Roberts and other expensively suited court-artists of the old school.

He turned away from the pier-approach. Posters for the Pavilion pantomime were torn and weather-stained by the

gales of February. Felt-tipped pens had added sexual protu-
berances to Sharon Rees and Wadman. Their performance
on the fairyland posters would have made the Squire and his
clients blush.

Hoskins followed the Cakewalk towards the neon sign of
Nono's, its restaurant front decorated in the Italian national
colours of red, green and white. Lesley was coming by metro-
rail from a yoga class in Canton. Hoskins, on his rest day, had
paid a call on Charlie Blades. Blades was off sick. Sick of the
Elaine Harris case, Hoskins guessed. The agony of Mrs Walker
on the previous day was headline news. Hoskins had given his
own evidence two days earlier.

In a single statement to the police, read out in court,
Walker stuck to his story of being at home on the Monday
evening, the first of the days on which it was forensically
possible that Elaine Harris had been killed. He denied all
knowledge of the skirt and tie. So far as he knew, his
donkey-jacket and blue trousers were still around. If not,
he could not account for their disappearance. He was just
an ordinary citizen with a legitimate interest in tales of sex
murder as the press reported them. He liked taking photographs. In particular, he liked taking photographs of girls.
So did other men. Girls in school uniforms. In swimming
costumes. In shrink-fit jeans and tee-shirts. Never naked. As
for the broken alibi, his wife was a liar. Her sister was a liar.
He could not explain their motives. But he was innocent.

The Elaine Harris murder trial was one of the few cases
Hoskins had attended in which he felt the verdict might go
either way. But Walker faced one powerful disadvantage.
He was the only witness for his own innocence. Under
other circumstances that might not have mattered. But the
solution of the Elaine Harris murder might close the files
on Rachel Lloyd and all the others. Someone had murdered
them. There was evidence against Walker. As the newspapers
and television highlighted national alarm at such crimes, their
readers and viewers demanded results. Walker was a potential
result. Someone had murdered Elaine Harris. If that person
was not Walker, who else was it? He was far and away the
most likely candidate. To many Cantonians, he was better
than no one at all.

Lesley was at Nono's before him. Hoskins slid into the other side of the booth. The Cakewalk looked summer-warm again through plate glass. Their hands met under the table. It was their first public appearance together. A weekday lunch at Nono's, they had agreed, was probably safe.

'Sorry,' he said. 'I went to see Charlie Blades at Area Forensic. Just a nod and a smile for helping out. He wasn't there. Just as well or I might have been phoning you from a boozer.'

Her fingers twined in his under the cloth.

'I thought you might have to go back to the trial.'

Hoskins grinned and took a menu from the waiter.

'I've had my star billing. Day before yesterday. Now it's all down to Walker and the closing speeches. I'm clear until tomorrow night.'

Her knee, under the long skirt she wore, touched his. She brushed her fringe straight with her free hand.

'What happens tomorrow night?'

'The team gets together. If it's an acquittal, we scratch our heads and decide what to do next. If he goes down, then we have a raving booze-up for the lads. Not your scene at all. Clitheroe cross-eyed, glass in one hand, dancing on the table with his trousers down round his ankles. Recitals of *Eskimo Nell*.'

'Really?'

Hoskins shook his head.

'No,' he said thoughtfully. 'I shouldn't think Clitheroe's trousers have budged since the day he was born. Probably came into the world wearing them. More likely to be a handshake and a small glass of dry sherry all round.'

'I'd like that now.' Lesley tried to get her knee between his legs. 'A dry sherry.'

'Right. And, by the way, this table-cloth might not be quite as long as you were thinking.'

Lesley sighed and jigged the knee impatiently.

'If anyone had ever told me I'd end up doing this to a policeman . . . '

'I told you,' Hoskins said with facetious long-suffering. 'We survived a holiday and a Christmas. There's nothing worse than those two. The rest is plain sailing.'

Lesley looked at him expressionlessly.

'We might try a little sail this afternoon.'

Hoskins stared at the menu.

'In that case,' he said, 'stay off the pasta.'

When the meal was over, he went to collect their coats.

'You had the *Canton Globe* this afternoon, Freddie?'

'Just now, Mr Hoskins.'

'Give us a look at page one.'

The type was thicker than the *Western World* but the news not unexpected. 'ELAINE MURDER: ACCUSED TO STAY SILENT'. 'Today's hearing of the Elaine Harris murder trial began with a surprise move by Mr Toby Raven QC for the defence. Opening his case, Mr Raven revealed that the accused man would not be going into the witness-box. Addressing the jurors, Mr Raven insisted that there was no case for his client to answer in this way. It is not clear whether Mr Walker will make an unsworn statement to the court. If he does so, he cannot be cross-examined on it . . . '

Hoskins held Lesley's coat for her.

'Toby Raven's been shot in the back,' he said cheerfully. 'They can't put old Walker into the box.'

'Oh?' She turned almost into his arms.

'He's been half-way round the twist all the time. Perhaps being in court finished him off. Looks as if Toby Raven's scared to let the other side get at his client. I'd hate to think of Walker being cross-examined by Russell Proctor. Right bit of blood-sport that'd be.'

'So what can they do?'

Hoskins opened the door, waved to Freddie, and shepherded Lesley out into the cold seaside afternoon.

'He'll just say there's no evidence against Walker. Photos and press cuttings aren't evidence. Mrs Walker's sister could back her up about not being home that Monday. But that means Mrs Walker lied to begin with. There's no corroboration about having mud on his clothes or throwing that skirt and tie in the bin. He could make an unsworn statement from the dock. Can't be cross-examined on it but it wouldn't do him much good. Looks as if he's hiding something. Or his brief could just use the statement Walker made to the police. Raven sat next to him while he did it. Almost wrote it for him. But a police statement sounds better to a jury.'

She shivered in the sudden cold and turned to him.

'So did he do it?'

Hoskins smiled and urged her on towards the car.

'I'm glad I don't have to say. With hindsight, Raven might have done better saying Walker was unfit to plead. That means they'd lock him up as a loony, if the submission was accepted. Too late for that now.'

'And what if he was innocent?'

'Bad luck,' Hoskins said. 'That's why Raven didn't do it, I suppose. Must have thought at first that he could risk Walker in the witness-box. Now he realises he can't. But he's stuck with the case as it is. If he suddenly turned round now and said Walker was a loony after all, he'd have trouble with the prosecution. The defence has to enter a plea like that before the case goes to court. Disclosure of documents it's called. Something of that sort. Producing evidence out of a hat only happens in films. Judges don't allow it.'

Lesley wriggled her arm through his.

'It makes me feel sorry for him,' she said. 'I never thought I would.'

'Not even if he was innocent?'

'No,' she said, 'not even then. That business of keeping newspaper stories about girls that were murdered! And following girls and taking pictures of them! That gives me the creeps.'

'I might give you the creeps as well,' Hoskins said cheerfully, 'unless I can get some warmth back into my hands before we stop off in Lantern Hill.'

He spent the night with her and most of the following morning.

'Rest day,' he said as they parted at the door. 'I'll go home and build my strength up again.'

Lamb's Chambers seemed cold as he opened the door. He went to turn up the heating. Whatever might be happening in Bermuda or the Bahamas, winter was holding its own down St Vincent Street. He was opening the morning's post when the phone rang.

'Sam?' It was Ripley.

'Yes, Max. I've just got in from a family visit.'

'Good,' said Ripley, as if he genuinely approved. 'You're coming in this evening? I know it's your rest day but I thought we could count on you.'

'Will they finish by tonight?'

'They finished about twenty minutes ago, Sam. We've got him. Guilty. Jury unanimous, surprisingly. Sentence postponed for psychiatric reports.'

'Just like that, Max?'

'No, Sam, not just like that. Poor old Toby Raven's case came apart in his hands. Walker threw some sort of fit and refused to go into the box. Swore that he never killed her but glad someone had done it. Said he wouldn't be put on show like a caged animal. Started screaming about no case to answer. Prepared to be hanged rather than talk. If he's so far gone that he can't remember hanging's abolished, it's as well he didn't give evidence. Vowle summed up very fairly, I thought. Really gave Walker every chance. But the jury was back in no time at all. Unanimous. That's the end of that.'

'Yes,' said Hoskins thoughtfully, 'I suppose so.'

'Anyway,' the Ripper said encouragingly, 'it's turned out handy for Clitheroe. And for you, Sam, come to that.'

35

That night's celebration followed the tradition of divisional CID. Hoskins, Clitheroe, Nicholls, the ACC Crime and the Ripper himself were gathered in the comparative calm of Ripley's room. There was sherry after all, though ACC Crime was drinking tomato juice. From down the corridor, beyond the open door, came the rumble and laughter of the briefing room where the sergeants and constables were packed in.

'One spin-off that's welcome', Clitheroe was saying, 'is the business of Scott. The complaint Walker made against him. That's well and truly dead and buried now. I don't think even Toby Raven would want to raise it.'

'Speaking of which,' Ripley added, 'I asked Russell Proctor along this evening. I don't think he can manage it. He's got the two cases of unlawful killing to prosecute next week. Canton City in the league quarter-final.'

From down the corridor there was a shout of approval and a bellow of laughter. Ragged at first, the voices came together in rough unison.

> If I were the marrying type,
> Which thank the Lord I'm not, sir,
> The kind of man that I would wed
> Would be a rugby full-back . . .

'I think it would be politic presently,' said ACC Crime, 'to pay our respects to the sergeants' mess.'

> He'd find touch, I'd find touch,
> Both find touch together,
> We'd be all right in the middle of the night,
> Finding touch together . . .

'Your glass looks empty, Sam.' Clitheroe came over with a bottle and clapped Hoskins on the shoulder. Hoskins decided that he could just about stand Clitheroe in his usual mean and narrow mood. Clitheroe being matey gave him the shivers. Sherry splashed into his glass and he murmured his thanks. From the other room the voices gathered energy, several fists thumping tables in time to the song.

> The kind of man that I would wed,
> Would be a rugby scrum-half . . .

ACC Crime winced.

'Perhaps we should make ourselves known before this gets any worse.'

As they went out into the corridor, Hoskins seemed to hear Jack Chance's voice distinctly among the others.

> I'd get it out, he'd get it out,
> Both get it out together,
> We'd be all right in the middle of the night . . .

The voices fell away as the senior officers entered. Then the babble resumed. Hoskins pushed his way over to Chance.

Several constables gathered round ACC Crime. There was a burst of laughter and a derisive cheer. Bottles, cans and glasses transformed the tables and chairs of the mundane briefing room into a bar-parlour. There was a scent of savoury grease from the pies that had been sent by the Irish Harp in Rossiter Road.

'You staying to the end of this, Sam?' Chance raised his voice to be heard above the noise.

'Probably have to, Jack. Why?'

'Old Dudden says he'll give us his well-known impression of a one-legged jockey riding the Derby winner and then we'll push off down the Shalimar in Balance Street and have a curry supper. Not a bad place. Under new management. Take a few jugs of the ale with us.'

There was a cheer for Ripley and someone knocked over a chair.

'Don't think I can just bugger off, Jack. Not with the brass here. Could have the Chief Constable as well before this lot's done.'

Wallace Dudden, with his prematurely white hair, red face and rolling gait, was the centre of a small group, his arm round the shoulders of McArthur.

'There's this one about Eve Ricard and Councillor Leroy on a desert island.' His face was flushed with the effort of making himself heard. 'Anyway, they get shipwrecked there. The only thing is it's very low-lying and they have to have sea-defences to keep the place above water. And there's no one else except this gorgeous native girl. And she's almost round the twist because the coastal defences keep leaking. And she asks Eve Ricard if she'd mind showing her how to keep her finger in a dyke. Anyway, Ricard says—'

'Good evening, gentlemen,' said Ripley in a powerful voice at Dudden's elbow. 'I believe we're just in time for the floor-show.'

A glass fell from a table, rolling and rattling against the skirting.

'Someone ought to stop Wallace Dudden,' Hoskins said to Chance. 'There's going to be a row one day.'

'Live and let live,' Chance said amiably. 'What're you drinking?'

'Dry sherry. Can't stand the stuff. Always tastes like Ronson lighter-fuel to me.'

'Serves you right,' Chance said. 'I could fancy getting out of this lot.'

'So could I, my son, but it's not on.'

There was a cheer at the far end of the room, half congratulatory and half derisive.

'ACC Crime's pushing off,' Chance said.

'He is too.'

Someone was starting a chorus of 'For He's a Jolly Good Fellow'. Hoskins thought at first it must be in honour of ACC Crime. Then he saw it was to encourage Dudden, now straddling a chair back to front, cheeks inflated, and prepared to do his impression of the one-legged jockey winning the Derby.

'Every time,' Chance said with a yawn. 'Every time we have this. You been out Lantern Hill today?'

'I called in.'

'Lucky devil. I met this dark-haired girl Marilyn last week. She says she's a research student. I can't see it. Seems all right to me.'

'Oh, yes?' Hoskins watched the display. Dudden's performance continued, encouraged as a tribal ritual even by those for whom it held no surprises. Clitheroe's face was rigid with distaste.

'She says most policemen kick the bucket within five years of retiring. Says it's a well-known fact. Did you know that, Sam?'

'Can't say I did, Jack.'

There was a roar of laughter and a crash as Dudden and the chair went over together.

'Silly bugger'll break his leg one day, doing that,' Chance said. 'There's Mac off out through the door. I'm going with him, Sam. Get some grub. See you down the Shalimar later, if you fancy it.'

As Chance disappeared, applause signalled the end of Dudden's performance. Several of the sergeants and constables followed Chance. Clitheroe came up to Hoskins. Even in his generous moments the tight pristine line of the mouth and the poisoner-moustache were inflexible.

'You did well, Sam. I can't say we should never have managed without you. No one is indispensable. All the same, that line of inquiry through the magazine photograph was really professional.'

'Jack Chance found the photograph.'

Clitheroe looked about him.

'I know that, Sam. But cases are made or broken at your level of command, not his. It was a nice piece of work.'

Hoskins tried to think of some reciprocal piece of flattery. There was nothing. His mind went blank.

'Sometimes,' he said vaguely, 'we get the breaks.'

There was a disturbance at the doorway. Chance was back, pushing towards him. The Sergeant's full red face was drawn in lines of anger and dismay.

'Sam!'

Hoskins turned away from Clitheroe. Jack Chance reached him.

'Sam, there's no one answering the phones up here. Lucas has been trying. It's that stupid bastard Walker. He's topped himself.'

'What?'

'In the remand cells. They had to take him back there because there's been no prison sentence passed on him yet. He was searched. No one found anything. Seems he had half a razor blade. Went through both wrists. Found him about half an hour ago. Arms under the blankets. Really made a job of it.'

Ripley pushed through.

'What's this, Jack?'

Chance elaborated the story for the Superintendent's benefit.

'It's Walker, sir. He's killed himself. Cut his wrists. They thought they'd checked the razor-blade back in the packet this morning. Saw it there. But he'd broken off one edge. They reckon he actually hid it in his hair. No bigger than a fingernail. No one thought of combing him out when they searched him. That's what they reckon.'

There was a moment's silence.

'Under the circumstances,' Ripley said, 'I think we'd better get back to work.'

Several of them began to clear glasses and cans from the tables.

'There's another thing, sir,' Chance said. 'They think he wrote a letter to someone. Gave it to Mr Raven's clerk to post before they took him down. Might be to Claude Roberts. Might be to anyone. Whoever it is, it could be bad news, sir. He'd got a lot of spite to work off. Anyone could see that. And even when they got him to the remand wing, he was still going on about being innocent. Very uptight and bitter, they reckon. Said he was innocent but even more glad now that someone did her and the rest of the girls.'

'Right,' said Ripley. 'I think we'd better take it from there.'

Hoskins saw Clitheroe's face. It was white and stiff with anger. Clitheroe had savoured his glory quietly but anyone could see, Hoskins thought, that he savoured it to the full. Now it had been taken from him, in the very moment of its celebration. Walker had gone down. But in his final self-destruction he had taken something of Clitheroe's reputation with him. A man who killed himself to demonstrate his innocence had earned a re-examination of his case in the minds of the newspaper readers and television viewers. His death would change nothing legally or formally. But the bright shield of Clitheroe's reputation was blemished by doubt and second thoughts. It would begin to look as if the weakness of the defendant rather than the strength of the evidence against him had brought about his conviction.

Dudden and the others who had left for the Shalimar now straggled back self-consciously like children caught playing truant.

'That's all right,' Clitheroe said crisply. 'We shan't need you all. Mr Hoskins and I will deal with the immediate situation. Inquiries and investigation. Perhaps Sergeant Clarke and Sergeant Percival would help us out.'

He was trying to be brave and decent about it all. But there was no doubt that the bar-parlour transformation of the briefing room now had the look of a wake rather than a triumph. Hoskins was aware of an unworthy but warming satisfaction at the thought.

36

A quirk of wind rippled the brown surface of the Town River, between the cold mudflats and disused wharves. Gerald Foster stood by one of the grey preserved capstans of Victoria Quay, where the street ended on the waterside. Downstream, the traffic bound for the docks rumbled over the Industrial Revolution ironwork of Balance Street bridge. There was a distant scuffing walk of the first lunch-time pedestrians from banks and insurance offices filling the snack-bars and pubs, the wine lodges and bistros of Canton's commercial quarter.

Foster held a single sheet of paper in his hand.

'Right,' he said to Hoskins, 'this is what it says, Sam. "In death, as in life, I defy my enemies who have brought me to this. Those who have given evidence of my guilt know, beyond question, that I am innocent. Why they should have perjured themselves, I do not know. Why the police officers concerned should have accepted the perjury and renounced the truth, is a question they must answer. Expediency, reputation, and an unprincipled attempt to deceive the public are a sufficient explanation."'

'That's nice,' Hoskins said. 'That's about all we need.'

'There's worse to come, Sam. Just listen. "To those who wonder why the police should support false evidence against me, I also offer this explanation. In August, I was viciously assaulted by a police patrolman, Scott, at Ocean Beach. The details are on public record. It was an unprovoked attack. I entered a complaint against Scott. A further complaint against the police was in preparation for their failure to pursue the first one. By pinning on me a crime of which I was innocent, the police avoided answering for their misconduct. I was advised, wrongly as it seems now, not to raise police corruption in the course of my trial. I was told it would prejudice Justice Vowle and the jury against me even more than they were prejudiced already. I never killed anyone. I cared nothing for Elaine Harris, alive or dead. But she was no loss. The way she acted, she had this coming to her.""

'Right,' Hoskins said, 'that lets everyone off the hook. No one's going to listen to a raving loony who's glad the girl's dead.'

Foster turned his back to the warehouse galleries on the far side of the river.

'There's another bit, Sam. "The police told me what awaits me in prison. The scum of the earth are encouraged by prison officers and the police to feel self-righteous towards men like me. They say the attacks will happen while prison officers and police (mostly scum of the earth in uniform) look the other way. But it is not from fear that I choose to die. I do it to advertise my innocence. Also to renounce the power of my enemies over me. I win the last battle after all. Let my wife and those who have sworn my guilt live as liars and cheats. Having a whore's vindictiveness, she was prepared to let a scoundrel like Clitheroe prostitute her honour. I hope they both rot in hell, though I doubt it. To me death is an end in itself. I need no fairy-tales from religion. To die now rather than later is nothing. Those who read this message will be joining me soon enough.""

Folding the paper, Foster looked up and pulled his coat tighter about him in the chill breeze.

'That's it?' Hoskins asked. 'Just ends in mid-air?'

'Yes, Sam. Unless he added a PS that hasn't come our way yet.'

Slowly they turned back from the deserted quay towards the Porter's Lodge.

'Where'd it come from, Gerald?'

Foster paused before they reached the lunch-time crowds, where Victoria Quay widened into a main street.

'It got to Claude Roberts's office two days later. Second-class post. Seems Walker must have made up his mind even before the verdict. If he went down, certain letters were to be posted. Claude had copies made. Ours arrived by hand this morning. I should think Clitheroe or Ripley must have one by now.'

'I'm getting a copy of it, am I, Gerald?'

Foster chuckled.

'When they fireproof me, Sam. You're not even supposed to know about it. Even reading it to you has a distinct smell of personal favour. I was hoping it might buy me lunch.'

They crossed the street. Hoskins pushed open the mullion-windowed door of the Porter's Lodge. Just after twelve, several of the high-backed mahogany booths were still empty. The two men sat down.

'You reckon you'll splash this across the front page of the *Western World*, then, Gerald?'

Foster shook his head. Hoskins beckoned one of the waitresses in her porter's uniform of bowler hat, blouse, tall boots and knee-breeches. Foster waited until she had taken the order back behind the bar.

'Conference this afternoon, Sam. Counsel's opinion. The feeling is that we can refer to the letter and Walker saying he's innocent. That's bound to come out when they reconvene the inquest. Might even quote a line or two. On the other hand, there's the matter of him calling Mrs Walker a whore and Clitheroe her pimp. Distinctly dodgy. Libel writs falling thicker than autumn leaves.'

'What if it's read out at the inquest?' Hoskins asked. 'You're entitled to report proceedings.'

Foster pulled a face at the difficulty of it all.

'Depends on the coroner. He could make it a document available to the jury but not read out *in extenso*. After all, it doesn't alter the fact that Walker committed suicide. Won't alter the verdict. Might be reporting restrictions, we're told. Same as they do with children sometimes. Protect the innocent.'

The warm lunch-time vapours of the bar enclosed them. Standing-room was soon packed with pin-striped brokers and tastefully painted companions, thrusting young account managers and hopeful clerks. The rumble of talk and the cigarette smoke rose to the stained dado above the Brazilian mahogany. The girl porter in her uniform brought two pints of Jupp's Special Brew with plates of sausage and mash. Hoskins asked Foster, 'You'll print it if you can?'

Foster reached for the mustard.

'Wouldn't you, Sam? A lot of juice in that. Dare say the poor bugger was round the twist – but still a good story.

240

Mind you, I don't think our readers like being told they're all going to die soon. Might leave that bit out.'

'And you could always remember to tell them that the jury found him guilty. So balls to him. Us police just passed the case to Russell Proctor's lads.'

Foster, his mouth full of mashed potato, waved his fork dismissively.

'No need to worry, Sam,' he said presently. 'I reckon old Walker put his head in the noose, so far as our readers are concerned. That bit about being glad someone had bumped off Elaine Harris. As you say, not exactly going to win many converts. Nice to see Judge Vowle get a kick up the arse, though.'

'And what about Mrs Walker?'

Foster shook his head again.

'We've been keeping an eye on her, in a general way. Sharing expenses with a friend in Fleet Street. Nothing obvious. Just a quiet interest in her.'

'And you'll be passing on any information to friends at "A" Division?'

'We might,' Foster said vaguely. 'Depends what it is. Tell you one thing, though, Sam. We're definitely not giving presents to the assorted nancies and pussy-bumpers of Coastal Television. No way. And not to Big Auntie either.'

The two friends finished lunch and walked away from Victoria Quay. For the first time that year the shopblinds of the department stores in Great Western Street shaded the pavements from the cool spring sunlight.

'You seen ACC Crime lately?' Foster asked.

'He was at the piss-up after Walker went down. Why?'

'How did he seem?'

'I don't know, Gerald. How does he ever seem? Looking at his watch. Waiting for it all to end. Why?'

'There's a story going round the village that he's on the out.'

Hoskins stepped round an abandoned push-chair.

'That's right, Gerald. Two more years. Same time as Ripley.'

Foster stopped and looked at him, as if Hoskins had suddenly gone stupid.

'No, Sam. A real outer. Boot Hill. The lads chipping in for flowers.'

A cloud wiped out the fragile sunshine.

'Not that I've heard of, Gerald. Where'd you get the story from?'

'I didn't,' Foster said, 'but it came to one of the staff reporters from a source close to the Chief Constable. I think that means Mrs Chief Constable with a couple of gins inside her after an official reception.'

'Nothing's been said, Gerald.'

'Nor to me neither, Sam. But the story is that he's had hospital tests. Something nasty in the guts and six months to put his affairs in order.'

Hoskins screwed his face up.

'Are you sure of this, Gerald?'

'Of course I'm not sure, Sam. That's why I asked. On the other hand, it has a reliable sound to it. Poor old devil.'

'I'll keep an ear to the ground.'

Foster nodded.

'Might let us know if you hear anything, Sam. Just as background. Off the record. Utmost discretion.'

'You're on the office blower this afternoon?'

'Not likely,' Foster said. 'I'm home to bed for a few hours this afternoon. Ten till eight on the night-desk means this is pyjama-time for me. What we had just now may be lunch to you, young Samuel Hoskins, but it's supper to me.'

They parted at the *Western World* office on King Edward Square.

It was almost the end of the afternoon when the Ripper called for Hoskins.

'How's the pirate broadcast business, Sam?'

'We're keeping after it, Max. At least it's just radio, so far.'

'They'd hardly be able to start a TV station.' Ripley smiled at the notion.

'They don't need to,' Hoskins said. 'Just overcome the existing signal and there they are. On the screen in the middle of BBC news. Happened twice in Chicago lately. A bloke in a Max Headroom mask, gibbering obscenities. Held the screen for a minute and a half before the engineers got their signal back.'

'Yes,' said the Ripper glumly, picking up several Form 52 incident reports as if about to read them out. 'Well, that's up to the engineers. Thing is, Sam, we might need you on stand-by for a little side-show. Kids in Barrier holding up local shopkeepers with knives and imitation guns. Little shops, as a rule, where there's a woman or a man alone behind the counter. Tom Nicholls and McArthur are on the inquiry. If something breaks suddenly, though, we might need back-up quickly, we'll have to call out the reserves.'

'I'm a bit busy, Max. Hit-Back comedians and the Hassan case not sorted.'

'I know, Sam, I know,' the Ripper said sympathetically. 'Just in a crisis, that's all. You and Jack Chance in at the kill, if we're short-handed.'

'I'll try and give it half an hour when the time comes, Max.'

Ripley laid aside the Form 52s. He got up and turned to the window, uncharacteristically keeping his back to the Chief Inspector.

'Something else you'd better know, Sam. Walker wrote a suicide note. A copy went to Claude Roberts. We didn't know until this morning. It doesn't affect the case, except that Walker protests his innocence, as you'd expect. Doesn't offer any rebuttal of the evidence. Unpleasant remarks about the police and Mrs Walker. It's extremely unfortunate. Bound to leave a nasty taste with the public if it gets too far. The bastard brought up that story of Scott hitting him. That's not going to sound too clever, if we let it out and about. All spite and malice but, unfortunately, that's what some of our critics want.'

'Off a duck's back, Max.'

'Oh, sure, Sam. Sure. But you've spent your life in this town. Must have known more people for more time than any of us. I thought if your friends in the press happened to raise the topic, you might ask them to ease up a bit. Just until we get the inquest on Walker sorted out. Just a week or two.'

He turned round again.

'Have we got a copy of this note?' Hoskins asked.

'No,' said Ripley, a little too readily. 'I certainly haven't seen it.'

'If a man is prepared to die to show his innocence,' Hoskins said quietly, 'there'll be some questions asked.'

243

But Ripley looked pained and dismissive simultaneously.

'Oh, I don't think so, Sam. I hope the media people will take a responsible attitude. After all, they howled long enough and loud enough for someone to be caught and sent down. And we caught him, or at least Clitheroe did. I don't think Walker can expect much sympathy from them now – dead or alive.'

'I thought,' Hoskins said gently, 'questions might be asked in this building.'

The Ripper hastened to reassure him on that as well.

'I wouldn't have thought so, Sam. We've still got the same evidence. Nothing in the note – as reported to me – alters that.'

Which left the other matter, Hoskins decided. He took Ripley head-on.

'I'm told ACC Crime is on the way out, Max. Hospital tests.'

Ripley looked aghast. Not at the news, Hoskins thought, but that anyone might know.

'Told by whom?'

'It's a story going round the building.'

Ripley sat down again.

'Then I'd rather it stopped with you, Sam. ACC Crime is as fit as a flea, to judge from his energy. Still, for your ears only, he's wanted to quit since last summer. Two years off retirement. There's been negotiation. Obviously I'm not privy to it. In the end, I hear, they made an offer he couldn't refuse. A lump sum to make his pension up to salary level for those two years.'

'No hospital tests?'

'I hope not, Sam.' The sincerity was just a little too earnest. 'Nothing that I've heard.'

'And a new ACC Crime?'

'Yes,' said Ripley with a sigh, 'and thank God it won't be me. Not long enough to do, Sam. We're looking at a bungalow near Lymington this weekend.'

Hoskins had turned to leave the room, when Ripley had an afterthought.

'By the way, Sam. Clitheroe's signing off the Elaine Harris case on television tonight. Just in case you're home. Half-ten. On this week's *Coastline*. Chance to thank the media and the viewers for their help. Shows what we can do if police and community work together. That sort of thing. Might do us a bit of good with the public. Rather neat, I thought.'

37

In the aftermath of the Canton rush-hour, Hoskins drove out to Lantern Hill. The ocean sky was smoke-grey again with a salmon-coloured flush of light that would have made a fashion designer's fortune. From the docks across the water came a smell of oil and dry grass, fresh paint and warm metal, that he always associated with the onset of spring. Everywhere there was a resurgence of life. Except perhaps in the worn and corrugated entrails of ACC Crime.

Nothing that Ripley had said about ACC Crime reassured Hoskins. If a deal was being concluded that fast, it suggested the Commander was on his way to Parklands Cemetery rather than an Ocean Front apartment. Hoskins turned up Lantern Hill as the light faded and the first streetlamps glimmered.

They watched television in bed. By the time Clitheroe's glory came on, Lesley was reduced to the upper half of her Christmas nightwear, just to keep her shoulders warm.

'I don't feel that sorry for him,' she said, 'even if he was mad and committed suicide. I don't care if he killed her or not. He obviously wanted to.'

Hoskins stroked the pearly resilience of her thigh with a frown of concentration.

'They don't let us lock people up for what they want to do,' he said thoughtfully. 'Otherwise even I might have to turn myself in.'

'That's not what— '

'Shut up a minute,' he said gently, 'I want to hear this last bit.'

'Obviously,' the youthfully grey-haired and tough-chinned presenter was saying, 'quite obviously we can't investigate or try cases on television. But may I ask you whether you now have any ideas as to how Rachel Lloyd, Jane Page and other young women met their deaths?'

Clitheroe was relaxed, like a man after a good dinner. The lines of the Edwardian-poisoner mouth were easier. Here was an anecdotal uncle the viewers could trust.

'We have very firm ideas,' he said comfortably.

'All right,' said the presenter cautiously. 'May I press you a little further on that? We have seen the conviction, indeed the death, of Mr Walker. In the light of the evidence available, how do the other cases stand?'

Clitheroe's smile suggested he might be rolling a marble round his teeth.

'I'd have to know which cases we're talking about.'

'Well, Rachel Lloyd and Jane Page, for example.'

'We've been able to conclude our inquiries in both those cases.'

'And in others?'

'And in certain others.'

'Without a public hearing?'

'There are circumstances', said Clitheroe thoughtfully, 'in which a public hearing is neither practical nor appropriate. In a sense there has already been a public hearing. There were, of course, the murder verdicts returned at the inquests.'

'On a parallel issue, Mr Clitheroe. Would it be fair to say that the conviction of Derek Warren for murder and events associated with that have removed a serious threat of criminal violence – perhaps even violence between criminals – in this area?'

'We think it will have assisted in that. Yes.'

'And all these results mean that the people of Canton can walk the streets with more confidence and in greater security than perhaps they did a year or two ago?'

'We hope so,' Clitheroe agreed. 'Time will tell. But with the degree of co-operation we have received from the public – and from our friends in the media – we believe so. But let me make one thing plain. The right of the ordinary citizen to go about his or her business unmolested is never to be taken for granted. It can be preserved only by constant vigilance.'

'Of which you will continue to be a part, I'm sure, Mr Clitheroe, even though from a more lofty vantage-point.'

Clitheroe's smile was thin and mean again, as if he disapproved.

'From whatever vantage-point seems the most appropriate, Mr Howells.'

The presenter turned full-face to the screen with an awkward smirk. Hoskins sat up.

'Vantage-point?' he said suddenly. 'Can I use your phone? I want to make sure Gerald Foster's not pulling some stroke.'

'Use the point in the hall.'

Hoskins went down, dialled the *Western World* and asked for the night-desk.

'Gerald? Sam Hoskins. Did you just see Clitheroe on *Coastline*?'

'Never miss it, Sam.'

'What's this "lofty vantage-point" rubbish?'

'You tell me, Sam. I was going to ask if you knew. I might be wrong, but it sounds as if they've got their successor for ACC Crime.'

'Clitheroe? ACC Crime? Bloody parking-warden?'

'I did warn you, Sam. Former Politburo. Surveillance on the docks for the boyos with their rocket-launchers. Clears up a series of long-standing sex-murders in no time at all. Puts an end to gang warfare between the new boys and the old boys. He's not the stumble-bum you all like to think he is. No use as a policeman, I grant you. But sharp. A chancer. A natural instinct for the ladder. How to trip the one above him while stamping on the fingers below him. Nasty, Sam. Real rat-poison. But he's got a rat's instincts too. Any news on our present ACC Crime?'

'He's definitely going, Gerald. Only, you didn't get that from me. The official story is that he's being offered a lump sum to retire two years early. I think Ripley was flannelling. You're probably right about the hospital business. It's all happened too fast for anything else.'

'And if Clitheroe steps in and they freeze Clitheroe's present post, Sam, that saves them one very expensive salary. Right? He's not only riding high just now – on the backs of the rest of you – but they get a new ACC Crime for almost nothing. Very popular with the Police Committee and the ratepayers. There's your new supremo, my friend.'

'I hope you're bloody wrong, Gerald.'

'If I am, Sam, I'll buy you dinner on the main menu of the Paris Hotel. A new ACC Crime on the cheap is just what the Whitehall boot-boys go for. Good news for their political masters and mistresses.'

'He could still land up in the cess, Gerald. This Walker business with the suicide note could explode under him.'

Foster chuckled down the wire.

'You don't get it, Sam, do you? It's you and Jack Chance and the rest of the lads sitting on that now. You'll be the ones that catch the blast. Clitheroe's going to be way out of range. Two floors above you. Making his move now before the detonation. Perfect timing.'

'Sod it,' said Hoskins miserably. 'I'm going back to bed.'

Lesley was lying face-down, bending her knees and flexing the muscles of her calves for practice. He patted her on the bottom and she turned towards him.

'Well?'

'Looks like Clitheroe could be the next ACC Crime. Should have Cooney and Pruen in stitches.'

'Oh?'

Hoskins drew a deep breath. He patted her again and relaxed.

'Oh, what the hell!' he said philosophically. 'Perhaps one of my Hit-Back experts might get to him first.'

38

At last a distant warmth of sun lay in the softer spring air. Hoskins sat well down in the passenger-seat of the parked car, next to Chance. The flat terraced streets of Barrier had no horizon but their own rooftops and chimneys under a limitless sky of Atlantic blue. It was the last land before the ocean, mudflats drained a century before. There was brine in the air and the soil was sand or silt. Mop-headed acacias along the pavements of residential roads were almost the only trees in this area of coastal Canton.

Hoskins narrowed his eyes, squinting down Ferry Road. Beyond a small Methodist chapel built of cream corrugated iron with a wooden spire, there were half a dozen shops in a shallow parade of their own. But Monday morning shopping was over in this quiet area of grey-stone houses, near the Barrier embankment against the sea. In the hour before lunch the world slept.

He let out an impatient breath for Chance's benefit.

'If we're down here for nothing again, Jack, I shall be bloody furious. I'll want the fancy bits of Tom Nicholls on toast for my tea. It's not our case.'

'He seemed certain, boss,' McArthur said from the back of the car.

'He's been certain five times in the last three weeks.'

'Yes,' McArthur said, 'but two of them bought Mickey Mouse masks in Hamleys. An hour ago. They went in on the 28 bus. That comes back here.'

'Kids!' said Hoskins bitterly. 'You'd think it was Dutch Schultz or Machine-Gun Kelly. I'd box their ears hard enough to keep 'em dancing for a week.'

Chance yawned.

'That's child abuse, Sam.'

'It would be if I was handing it out. I'd make sure of it.'

The radio spluttered into life and Nicholls's voice filled the car.

'Blue Leader to all mobiles. Two suspects on 28 bus going in the direction of Ferry Road. Proceed to positions. I am behind bus in Seawall Road.'

Hoskins put the condenser microphone to his mouth.

'Blue Four to Blue Leader. Message received.' He turned to McArthur. 'Right. When those two get here – if they do – they'll find three of the shops open. The sort they like. Wilkins the tobacconist, Atlantic Video, and the Sub Post Office. WPC Cummings behind the counter in the first, DC Jones in the second, and WPC Booth in the Post Office. Mac, you take charge of the team in the lane at the back. Jack and I will be in Wilkins's, watching through the window. Leaves Dudden and Browne to block the escape. The minute they approach, we get the news on Dudden's radio. If it's not Wilkins's place, Jack and I follow them into the one they go for. You'll be coming through the back of the shop. If either of them makes a move, Jack and I take them from behind.'

'Right, boss.'

The three men got out of the Fiesta, slammed the doors and locked them.

'And another thing,' Hoskins said gloomily. 'Catch them both quick. Those imitation guns are sometimes made of liquorice or whatnot. I don't want the little bastards eating the evidence before we can nab them.'

'Right-oh, boss,' McArthur said.

They went their separate ways. Hoskins and Chance waited with Gilly Cummings in the overheated space of the little tobacconist's. Beyond the narrow shop-windows, the mild sunshine lit Ferry Road. It was quiet enough to hear sparrows chattering in the mop-headed acacias.

'Come on! Come on!' said Hoskins furiously to the invisible thieves. The phone on the counter rang. He picked it up. 'Who? Yes. All in place. Tom Nicholls is having a drive-around somewhere between here and Hamleys. Yes, we're fine. No, you can tell the Tactical Support Unit to go back to sleep.'

He covered the mouthpiece and turned to Chance.

'Clitheroe's fallen out of his tree again. Do we want armed officers from the Tactical Support Unit? All telescopics and baseball caps!'

He returned to the phone.

'Max, if Clitheroe sends them, who're they going to shoot? There's only a couple of schoolkids or a couple of us. Or possibly a bewildered passer-by. We've had enough news of trigger-happy cops in other places. Thanks, anyway.'

'Wake up!' Chance said. 'I think they're here. Coming from the bus stop.'

Hoskins edged to the side of the little shop-window. In jeans and anoraks, a pair of children were walking casually towards the shopping parade forecourt. One was a ginger-haired ten year old, cropped and freckled. The other, with straggling dark hair, looked about fourteen. They stopped on the kerb outside the row of shops, looking up and down the road as if waiting for a lift home from school. The dark-haired boy drew something from his pocket.

'Give us the glasses, Jack!' Hoskins said. He scanned the fourteen year old from the shelter of the window's cardboard advertisements for cigarettes and sweets. 'That's not an imitation, my son. Too well-used. There's even been oil on it. I'd say he's carrying a .455 with the barrel sawn short.'

Chance was on the radio to McArthur.

'Blue Four to all units. Two suspects now on forecourt of shops. One ginger hair, one dark. The big one with dark hair has a gun in his hand. Watch yourself, Mac. We think it's a real one. They're turning. They're turning now. It's the tobacconist's. Definitely. We're taking cover.'

'Where's Dudden?' Hoskins asked. 'He was supposed to give the alert.'

Concealment had been improvised by two piles of unpacked cartons at the side of the shop. Hoskins took one, Chance the other. Two sunny-smile Mickey Mouse faces turned from the pavement and peered through the glass of the shop door. Gilly Cummings behind the counter pretended to read a magazine.

The two boys came in slowly, pressing the counter with their hips.

'Don't scream and don't move,' the fourteen year old said in a hoarse voice. 'Not unless you want a second belly button a lot bigger than the first. This is loaded and it works. So you open the till nicely and you hand my friend the money. Then you turn your back and we tie your wrists. And if you're really good, we don't even leave a mark on you. See?'

There was a sound from the back room of the shop and the boy moved his eyes. Hoskins stood up and crossed the six or seven feet in a couple of movements, ready to grab the elder boy and fling him face-to-the-wall with his arms behind his back. Before he could do it, the boy turned to him, eyes narrowed in a fury of resentment. WPC Gilly Cummings took him from behind, across the counter, her arm round his throat bending him back until the boy's head struck the wood. The gun hit the floor and the boy lay obediently on his back, staring at the ceiling as if in hysterical spasm. The ginger-haired child began to run, collided with Chance, and rebounded, tumbling to the floor. The Sergeant raised him by the collar.

'Right-oh, Sonny Jim,' said Chance encouragingly. 'You are nicked.'

McArthur, coming in from the back, handcuffed the elder boy and patted him down. By the tip of its barrel, he picked up the gun from the floor.

'Bloody comedians!' he said scornfully for Hoskins's benefit. 'Not even took the safety catch off, boss.'

But Hoskins was not listening.

'Mac,' he said quietly, 'I might be wrong. I don't think I am. That piece of ironmongery has a distinct look of what Sonny Hassan was carrying in Prince of Wales Road. Treat it gently.'

Half an hour later, Hoskins and Chance sat either side of the handcuffed fourteen year old in the parked police car. A purse with a Canton Corporation season-ticket had yielded his identity, address, and school.

'Simple question, Kevin,' Hoskins said. 'I want to know where the gun came from. A simple answer, and it might be Christmas for you. A telling-off and out the door.'

'Nothing to say.'

'Don't mess me about, my son. I don't care about you doing Jesse James round the local sweetshops. Whether you say anything or not, I can do you for armed robbery any time. Five or six years down Grove Park detention centre. Army drill and face-slapping. A bed smelling of disinfectant and other people's sweat. Being some greasy tearaway's sweetheart into the bargain. All I have to do is sign the charge sheet. Only reason you're getting a chance is I'm more interested in the man who had the gun last than I am in you.'

The boy flicked back the long dark hair.

'Bollocks. You can't do anything to me.'

Hoskins shook his head sadly.

'You're an amateur, my lad. You didn't know how to get the safety catch off. So I don't fancy you sawing off the barrel to fit your pocket. It's a .455 Eley. Not that you'd know the difference between that and a water-pistol. Old-fashioned army service revolver. Not many about.'

'You can't do anything to me, so stuff it.'

Hoskins patted the boy's knee sympathetically.

'I shan't try, Kevin. If this is Sonny Hassan's gun, you'll meet the real professionals. Hassan was a hard man. A killer. Slipped up on a job. Put some big names in danger. That's a death sentence in his circle of friends. Before the firm killed him on Christmas Eve, they did things I could hardly describe to you. Spent all afternoon on him. Tied him up for a punch-bag. Broke his nose with brass knuckles, knocked his teeth out. When they find you, Kevin, you'll think you're having a bad dream. They took his clothes off and let a knife-artist loose on him. Nothing personal. But he had to be made an example. You won't believe you're seeing it, when they start that. Bits of you coming off like peeling an apple. And then they made him kneel. Put the muzzle of the gun to the back of his neck. He was found strung up under the New Pier at Ocean Beach on Christmas morning. If you think I'm having you on, Kevin, we'll let you see photos of Sonny Hassan when he was in the mortuary.'

'Why'd they want to do anything to me?'

'Because, Kevin, that gun could convict a man of murder. A very important man. Been in this town a long time. Very rich. Never caught. A hundred people work for him. Whoever knows about the gun has to go – the hard way.'

The boy was frightened. Not too frightened, Hoskins thought. The voice trembled just a little. Just coming to the boil.

'What's it got to do with me? I don't know any of them.'

'It's got this to do with you, Kevin,' Hoskins said in the same gentle voice. 'I want to know where you got that gun. I don't want fairy-stories and I don't want to be messed about. I can let the papers and the television people know that you had Sonny Hassan's gun. That you knew him and who killed him. That you've promised to tell us everything. I'll give them your name and address, so everyone knows where to find you. And then I'll let you out on bail with a hundred underworld bounty-hunters looking for you. A bit like turning you loose in the safari park at feeding time, Kevin. I reckon we'd find bits of you everywhere from Mount Pleasant to Lantern Hill. We found most of Sonny Hassan. Except his tongue. He must have lost that early on.'

'I thought you were supposed to protect people!' The voice was shriller now.

253

'If they ask us to, Kevin. As I understood it, you don't need us. You're right, there's nothing we can do to you. Not allowed to beat up suspects. But whether we forget we ever saw that gun – or whether we tell the world – that's up to us. Now, don't piss me about, lad, which is it to be?'

'Don't be a prick,' Chance said encouragingly to the boy. 'We've got better things to do than chase after penny-ante thieves like you. We don't bother with less than murder. So we want to know where you got the gun. That's all.'

'Found it,' the boy said.

'Oh, yes? Lying in the street, I suppose?'

He looked up at them glumly.

'In a hut. Down the East Sluice.'

Hoskins caught Chance's eye.

'Which hut?'

'Fishing-hut,' Kevin said bitterly. 'How do I know who owned the poxy thing?'

Hoskins beamed.

'You are a lovely boy, Kevin,' he said quietly, 'and you have just done yourself a favour. Or cut your own throat if this is a try-on. We're not going to take you to the police station yet. You and me and Mr Chance are going for a nice drive to the East Sluice. You're going to show us this hut. We might be able to see this larking about with shopkeepers as a bit of a joke that went too far. All right? Could be no worse than a slap on the wrist. Magistrates don't ask about things like the make of gun. We might just say it was surrendered and destroyed. Fair enough?'

Hoskins got out of the car and spoke to Nicholls. Then he came back.

'Reckon you could find this hut again, do you, Kevin?'

'By that wooden footbridge over the Sluice. One with the rope rail.'

Hoskins nodded and switched on his radio.

'DCI Hoskins in mobile Blue Four to control. I'm proceeding from Ferry Road to Eastern Sluice. I have with me Sergeant Chance and a witness. I want a duty team on call to isolate a search area. An angler's hut by the Sluice footbridge. And I want a forensic team from Ocean Beach on immediate stand-by. Preferably with Dr Blades in charge. The duty team will rendezvous, if called, on the hard shoulder of the Eastern Causeway bridge. Fifteen minutes' notice. Inform Mr Ripley. And a complete press blackout. Any questions?'

'Message received, Blue Four. No questions.'

Chance moved to the driving-seat. Hoskins beckoned McArthur.

'Sit the other side of our young friend Kevin, Mac. He's holding his hands nicely behind his back, but I'd hate to lose him out of the other door.'

'Right-oh, boss.'

'And be nice to him, Mac. Seems he might be on our team, after all.'

39

The tide was at the ebb that afternoon. The East Sluice lay at the bottom of a brown canyon, a dribble of water almost enfolded by flanks of mud. A warm breeze stirred the tall grasses that screened the stark outlines of Atlantic Factors and the mirror-glass fingers of the new finance towers in central Canton. Their image of the city hovered on the far edge of the Eastern Levels, remote and unreal as a postcard of Paris in the Belle Époque.

The forensic search was like a circus come to town. A tent of silvered polythene had been erected over the little fishing-hut. The racket of a generator vibrated in the stillness of the wide moorland. Several squad cars had parked along the raised track that bordered the sluice. Everywhere there were flat-hats and white tapes.

Hoskins turned to Blades.

'What's it look like, Charlie? Anything at all?'

'Nah,' said Blades disparagingly. 'Not that quick and easy. You picked a real bugger here, Sam. Neap tides. Spring floods. Several days there's been water up through the floor of that little home-from-home. What you need here, my friend, isn't Forensic. More like the gipsy queen and her crystal ball.'

With the rest of his team, Blades wore white overalls of a tracksuit pattern, like a boxer out on roadwork. Only his olive-green gumboots spoilt the illusion. His thin, creased face looked more depressed than usual. It was no secret that he disliked being out of doors under any circumstances.

The fishing-hut was one of a dozen along the East Sluice. Its thin wooden planks were dark and rotting. The felt and bitumen that had formed a rough shelter over it now leaked copiously. Hoskins could see that it was a forensic scientist's nightmare after months of neglect.

'Still,' he said cheerfully, 'there's one thing, Charlie. Not a big area to cover. The floor can't be more than six feet by four.'

'It won't be the floor where we find anything now, Sam,' Blades said sourly. 'That's been flooded too often. More like the shelves where he kept his lines and his bait. Where exactly was the gun?'

'According to our little friend, it was on the top shelf, wrapped in a cloth. He's a busy boy, so he can't remember quite which day he came here. Seems these places get looted quite regularly by lads from his school. He just wrenched the padlock off. Practising for his O-level in housebreaking. First half of January, he reckons. I don't think he ever fired the gun in earnest. Couldn't even find the safety catch this morning, fortunately.'

Blades sniffed.

'Jack Chance says you went over the top with that kid. Telling him you'd turn him loose for Cooney and Pruen to work on. How they cut Hassan's tongue out before they started on him. That's bollocks, Sam. Jack reckons you scared that little yob witless. He'd say anything. And that's no good to anyone. We could all be wasting our time out here.'

'I don't think so, Charlie. I'd rather have a bloke that'll say anything than one who won't open his mouth. Actually, it was when we offered to show him the post-mortem photos of Hassan that he went all green and started gurgling. He didn't sound like he was having us on about the gun being here.'

'Got the cloth he says it was wrapped in, have you?'

'His mum and dad's place is being turned over this minute,

Charlie. Going on something awful, they are. Seems he was a proper little Sunday School angel.'

'I'll bet,' Blades said. 'Well, Samuel, I'll see what we can get out of this cosy little slum in the next couple of hours, then take it home and play with it. We'll get fingerprints, of course. Most of them belonging to the owner and a few to your young friend, perhaps. Who's the merchant who wastes his time with this lot?'

'We're filling in the picture as we go along,' Hoskins said evasively.

Blades shook his head and his mouth tightened in contempt.

'You spend your time out here in all the draughts and wet, would you, Sam?'

'Not a great one for fishing. No, Charlie.'

'He sat out here getting rheumatism and what else besides, when he could have been back in a nice warm room with a young lady being friendly over the end of the sofa? Makes you wonder what the world's coming to.'

'Does indeed, Charlie. Hang on. That's Jack Chance's motor turning off the causeway. I'll ring you later.'

Chance waited for him in the car, shuffling through papers. And that, Hoskins thought, meant that something had come to light.

'What's the gen from the other search, Jack? Anything turn up at young Kevin's place yet?'

'Not that I heard.'

'Charlie wants the cloth that Kevin says was wrapped round the gun when he found it. Get Mac on the blower when you've briefed me. Tell him if a likely bit of rag turns up in the boy's house, it goes straight to Forensic at Ocean Beach. Special delivery. Now. What's the rest of the story?'

Chance shook his head.

'There's some bloody odd stuff coming up, Sam. We're back with this character Jonas. The same one that reported his wallet lost in Ocean Beach the day Ma Pruen was killed. He rented this hut two years back. Paid his sub regularly. We've got an address for him from the angling club. Shannon Street, down the Peninsula.'

'A mug who went bail for Cooney's boys on gaming charges! Tastes like flavour of the month to you, does he, Jack? Run him past CRO, did you?'

'Not half,' Chance said, flicking over the papers. 'Turns out he's got form. Not much. And not round here. Seven years ago in Swindon. After his time as bail for Cooney's friends. Probation report said he'd worked his way up. Hotel butchery assistant. Chicken factory. Betting-shop manager at the time of his trouble. Indecent assault, it was. Touching a woman's leg in a bus queue. She said he did, he said he didn't. Magistrates decided he did. Fine and probation. Nothing since.'

Hoskins stared out across the level horizon of mudflats to a distant sparkle of low tide.

'Now that,' he said, 'is more like it. But I don't know about Cooney risking an indecent assault merchant on his pay-roll. Got his reputation to think of.'

'Perhaps he didn't know,' Chance said. 'Perhaps he couldn't be choosey this time. Not everyone knows the slaughterhouse trade. Not even in Cooney's mob. I'd say being in butchery was more important than him touching a lady's leg.'

Hoskins twisted his mouth sceptically.

'Let's turn over the stone that Mr Jonas calls home and give him a tug.'

'Half a minute, Sam.' Chance reached over the seat for another folder in the back of the car. 'There's more. We've got Jonas's prints and mug-shot from the bus-stop business. Round-faced, dark-haired, bald down the middle.'

'So?'

'That Sunday last summer, the day Jonas said he'd dropped his wallet somewhere in Ocean Beach. Hoped someone might hand it in. No one did.'

'Still not with you, Jack.'

'Walker was in Ocean Beach that day, taking his pictures of girls on the pier and the beach. Two or three gems of Elaine Harris we collected from his house. There's one that needs looking at again. Walker only printed the part of the negative that had Elaine on it. Blew it up to fill the plate. We never bothered with the rest, the background and all that. No reason to then. But I had a look at the whole negative today. Got Jimmy to do a print. You take the magnifying glass and look close. There's Elaine on the pier. A face as if she's just trod on something nasty. Two blokes with backs three-quarters to the camera. One could be Hassan. The other I'd bet is Del Warren. Right?'

'Warren definitely,' Hoskins said. 'Could be Hassan. Seeing that they all went round together, I'd say it was Hassan. It's got to be.'

'Right,' said Chance again. 'Now there's a bloke in the middle between Elaine and the other two, looking sideways at Del. I reckon they're saying something to him. One of 'em's just attracted his attention. He's with an older woman but he's looking at them.'

'Okay.'

'That's Jonas,' Chance said simply. 'Changed a bit the last seven years, but not that much. And if I'm right, guess how he came to lose his wallet?'

'Pocket picked? We know that. But not while young Elaine was trembling his knees. Not if he had another woman with him already.'

'One thing,' Chance said, 'it's definitely that day. Walker's camera was expensive. You can read a headline about a dead baby in the post. I told our press office to check. It is definitely that day's headline.'

'I'm not going into court, Jack, and tell a jury he murdered two people because they picked his pocket. Even if it's true, they wouldn't believe me.'

'No, Sam. But suppose he spotted Elaine again weeks later, when she and the other two were on the run from us and from Cooney. He reckoned she owed him for the wallet. Cornered her somehow, knowing she'd be scared that he might tell the law or turn her over to Cooney for a bumpy ride to Boot Hill. Forced her out here for a bit of fun that turned lethal. He might even have decided at the start to top her as the grand finale. Remember Walker and what he fancied doing to her in his notebook? I shouldn't think he was one of a kind in a city this size. Afterwards, perhaps Jonas had to hit Hassan on the head and plug him with his own gun to be on the safe side.'

Hoskins stared out to sea. His mouth tightened as if he disapproved.

'Betting-shop manager, he was, Jack. Part of the Cooney and Pruen trade. Along come Del Warren and Sonny Hassan. Shouting the odds round the clubs and boozers about how they're going to take over the business. Not hard to imagine Cooney having them watched on the cheap by a betting-shop dodger like Jonas. Sonny and Del were fully paid-up dumbos. They were thick enough, Jack, not to know someone watching them from a punter ready to be ripped off.'

'His pocket picked and Ma Pruen killed the same day, Sam? Bit coincidental.'

'If I was putting money on this, Jack, I'd say it's not coincidence at all. A distinct pattern. Jonas and a few other no-hopers could have been hanging around as Cooney's eyes and ears. And, in Jonas's case, as slaughterman.'

'Could be,' Chance said. 'Certainly looks like Sonny Hassan got the last rites from butcher Jonas. Courtesy of Carmel Cooney. Handed over gift-wrapped for a thumping, the chop and disposal. Seems like Elaine had to go too. But no reason our genial neck-wringer and throat-slitter Jonas shouldn't enjoy himself with her along the way. One step up from strangling chickens and gutting pigs. I think Cooney might enjoy the idea of that.'

Hoskins watched Forensic in their white tracksuits scooping Canton clay into plastic bags.

'An afternoon down the Peninsula for us, Jack. With Mr Jonas in Shannon Street. Any case, there's nothing doing out here at the moment. Just old Charlie Blades moaning because it's draughty.'

They took the Eastern Causeway past Atlantic Factors and on to the Peninsula by a tunnel under the Prince Consort dock. Shannon Street was one of fifty terraces that ran from the drab spinal length of Dyce Street. The sooty lintels of its doorways stood over an uneven and neglected paving. Shannon Street itself was a cul-de-sac, cut off at its end by the wall of the Western Reclaim scrapyard embellished with cloudy letters of popland graffiti.

'You got a number for him, Jack?'

'Thirty-eight.'

Hoskins peered sideways from the car.

'Even numbers my side, by the look of it,' Chance said.

There was a pause. Then Hoskins gave a sigh of despair.

'Bloody hell!' he said miserably. 'Will you look at that?'

The last four houses in the terrace, including thirty-eight, had the air of a film set. There was a skip outside, piled with gutted wood and fireplaces. The buildings themselves were reduced to a front wall whose doors and windows showed demolition within. Floors and roofs had gone. Smuts drifted from the bonfire of the demolition team. A steel ball swung on its chain and another section of wallpapered bedroom crashed down within the doomed shell.

'Must have been condemned years ago,' Chance said. 'He could be anywhere.'

'He could be, Jack. I reckon he's still around here. A zombie like him. If he's lucky, Pruen or someone is keeping him warm. If not, he could be dossing. I want a photo and a public appeal. Sought for interview in the case of Sonny Hassan. Leave it at that. He might discover he's got no friends after all. We could even find him wandering around glad of a nice comfy cell.'

By seven o'clock that evening, Jonas the betting-shop manager and ex-slaughterman was still a face on a photograph. The houses had been empty for two years. The housing department had no record of rehousing the tenants from number thirty-eight. Jonas was no longer employed by any betting-shop in the Canton or Ocean Beach licensing areas. Hoskins checked the entry of the Luck's-Inn Betting-Shop, where Jonas had worked at the time of his indecent assault conviction seven years before. There was no evidence that it had been owned by Pruen or Cooney.

'There wouldn't be evidence,' Chance grumbled. 'They're not that simple.'

'Matthew Protheroe, it says here. Could have been their nominee.'

'Yes,' Chance said sceptically. 'Still, seeing old Protheroe kicked the bucket about eighteen months ago, that rather puts the mockers on that.'

Hoskins waited until eight o'clock. Then he phoned Charlie Blades.

'Charlie? Sam. I don't want to be a nuisance, but is there anything yet?'

Blades grunted.

'Only what we thought. Definitely Hassan's gun. Test-fired it and did the comparison-microscope bit. We also had Mr Jonas's fingerprints sent over from when he was indecent. They're all over the hut. None on the outside of the gun but they're inside, where he broke it open to load it, I suppose.'

'Who else?'

'There's Elaine Harris's prints in that fishing-hut. And that kid you pulled in this morning. He was there all right. But not Hassan and not Mr Walker.'

'So Hassan wasn't taken there?'

'Not unless they made him wear gloves, Sam. In any case, there's nothing else we've found that matches him. If he died there, we'd have something.'

'And Walker?'

'Nothing, Sam. Even if he wore gloves start to finish. No trace of him.'

'Listen, Charlie. This is getting delicate, as they say. Could Jonas have screwed her in there, let her go, then Walker picked her up and killed her?'

'Not in my book, Sam. There's more about the gun. We got the cloth that Mac sent from the search of the boy's house. Torn off a man's old cotton vest. It's had the gun in it. Oil stains. And they're not recent. A few months.'

'You reckon it was Hassan wrapped the gun in it?'

'No, Sam. That cloth was in Jonas's hut before he ever got hold of the gun.'

'How's that then, Charlie?'

'There's other stains, Sam. Saliva marks that match Elaine Harris's group. More to the point, there's two hairs in it. Well, more than two but two special ones. We've had them under the 'scope. They are hers and only hers. If you want volume three, the cotton thread in her mouth is a ringer for this bit of vest. Can't say who killed her, Sam. But she was definitely tied and gagged in that hut. Imprints on her wrists from nylon twine on his top shelf. Another of her hairs snagged rather low down on a rough edge of wood by the door. Perhaps when he was carrying her out and her head was drooping.'

'Just to complete my misery,' said Hoskins quietly, 'you didn't by any chance find her skirt and tie there?'

'Can't say we did, Sam. Why?'

'Because I want to know, Charlie, where all this leaves the late Mr Walker.'

Blades gave a deep humourless chuckle.

'Oh no, Sam! No, no! Mr Walker is definitely down to you lot. I don't even want to hear about him. I've spent the whole afternoon splashing about in excrement down the East Sluice. The rest of you can have a turn in it now.'

'Thanks, Charlie,' said Hoskins wearily. 'I knew we could count on you.'

He put the phone down and sat for a moment, staring out at the light-patterns of Canton after dark. Then he dialled the *Western World* night-desk.

'Gerald? Sam Hoskins. A favour. Your eye that you're keeping on Mrs Walker. Has it seen anything interesting?'

There was a breath that had the sound of a smile as Foster answered.

'Not a lot, Sam. Mrs Walker used to visit her sister once or twice a week, according to our informant in the neighbourhood. A gentleman used to go at the same time. Grainger. Salesman of industrial paint. Having got over her bereavement in short order, Mrs Walker is now to be the new Mrs Grainger.'

'She could have shopped him for that,' said Hoskins helpfully.

'Don't think so, Sam. It was when she found out about his nasty little ways that she shopped him. Natural female revulsion, they call it.'

'Giving him an alibi and then taking it away? Bit calculated.'

'Could be a genuine mistake, Sam. They usually met at her sister's Monday evenings. But that Monday, Mr Grainger was in Leicester at a company dinner. We confirmed it. Perhaps that confused her at first. Then she realised later that she went to her sister on her own. Us civilians do get confused sometimes, Sam. But she didn't say anything until she found those sex-crime press cuttings and the photos of girls he'd taken. And when she heard where the skirt and

263

tie had come from. And when you lot turned up to nick Walker.'

'Let's hope you're right, Gerald. Supposing her story about seeing the skirt and tie in the dust-cart wasn't made up just to sink Walker without trace.'

'Jury believed her,' said Foster philosophically. 'Now, Sam, I'd like the news about Ferry Road this morning and the East Sluice this afternoon. I've had a bigger load of horse manure from your press office than I can ever recall.'

'Not a lot to it, Gerald. Two kids with toy guns sticking up old ladies behind counters of corner-shops down in Barrier. We tidied the pair of 'em away this morning. Both juveniles, so you'll have to watch your reporting. This afternoon was different. We had a tip-off anonymously that we'd find a gun in a fishing-hut down the East Sluice. We turned one up. I've just had a test report. It's definitely the weapon that said cheerio to Sonny Hassan.'

'Which means you want to speak to the complete angler?'

'Which means, Gerald, that we want to speak to the owner of the gun.'

'Right,' said Foster eagerly. 'Thanks, Sam. I owe you one down the drinker. Remind me next time, in case I should forget.'

40

The next evening was the only time Hoskins had seen the Ripper's face quite as red with anger. It was also one of the few occasions when he had remained seated at his desk with Ripley in his room.

'Do you mind telling me, Sam, just what the hell you think you're doing? I don't pull rank. God knows I've never tried to work in that way. But I'm not standing for this. Your friend Foster in the paper tonight. You've read what we're supposed to have told him? We're not satisfied that Walker killed Elaine Harris! Case to be reviewed! What in hell possessed you, Sam?'

'Nothing possessed me, Max. That's all Gerald Foster. Whether Walker killed her or not, only Walker could tell you. I doubt if he did. But that's a private opinion.'

Ripley's eyes narrowed and he wagged a finger.

'This is Clitheroe, Sam. Isn't it? You have had your knife into him since the day he set foot in this building. You and Chance and McArthur and the others. Each of you likes to think he's Jack-the-Lad. Down the pub with the reporters. Showing the vice squad seizures on the briefing-room projector. Well, I tell you this, Sam. You take on Clitheroe now, as ACC Crime, and you are going to be annihilated. The evidence against Walker went through the prosecution service. They tested it. It went before a jury. They believed it. Just who the hell are you to start something like this? If you think, to gratify your personal enmity, that the cases of Elaine Harris, Rachel Lloyd and the rest are going to be reopened, you have put your neck under the chopper.'

'I don't think anything, Max. All I know is that Elaine Harris was bound and gagged in that hut, where Jonas had been and where Walker never was.'

'You know the gag was left there,' Ripley said sharply. 'You know the twine came from there. You don't know anything else at all. You don't know who was with her.'

'I know Jonas had Hassan's gun,' Hoskins said quietly. 'That's all.'

'And that clears Walker of murder? You think the Chief Constable's going to back you against Clitheroe with that?'

'I'm not asking anyone to back me, Max. I want to pull Jonas in and question him. If there's a case against him for killing Elaine Harris, so be it. And if that case stretches to Pruen as accessory before and after the fact – or to Carmel Cooney – so be it again.'

'Cooney?' There was a glimmer of fright in Ripley's eyes. 'You propose to arrest a public figure in local politics and charge him with a murder for which another man was tried and sentenced? Do you have any idea of what that means in the real world, Sam? The world outside this building?'

Hoskins sighed.

'I'm not going to arrest or charge anyone just for fun, Max. Not even Jonas. Not unless there's a case. Elaine Harris is a side issue. I want the man who killed Hassan and, if necessary, the men behind the killer. And if those men also killed Elaine Harris or anyone else, I want them for that as well.'

The Ripper's energy went suddenly, like water down a plughole.

'All right, Sam. I'll just say this. Until there's been an inquiry into the Walker case, no one from this building is going to seek a warrant for the arrest of anyone else for the murder of Elaine Harris. That's flat. If Jonas killed Hassan, fair enough. But you try arresting Jonas – let alone Cooney – for the girl's murder and what happens? You'll have to prove Mrs Walker perjured herself. You can't do that. You'd need new evidence. You haven't got it. The girl could have been letting men screw her for money in those huts. Girls of her age do that, Sam. Grow up! Walker could have worn gloves. Tied her with the twine. Gagged her with a cloth that was lying in there. Killed her on the ground outside. Tossed the cloth back in. Carried her body up and hidden it in the long grass. What you found yesterday doesn't alter that.'

'We'll see what Jonas has to say. If we find him before Cooney does.'

Ripley sat down, tired and softened.

'Sam, every plain clothes and uniformed officer in the city is looking for Jonas. You're the only one with this obsession about Cooney – or Pruen for that matter. There's not a shred of evidence against them. Nothing. And worst of all, it's blinding you to the facts.'

He stood up and walked to the door.

'Let's see, Max,' said Hoskins wearily.

'Right,' the Ripper said. 'All I'm saying, Sam, is that you're doing good here. Don't throw it all away over some vendetta against Clitheroe. You won't win. You can't win. As it is, you make people think you're sulking in your tent because you lost the glory and he won it.'

Hoskins tightened his mouth as Ripley went out.

The Friday evening rush-hour was over but traffic was queueing for the late-night shopping parks by the time Chance returned.

'So,' Hoskins said. 'What's Del got to say for himself from behind bars?'

'He's not saying nothing.' Chance sat down. 'I thought you scared young Kevin yesterday. But our Del is one big blond flabby jelly. Sweaty and quivering.'

'You think they got to him that fast?'

Chance shrugged.

'I'd say they got to him a long time ago, Sam. I think he's been made an offer. If he's a good boy, does his time and keeps his mouth shut about Elaine and Hassan, they might only blow off one kneecap rather than two. Might even just give him a smack and let him go. But if he talks to us or anyone else, he'll feel knives tickling him where he didn't even know he'd got anything to feel 'em with. He is shit-scared, Sam. Honestly. And from now on he says he's refusing to see us. If we come pestering, he'll ask for his brief.'

Hoskins sucked his teeth in resignation.

'I've had the Ripper here, Jack. Telling me not to make waves over Walker's conviction. He's got a half-cock notion of Walker killing the girl with gloves on, hence no fingerprints in the hut. Otherwise we've got to do Mrs Walker for perjury and unstitch Clitheroe's reputation. All the other killings he lumbered Walker with come popping up again. And that means whoever did 'em is still stalking the streets of Canton laughing his head off. Which, of course, he is.'

'So?'

'So if I push it, my son, Clitheroe and the Chief Constable are having one of my knackers each. Mounted in their hat-badges for ceremonial occasions. I reckon that's about it. Our friend Jonas is allowed to murder Hassan. But the name of Elaine Harris is not so much as to be mentioned in his presence.'

'Sod that,' Chance yawned. 'You fancy a beer, Sam?'

'I'd fancy anything that'd get me out of this bloody place, Jack. I'm about due for a meal-break. Mind you, Gerald Foster's got a bit to answer for. Phoned me last night about Mrs Walker. She's getting married again to a bloke who was screwing her long before any of this happened. We talked about whether she could have put Walker in the frame deliberately. No evidence that she did. Next thing, this sod Foster puts a column in tonight's *Canton Globe* saying the police are reconsidering Walker's case. Which is bollocks. Last thing they'd do. Trouble is, I'm known as Gerald's long-time friend. So the police means me. I am nostril-deep in the constabulary cess-pit, my son. With Clitheroe and Ripley dancing on my head.'

They walked down the stairs together and into the main lobby. The Mall was dark beyond the glass doors, the ornamental lamps like pale moons among the evergreens of the Memorial Gardens.

'Sam!'

It was Crowther on duty at the main desk, cradling the telephone receiver. Hoskins walked across.

'Someone want me? I'm on my break.'

'No, you're not, Sam. I just tried phoning your office. You must have been on the stairs. Take the first car. They've seen Jonas.'

'Who saw him where?'

'Mr Calverley. Store detective in Lewis's, down Longwall Circle.'

'Store detective? How come?'

'Ripley issued all the chain-store security officers with Jonas's picture.'

'How does this bloke Calverley know it's Jonas for sure?'

'He was using his store card to buy a Walkman in the Audio Department. He's Jonas all right. And he's our Jonas, what's more.'

'Right, Jimmy. Issue the car keys to young Mr Chance. Come on, Jack.'

'Calverley was still following him, Sam. Somewhere near Market Cross. We told him not to approach in case Jonas is carrying one. So he's with WPC Barton, foot patrol. They're waiting for the cavalry to arrive.'

41

Chance turned the car from King Edward Square into the eastern length of Longwall.

'All I'm saying, Sam, is that Clitheroe could be right this

time. Jonas could be carrying one. There could be trouble. No loss in having armed back-up.'

Hoskins grunted. Neon and sodium glared the length of the street where the Friday night shopping traffic lurched and braked towards the car parks.

'You fancy one of our Desperate Dans in his macho suit, loosing off a Smith and Wesson or a pump-action shotgun in the middle of these family outings?'

'I don't fancy giving Jonas a chance to do it first.'

Hoskins gestured at the traffic in front of them.

'Friday night punters sitting in their cars and playing with themselves. Give 'em a tune on the hooter, Jack.'

Chance pressed the switch and the street filled with the hee-haw of the car siren and the faint reflection of flashing blue. Several drivers woke up and nosed into the pavement as Chance edged by. The far end of Longwall, wrought-iron Victorian shopping arcades, had been levelled by German bombers in 1941. Longwall Circle had risen in the 1950s, a double curve of chain stores in the grey cement rendering of Stalinist cityscape. Its pavements colonnaded in square concrete pillars, it stood vast as some great cathedral square of southern Europe. At night, with the pavements crowded and the fairground colours of neon above bright display windows, Longwall Circle became what its promoters liked to call a 'fairyland' arena of consumers' delights.

Chance slowed down, turning off the siren and the light. The road branched round either side of the central lawn and monument, a Henry Moore mother and child. A four-lane underpass, joining Canton centre to the ring road, ran through twin tunnels beneath the shops. It surfaced in the urban motorway interchange of Market Cross at the far exit of Longwall Circle.

'If they spotted him in Lewis's, according to old Crowther,' Chance peered ahead at the busy pavements, 'where'd he go from there?'

'DCI Hoskins to control. We're in Longwall Circle, looking for Jonas and his shadow. Someone please guide us if they can. He was coming out of Lewis's, going towards Market Cross on foot, the last we heard. We're just driving past

'Nope,' said Chance. 'But seeing he's got a radio sticking out of his pocket, I reckon it must be him. Not too clever, that, in full view of Mr Jonas.'

Hoskins watched as Chance edged to the inner lane of traffic and turned on to the shallow forecourt of the Holiday Inn.

'There he is, my son. Stupid-looking but big. Seeing as he's probably more scared of the Blessed Carmel Cooney and "Horse-Parlour" Pruen than he is of us, let's keep it all cool. He could be looking for a lift but I don't fancy waiting to find out.'

Chance stopped, temporarily blocking the approach. He and Hoskins got out on opposite sides, closing the car doors and carefully looking away from Jonas. Their target stood thick-set and round-shouldered, a bald strip between two flaps of dark hair clearly visible. He was baggy-trousered and anoraked.

Hoskins and Chance turned together. As they did so, Jonas glanced at them. He met Hoskins's eyes without expression. Then, looking away, he moved with sudden and improbable speed, crossing in front of a slow taxi and sprinting up the pavement towards Market Cross.

Hoskins swore and broke into a run, hearing Chance's feet thumping on the pavement behind him. He was never to know how Jonas recognised him. So far as he knew, they had never seen one another before. The eyes. He supposed there was something in his eyes, an excitement or purpose that betrayed him.

The taxi blocked his way and he had to dodge round it. The uphill stretch of pavement towards the interchange vibrated with the din of Friday night traffic. Two lanes rumbled up towards the crossing and two lanes whined down from it. In the earth below, four lanes of traffic shook the shop-foundations from the Longwall underpass. The emerging cars and buses rose like a double chain of rubies beyond the interchange, mile upon mile of rear lights dwindling towards semi-detached Clearwater and high-rise Peninsula.

'Squad car behind!' Chance was gasping and gulping already. Hoskins kept his eyes on Jonas. The first tell-tale ache in his chest had begun. Why a DCI of his age should be panting after suspects on foot through Friday night shopping crowds rather than keeping a chair-seat warm in his office was the kind of question that occurred to him on every such occasion.

Still, Jonas was no problem. Anyone could outpace a beer-gutted, duck-footed dumbo like Jonas. But Jonas looked back, danced round two window-gazing couples and began to put on speed. To Hoskins's dismay, the man was pulling away. Where was Chance? Where in bloody hell was Jack Chance? Not daring to look back, Hoskins drove his legs faster, heaving in great gulps of petrol-layered air. Pollution. That was another thing he must start taking seriously. It was like having his head stuck down an oil-well. To one side and behind him, a man's voice squawked, 'You push me like that again, and I'll give you in charge!'

Jonas was on the brow of the pavement, level with the four-way interchange of cars and pedestrians. He dropped from sight, somewhere in the maze of pedestrian subways. Hoskins galloped on, snatching his radio from his lapel.

'Hoskins to all units. Seal off the Market Cross subways and bridge. All exits. No one in or out. Jonas is down there somewhere.'

Where the hell was Chance? To his astonishment, Hoskins saw him on the far pavement. Somehow or other Chance had negotiated four lanes of traffic and was trying to head off the fugitive. But he was going the wrong way. Another divisional fiasco was in the making. Hoskins plunged down the steps into the cement-floored subway with its ceramic-faced walls and a reek of stale urine. The long tunnel ahead of him was empty. Purse-snatchers, dope-addicts and dealers in grievous bodily harm had long ago driven off the shoppers.

To either side, tunnels led to pavements on other approaches to the intersection. Hoskins thumped on, glancing down each one. Empty. Empty. Empty. KILL THE RICH AND SMASH THEIR CARS! Like a nostalgic postcard the graffiti recalled a warm summer night of sea air and the Hangman's concert.

Jonas! Coming out at the far end of the main tunnel. He saw Hoskins and dodged back.

'Hoskins to all units! I want some support down here! I can't search the entire underpass network single-handed. He's down here, but he won't be for much longer.'

Presently, a footstep far behind him. Jonas at the other end of the tunnel, the point where they had come down. Jonas raced for the steps. Up them and into the arms of Jack Chance with any luck. Hoskins pelted after him. Up the steps and there was Chance. Red-faced, plump, winded, stooping to relieve the ache.

'Where is he, Jack?'

'Fuck knows, Sam! I thought you'd got him.'

'If he didn't pass you, he's on the bridge! He's got to be! Get up this side and close the gate. I'll go up the other way.'

Leaving Chance the easy job, Hoskins took off at a sprint, down the subway under the main traffic flow and up the other side by Coastal and Metropolitan Insurance. He sprang for the double escalator that carried the citizens of the New Jerusalem up to the walkway over Market Cross. The metal stairs were motionless. Someone had switched off the machinery. Pounding up past the arpeggios of graffiti on the tiled walls, the blood splashes here and there from needle-pops, he saw Jonas above him.

And then Hoskins knew he had won. Chance would have closed the metal grille on the far side of the pedestrian bridge. Jonas turned and began to run back up the steps again. But Hoskins slowed down. It was all right. It was going to be all right.

He came out into the fresher night air. The wide walkway above the four-lane traffic flow had a waist-high concrete wall either side. Sleek and graceful, nose-to-tail cars moved in their double lanes. White lights and red lights two and two, two and two as far as the eye could see. From underground more double lanes flowed into them, weaving and changing like streams of jewelled fire in their concrete runs. High above, the austere oblong of the Holiday Inn and Coastal and Metropolitan soared among the stars.

It was an astonishing sight. When the walkway was first built, families used to come on visits and stare at their dream-city in motion. Hoskins looked about him. Jonas had found the grille of the far gate closed, with Chance visible on the other side. Jonas began to walk back towards Hoskins, hunching a little as if he might fight. At least that meant there was no gun.

'Just relax,' Hoskins said firmly. 'There's no point doing anything silly now. No point in making things worse than they are. You can't get out of here. There's a block on every exit. You won't even get down the stairs. Take it easy and you'll be all right. Just a few questions, that's all. If you start carrying on, people are bound to think you've really got something to hide. It's a wallet you reported missing last summer. We found it somewhere that seems odd. That's all.'

'No!' It was a grizzling whine, aggressive and yet self-pitying. 'It's not. It's not.'

Hoskins took a step forward, about fifteen feet from where Jonas was standing.

'All right,' he said quietly. 'Then you tell me what you think it is.'

'It's not that! You want to lock me up somewhere and let them kill me.'

Another step forward.

'Now that's just silly, Mr Jonas. Isn't it? Why should we want that? It wouldn't do us any good.'

'Keep away from me! Keep away!' It was almost a scream now. A scream of fright, Hoskins guessed, at the thought of vengeance as dispensed by the likes of Cooney or Pruen to those who failed them. But he took one more step. Jonas let out a belligerent howl and scrambled up, standing on the waist-high concrete wall of the walkway. The empty night-sky behind him was flushed acid bronze by the sodium lights. From the corner of his eye, Hoskins could see Chance tugging unavailingly at the metal grille. The gate had locked automatically. It would need a key to open it now. Hoskins stood still.

'Now that's just silly, Mr Jonas,' he said gently. 'You come down and stand on the walkway. I'll go back to the far side. All right? And you just come down and stand there. I won't touch you. And we'll have a quiet talk. How's that?'

But the face was crumpled like a child's on the verge of tears.

'You'll kill me! You all want to kill me! You're going to kill me!'

The eyes looked aside from Hoskins. Glancing back, Hoskins saw a figure in ski-wear and baseball cap, clasping a pistol with both hands. Hoskins spoke from the corner of his mouth.

'Get out!' he said furiously. 'Get out and stay out!'

The Cuban-moustached marksman withdrew as silently as he had come on his crepe soles.

'Now, Mr Jonas. How's that? Just you and me.'

'No!'

Was it a refusal or an intercession? To his dismay, Hoskins saw the man's feet perform a sudden skittering dance on the smooth and slightly rounded top of the low wall. Jonas swayed, held himself for a moment with a look of horror, and then fell back into space.

Hoskins reached the wall in time to see Jonas's fall broken, about twelve feet down, by the cab-roof of a lorry. He slithered down forwards, down the windscreen and radiator to the ground. The lorry stopped with a jerk in the outside lane. At first Hoskins supposed that Jonas must be dead or unconscious. But he was pulling himself up, one knee bent, the other on the ground as if genuflecting. The traffic had stopped or slowed, the lane ahead of the lorry now clear. Jonas seemed to be trying to pull himself towards the pavement by the Holiday Inn, where he had first been standing. He was still kneeling, one hand raised, like a devotional figure giving a blessing.

At that moment a car pulled out from the forecourt of the Holiday Inn. With a supreme effort, Jonas got to his feet, staggering and with legs wide apart. He seemed to cling to an invisible support in the air above him. The car came on, accelerating as if to take advantage of the empty lane in front of the stationary lorry. Hoskins waited to see if it was, after all, Jonas's lift. But instead of drawing up, the car gathered speed. It caught the injured man with a bone-shattering impact, throwing him back against the lorry's front wheel. The soft thump of the impact was audible on the walkway. He lay almost shapeless, a heap of dark clothing in the tarmac arena of a traffic accident. Because he had been caught between car and lorry, those on the pavements and in other vehicles had not even yet registered that the car had hit him.

By the time Hoskins got to the other side of the bridge the car was lost, one of several thousand in the moving chain of lights returning to Barrier and Peninsula, Hawks Hill and Mount Pleasant, Clearwater and Orient, Lantern Hill and Ocean Beach, Harbour Bar and Highlands. Back in their snug cushioned living-rooms, the punters unwrapped and unboxed their micro-waves and VCRs, their electric coffee-pots and single-lens reflex cameras. By the time the first instant meal was cooked, the first coffee made, the first shutter pressed, the car that had done the bidding of Carmel Cooney or "Horse-Parlour" Pruen or half a dozen other names would be under the silt of the Railway Dock or reduced by a Western Reclaim crusher to a cube of tinfoil.

Hoskins turned and walked down past the armed marks-men who stood silent and braced on the escalator. Chance was standing at the bottom.

'No one got the number in time,' he said helplessly. 'Not even the make. Bloody hell, Sam! No one was expect-ing that!'

Hoskins nodded.

'Including me,' he said comfortlessly. 'Including me, my son.'

42

'So that's it?' Gerald Foster said as they parted outside the Porter's Lodge in the next day's lunch-hour.

'Yes, Gerald.'

Foster shook his head and stared at a gleam of brown river-water beyond the preserved and silent waterfront of Victoria Quay.

'Apart from Warren, they're all dead. Muriel Pruen and whoever killed her. Elaine Harris and whoever killed her. Sonny Hassan and whoever killed him.'

Hoskins stretched and yawned.

'We can put names to it, Gerald. Warren and Hassan half-drowned Muriel Pruen in that bowl and left her to die.

Charlie Blades and Forensic proved it. Pruen was there too. That's what we can't prove, with Cooney's witnesses paid to give Pruen an alibi. Cooney didn't want the law interfering in his private war.'

'And Jonas?'

'One of Cooney's mugs that watched the likely opposition. A man that could kill without hard feelings, if someone told him to. If he hadn't had trouble that morning over his wallet, I suppose he might have been on watch that night. Del and Sonny might never have got near Pruen.'

The insurance brokers and bank clerks scurried past them, returning to duty from wine and cheese. Foster shook his head doubtfully.

'Cooney wasted time watching amateurs like those two and their girl?'

'Amateurs are dangerous, Gerald. At his age, Cooney needs to protect himself. He must reckon that a few impatient young bucks will try to shaft him now and again. But Jonas wasn't just a watchman. He also killed Hassan. His prints were inside that gun. We think Hassan was tricked into going to the Paris Hotel on Christmas Eve. Expected to see someone else. Anyway, we've got a sighting of Hassan and Jonas in the brasserie, separately. Identified from photographs by Joyce Talbot, the cuddly waitress with the dark hair. And there was a noise in the hotel car park afterwards. Chap who saw it thought they were office-party drunks. Two men helping a piss-artist into a limo. Jonas identified as one of the helpers. Hassan was the one who was already drooping. I reckon they'd given him a swift bash or two in the toilet corridor to keep him quiet and dragged him into the yard through the back door.'

'Just sightings, then?' There was no mistaking the disapproval in Foster's tone as he stared at one of the bank-girls tottering past in skin-tight crimson boots with acrobatically high heels.

'And there's Charlie Blades, Gerald. He's red-hot forensic when he can get his mind off his new missus. There was a pair of kid gloves in that fishing-hut. The gloves belonged to Jonas except for the dried blood on them. That belonged to Hassan. Liked to keep his hands clean, did Mr Jonas. And it's Sonny on the gloves all right. Genetic fingerprint, as they say. He wasn't killed at the hut, Charlie says. Probably took him to a shed down the docks. Shoved a rag in his mouth and gave him a thumping that would turn your stomach to hear about. Broke a few ribs. Bled him on the razor while he was still alive. No hard feelings, but he had to be left in a state to show the younger generation the kind of spanking Cooney hands out. Then forced to his knees and bullet through the back of the neck – Russian style. Strung him under the pier at Ocean Beach. A warning to other young chancers.'

'And the girl?' Foster asked. 'Who's favourite for killing her?'

'Mr Walker or Mr Jonas. You pays your money, Gerald, and you shuts your mouth. At least you do if you think it was Jonas. Which Charlie Blades says it must have been. Walker was nasty, right enough, but all in the mind. Probably pass out cold at the sight of real blood. Still, if Walker starts looking innocent, that opens up all the other cases of sexual mayhem not proceeded with at his trial. Very bad news in this city. Means whoever did them is still walking round free as air and giggling like mad. Makes it look like Clitheroe took the chance of lumbering Walker with everyone else's previous. All you have to do, Gerald, is convict a man on one count. Charge him with the rest you can't prove. At the trial, you don't proceed with them. Or you just announce that the files are now closed. Tip a wink to the punters on one of those help-the-police telly shows. The rules won't let us prove it, folks, but down the nick we all know the bastard was guilty. Clears up crime at a stroke. Puts Clitheroe on course for Commissioner.'

'And Jonas?' Foster asked softly. 'Who killed him?'

'That, Gerald, is something we're not expecting to find out. His minder must have been driving that car. Someone that was looking after him for Cooney or Pruen. Jonas was dropped off to do a little shopping. Must have thought he was safe in those crowds. We found him standing by the Holiday Inn waiting to be collected. By the time his car arrived, the driver saw Jonas in the arms of the law, so to speak. The fall hadn't killed him. But if he lived, he might start chatting to us, sooner or later. Only one thing to do. Foot down on the throttle and aim the bonnet for his navel. I couldn't tell you,

Gerald, whether the bloke driving that car got a gold medal or a rabbit-chop for killing Jonas. You'd have to ask Cooney or whoever takes orders from Cooney.'

'That's as far as it goes then, Sam?'

'Looks like it, Gerald. Except that I don't think I'd want to issue life insurance on young Del when they let him out in seven or eight years' time.'

'You might have banged up Carmel Cooney by then, Sam. Not to mention Pruen.'

Hoskins gave a quiet derisive chuckle.

'Pruen's going to die of old age. And I keep telling everyone, I don't think people like Cooney get caught. They get bought off. By being on the council. Knighthood for services rendered. Perhaps the car that finished off Jonas had nothing to do with Cooney. Some other score being settled. But you can bet the bloke driving it couldn't tell you one way or the other. Just a chauffeur. The chain of command goes back from here to infinity, Gerald.'

'Still, you got Elaine Harris and Ma Pruen tidied away now.'

Hoskins pulled a face.

'When I was busting a gut along those subways, I thought what a bastard this whole thing's been. Not much like crossword-puzzle murder stories. Just one killing fading into another, fading into another. Like a kid's toy. Or a diseased root-system with Cooney sitting at the centre, laughing his head off.'

'They picked him for Canton Peninsula, by the way,' Foster said. 'That's definite. Parliamentary candidate. If he gets in, he'll be the first Conservative that's ever won the seat. Liberal until nineteen twenty-two. Labour ever since.'

'He'll get in,' Hoskins said wearily. 'You can count on it.'

'Conservative? Down the Peninsula?'

'No,' Hoskins said gloomily. 'Carmel Cooney down the Peninsula. The label doesn't count. He could run as a Basque Separatist or the Mujahideen for all it matters.'

They walked to the end of Victoria Quay.

'I'm not going back to the Mall, Gerald. Walking home. My afternoon off.'

'That's nice,' Foster said. 'See you soon. You going to the funeral on Wednesday? ACC Crime?'

278

'We all are, Gerald. Sunday best.'

'Poor old devil.' Foster shook his head. 'Might see you there, then, Sam. Take care.'

'You too, Gerald.'

Hoskins walked back over the Longwall river bridge to St Vincent Street and Lamb's Chambers. He let himself in. Lesley was sitting in an armchair, barefoot but still wearing her singlet and a pair of plain briefs.

'I think you might have to get another key cut,' she said gently. 'I could hardly open the door with your spare one.'

'I'll see to it.'

She got up and came towards him. He patted her on the tight blood-warm cotton of the pants as they put their arms round one another.

'Is it all over?'

'More or less,' he said. 'As far as anything in this bloody city is ever over. I was saying to Gerald Foster, whoever murdered Ma Pruen or Elaine Harris or Sonny Hassan is dead now, except Del Warren. And he's doing a life sentence for murder anyway. I reckon this particular roller-coaster ride is finished. No one's asking questions any more. Carmel Cooney's alive and well. Next Tory MP down the Peninsula.'

She shook her fringe and looked up at him.

'Peninsula? That's where Eve Ricard's been chosen.'

Hoskins chortled.

'Tell her not to bother.'

'But it's solid Labour.'

'Still tell her not to bother.'

Later that afternoon, she turned on the bed and faced him.

'There was a telephone message for you while I was waiting here,' she said innocently. 'A Mr Chance. I said I'd tell you when you came back.'

'Jack Chance? What'd he want?'

'Wanted you to go back to your office, I think.'

He stroked the cool pearly smoothness of her hips, half listening.

'Why's that?'

Lesley frowned a little, as if with an effort of recollection.

'You know the one on Coastal Network that reads out names and addresses of people convicted for drinking and driving? They don't give his name any longer, but you know the one I mean?'

'Yes,' said Hoskins uneasily. 'What about him?'

'He parked his car in Balance Street multi-storey this morning. When he went to drive off, it seems that someone had got into the car while he was away and hidden behind the driving seat. They hit him with a hammer. Very hard on the head. He's in the Royal Infirmary. Intensive care. A fractured skull and a brain haemorrhage. Mr Chance seemed to think you'd like to know, even though it's your rest day.'

Hoskins propped himself on his elbow.

'And you deliberately didn't tell me until now?'

'That's right,' Lesley said, brushing aside her fringe, leaning over him on her elbow and staring into his eyes. 'I thought what we've just done mattered more. You're not the only policeman in Canton. It's your rest day, after all.'

Hoskins lay back and stared at the ceiling.

'Well done,' he said quietly. 'It's what I've always wanted. To meet a girl who'd got her priorities in the right order. Jack Chance can handle this lot till tomorrow. He's a big boy now.'

>>> If you've enjoyed this book and would like to discover more great vintage crime and thriller titles, as well as the most exciting crime and thriller authors writing today, visit: >>>

The Murder Room
Where Criminal Minds Meet

themurderroom.com